SILENCE IN THE STONE

The Lost Pharaoh Chronicles Book IV

LAUREN LEE MEREWETHER

Edited by
SPENCER HAMILTON

LLMBOOKS
PUBLISHING

LLMBOOKS
PUBLISHING

eBook ISBN: 978-1961759190
Paperback ISBN: 978-1961759206, 979-8643826590

CONTENTS

PROLOGUE
THE TIME OF REMEMBERING

"YOU CANNOT SIMPLY FORGET SOMEONE YOU LOVE," PHARAOH Horemheb whispered as the cool water ran down his back. *But Egypt will forget. Its people will never remember her . . . them.*

He closed his eyes and steadied his breathing.

"I miss you, Nefertiti. Do I wish you here? Yes, but you are not." He mouthed the words more than spoke them, so that the servant pouring his morning shower over him would not hear. "But if your ka still roams this palace, be with your sister, my wife, my sweet Mut. Comfort her as she will not let me. Make her see the truth."

He balled his hands into fists against the stone wall.

"The *truth*," he whispered and thought of the retelling. He had told all; he had spoken every truth he knew. The weight of what he had to do that night pressed against him. "Forgive me, my love."

He shaved, oiled his face and body, and applied his own kohl and scent, after dismissing the servants. He dressed in silence, his mind numb as he tied his royal shendyt.

Time seemed to stop as he sat on his throne, waiting for the first day's light. Mut entered before the five prophets of Amun and took her place by his side. Lotus blossoms covered her freshly bathed body in their perfume, and he closed his eyes and dipped his head as his mind struggled to separate Nefertiti from her sister.

"Thank you for coming this last day," Horemheb whispered and peered at Mut. He gestured to his guards to stand outside the council room.

"I told Pharaoh I would stand by his side as his Queen." They locked eyes, and as the guards stepped outside, she continued. "*I* keep my promises."

"As do I." Horemheb's brow furrowed as he watched her lips contort into a scowl. "One day, I hope our goddess Ma'at shows you the truth."

"She already has," Mut spat, and looked him up and down. "By your own words."

"My words were of a love that happened ten years ago, and just this morning, my words were of a love I feel for my wife—my wife who stands before me, calling me a liar." Horemheb stood to face her.

"I cannot believe you anymore," she said, remaining in her seat. "I have always been in Nefertiti's shadow. Even my own parents favored Nefertiti over the rest of us. She was the standard. She was the one to live up to—and she was *Pharaoh*! We would *never* compare. It is no different with you. I heard the way you spoke about her. I heard the longing for her in your voice. You fathered a son with her. You promised her you would marry me and take care of me. The only reason you say you love me is so you may feel assured her last wish was met." Mut shook her head at him. "You disgust me. After everything you told me all these years . . . you disgust me."

Horemheb chewed on his bottom lip and scratched his chin. *How to make her see the truth and believe me when I tell her I do love her?*

His hand dropped as he opened his mouth to speak, but the First Prophet of Amun, Wennefer, stepped into the council room's light, followed by the remaining four prophets of Amun.

Pharaoh's guards entered behind them and took their place behind the throne. Horemheb looked at the prophets, focusing his glare on the one who attempted to sit while Pharaoh still stood. When he made sure they knew to only sit after Pharaoh, he sat, and then the five prophets followed.

"Pharaoh," Wennefer spoke and bowed his head. "Surely this is the last day of retelling? There is but one Pharaoh left whose account is to be retold?"

Surely, Horemheb thought.

Horemheb rubbed the gold in the throne's arm, as Tut had done only six short years ago. *There was no more need to retell Pharaoh Akhenaten's heresy, nearly causing the empire's collapse. His wife, his brother, his son . . . they had all met the same fate as he. Akhenaten had cursed them all to a truly eternal death among the living, for to live eternally was to have their names spoken on every Egyptian tongue for all eternity.*

You have forced my hand to take that from them, Akhenaten. You make me erase their names alongside your own. Akhenaten . . . Smenkare . . . Nefertiti . . . Tutankhamun . . . Ay . . . and all the others. Curse you, Akhenaten.

His stare bore into the great god Amun's face.

Curse him.

"Pharaoh," Wennefer spoke again at Horemheb's silence, "the last three days have been long, and we, the prophets, have grown old. We must finish the recounting and begin the erasure, so that we may restore faith in Amun's priesthood and reverence and power for Pharaoh."

"Yes." Horemheb nodded, knowing his days of stalling had come to an end. "Today, we shall remember Pharaoh Tutankhamun's chief royal wife, Ankhesenamun, the last child of Pharaoh Akhenaten and Queen Nefertiti. We shall also remember Pharaoh Ay. But after today, we shall remember them no more."

❦ I ❦

THE TIME OF DEPRAVITY

WASET, 1324 B.C.

ONE DAY WAS ALL HE NEEDED.

Pawah planted his feet outside the palace doors of Malkata as he peered over his shoulder at the two royal guards escorting him away, Ineni and Amenket.

"In the morning, we will tell the chief royal guard you have escaped." Amenket glowered at Pawah, gripping his spear with both hands. "Then we will have paid our debt."

Ineni nodded, his knuckles growing white from their firm grip upon his own spear.

Pawah leered at the two men. *Your debt will never be repaid.*

Their eyes bore into his own, but Pawah knew he still held the upper hand. He needn't remind them that their letters to him indicted them in the murders of Pharaoh Akhenaten and Pharaoh Smenkare.

Ineni spat at Pawah's feet as they closed Malkata's doors to him.

"Fools," Pawah whispered under his breath, and began to calculate what needed to be done prior to the morning. He stared at the sun in the sky. *Midday.* He wrapped his robe tightly over the bleeding dagger wound in his chest and wiped his chin with his forearm, letting his sleeve fall to cover the blood on his arm. *Curse Ankhesenamun and her dagger.*

He went and stooped at the Nile's edge and lapped up some water to wash his chin free of any smeared blood. His mind raced. *What to do? What to do now?* His plans to take the crown thus far had failed. *First, I need to hide.*

Narrowing his eyes against the sunlight, he made out the barge to take him across the Nile to the city of Waset. He needed to stop by his stolen estate first and gather some needed items before the royal guards came to arrest him. *Do I run? Flee Egypt?* His nose wrinkled in response.

"I have come too close to give up now," he whispered from the depths of his chest.

He began to walk toward the barge.

Blood drizzled from his lip, but his tongue lapped it up.

You will pay for that, little girl.

The barge worker looked the other way as Pawah boarded.

At least I have a few still loyal to me, he thought as he stood at the end. He peered over the Nile to the city of Waset in the east. *I have more than a few. I can always secure loyalty other ways, but my funds are running thin.*

He ran his thumb over his finger pads as he looked into the waters of the Nile. A crocodile sat nearby, waiting for something to be snatched up.

Waiting . . . He shook his head. *I waited too long. I should have seized the crown when I had the chance, when we could have killed all of them in one night, instead of saving Egyptian blood and giving Nefertiti the hemlock-laced wine to take to her husband. Why didn't I let the rebels storm Aketaten and kill the royal family? I would have been King. All of it for naught!*

His fist made contact with the barge's railing.

"No," he whispered. *I have come too far . . . too close . . . but how do I give myself another chance? How? How?!*

He watched as the crocodile's mighty jaws snapped from the water with a fish in tow.

That's what I do. I am done waiting. A frustrated breath accompanied his thoughts as he remembered his long-held motto: strike only when you can win. *But look where that got me. I am out of ideas. Think, Pawah. Ay is Pharaoh. Ankhesenamun is Hereditary Princess—but, unfortunately, I will have to do away with her like her mother. If she only did not refuse me . . . and Ay, he has no sons. Horemheb is dead, as well as that wretched boy Tut, so there is no Hereditary Prince.*

A thought struck him.

Hereditary Prince . . . yes . . . I must make Ay name me Hereditary Prince . . . but how? He won't name me on his own accord . . . and his daughter is dead so there will be no Hereditary Prince by marriage.

A small flash of jealous lust came over his eyes. "Nefertiti," his lips crooned. "Why did you refuse me?" His head slung back and forth; he both hated her and wanted her. "We could have been great, you and I . . . me as Pharaoh, you as my wife." His mind flashed to all of the desires he'd held for her in his own twisted imagination.

Then he stopped as a realization dawned on him: Nefertiti had a younger sister. *What was her name?* He watched the crocodile yet again prey on an unsuspecting fish as the barge moved toward Waset.

"*Mut.*"

He held his chin up and thrust out his chest, standing as tall as the statues in Ipet-isut.

"Mut . . . Horemheb's wife." *His widow.*

He knew then exactly where he was headed: Men-nefer.

He stepped foot on the other side of the Nile and went straight to his stolen estate.

Would the old Pharaoh die with two daughters' lives on his conscience? No, he thought not. Leverage Mut's life for the crown, and then his final goal would be achieved.

Good things come to me, he thought, *when I take what I want.*

Victory tingled his lips as a smile spread over them.

As he threw open his door, Merka, his servant, dropped his head. "Are you our new Pharaoh?" he asked, his mouth pinched and his voice holding a certain tone of mockery.

"No, you ridiculous buffoon," Pawah said, his prideful beam falling from his face. He slammed the door closed. "Do you think if I was Pharaoh I would come back here?"

Merka pushed his lips forward and shook his head in a failed attempt to hide a smirk.

"Fetch me gold for a trip." Pawah shook his fingers at him to shoo him away. *I cannot deal with you right now,* he added in his mind, *but you will pay for your insubordination.*

"Where are you going?" Merka asked, not moving.

"You do not ask questions!" Pawah grabbed his collar and half pushed, half pulled him in the direction of the estate's treasury.

Merka sighed and went and measured out a few deben gold.

"Here are ten deben."

Pawah held out his hand, but Merka dropped the linen sack on the table just out of Pawah's reach. Merka's uncaring eyes and finger-tapping on the table almost caused Pawah to slap him.

"Get me twenty more," Pawah said, dismissing Merka again, and then leaned forward to yank the sack from the table.

One copper deben should be enough to make it to Men-nefer, but I may have to leave the country and will need a good stash should I find myself in exile again.

Merka came back, dropping two more linen sacks on the table, both again just out of Pawah's reach.

"You wretched servant!" Pawah growled at his subordinate and then whispered under his breath, "I would have killed you by now if we were in Aketaten."

Merka shook his head uncaringly. "But we aren't." His voice was monotone and flat.

Pawah drew near and slapped Merka across the face. "Do you know how many lives I have taken? As if yours would mean anything to me."

"Then why do you keep me around?" Merka leaned forward so his nose almost touched Pawah's.

Because I am running low in support and those I can manipulate.

But he couldn't admit that. Instead, Pawah wrenched Merka's collar in his hand. "When did you become this way?"

"When you refused to pay the soldiers what you promised. I joined you because I did not want an heir of Akhenaten on the throne. That horrid man we had to call Pharaoh stripped us of food, work, and decency. He robbed Egypt of faith. My only son joined the army ranks and went to the Field of Reeds in one of his border crises because he refused to set up proper defenses."

Merka's breath was hot on Pawah's nose.

"That was why I joined you. You gave my family bread to eat. You paid me to work for you in the People's Restoration of Egypt. You protected us in our worship to Amun." Merka narrowed his eyes. "I've killed for you, helped you to kill several royals, and you aren't even loyal to those who do your bidding." He spit at Pawah's feet. "You left Sitayet's, Ebana's, and the other's families without grain after they were killed in their assassination of Pharaoh Tutankhamun and General and Hereditary Prince Horemheb. You had promised them their families would be taken care of. You threatened their families' *lives* if they did not do what you asked."

Merka shook his head and pushed off Pawah's hand around his beaded collar. "My mother gave me this collar when I took a wife, and I'll not have you ruin it." Merka leaned past Pawah and grabbed his reed brush to take note of the withdrawal of funds. "Now do you want me to dress you in linens with fewer decorations?" Merka asked, not bothering to peer up at Pawah. "For your travel."

Merka's eyes widened, seemingly noticing the blood stains on Pawah's chest, and his gaze jumped to his chin. "What happened at Malkata?"

"I was . . . caught," Pawah muttered.

Merka snapped his reed brush accidentally. "You were . . ." Merka grunted; his hand crumpled the papyrus as it curled into a fist. "I want no more to do with you, but my hands are as bloody as yours and I am tied to you as you are to me. I know you will not kill me, because you *need* me. I am one of the few you have left."

Pawah went completely still, his eyelids held heavy over his eyes, and then, with the force and swiftness of a crocodile, he swatted the papyrus and brush from Merka's hands and grabbed him with both hands, again by his precious collar.

"You're wrong."

Then he pushed Merka into the wall and bashed his head against the stone until Merka fell to the floor in a seizing heap. Pawah chuckled to himself as he squatted down so he was eye-level with him, watching the life leave his body. He tilted his head, slightly amused at the way Merka's body lay dying and slightly in awe of his handiwork against the stone wall. His gaze finally fell from the blood spatter back to Merka, whose life drained from his eyes.

"I don't *need* you, and I tire of your ungratefulness."

He stood and kicked Merka's body after he was gone.

"Really, you should be thanking me. If someone comes looking for me in the morning, I've just spared you the impalement . . . but mostly, I don't want you to give anyone any details of our happenings."

Pawah burned the papyrus. No more would he have to keep records of how much he had taken from the royal treasury for his own estate to supply the movement once the priesthood's funds had run out so long ago. No more would there even be proof of such a thing.

He peered over to the large chests of gold, copper, bronze, and grain. He would take as much as would fit in his sling. Smiling, he went up to his room on the second floor and gathered up his lists and records of who did what in the movement—

"Pawah, my handsome man," a woman's voice crooned. "Where are you going?"

He twirled around to face his mistress from the night prior as she lay in his bed. "Ah, my beautiful . . . Nile reed." He added in his mind, *Because I cannot remember your name. There are so many of you.*

He helped her to stand and slid his hands around her waist, placing a kiss on the base of her neck like he did with all of the women he brought into his bed. This woman was no different. He pulled her close and peered out the window to gauge the time. His lips turned into a scowl.

Not enough daylight left to be with this woman.

"Why is your travel sling packed?" she asked. "Why . . . you're *bleeding*!" Her finger graced the wound on his chin.

He winced. *I don't want to kill you, but if you ask any more questions, I may have to. I can't have loose ends around Waset.*

"My lily flower . . ."

He ran his fingers down the outline of her jaw. *She is naïve enough to believe whatever I say. Neglected wives are so desperate for love.* He titled his head as an idea came to him.

"I must go to Nubia."

"Nubia?" Her eyes danced. "Why? Don't you want to stay here with me?"

"I do," he whispered, and pulled her mouth to his. "But," he said, pulling away, "I have been reinstated as Vizier of the Upper, and Pharaoh Ay needs me to go and reconcile the border disputes. You make plans to divorce your husband and I will bring you to the palace with me."

He gave her his charming grin and got a small thrill at what this brainless woman would do in his absence. Not that he cared, but it was amusing, nonetheless.

"Oh!" She smiled and giggled, her shoulders rising at the possibility of living in Malkata. "I am beside myself!" She pulled his hands to her chest. "We must celebrate!"

"I want to." He hummed as his eyes ran over her bosom. It was no lie—he certainly wanted to. "But I must be going. I'll let you out the window and down the tree. We don't want you getting in trouble should anyone see you coming from my estate door. I don't think your husband would take too kindly to that." He winked at her, thinking, *Nor do I want you to see Merka's body lying in the main room.* He waited for her to object to the window, but she didn't. That was why he kept this one around.

She took a deep breath and nodded. "I am always so careful."

"I know you are, my charming anemone."

She giggled again at this, playing with her wig.

"I shall be back at some point in the future. I'll send you my usual call."

He winked at her as he patted her cheek, then hurried her out the window to let her down. She blew him a kiss and he in return once she was at the base of the building.

He turned back to his room and gave a soft chuckle at the ease of it all. He finished putting the papyrus scrolls in his sling. If he were to be taken in, then he had his records of those who would join him. His very last resort of evading arrest and impalement.

After stitching his chest and rubbing honey into his chin, he changed his clothes to look like a noble. He looked at himself in the polished copper mirror as he thought about what lie to tell people.

"I cut myself shaving," he said, his voice dripping with

ease and charm, "because I was too burdened with the report of Pharaoh's untimely demise."

He descended back to the first floor, opened the door to his estate, and then yelled to Merka's body, "Make yourself useful while I am gone!" He walked out of his estate with a sneer on his face. A bark of laughter followed, and he muttered under his breath, "When I become Pharaoh, I will return for my gold."

He headed to the nearest dock, his mind focused on one person.

Mut.

How would he get her to let him inside? He could bring word of General Horemheb's death. *No. She probably has already received that news . . .* His mind whirled as his feet took him where he needed to go. *I will be his estate trust, that's it! I need her to review legal documents for his estate. Yes, she will let me in, and then, once I force her into submission, I will send word to Pharaoh that Mut is ill and needs her father to come at once.*

He laughed at the ease of his plan and then snorted, wishing he had done the same years ago with that cursed Nefertiti. He had been a different person then, but he cared not now for the blood of Egyptians. He cared not for the diplomacy.

I will take what I want at any cost!

He stepped onto the barge to Men-nefer, paying his toll, and looked across the Nile to the grand Malkata. Ankhesenamun's words hung in the back of his mind from that morning's attack. Had it really only been just that morning? It seemed a life away now. *No one will ever remember the man who began his descent as the Fifth Prophet of Amun. I curse you to be erased from all of history.*

Fear of her curse coming to life began to muddle his vision, so he pushed it aside as he planned out his great victory. *I will be remembered, girl—always. It will be you, Ankhesenamun, who they will forget.*

He looked to the sun and smirked. One day's head start.

ONCE IN MEN-NEFER, PAWAH TRAVELED QUICKLY, QUIETLY.

He looked up at the wooden beam overhanging the entry into Horemheb's estate and the walled gate around his courtyard. "Too bad he is dead," he muttered with a sneer.

It had taken three decans, thirty days to get there, as the season had not been kind to the Nile. And nothing but a light scar remained on his chin and chest.

He put his hand on the wall, admiring the craftsmanship; he knew, however, even as nice as this estate was, that it would not have satisfied his own desires for a palace. He looked across the courtyard to the main house, and his eyes sparkled at the thought of what he would do to Mut as he held her hostage, waiting for her father to arrive. He arranged his travel sling and adjusted his shendyt and robes, feeling the weight of the gold tied to his waist. A scowl came to his face, for still, his gold was not enough to quench his desire for more. And even more so, his gold did not hold authority over all, which was what his soul truly longed for since he had nothing as a boy.

Putting the lacking gold from his mind—for the moment —he strode to the door. His eyes darted between the windows of the house. His plan wasn't entirely together yet, but it was something along the lines of: persuade the servants to let him in, get Mut alone, either seduce her or force her depending on what she knew about his murder of her sister to send for Ay . . . where he then would have Ay name him Hereditary Prince and then drink poison to save his daughter's life, leaving Pawah as Pharaoh and husband to Ankhesenamun, whom he would dispatch shortly thereafter. Maybe take Mut for his wife . . . or, better yet, dispatch her too.

Can't have anyone alive who knows I killed Pharaoh, can I? Yes, that should work. And if not, I might be out of options. He stopped at that thought. *No. I will have what I want because I am the best. Nothing can stop me.*

With his feet planted before the door, he knocked.

Once.

Twice.

Three times.

Then he pounded.

Finally, a servant came and opened the door.

"Where is the Mistress of the House?" Pawah demanded.

"She has left by command of Queen Ankhesenamun to visit Malkata to share in their grief." The servant lifted her chin as she spoke, eyeing the stranger.

"I see." Pawah put his hand on the door to hold it firmly open. "Then I shall wait here until her return." He pushed himself inside, knowing the wealth of his dress would command no questions from the servant.

But he was wrong. "Who are you?" the servant asked, a quiver in her voice.

"You dare ask my name?" Pawah spat at her. "Fetch me some wine. Do not dishonor your deceased master by treating your guests to die of thirst!"

The servant clenched her jaw, bowed her head, and did as she was told.

He looked around, waiting for the other servants to dare try him.

Sure enough, one did: "Who are you? Why do you not tell us who you are?"

At first, a rage built behind his eyes, but this servant stood tall with a pretty face. "I'd rather not deal with these matters until the Mistress of the House returns." Pawah cocked an eyebrow, leering at each of the servants who had come to see who stood in their home, before his gaze fell back to the one who spoke. "But if you must know, I have come regarding

General Horemheb's estate. There were debts he owed, and they must be squared away with his benefactor."

"Your kind waste no time," the servant said under her breath. "No respect for those traveled to the Field of Reeds."

Pawah chuckled as he eyed her slender frame. "None whatsoever." Then he rested his eyes on her face. "What is your name?" He smirked, undressing her with his eyes, all while keeping a smoldering gaze upon the servant, thinking, *I shan't be bored waiting for Mut's return.*

"Bakt, Head Steward," the servant said, lifting her chin. "And yours?"

"I may tell you one day"—he grinned—"Bakt."

She ran her eyes over him. "You disgust me."

"You may come to think differently," Pawah murmured. He snapped to another servant: "Make a bed for me and prepare something to eat. I have traveled a long way and will be treated as an honored guest."

He could feel the other servants' eyes burn through him, but he cared not, for they would do as he said regardless of their lowly opinions of him. He turned his whole attention again to Bakt and shooed away the others. He racked his memory for the information he'd acquired about Horemheb over the years . . . and landed on a piece that may strike a chord in this servant.

"Now, High Steward Bakt"—her name flowed over his lips like honey—"I heard General Horemheb had another wife?"

She stiffened and crossed her arms over her chest. "What has Mistress of the House Amenia to do with this? Let her ka rest in peace."

"Ah . . . Amenia." Pawah gestured for her to show him to the dining room. "Come tell me about her while I eat."

Bakt cautiously approached, led him to the dining room, and sat at Pawah's invitation.

Just like fishing. Easy.

Pawah's lips held a warm smile as he began to take on her mannerisms—the same curled fist under the chin, the same furrowed brow, the same pursed lips.

"Now, Bakt—may I speak to you without the title?" He continued without letting her respond. "Bakt, tell me more about Amenia and this new wife, Mut."

"You will not disgrace the name of Amenia," Bakt whispered with a harsh tone. She wagged a finger in his face. "She was a great Mistress of the House. You will not—"

"I am not here to disgrace her, my darling Bakt." He gently grasped her hand in his and lowered it to her lap, letting his hand linger on her knee. "But I would like to get to know you a little better. How about over some dinner?"

"Why do you ask about her? Did you know Amenia?" Bakt said, ignoring his invitation.

"Yes, I knew Amenia. I feel that what General Horemheb and his new wife did to her was despicable," he said, playing off of Bakt's emotions and hoping what he said made sense to her.

Bakt's jaw clenched, and he knew then he had struck a familiar chord within her. "Yes, it was."

"Please tell me what happened. I only know from hearsay."

Pawah patted her knee and then leaned both elbows on the arms of the chair to listen to her speak. Bakt began recounting Amenia's plight with so much passion in her voice and her hands.

Well, that was easy. I may enjoy my stay here, he thought, imagining the same passion she would surrender to him in the evening. *At least before I move into the palace as Pharaoh.* His lips drew into a pensive smile to keep up his façade with Bakt. This plan would surely be the way to the crown. He would leave nothing to chance this time. He was done waiting and now had nothing to lose.

THE CHIEF ROYAL GUARD, DJAR, CAME TO PHARAOH AY AND bowed. "Pawah has escaped." There was no introductory title, no acknowledgment of Ay's crown; just the dreadful report.

Ay narrowed his eyes, pressing his lips into a thin line, his stomach churning. "What do you mean, escaped?" Tension flooded his aged shoulders.

"He is no longer in Malkata. He is no longer in the royal guard's custody. There will be no execution for him today." Djar stood straight and looked Pharaoh in the eyes and appeared to anticipate Ay's next question, for he mumbled on rather quickly: "He escaped during the night. I do not know by whose hand."

"Who was on guard?" Ay barked, and slammed a fist into the throne's arm.

"Several men." Djar shook his head, keeping a clenched jaw as he spoke. "I don't know how it happened. There was evidence it was not *my* men."

Ay stood and let out a guttural groan. The crack of his knuckles echoed through the throne room as he surveyed the room's pillars.

"Tell no one of this, Djar." Ay's voice deepened as his cold, hard stare fell upon his chief royal guard. "I want you and your trusted guards to hunt him down. Bring him to me alive, so that I may slay him myself."

Djar bowed and turned to leave without Ay's dismissal.

"Do not make mention to Queen Ankhesenamun," Ay called after him.

Djar spun back around to face Ay. "Thus Pharaoh says."

"*Now* Pharaoh dismisses you, Chief Royal Guard."

Djar stood straight for a moment, then placed a fist over his chest before turning to leave.

Ay watched him pass through the wooden throne room

doors and wondered if he had advised Tut in error when naming the new chief royal guard. The last one, Jabari, had led his daughter to her murder.

A shroud of sadness still hung heavily over his heart for his lotus blossom—his Nefertiti—and, within her, his first wife, his beloved Temehu. He eased back into the throne with a stone face.

"Amun-Re, if you hear me," Ay whispered, "if you see my family has done nothing but try to honor you the best they can, to regain power for your divinely appointed . . ." He closed his eyes and clamped his jaw so that his whisper hissed through his teeth. ". . . then give me your false prophet, Pawah." His eyes slowly opened, and he lifted his chin. "Let him die an agonizing death for the pain he has caused my family, the wrongs he has dealt to your appointed."

👼 2 👼

THE TIME OF QUESTIONS

ANKHESENAMUN WAITED FOR MUT TO DISEMBARK FROM HER barge in Malkata's harbor with red, swollen eyes and slack cheeks.

"My Queen." Mut's raspy voice floated in the breeze as she hinged at the waist. She lifted her head, and they found each other's gaze. Mut saw the quiver in her niece's lip and realized her own lip was still. She had grieved Horemheb, but it seemed as though Ankhesenamun was not finished with her own grief. *Should I be grieving longer?* Mut's unspoken question resounded in her mind.

Ankhesenamun waved off the servants. As they all turned their backs and went a ways off, she ran to Mut and threw her arms around her neck, and Mut wrapped her arms around Ankhesenamun's body.

"I cannot believe they are gone," she whispered to Mut, her voice breaking.

Ankhesenamun's grip around Mut's neck pulled tighter, as if she would fall if Mut were not standing to support her. Mut could only close her eyes in response and squeeze. She remembered the day the messenger came to her home to tell her Horemheb was slain in battle; she had wept with an overwhelming emptiness, but at the end of that day, her eyes were completely dry. She had not shed a tear since.

Horemheb had not been back to her once since they were married. She tried to reason with herself that it was because the royal family needed him, and he was acting as he should in the eyes of Amun-Re. He did write her several times, but letters took time to be delivered, and then responded to, and then returned. His words always seemed forced and polite. She wondered if he really even wanted her as his wife; after all, they had never even consummated their marriage.

She remembered her tears then. Why wasn't he the man who had rushed to her when Nefertiti's body lay on the floor, to shield her from the bloody scene? Did he care for her? Or was he just being kind? Or only protecting her? She had begged her stewards, Tener and Raia, to tell her she was not foolish for marrying him, to tell her he would come back to her, to tell her he loved her, to give her any answer as to why his letters were always so devoid of feeling, why he had left her alone the eve of their marriage and fled Men-nefer the day after. Their responses gave her little consolation, for all they could do was pat her back and tell her what she wanted to hear.

The servants of his estate treated her with disdain: throwing linens at her and her inherited stewards, dropping the plates onto the table so that food would spill, slamming cups down so the wine would stain her clothes. She had dismissed one from the estate, but the servant had just laughed and stayed. For the past couple years, she had locked herself in her room, making Tener and Raia endure their hatefulness and bring food to her. But even then, when she dared venture out on a particularly sunny day, she had still heard the whispers in the house about Amenia, Horemheb's late wife.

But, she had always ask herself, were they true?

Horemheb had left her there alone in his estate for

almost two years, just as he had done with his first wife. If anything, anger gripped Mut's mind now, after her heart had mourned him and what could have been their life together. There had always been a hanging doubt that lingered in the back of her mind that he had only married her to keep her safe . . . but from whom? Pawah? Others who wished her harm because of her relation to Nefertiti? But, as Ankhesenamun had so pointed out when they were younger, Mut wasn't royalty. Her father hadn't named Mut as Hereditary Princess but again named Ankhesenamun. Even with her relation to her father now that he was Pharaoh, she still wasn't royalty, married to a commoner. Maybe her father did not think of her as much as he thought he might have. Maybe he was keeping her safe as well.

None of that mattered now. Horemheb was gone, and Ankhesenamun needed her.

At least she and Tut actually loved each other. Mut rubbed Ankhesenamun's back. *I was just a silly girl infatuated with a man—a man who helped kill Pharaoh Akhenaten and justified, along with my father, covering up my sister's murder.* Ankhesenamun clung to Mut, her tears wetting Mut's neck. Mut resolved her anger in the moment with a soft resolve. She would be there for Ankhesenamun in her friend's time of sorrow.

"I am so sorry, my Queen," Mut whispered back.

Ankhesenamun pulled back and wiped her tears. "Mut, you know to call me Ankhesenamun when we are alone."

Mut nodded, and together they walked to the Queen's bedchambers and sat in the living area.

"I miss Tut so," Ankhesenamun finally said, drawing her hands close to her chest. "I dream of him often . . . only to wake up and realize he is not here." She looked at her bed in the distance before her eyes fell to the floor. "Maybe it will be easier when I move back to the royal harem and my grandmother takes this room." Her eyes swept the grand Queen's apartment. "Maybe it will be better that way."

Mut stayed silent, listening with shoulders forward.

"I begged him not to go." Ankhesenamun's eyes glistened. "He told me he would come back to me."

Mut felt a burning in her chest and on her cheeks. Horemheb had left her before she could say goodbye. He, too, promised he would return, but at an undefined date. That had been almost two years ago. It seemed so long that she had nearly lost count. Why had she not divorced? Because she knew that there would be no one else. Perhaps it was fear that kept her in his estate.

"I saw our future together." Ankhesenamun dropped her head as a slight smile took over her lips. "I would bear him an heir. We would grow old together, be entombed together, and join Re together." She interlaced her fingers as if remembering his touch. She drew a deep breath and, with an unfocused gaze, lifted her head as her hands dropped into her lap.

"What will you do now?" Mut asked, crossing her arms over her chest and wishing Horemheb had shown her any inkling of love so that she could have believed the same future for her and him—so that she could have been as sorrowful as Ankhesenamun.

Ankhesenamun's shoulders lowered and loosened, and her voice fell flat. "I am the last Hereditary Princess. I only assume I will marry whomever your father names as Hereditary Prince." She squeezed her eyes shut and grimaced. "I just cannot think about being with someone else right now. It hurts too much."

Mut nodded.

"Surely you know what it feels like?"

"Yes," Mut replied but her thoughts were elsewhere: *My first husband . . . Menna . . . taking another woman as he did, though I suppose I pushed him into her arms. But yes, Ankhesenamun, after that and my second husband having nothing to do with me, I know what that feels like. I do not think I will take a third husband. There is no one I want to be with. If I am alone, no one can hurt me.*

Rolling her shoulders back and her neck in a circle, she only longed to sleep. Her trip from Men-nefer had been long. She was done crying. She was done caring. A pang of guilt struck her—she selfishly wanted Ankhesenamun to find another friend to whom she could speak her sorrows. She had told herself she would be there for Ankhesenamun, but it was proving to be too much for her.

"Who will Pharaoh name as Hereditary Prince?" Mut asked, leaning back in the chair and crossing her ankles.

"He said anyone I choose." Ankhesenamun's body sagged in her chair as if her muscles had become loose.

"Anyone?" Mut raised an eyebrow. *To be so lucky.*

Ankhesenamun nodded but shrugged. "If the people did not want my mother as Pharaoh, I do not see how anyone being named Hereditary Prince will do. At least your husband was General of Pharaoh's Armies when he was named Hereditary Prince, and my grandfather was Vizier of the Lower when he married me to take the crown." She turned away, her gaze on the bed. "There is a lack of established men, it seems."

"Has Father chosen a vizier yet?" Mut's toe tapped back and forth in the air. She felt sorry for Ankhesenamun, and yet she also did not.

If he has not chosen someone, then Ankhesenamun could choose her husband. A royal woman choosing her husband . . . a luxury unheard of!

Mut closed her eyes with a slight shake of her head.

Why am I like this? She lost someone she loved and will be forced to marry another! I, at least, do not have to deal with much heartache, and I can stay unmarried if I so choose.

"No, Mut." Agitation plagued Ankhesenamun's voice. "Tut's body is not even back yet. We cannot even send him to the afterlife with a burial preparation fit for a King. They are performing the preparation in the Mitanni lands with *battlefield* priests."

Mut nodded, contrite in her own ignorance. Her father needed to perform the funerary rites first; otherwise, it would be in poor taste.

"I am sorry, Ankhesenamun."

Mut spoke the truth. She was sorry—*and* jealous but not at the same time. She took a quick inhale to silence her self-reflections. Ankhesenamun was in pain. Ankhesenamun was her niece, although older than her, and Mut was going to be there for her as the Queen's aunt.

Ankhesenamun shook her head. "It is not . . . I am . . . I just do not know what to do." She buried her head in her hands, and her shoulders shook out silent tears.

Mut came, wrapped her in her arms, and pressed her head against her shoulder.

"The gods will be with us." It seemed like the right thing to say.

"Ah, the gods." Ankhesenamun pushed Mut away as tears fell afresh down her cheeks. "The gods take my two children and then strip me of my parents and my sisters and the man who finally realized he loved me. Are we still paying for the crimes of my father? Do they have no mercy?"

She stood and shook a fist at the ceiling. "Do you have no mercy?!"

Then she collapsed to her knees and bent her back so she rocked on her knees and elbows. "Please . . . give me peace . . . give me peace." It was the only thing she repeated, a litany to the gods.

Mut looked at the figurines of the goddesses on the table by the door. She was not even sure the gods listened to them. Half her life had been spent worshipping in secret from the tortuous prosecution from Pharaohs Akhenaten and Smenkare, the rest spent learning about all the festivals that accompanied each deity and trying to remember how to worship them properly. It seemed like a lot to her. So many people worshipping so many gods—the same gods who did nothing but punish her family, let men like Pawah escape justice for murdering her sister—Pharaoh, of all people, Amun's divinely appointed.

Mut's gaze fell back to the sobbing Ankhesenamun. Akhenaten was gone now. He had paid for his crime at Nefertiti's hand. Why should the rest of his family pay for his transgressions against the gods? Ankhesenamun's question repeated in her mind:

Do the gods have no mercy?

If not, she felt that they need not be worshipped. There had already been too much pain and suffering in Egypt.

Mut knelt beside her niece and put a hand on her back. "The gods will bring you peace. You have suffered much for them."

She almost believed her words, but then she looked at the figurines again—how would they grant peace? They were just little stone statues.

Ankhesenamun stopped rocking and rested her head on her hands as her body sank to the stone. "There will be no peace for me." Her solemn whisper reverberated from the stone floor. "I have lost everything. I will marry the next man who succeeds my grandfather after however much longer he shall live. I will bear the next Pharaoh his children, perhaps, just his heir. And then I will die an old woman, alone and fat from luxury." She sat up and took a deep breath as she stared at her bed. "I see no more happiness in my life. I managed only a taste of it at the end with Tut."

Mut wished to speak but held her tongue. *At least you have experienced happiness with a man who loved you. My husbands had nothing to do with me.*

Ankhesenamun stood, rigid, as if accepting her fate. "I cannot change what has happened. Both of our husbands are gone." She placed her hands on Mut's shoulders. "I am trapped in Malkata, but you, Mut, you are free to remarry when and to whom you want."

Mut shook her head. "No, I will not marry again. My father told me only to marry if I was happy. Maybe he will tell you the same."

"I am Queen." She laughed, trying not to cry. "I *must* marry the next Pharaoh. There is no heir. I am the sole child of the royal bloodline."

Mut lowered her chin.

"Do you not see, Mut? I am trapped here to live as Queen, only hopeful the next Pharaoh does not make me his bed slave, hopeful the next Pharaoh at least treats me well."

"But Father has said *you* choose Hereditary Prince."

"Who would I choose, Mut? There is no vizier, no General. Who would I choose that the people would so accept? A guard? A goldsmith? A *beadmaker*? I will be as my mother, rejected by the people, and probably slaughtered like her too."

Mut held her breath, remembering the bodies in the council room and Horemheb rushing to her to shield her from the blood. She shook the memory from her present.

"At least Pawah is to be executed, no? You will not have him to deal with."

"Another will rise in his place." Ankhesenamun sliced the air with her hand and then began to pace. "My mother spoke of trying to return power to the position of Pharaoh, and I see now their attempt. I see now my father's folly." She stopped and dropped her head. "I am stuck." With her exhale, more tears trickled from her eyes. "I cannot move. I cannot breathe. I cannot sleep. I do not know what to do."

"Grieve. It is all you *can* do right now."

Ankhesenamun shook her head. "It hurts too much."

Mut sighed. *I do not envy her pain, but I wish I felt what it was like to be loved in return by someone I loved—or at least thought I loved.*

After taking a few moments to compose herself, Ankhesenamun asked, "What are you to do, Mut?"

Mut shrugged and shook her head. "I suppose I will go back to Men-nefer at the right time and then do as my father told me long ago: do what makes me happy."

Ankhesenamun wiped her cheeks. "What makes you happy?"

"I do not know. He told me to be a scribe or a physician or a priestess." Mut snorted at that last one. *Maybe it would do my faith some good if I studied to be a priestess for one of the many gods,* she thought.

Ankhesenamun rubbed her arms and let out a breath. "You are smart. You are talented. You will find what makes you happy."

Mut's lips curled into a sad smile as her feelings once again bubbled over.

"In my ignorant youth, I thought happiness was marriage and a life with Horemheb . . . but Horemheb refused me. Later, when he *did* marry me, he told me I would be safe at his estate, making me question his motives in marrying me. I cannot ask him anymore, and I will never know for sure, but he left me for years. So maybe it is best that I do not know."

Tears welled in her eyes at the pain of rejection, of always being second in others' eyes, of falling in someone else's shadow for all her life, never amounting to that which she was expected.

"At least Tut loved you." Mut's breathless whisper accompanied the tears that finally broke free.

Ankhesenamun's mouth contorted into a grimace as she pulled Mut into an embrace. "I am so sorry, Mut."

THE NEXT MORNING, MUT AND ANKHESENAMUN WALKED around Malkata's courtyard, trying to enjoy the bright sunshine in lieu of the darkened bedchambers.

Ankhesenamun stopped as she focused in on Sennedjem across the way. It had been months since she had seen him, and a flood of memories rushed upon her: Her husband's doubt that she had stayed true to him while he was off at war, placed there by the plotting Pawah. The years spent telling Tut there was nothing between them and the pain of Tut pushing her away.

With Tut gone now, it seemed to her it may be taboo to even acknowledge Sennedjem, for what if those same accusations resurfaced? What would the palace think? Would they see a glimmer of perceived truth in Pawah's lies? Ah, she could see it now: the pointed fingers and hushed whispers behind her back.

"Queen Ankhesenamun had her husband killed so she could be with Sennedjem!" they would say. "And to think she lied her way into Pharaoh Tutankhamun's bed!"

But did she even care at this point?

Her heart missed Tut, and she had never strayed, not even in thought.

Sennedjem saw her and began to make his way to them.

Her heart pumped within her chest. *Why am I reacting this way to him? I have never felt anxious being around him before!*

"The Overseer of Tutors is approaching," she whispered to Mut, who glanced first at Ankhesenamun and then to Sennedjem as he drew closer.

He came to a halt in front of Ankhesenamun—at a respectable distance—and bowed. Upon rising, he glanced for a moment at the royal guards, Hori and Ineni, who were escorting the Queen and her guest.

"My Queen, I am sorry to hear of Pharaoh Tutankhamun's passing. May he journey well to Re."

Her eyes glistened over, and she lowered her chin in

thanks. There was a sadness in his voice that triggered a memory, something he had said to her after losing her second daughter to the Field of Reeds: he, too, had lost his wife. Maybe he could have some encouraging words. For, after realizing Horemheb may not have loved Mut, she tried not to voice her sorrow so much in front of Mut. But no—she would have to ask Mut to leave to speak her feelings with Sennedjem, and she could not let her guards hear her speaking like this with him . . . if she did that, then she might as well start the rumors herself. She glanced at Mut and realized she and the tutor had not met.

"Sennedjem," she began in a soft voice. "Overseer of the Tutors, this is Mistress of the House Mut. She was married to General Horemheb."

Sennedjem nodded to show his condolences. "May the General make a good journey as well."

Mut stayed silent but dipped her chin in gratitude.

Ankhesenamun hesitated, but then her sorrow forced her to speak.

"Please leave us, royal guards Hori and Ineni."

They bowed and walked out of earshot. She stole a quick glance at Mut again and thought it better for her to stay—for Ankhesenamun's own selfish reason, true, but better nonetheless. She only hoped she did not further agitate the wound Horemheb had left upon her aunt.

"Sennedjem—" Ankhesenamun's voice cracked. She took a deep breath and pulled her shoulders up again to retain her composure. "How did you overcome the loss of your wife? I know you told me before, but I . . . I cannot . . . I could not understand until now. I find . . ." Her voice caught in her throat. "I find the loss unbearable."

He nodded, and it seemed as though he had known the question was coming. His feet shuffled before he answered. "In many ways, I did not . . ."

He paused, half smiling. His eyes did not glisten, but the

sound of his voice made her want to cry. Her eyes blinked to keep the tears at bay as he continued.

"I engrossed myself in my career as a military man, took chances I should not have." He nodded and pursed his lips. "I stayed busy because if I did not think of her, I did not remember her. But when the nights came, and I lay idle with my thoughts, I hated myself for not constantly remembering her."

Mut shuffled to the side, as though perhaps she did not want to be part of this conversation. Thankfully, Mut did not actually leave them but only stooped to look at the flowers. In this way, Ankhesenamun felt she could continue without garnering stares or whipping up gossip.

"How do you . . . ?" She paused, finding his gaze again. "How do you live every day with the burden?"

"I . . ." He shrugged and gave a slight shake of his head. "I found beauty in other things." His eyebrows raised as his eyes traced her face. "I found I could still make a difference and was a better teacher. I found purpose in teaching my students so that they might not take the ignorant chances I took while on the battlefield." He dropped his head and took a pained breath before lifting his eyes once again to her own, a grimace now etched on his features. "I am sorry to have failed with some, including our late Pharaoh." He looked to the ground once again. "I beg forgiveness, my Queen."

Her lip trembled as she stared upon his bowed head. "You did not fail him." Her words were strong and firm. "He fought through two wars and lived."

He lifted his head.

"There is nothing to forgive, Sennedjem, Overseer of the Tutors."

His mouth held no smile, but he nodded, breaking eye contact right as Ankhesenamun found comfort in his eyes.

"You are most kind, my Queen."

She stared at him. He held an attractive face and body, and

his heart was pure and loyal. She shut her eyes, wishing she did not have to think about a future Pharaoh, longing for this time to grieve her husband instead. It would be only a matter of decans before Tut's burial, and her grandfather would have to name a vizier and a General, one of whom he would then name Hereditary Prince. Sennedjem would not qualify, in the people's eyes, for either position. He would never be accepted as Hereditary Prince. Looking into his eyes, she saw an admiration there and wondered if he knew the same.

They held each other's gaze for a long while, enough time for Mut to stand and begin looking around. Mut finally cleared her throat, breaking the silence, and Sennedjem spoke.

"My Queen, if you ever need a reason to train again, I will be in the training yard." His words were rushed and whispered. He then went silent, as if waiting for her dismissal.

She wished to tell him that he was her only friend left in the palace, that she wished she could sit alone and speak with him again, as they once did, that she wished she could share her sorrow with someone who truly understood, but fear of rumors lingered in the back of her mind. The next Pharaoh should have no doubt about whose bed she shared, for the next Pharaoh may not be as slow to punish as Tut had been.

She nodded and let him go.

As he walked away, Mut looked at Ankhesenamun. "It may be too soon," she whispered, "but how do you think the people would feel about an Overseer named as Hered—"

"They would not accept him." Ankhesenamun blushed and averted her gaze. Pinning her arms against her stomach, she tried to suffocate the guilt that lived there: the guilt for thinking the same, especially after receiving news of Tut's passing only a few months ago. She bit her lip and straightened, regaining her posture once again. She would not be sorry for thinking those thoughts. Tut was gone, and in the very near future, she would be forced to live the rest of her life as the wife of someone else.

Her eyes lingered on Sennedjem as he walked across the way, and just before he turned the corner, he looked back. They locked eyes for a moment. Then he vanished behind the stone.

"I am sorry, Ankhesenamun." Mut clasped her hands together over her stomach. "He seemed to favor you."

"What?" Ankhesenamun asked, her train of thought failing her. "How do you mean?"

Mut shrugged. "In the way he spoke to you . . . I assume you have spoken before—and not as Queen and Overseer of the Tutors."

"Yes, we have on several occasions. When Pawah was in Aketaten, Sennedjem trained me per my command. I found his loyalty then. Pawah, of course, used that as a seed of doubt he planted in Tut's mind—that I had been unfaithful to Tut with Sennedjem." She frowned at the remembered heartache. "Pawah also told Tut that I killed our daughters." She lowered her head and pressed her lips into a grimace.

Mut's eyes watered. "I am sorry."

She shook her head. "No . . . it was hard and difficult. I thought I was all alone, but Sennedjem and Hori"—she peered over her shoulder—"I found I could trust. They helped me see through Pawah's hold over Tut." She found Mut's eyes. "I would never have known Tut, in the end, would choose to believe me and love me despite all the rumors and lies and the so-called lists Pawah had that verified his accusations."

Ankhesenamun paused in thought. She and Tut were so happy in the end. She wished she could tell Mut, but did not want her to hurt more. She did not want Mut to compare.

"Sennedjem became my friend . . . but now I fear, with Tut gone, the people will only remember the accusations. I must distance myself from one of my last friends I have in the palace."

Silence befell them as they each shared a pained look, knowing words would do no good.

———

ALMOST A SEASON HAD COME AND GONE AFTER RECEIVING NEWS of Tut's passing until finally, his mummified body made it back to Malkata. Ay had ordered the masons working on Tut's tomb to work triple their speed, but still it was not done, still needing one or even two more years.

At the realization, Ay ordered that his own tomb—much smaller and lacking in splendor, but completed—be given to his predecessor. While the tomb was modified for a Pharaoh's afterlife, King Ay performed the funerary rites.

Ankhesenamun watched, glad the battlefield priests at least had the dignity and the foresight to make Tut's body like that of Osiris. Black tar wrapped his body, and cornflowers adorned his neck.

"In the afterlife I shall meet you again, my love," she whispered as Ay's aged voice still boomed out amongst the people. Her face slack and expressionless, she kept her hands from shaking by curling her fingers and hiding them beneath the pleats of her long royal dress.

The sun's heat fell upon her brow, causing her to lose herself in her thoughts: remembering Tut's touch, his asking of forgiveness, his kiss. She drew an inhale, remembering still further back into his childhood, in the Kap, as he learned from Sennedjem. *"I'll protect you, Ankhesenpaaten!"* His child's voice rang in her memory. A smile tried to form, but a frown took its place.

"I miss you," she whispered to his ka.

Her grandfather said the last rite to open Tut's mouth so that his body would have food and water on his journey to the afterlife. Then the servants began to move Tut's coffin down into the tomb in the Valley of the Kings. The nobles and the people stayed and watched them until the tomb was sealed.

Ay stayed with Ankhesenamun until finally, the sun set in the west, and darkness encroached upon them.

"My granddaughter, we must leave now," Ay whispered into Ankhesenamun's wig.

She struggled to find her breath. "I had seen a future for us, Grandfather. I believed there would be a future for us."

"As did I with my Temehu," Ay whispered, "but . . . life never happens as we plan it." He looked up to the sky, now beginning to prickle with stars. "Nothing as we plan." His thoughts drifted to his first wife, his firstborn, his role in removing kings—none of which had gone to plan—and a frown accompanied his thoughts. "Tut will be with Re, and one day you will see him again."

Ankhesenamun's breath hitched.

"Granddaughter, I love you," he said and wrapped his arm around her shoulder. "At least the people cry real tears for his passing, unlike your father's. Tut was a good King. Hold onto that."

She nodded and let him lead her back to Malkata.

℁ 3 ℁

THE TIME OF PROMISE

AT ANKHESENAMUN'S CONTINUED SILENCE IN THE FOLLOWING days, Ay declared Paramesse as General, Nakhtmin still as Master of Pharaoh's Horses, and the aged Nakht as his Vizier of the Upper and Lower. They were the most logical choices, and all three were powerful men. Ay also appointed Tey as his chief royal wife, which in turn demoted Ankhesenamun as royal wife—yet, still, if there was no offspring from Tey and Ay, which was not likely, Ankhesenamun would remain the sole Hereditary Princess even though she was now Great Chief Wife to two past kings, her father and her half-brother.

Ankhesenamun looked out her window to one of Malkata's many courtyards and then around her new bedchambers—she had been sent back to the royal harem now that Tey took the queen's bedchambers in the main palace. It was large enough, but it held no memories.

Maybe that is for the better, she thought as she looked to the dunes that hid her late husband's tomb in the distance. Her grandfather had ensured her room was uncommonly private, and she wanted to kiss him for that. No one would see her tears there.

A knock came on the door of her new room. Her new

steward, Ahset, answered it. Her grandfather's voice cut through the silence. "Leave Pharaoh and his royal wife."

Ankhesenamun heard the scurry of feet but remained facing the window. The door closed.

"It has been two seasons since we received the news of Tut and Horemheb's passing." Ay came up beside her and looked out at the courtyard and the skies beyond as well, taking in a breath of the fresh air. He placed his hand over hers on the window sill. "I know it is not easy for you. I remember the pain of losing Temehu, your grandmother . . . but I am getting old, and my years are limited. Please, Ankhesenamun, name a Hereditary Prince so that before I journey to Re, I can bring happiness to the last remaining daughter of my Nefertiti. Please grant me my last wish."

Ankhesenamun pressed her lips into a smile and pushed her brows over her eyes. With a soft laugh and shake of her head, she whispered, "It is hard to find happiness now." Her mind drifted to Sennedjem—as the days wore on, he was the only one she could even attempt to see herself with. But still, her words spoke the truth: "I do not want anyone."

"I know," he said and pulled her into a side embrace. "The days, although the sun shines brightly, are dark. I lost myself, too, remembering Temehu." He chuckled in his sorrow. "I could not even bring myself to look upon your mother for a long while. You have lost much, my dear. What can I do to bring you some happiness?"

"Nothing, Grandfather. If anyone I name is not as Pharaoh should be, the people will not accept." She leaned with both hands on the window sill, jutting her head out of the window to feel the sun's rays on her face; they evoked memories in her of her father's worship of the Aten. Such a simple time her childhood seemed to her.

"The people cannot refuse Amun's divinely appointed."

"They refused Mother. I have seen the disrespect they show you as Pharaoh. Only a few still show you the respect

Pharaoh deserves." She dropped her head; the warmth vanished from her face.

She had pleaded with her mother for the truth, and when she finally got it, she knew the times of laughter and play were over. *A new day means new beginnings,* she had told her mother in her attempts to comfort her. Except now, it seemed each day had the same beginning—one without Tut. She longed for her mother; just like Tut, they had become close at the very end. She foolishly believed a lie that had brought her peace: a bright and happy future with the both of them.

Look at me now, she thought bitterly.

She stood back and removed his hand from her shoulder. "She told me of the plan to take power from the Amun priesthood and return it to Pharaoh . . . I guess it has all been in vain."

Ay clenched his jaw. "Not all, but . . ." He trailed off and shook his head. "But certainly most. It caused much pain and sacrifice." He rubbed his face and then pulled his hand away, taking a deep breath. "At least now Pharaoh appoints the First Prophet of Amun again." He sighed in frustration as he lifted his eyes to the Aten. "I curse you, Akhenaten, for bringing so much destruction. If you had done what we planned, none of this would have happened." The tension in his shoulders fell with his head. He squared his shoulders to Ankhesenamun. "I know the pain . . . but please let me give you some semblance of happiness, of peace. Name your Hereditary Prince."

She shook her head. "I have none. Tut is gone. He was my prince."

"I swear to you, Pawah will die for what he has done."

"Has he not already?" Ankhesenamun's head snapped to Ay, whose body froze. "He was to be impaled outside the temple. Was he not?" Her voice rose as her heart prepared to scream. "What happened? Did he escape? Did you let him go?!"

Scowling, Ay locked eyes with Ankhesenamun. "I swear to you on the grave of my Temehu, I did no such thing."

"Then what happened? Why was I not told?" Ankhesenamun grabbed Ay by the arms, her eyes searching his until, finally, he let go of the truth.

"He escaped the morning after I ordered his sentence. The guards have swept Waset, and they cannot find him. They are searching both the Upper and the Lower as we speak." He chewed his lip as if there were more.

Ankhesenamun's eyes grew big as her heart raced in her chest. "Mut left the palace . . ."

"I sent guards with Mut on her journey home in case, for some reason, Pawah wanted to hurt me more."

"Hurt *you* more?! He would be hurting *Mut*! You should not have let her leave Malkata," Ankhesenamun said through her teeth. "She was at least safe here. Pawah killed my mother because of guards we trusted. Pawah *escaped* from guards we trusted!"

Ay let out a captive breath, seemingly to calm himself. "I tried to keep her, Ankhesenamun, but Mut wanted to return. She wanted to find peace in her new life, especially now that Tut was entombed. She needed to know if Horemheb's body had returned to Men-nefer, and she needed to put him to rest." He shook his head. "I tried to keep her here. She is so stubborn. Like your mother."

"Did you at least tell her Pawah was in hiding? He could strike at any moment!" Ankhesenamun's grip hardened on Ay's robes.

"I did as a last resort. She assured me she was nothing to him. She left, Ankhesenamun. What was I to do? Hold her in Malkata as a prisoner?"

"Yes, if need be. You lock her in the royal harem with me." Ankhesenamun narrowed her eyes. "You *let* her leave." She threw her grip off of Ay and rubbed her forehead with her finger and thumb. "I am going after her."

"You will do no such thing. As Pharaoh, I order you to stay," Ay said and pointed a finger to the ground.

Tension wrapped her vocal cords. "And you could not have done the same with Mut?"

"You do not understand. She is my daughter. She needed to bury her husband."

"And I am your daughter's daughter. We delayed in Tut's burial—she can delay Horemheb's." A rage grew behind her eyes. "Order her home now."

Ay shook his head. "You do not understand. Pawah needs you, not Mut, to become Pharaoh. You are the last Hereditary Princess. If you should travel to the Field of Reeds, then Mut would take your place, but for now, she is useless to Pawah. You will stay here at Malkata where you are safe." He turned to leave. "But I will send word to order Mut to Malkata once she has buried Horemheb."

"Do what you will, but I will not have her murdered by the same man who took my mother. I would think you want the same." Ankhesenamun's fingers curled into her palms as she leaned toward her grandfather.

"I do," Ay said, nodding. "But"—he held a finger in the air—"Mut would never forgive me if I did not let her bury the man she married."

"Would she forgive you if Pawah *killed* her?" Ankhesenamun snapped.

"My daughters made and make their own choices in this life. For Nefertiti, it ended in an early journey west." Ay swallowed. "And for Mut, I hope it does not end the same way."

He shut the door after him before Ankhesenamun could speak again.

ANKHESENAMUN RACED DOWN THE CORRIDOR, HORI AND INENI running after her, toward the training yard. She found Sennedjem cleaning the training daggers. He jolted to standing upon seeing her and then bowed before Ankhesenamun.

"In peace, my Queen," he whispered, a little startled at her sudden appearance. "How may—"

"Did you ever teach Mut to defend herself while she was here? Did she ever come to see you?"

He blinked several times and then shook his head. "No, I did not, and she did not."

Ankhesenamun's shoulders dropped.

Sennedjem looked to Hori and Ineni, who stood behind her, and they shrugged.

Ankhesenamun went to the bench in the shade and plopped down. Sennedjem followed and knelt—a respectable distance from Ankhesenamun, as was his position as Overseer.

As she stared at her wringing hands in her lap, Ankhesenamun whispered, "If Mut is killed, I would like you to end my life."

Sennedjem shot a pointed look at Hori and Ineni, who both quickly turned their backs against the conversation. He stood and sat down next to her, still with distance between them.

"I took an oath never to harm Pharaoh or his royal family. In fact, I took an oath to *protect* them, to *die* for them." Sennedjem's voice was soft and smooth, free of judgment.

"I will have no one left if Mut is killed. My grandfather will not last much longer. Same for my grandmother. My sisters are all gone. My husband lies in the Valley of the Kings. I have no children." A tear fell down her cheek. "I am all alone."

"My Queen, I have said before . . . you are not alone. We

are here. Hori, Ineni—" He gestured, and then added, "And me."

She closed her eyes and shook her head. *No, I am alone,* she thought. *Tut is gone. I cannot be with him anymore, and if I am forced to choose a husband . . . I would choose you, Sennedjem. Nakhtmin and Paramesse are twenty years my senior, with wives already, and Nakht is almost my grandfather's age. I do not see a happy life with any of them.*

Then she spoke: "I will be married to whomever Pharaoh names as Hereditary Prince. In such a life, I see no beauty as you have found in yours. I see no path to make a difference." She licked her lips, dry in the heat of the day. "I would rather journey west than live that life."

She wanted to say, *I will spend the rest of my days in the royal harem as a secluded royal wife, unable to speak to you alone, to have you as my friend . . . unable to influence Pharaoh in his decisions, unable to make any impact in Egypt. I will be alone.*

"Another husband could give you children," Sennedjem offered, but upon her silence, he continued a different path. "My Queen, I was not wholly truthful the last we spoke. If I may be so bold as to compare, there was a time I wished to end my life as well."

Her jaw tensed, but still, she said nothing. She turned her head to look upon him and nodded for him to continue.

"I was as you, my Queen. No spouse, no children, a dim future that I did not want. In fact, it was an entire two years after they had gone to the Field of Reeds, during which I did not want to live. I trudged on each day, hoping someone would kill me in battle. I was a Captain of the Troop and made foolish decisions. I believed I was costing the lives of my men and thus resigned to become a tutor. As I tutored—as I told you—I found some reward there . . . but nothing revived the numbness in my soul. Then one day . . . " A soft chuckle and a distant gaze filled his pause. ". . . you came to my training yard wanting to learn to fight. 'What an odd request of a Queen,' I remember thinking."

He looked at her once again.

"When I learned Pawah had threatened you, and that what you had told Pharaoh Tutankhamun about your mother was true . . ." He shrugged his shoulders. "For once, it made me feel as though I were a part of something that mattered. *Protecting* someone who mattered." A small smile came upon his lips. "And I have not felt quite so numb since."

" 'Numb' is a good word," Ankhesenamun whispered. "I feel numb. I do not know how much more numb I can feel."

The only thing that maybe kept her from truly wanting Sennedjem to kill her was that she knew Nefe was somewhere out there, hopefully living a fulfilling life. General Paaten, hopefully, was also still alive, protecting her. Part of her wished she had gone with Nefe, to save herself from the heartache of gaining Tut and then losing him once he finally realized he loved her. She covered her eyes, embarrassed to cry in front of Sennedjem yet again—and this time with Hori and Ineni within earshot.

She jumped when Sennedjem placed a hand on her forearm. His gaze locked with hers. "The feeling of numbness does go away at some point. Maybe when you bear your next husband's child, or if you should love the Hereditary Prince, or find another purpose in life. It will never be the same, but you can find happiness again."

Her eyelids drooped around her puffy cheeks. "*You* did not."

He swallowed and pulled away his hand.

"Why do you tell me that which you are unsure of yourself?" Her voice came from her chest as she tried to calm her hitching breath.

"I found happiness in helping you," he whispered.

Tears hid behind his eyes, and Ankhesenamun's heart

dropped to the pit of her stomach. She had hit him hard with her words, and then he only smoothed honey in the wound. She turned her head away and fiddled with her thumbs in her lap.

"Why do you find happiness in helping me?"

"You are my Queen," he said, outlining her profile with his eyes.

She looked up at the guards and noticed Hori peering over his shoulder.

I want to talk to Sennedjem without ears listening in on our conversation, but I also do not wish for rumors to spread. She lifted her chin, making her decision hoping Ineni held the same loyalty as Hori.

"Please leave us," she told them.

Hori nodded, and they walked a distance away.

She took a small breath of reprieve as she surveyed the empty training yard.

"My grandfather has told me I could name my Hereditary Prince, but I know the people would never accept anyone but a General, a vizier, or perhaps a Commander." She shook her head. Taking a heavy sigh, she closed her eyes, and turned blindly to Sennedjem. "I had thought about asking Pharaoh to name *you* as Hereditary Prince . . ." Her voice trailed off, and she stole a look to see if he might have been happy at the request, but his face gave away no secrets. "It was only for a moment, because I believe the people would never accept you as Pharaoh."

"I do not believe they would either, but I am honored you thought of me." Sennedjem glanced at her lips. "I would be good to you, my Queen. I would—"

"I know." She nodded as bittersweet happiness sank into her heart at his reciprocity. "I try not to entertain any false futures. I miss Tut. I miss our daughters."

He nodded. "I miss my wife too."

A moment of silence passed.

Ankhesenamun gathered the courage to speak her mind,

knowing she had just said she would not entertain any false futures: "I know you would protect me, and I think perhaps we might even find it within ourselves to fall in love at some point—" Ankhesenamun's breath hitched. "But it would never be accepted."

"Pharaoh could appoint me Vizier."

Ankhesenamun chuckled, and Sennedjem smiled at the ridiculousness of it. Ankhesenamun shook her head. "Overseer of the Tutors jumping to Vizier to Hereditary Prince. The people would see through that."

"I know." Sennedjem's smile broadened. "It was worth a try. In truth, I do not want to be Pharaoh. I do not envy what you and Pharaoh Tutankhamun went through with former Vizier Pawah, and even watching Pharaohs Akhenaten, Smenkare, and Neferneferuaten and seeing the burdens they had to carry . . . I have no desire to fulfill that role, even if I were named Hereditary Prince."

Ankhesenamun dipped her chin. "I do not wish to be royalty anymore. It brings nothing but pain."

Sennedjem nodded again. "A life of luxurious loneliness."

"Yes." She paused. "You would reject being named Hereditary Prince."

Perhaps he only tells me this so I do not think of him anymore, as a future between us is nothingness—just as with Tut.

Her thoughts focused on him as her heart cried out to his ka.

Why, Tut? Why did you leave me? Doom me to a life where I can never find peace?

She noticed Sennedjem staring at her and remembered his stare after he hid his dagger in her belt that day in the Aketaten training yard, but it was different this time. Then, it was one of determination and a bit of anger that someone dared threaten her, but now, it was . . . what? Pity? Admiration? Friendship? She turned to face him, realizing conversations like these could only last as long as her grandfather were alive—until the next husband came along. Sennedjem kept his mouth closed, but a half smile grew on his face.

"You pity me?" she asked, trying to guess the reason for the smile.

He shook his head.

"Then what are you thinking?"

"This may be a little bold for an Overseer, and given the timing . . . maybe I should not say anything . . ." His voice trailed off, and he looked away. "It is not within my status to say."

"Sennedjem, please . . . I have told you things I should not have, and you are my only friend left in Malkata. Only you understand what it feels like to lose your spouse and your child. I am sorry I am the one who has blurred the line between us and our statuses. Please tell me what you want to say."

Sennedjem took a deep breath and looked at her once again. "If the position of Pharaoh came with you as my wife, I would take it without hesitation."

A smile crept over her lips, even though her eyes still held sadness. "That *is* a little bold," she whispered, and then her heart fell, for he would never be Hereditary Prince. "I wish it were not so."

"I am sorry, my Qu—"

She grabbed his hand. A deep breath escaped her lips as she rubbed his thumb. "For now, I will always wonder about the life I could have had with you." His hand was strong and warm in hers.

"As I have and will every day," he whispered and rubbed her fingers with his thumb.

They shared a moment of silence before Ankhesenamun felt the weight of her reality press upon her and looked to the guards to see if they watched. They did not, but she needed to end this now before she suffered any more heartache than she had already in the past two seasons.

She stood up abruptly, letting go of his hand. "I shall be married to whomever the people accept and Pharaoh names as Hereditary Prince." She and Sennedjem locked eyes. "I wish you to find your own happiness, my friend, Sennedjem." She dipped her chin to him as tears filled her eyes. Then she turned to leave.

"Wait," he whispered, standing as well.

She turned back to face him.

He stepped closer and peered over her head to ensure the guards did not watch and his training yard remained empty. He grasped her hands and brought them to his lips. "I am sorry, my Queen." He kissed one hand. "I will always be here to protect you and your family." He kissed the other. "That is my happiness, and I shall continue to admire from afar as I have done." He smiled and pulled her hands to his chest. "And most of all, I wish you to find peace in whatever life the gods give to you."

She nodded as he kissed her hands again.

"Whatever you do, my Queen, please do not end your life. You never know what the future may hold." At her silence, he added, "Pharaoh Tutankhamun would not want you to leave this life in unhappiness." He paused. "*I* do not want you to leave your life in unhappiness."

She took a deep breath and then nodded as he wiped a tear from her cheek.

❧ 4 ❧

THE TIME OF DOMINATION

MUT STEPPED OVER THE THRESHOLD INTO HER ESTATE AND TOOK a deep breath, secretly wishing the home smelled of Horemheb; but it did not . . . it never did.

It's not like he was ever here with me, his wife.

But she did expect there to be the smell of something: bread or fish, perhaps. She looked around the entrance of the main home. No servants came to greet her. She peered over her shoulder and saw the two royal guards, who had come with her from Malkata, standing beside Tener and Raia, who carried her travel slings.

"Do they still hate us?" Tener whispered to Raia.

Raia shrugged.

They walked the hallway of the main house shrouded in darkness. Tener began lighting the alabaster sconces on the wall to give some light as one guard walked ahead and the other behind the three women.

"Have the servants left?" Mut asked Raia.

"I do not know, Mistress of the House."

Mut let Tener and Raia go about the first floor of the home and light the candles with one guard while the other guard stayed with her in the eerie silence. She walked to the foot of the stairs leading to the second floor. Mut was about to step up, but then—

SLAM!

Her heart jumped out of her chest, and her face went white.

"It was me!" Tener cried at the front door. "I closed the door!"

"Oh! In honor of Bastet!" Mut yelled, grasping her chest as she peered over the railing down the hall toward Tener. "Do not scare me like that again!"

"Yes, Mistress of the House. I am sorry!" Tener said, and bowed.

Mut muttered under her breath, "Just stay calm. There is nothing to be afraid of." She shook her head and turned back to the stairs.

Before she could ascend, Bakt appeared at the top of the stairs. "I apologize. I have been tidying up for your arrival and did not hear you come in." She pulled her belt tight and adjusted her wig.

"It is all right. Where is everyone else?" Mut asked as Tener joined her.

"I let them all go home for a while. We did not know how long you would be at Malkata, and the estate only needs gardening and a light cleaning every now and then, all of which I could do myself. I will let them enjoy the decan, and then I will call them back now that you are home." Bakt hurried down the stairs and ordered Tener to the kitchen. "Why don't you go to bed? You look a little ill and must be tired from your trip."

"Yes, I'll go upstairs," Mut said, and began to ascend. Her sleepless nights alongside the Queen must be showing in her face for Bakt to insult her by saying she looked ill, but she also knew Bakt did not care for her much and probably meant it to be mean.

The guard stepped on the first stair behind Mut.

Bakt slapped his hand from the railing. "There is no one up there. Just let the poor widow get some sleep for tonight."

Mut was too tired to argue or chide her at the lack of use of her title, so she turned and nodded to the guard, reassuring herself: *Bakt may not like me, but she would never put me in harm's way. I am the Mistress of the House, after all.*

"We will be at the courtyard gate, Mistress of the House," the second guard said, tapping his spear on the ground. "Call from your window should you need us."

Mut dipped her chin in agreement and watched them both go out the door, and then, step by step, she went up the stairs. She peered over her shoulder to see Bakt staring at her with a small grin on her face. "Is everything well, Bakt?"

"Yes, everything is fine." Bakt's voice held no waver. "I just want to make sure you don't fall. You seem a little weak."

Mut pursed her lips. *Maybe she is trying to form some sort of relationship with me.*

"All right, well . . . thank you," Mut said and thought she should extend some sort of olive branch as well, so she added, "High Steward Bakt."

Bakt lowered her head. "Of course, *Mistress* of the House."

A half smile crept upon Mut's mouth as she continued up the stairs and down the corridor. *Maybe things will be different now,* she thought, replaying Bakt's last use of her title and her seemingly caring remarks—there had still been a tone of resentment behind her words, but it was progress nonetheless. *A few more years, and it will eventually go away completely. Maybe I can have a life here and find something to bring me happiness.*

She stopped as a sudden tightness gripped her chest.

I was so sure I would find happiness with Horemheb . . . but my mother was right, my father was right. She shook her head, standing there in the dim corridor and remembering the first time she entered the room. *I should have known then. I should have divorced him then, but why did I stay? Why did I stay?* she thought again. *Because even though Horemheb never loved me, I'll never forget him rushing to my side upon seeing Nefertiti's body in that council room. Something even my father did not do. Horemheb was a good man, despite leaving me after we married. I shall always remember him as that man. I have overlooked every wrong you did, Horemheb, because I believed you were the one for me.*

A tear slid from her eye as she whispered to his ka. "I will miss you. Rather . . ." she said with a soft, sad chuckle, "I will miss any life we could have had together. The life that I had envisioned for us. My mother was right. I was a foolish, infatuated child in love with a man who never really wanted me."

Mut let out a shaky breath, ready to move on.

Opening the door, she walked into her dark bedchambers.

The door shut behind her. A hand wrapped over her mouth. Someone pinned her arms behind her back. Pain seared down her arms and jaw as her heart caught in her chest.

"If you scream, I shall cut your throat," a whisper attacked her ear.

Her heart raced out of her chest as she tried to wriggle free, but with every move she made, her attacker's grip only intensified, until finally a sharp pain struck her neck. Her muscle had been pulled as tight as it could go. Her mind couldn't think—it went blank.

"Are you done?" the whisper came again.

She couldn't move. Her body was frozen.

"Good."

She felt his hot breath on her neck and squeezed her eyes shut, hoping he would just take the grain out back and leave her body alone. "Now, my dear Mut, you shall do what I want when I want it, and when the time comes, I shall present to your father an exchange for the crown."

Pawah.

Fear swarmed her legs as they almost gave up from

beneath her. Her racing heart rivaled that of a bird's wings flapping as she waited for the searing pain in her back from the sharp point of a dagger, but none came.

"Now, Mut . . ." The force over her mouth became unbearable as he shook her head to make his point. "I want you to tell your two servant girls to leave and come back in the morning. If you do not, I will slice their throats in front of you. I have nothing left to lose, and I will not blink an eye in killing everyone in this house. Then I will make you beg for death." He ran his tongue from her shoulder to her ear, and in the darkness, she felt his evil smile slither over her trembling body. "Do you understand?"

Tears fell from her eyes. She knew the truth: she knew he would probably kill her eventually. But at least she could save the three other lives in the house.

"Do you understand?" His hot whisper burned her neck as he shook her again for good measure.

She nodded and whimpered at the pain in her neck.

A knock came at the door. "Mistress of the House." It was Raia, speaking through the closed door. "Would you like for us to draw you a bath? Bakt said she could help while Tener finished in the kitchen."

Pawah shook her and squeezed her arms behind her back. Her eyes darted, trying to make out anything in the dark. *Why didn't Horemheb keep weapons in his home? Was he not Pharaoh's General?* But even if there were, she didn't know how to use them. She looked for a lampstand, anything, but her mind came up blank; all it saw were countless scenarios in which Pawah would kill her in her attempt to save herself.

Pawah elbowed her in the back, and she realized his hand was gone from her mouth.

"Mistress of the House? Are you well?" A small light graced the room from a slight opening of the door.

She thought about screaming for help, but then a pain in

her back sent out the words she knew she had to say. "Yes . . . Raia . . ." she finally said. "You and Tener . . . and Bakt . . ."

She paused. *Bakt. Bakt knew Pawah was here! She had to have known! She kept the guards from coming up the stairs. She betrayed me!* She clenched her jaw to keep her chin from quivering.

"Yes, Mistress of the House?" The door opened a little more, and Pawah held his dagger in front of Mut's face so the light glinted off the copper blade.

Mut's tongue tried to form the words, but her mind whirled until, at the last second, she blurted out the rest of what she needed to say to save Raia's life.

"Go with the other servants."

A pause.

"But we usually sleep here." The door opened more.

"Sleep in the second house!" Mut cried before the light of the corridor reached her toes. "I want the main house to myself tonight."

Pawah's hand wrapped back over her mouth with the dagger's handle pressed to her cheek.

The door paused. "Yes, Mistress of the House." Another pause. "Would you like for me or Bakt to draw you a bath or give you a shower?"

Pawah unwrapped his hand to let Mut speak.

Mut paused, trying to calm her breathing, and decided to hold her breath and speak to keep from sounding strained. "No, please. Leave me be tonight."

Pawah once again cupped Mut's mouth.

"As you wish," Raia said, and then, after a moment, she let the door fall closed again.

After they heard Raia descend the steps and the main home's door close, Pawah whispered in Mut's ear, "You follow direction so well—unlike your sister."

Mut struggled to free herself again, but Pawah slammed her against the wall and squeezed her neck.

"The women in your family love this position," he

whispered, his eyes so close their foreheads touched. Her eyes were adjusting to the darkness with the moonlight falling through the window.

"In the morning, you will tell your servants you are sick and to leave you be. They are to stay in the second house and check back in three days. On the third day, you are to tell them to summon your father, as you are very ill. Do you understand?"

"And if I don't?"

Her hands tried to pull his away from her neck. She tried to use her knees to pry him off of her, but he had pinned the whole of his body against hers. He kissed her lips as he drew the flat side of the dagger's blade along her cheek. Her nostrils flared, her body cringed at the touch, and she drew in a raspy breath.

Don't say a stupid thing, she chided herself. *He will take you in bed or kill you.*

"If you don't . . ." He hovered his face over hers. ". . . then what use are you to me?"

"I am your last chance of securing the throne," Mut said through her teeth, bracing her neck against his hand as if to compete with his squeeze.

He stabbed the dagger into the wooden wall next to her head. Mut felt the hot tears of terror fall down her face.

He is going to kill me.

She wanted to look around the room to see if there were some means of escape, but his penetrating lock upon her unblinking eyes kept her frozen. He released his hand around her neck a little so air rushed through her body, but just as he had released, he tightened it again.

"I still have Ankhesenamun. Your father won't live much longer, and until then, I just need to bide my time. Then I will force Ankhesenamun to marry me." His thumb grazed her temple as he pushed the dagger deeper through the wall.

"She will have nothing to lose but her life." Mut tried to shake her head. "You have to keep me alive."

Pawah clicked his tongue behind his teeth. "*Tsk-tsk.* Even a destitute dog fights for its life, my dear Mut," Pawah crooned. "How much more will the Queen?"

Mut tried to swallow the lump in her throat. *He is going to kill me.*

"But I think the easier option is to let you live and then exchange the crown for the Hereditary Prince title and watch your father drink poison before he can renege his appointment." Pawah pressed his mouth to hers. "How would you like to be my Queen?" he hummed.

"I am not yours, and I will never be." Mut's words came out on her breath.

"We shall see about that," Pawah said as his hand let go of the dagger stuck in the wall and ran over her body. "You look so much like your sister. Such a shame you were not as wholly blessed in the face as she. How was it as a child, Mut? Were you compared to her often?"

Mut's mouth turned to a scowl. "Stop it."

Mut had put to bed her resentment of her sister long ago —or so she had thought. Pawah was right. She had been compared. She had been favored less than her eldest sister. But none of that mattered now. Nefertiti was gone. Tears streamed down her cheeks. "You murdered her." Her breathless whisper felt hot on her lips.

"Yes . . . yes, I did." Pawah nodded, smiling. "I am happy, though." His hand stopped at her waist. "I'm happy you didn't make me kill you tonight. I would have hated to kill someone who resembles Nefertiti so closely. Some of her beauty needs to survive. But like I said . . . you are more of a cheap copy."

Mut's jaw clenched at the realization of her childhood fears—she could never compare to her sister, and now, long after Nefertiti's murder, even a stranger could see the truth.

She shook the doubt from her mind. She was not a cheap copy of her sister. She was her own woman. She was Mut.

Pawah sneered. "I wonder if that's why your husband never came home?"

Mut's breath hitched, her mind racing: *No. Be quiet. I can't hear this. I don't want to know. No! No, that is not the reason he never came home. He . . . I was just too young . . . he was the General and fighting wars . . . and he had other obligations to the royal family—*

"And after what you did to poor Amenia."

"Me?" Mut whimpered. She could barely speak; her breath caught in her quivering shoulders.

"You are horrible. Amenia journeyed west because Horemheb loved another woman and promised her to take care of you by way of marriage, and then you feign ignorance?" Pawah shook his head. "You are despicable, Mut. Everyone knows you were the other woman. How did you find out Amenia was infertile?" He smiled and squeezed a little harder. "Ah, I know . . . you are just as resourceful and manipulative as I."

"I am nothing like you. You speak lies." Mut's whisper came out with her raspy breath as she tried to pry his hand from her neck, digging her fingernails into the flesh of his skin.

His brow furrowed. "Ah, Mut . . . my dear Mut . . ." He leaned further into her, trapping her arms above her head with his other hand. "You will realize soon enough." He surveyed her face in the moonlight. "I waited for you all day."

Mut squirmed under his weight, not wanting to envision the coming night.

"But now I am tired. How about this? I promise I won't touch you if you quit trying to escape and do exactly as I say."

Mut felt a sigh of relief come through her lips, but

wondered if he meant what he said. Nevertheless, she nodded.

"Good." Then he spun her around and rammed her onto the bed.

"You promised—" She could barely get her words out through the tight grip he still had on her neck.

Pawah rubbed against her, reaching for something over her head. Before she knew it, he had looped her hand through a pre-tied rope, and then the other hand.

"I know, and I am a man true to my word. These are just in case you decide you are not." Pawah stood up and tightened the ropes so that her arms were pulled taut across the bed, each hand tied to the opposite corner of the bedpost. He ran his eyes over her body. "But you do entice me . . ."

"I shall scream until I cannot scream any more," Mut told him with her chin firm. "The guards will hear." *The guards,* she reassured herself, *the guards will hear.* She opened her mouth to scream, but Pawah, anticipating this, fell on top of her, clasping his hand over her mouth.

"You little demoness," he whispered, and pulled a linen cloth from the bedside table. "I thought I could trust you."

He stuffed her mouth with the cloth to the point where she almost could not breathe. Her body began to wretch, the more he stuffed, until finally he removed it. She coughed and breathed in the precious air.

"Now, my dear Mut, you will not scream. If you speak when I tell you not to speak, I will slice your throat and leave you to die." He wagged his finger in her face. "I have come too far to allow you to ruin this for me."

"Don't touch me, and I won't scream." She breathed in big gulps of air now, her mind racing to determine how she would get the guards' attention. She was in no place to barter: vulnerable and tied to the bed. "Touch me, and I'll scream. I'd rather die than have to live through you taking me."

Pawah cocked a grin. "We'll see in time. But for now, I am

tired. I will agree to it, but just in case . . ." He stuffed the linen cloth back in her mouth, but with enough room for her to breathe. He stretched and yawned and then rolled off of her, using her arm as a headrest.

After a few moments, Mut calmed her tears, believing the night's attack was over.

A while later, she heard his soft snores. She looked to the ceiling, her tears drying on her cheeks.

If you are there, she silently prayed to the gods she had dismissed in Malkata, *be with me.*

THE NEXT MORNING CAME. THE SMELL OF FRESH BREAD FILLED the upper room. Mut awoke to her fingers tingling and her elbows screaming. The night prior wasn't a nightmare, she realized upon seeing Pawah already sitting up and tracing the outline of her face with his finger.

"Good morning," he whispered. He yanked the linen from her mouth, grabbed her chin, and pressed his lips to hers. She tried to push her head back, but the bed and his grip kept her head where it was. Finally, he released her. "When your servant comes, tell her you are not well but to leave you be."

"If I do as you say, will you promise me you will not take me, and you will spare my servants' lives?" Mut wished she could wipe her mouth, but the ropes were tied tightly over her wrists. She moved her fingers, despite the rain of pricks attacking her hands.

"You ask a lot for a woman tied to a bed." Pawah smiled and ran his fingers down her neck as he threatened the linen cloth again.

She willed herself not to move. "You like making deals."

"I *love* making deals. I'll let you in on a little secret. I love playing games with people and letting them think they are winning."

A cold rock fell on her chest, and the color drained from her face. *I don't care,* she told herself. She was winning. He was not touching her. "Promise me, Pawah. Are you not a man of your word?"

Pawah hummed and seemed to think about it until steps could be heard outside the door.

"Pawah, tell me. You will not harm them, and you will not harm me if I do as you say," Mut said, trying to pull at the ropes to see if there was any give.

Pawah pursed his lips, still not answering.

A knock came at the door.

"Mistress of the House?" Tener asked. "We have made bread. Also, the servants have not come back this morning. Bakt has gone, I suppose to the market."

Mut felt her body tremble as she looked to Pawah for an answer. He only cocked his head and drew his thumb across his neck, and then pointed a finger to the door.

"Mistress of the House?"

"Yes, Tener," Mut called and swallowed the lump in her throat. "Please don't come in. I am not well."

There was a silence at the door. "Mistress of the House, you have never asked us to leave you while you are ill. Shall I call a physician and—"

"No!" Mut calmed her breathing as she stared into Pawah's eyes. He nodded her on. "Please just leave me. Stay in the second house."

"Shall I leave the bread by the door?"

"Yes, please," Mut said, looking at Pawah. She could only assume he was hungry, too.

"As you wish," Tener said, and the shadows of her feet lingered at the door before they disappeared.

Pawah brought his hands together in a silent façade of applause. "You are almost as good with your lies as I am."

"I am *nothing* like you."

Pawah curled his lips into a frown and tilted his head.

"That's no way to talk to your house guest." Then he smiled and gripped her chin again. "But that will change in time. I think you shall make a nice addition to my house . . . as my wife."

"I'd rather die." Mut spat at him, but it landed short of his face and fell to his arm.

"I see," he said, and wiped her spit from his skin and shoved it back into her mouth. While doing so, he pushed her head into the bed. "Mut, Mut, Mut . . ." He shook his head, and his hand crept over to include her nose. Mut's eyes grew big as she realized her air was being cut off. His eyes danced. "You see, I wish it wouldn't be like this. I . . ." He grimaced as Mut began to try to kick him off of her, but he leaned out of the way and then closer to her face. "I was hoping you would want to be with me, and I wouldn't have to tie you to the bed for fear of you leaving me."

Tears welled in her eyes as she jerked her arms, but the ropes held her tight. She stared Pawah in the eyes as he kept his hand over her nose and mouth. He lowered a little more, balancing his chin on the back of his hand as he watched her struggle. A muffled "Please!" came from Mut, and a sneer grew on Pawah's face.

"I thought you would never ask." He moved his pointer finger so a small bit of air could reach Mut's nostrils. Mut drew in as deep of a breath as she could, but he pressed against her chest, and the weight of his head on his hand pressed into her mouth. At least she had some air, as small as it was. Her breath made a rushing sound between his fingers with each inhale and exhale.

"Oh Mut . . ." Pawah shook his head. "If only you would stay of your own free will, we wouldn't have to play this game."

Another knock came at the door. "Mistress of the House, I have brought your bread. It is outside your door."

Pawah whispered in Mut's ear as he lifted his hand. "Thank the woman, and I will leave you alone."

Mut drew in a deep, shaky breath. *He kept his word last night,* she thought, and really, what choice did she have? Her servants would not be able to defend themselves against him, especially if he could beat them to the door and kill them one at a time.

"Thank you, Tener," Mut called, and when they didn't hear footsteps, Pawah whispered to her:

"Second house."

Mut closed her eyes and said again, "Please leave me. Stay in the second house for three days, and then come check in on me."

"As you wish," Tener said, and then she descended the stairs.

Pawah sneered and cupped his hand back over Mut's nose and mouth and whispered again to her, "Well done, my dear Mut." Then, finally, he let her breathe once more. "One of these days, you will do what I say simply because I said it."

Never. She wasn't going to risk him striking back at her again, so she kept that word to herself. But as if reading her thoughts, he smiled.

The door to the main home closed, and Mut closed her eyes, wishing she had not sent them away. Maybe they would have been able to fight him off. No—Pawah would have struck from behind because he was a coward. He would have ambushed them. They would have had no chance. And Pawah stayed too close for her scream to travel to the guards. Besides, they would probably brush it off as something small, like stubbing her toe.

"It looks like I am winning our little game of will," Pawah said, bouncing a finger on Mut's lips. "When your father arrives here, you will beg him to trade the crown for your life."

Mut longed to ask him what would happen if she didn't, but she already knew the answer and so kept her mouth shut.

Pawah smiled again. "You learn fast, dear Mut."

She wished for him never to speak her name again. It made her hate her name, and *hate* that the first time anyone used a term of endearment for her, "dear Mut," it was from Pawah. The thought ate at her insides. Nefertiti was "lotus blossom," but she was only ever *Mut*. Pawah's words returned to her: *You are only a cheap copy.*

Pawah put the linen cloth back into her mouth. He then got up and retrieved the bread, and ate it in front of her. "Did you want some?" He offered it to her but then pulled it back. "Ah, but how would you feed yourself?" He chuckled and took another bite as he sat down in the chair facing the bed and propped his feet on the bedside table. "Do you think the old man will know I am serious when you beg for your life in exchange for the crown if you are without injury?" Humming while he thought, Pawah tapped the bread against his lips.

Mut's eyes grew wide at the insinuation. *You promised.* Her mouth, unable to form words, focused on breathing with the linen stuffed in her mouth.

Pawah continued. "I *did* kill his daughter. You would think he thinks me plenty serious." He took another bite of bread and narrowed his eyes at Mut. "But I never know with him. I threatened Ankhesenamun. I threatened Nefertiti. I threatened Horemheb and Tutankhamun. But you see what happened with all of them? They didn't take me seriously. Three of the four died, and Ankhesenamun lost both of her children. I would hate for Ay to lose another daughter because he didn't take me seriously." Pawah popped another pinch of bread into his mouth.

"He knows you are serious," Mut tried to say through the linen as she grasped her hands around the ropes and tried tugging again. But it was no use—there was no give and her bed frame was made of solid wood; cursed be the luxury to have a wooden bed and not a cot on the floor. In that moment, she hated what riches bought her. "There is no need to do anything more to me!" she tried to scream through the linen ball in her mouth. A tear slid from her eye as her words came out mangled and unrecognizable.

She watched him eat without a care in the world, and knew, *knew* with utter certainty, that he was going to do something to her. Her mind played tricks on her as he ate and talked to himself, debating whether he should make his threat seem more serious.

"Well, you did send away your only help, Mut," he reasoned, taking a sip of wine.

"You threatened me and them," she tried to yell, but it was useless. Her heart quickened again as each breath became more shallow. Her mind jumped from one vision to the next of what he would do with her.

"You didn't call the guards. You let me tie you to the bed. You even let me sleep beside you. I don't think you realize the seriousness of my threat, Mut."

Mut watched his every move, not knowing how she would protect herself. She tried to move her legs, but they too were tied—not as tightly as her arms, but tied nonetheless. When had he done that? Before she woke. Her muscles grew taut, expecting the worse.

Pawah pursed his lips and then tore another piece of bread with his teeth. He lifted his head; his eyes held a distant gaze as he thought, and he used his tongue to roll the piece of bread into his mouth.

"Let's see . . ." He hummed in thought. "I've held back before because I thought it would be less . . . *messy* . . . and all that did was erase opportunities to take what I wanted." He lifted one shoulder, then the other, bouncing his head on each as if weighing his options. As he thought, he ate the last piece of bread. Dusting the crumbs to the floor, he examined the heavy Nile-fired clay plate. He grasped either side of it and hummed in thought again. He stood and walked to the side of the bed, lifting the plate up and down to see just how much it weighed.

Mut watched him, taking one shaky breath at a time. Her mouth trembled around the linen as she said a silent prayer to the gods she hoped existed.

He raised the plate above his head and brought it down. Mut lifted her legs to try to kick Pawah's arm or his body. The plate slammed into her shin. Mut cried out, but the linen in her mouth kept it a gargle. He raised it again and slammed the plate down again and again as Mut tried desperately to defend herself, but as she struggled to breathe, she saw her own blood on the sheets and passed out.

MUT AWOKE TO HER ACHING BODY AND SAW THE BRUISES, BLOOD, and broken skin. Her vision blurred together as she moved her head. She stopped at the image in the chair next to the bed. The blur's trail ended as she made out Pawah's face. He'd pulled the chair, so it sat at her bedside. A thick lump formed in her throat. She swallowed it. *Blood.* She coughed and wretched. Tears brimmed her eyes.

"Ah, you're awake!" Pawah said. "You missed the fun of it." He patted her hand and dabbed her face with water.

Realizing the linen rag was not in her mouth anymore, she breathed out in a gasping breath: "Fun?"

"Well, not fun for you, I suppose," he said. She eyed the blood-stained linen rag as he dabbed it near her mouth. "I am not going to gag you again unless you make me. I am an honorable man. I only do what I need to do."

Mut peeled her lips back in disgust as she winced from the pain in her legs and arms and face and body. Blood trickled from her lip. "You're an evil man devoid of honor."

He stopped wiping her face. "That is a very mean thing to

say, Mistress of the House. Have I defiled your bed? Have I killed you?"

"You killed my sister."

"She left me no choice, just as your father leaves me no choice." Pawah continued to wipe the blood from her swollen lip. "See now, I take care of your wounds, and yet you say I am devoid of honor?" He shook his head. "Perhaps *you* are the one devoid of honor."

Mut's eyes glistened. "*You* caused these wounds."

"Your father left me no choice. I could not have restrained myself the night you returned to Malkata, but I did. I know you are a grieving widow. I do apologize for that, by the way. If the boy had not named your husband Hereditary Prince, I might have let him live."

Mut's eyes grew wide as her nostrils flared. "You?" Her words came out a whisper through a slack mouth. Her stomach hardened. "You killed them?"

"Well . . ." Pawah chuckled. "Not me, per se, but I did . . ." He nodded and smirked. "I had them killed, just as I did with the last few Pharaohs."

Mut's heart raced out of her chest. She yanked her hand to go for his throat, but the ropes held tight.

"Calm yourself before you cause more injury." Pawah grinned and tapped the tip of her nose with the rag. "But I am glad to know their killings were taken as only war casualties. Maybe I was wrong not to pay Sitayet and the others' families . . ." He sat back and made himself comfortable in the chair. "No, I'm never wrong." He puffed up his chest as he surveyed her body and then found her eyes again. His dagger, sheathed on his belt, lay in his lap.

As much as she told him she would rather die than have him touch her, part of her did not want to die, no matter the consequence. *A destitute dog still fights for its life,* she repeated his words in her mind. *I hate you, Pawah.* She shook her head at him, clenching her jaw, as hot tears rolled down the sides of her face.

He only smiled. "I will not hurt you anymore or take what I want from you, unless you give me a reason, Mistress of the House. Remember that. So you need to watch your tongue and do as I say."

Mut caught a glimpse of her fingers in her peripheral vision. They were tinged with blue. *If* he hadnot already taken from her, while she was passed out. A man like him would never be satisfied with only a taste. She wondered how long it was since he had attacked her. "I will not say one word. Please, just let me go."

Pawah shook his head. He slapped his knees and then stood up. "I wish I could, Mut, but I just can't. I'm so close to what I have been working for since I was a child. You see, I saw the impoverished state of my parents. I saw the greed of the priests, and then I saw the corruption of the throne. All of these high status people, blindly following these gods, allowing priests and kings to take their hard-earned wages and food—for what? So they could say a prayer on their behalf? I don't think that is how a god should deal with his people. 'Give me your hard-earned wages, and I'll grant you your wish'? If a god was a god, would he need that barter system? Tit for tat? A god demands! A god's law is unswayed by mere mortals." Pawah opened his arms wide and twisted to showcase the bedchambers. "I see this same belief in yourself, Mistress of the House. I look around your room. There are no statues of any of the gods. Did you lose your faith as well? Perhaps we are more similar than you want to believe? When I am Pharaoh, I will make sure the gods are only worshipped enough to keep me on the throne. I will make sure all people are equally as wealthy. I will—"

"You?" Mut laughed but then stopped herself as he stepped toward the bed.

He lowered his chin. "I see myself as a reasonable man. Tell me your thoughts."

She swallowed and looked at her blue-tipped fingers again. In her heart, she knew he was going to make her his eventually, if he had not already. And if he had, at least he had spared her the knowledge of it happening. She took a quick inhale through a semi-bloody nose. It was all part of the game he played, but she would try to delay it as long as she could.

"If everyone is the same, no one will work harder. No one will have motivation to work."

"Then I will force them. Pharaoh's word is law."

"Did you learn nothing from Pharaoh Akhenaten? A people deprived of food and meaningful work, rebel. I know what my sister did to her husband. Your Queen would do the same."

He grabbed her chin and climbed into the bed. "Look here, Mut. Pharaoh Akhenaten, had he been more of sound mind, would have been a perfect role model, but he lacked enforcement. Pharaoh Smenkare had the right idea. You get rid of those who would rebel, those who break your law. You silence them for fear of their lives."

"Then why did you organize rebellion? Why did you take the Pharaoh's lives?"

"I needed to be the people's savior." Pawah shook his head at her apparent ignorance. "So that the people would name me their Pharaoh. I just had too kind a heart before and didn't seize the throne at the opportune time. Now I'm left with taking measures such as these. Do you think it makes me *happy* to do this to you? I should have killed the entire royal family, and then the people would have shouted my name to rule. I thought I could do it without spilling much blood, but, well, see how that turned out."

"Do you regret the blood you've spilled? Do you regret anything but not killing more?"

67

Pawah laughed and looked up dreamily. "No." He snatched his hand away from her chin, the impression of his grip left on her skin. "I think that is a gift I have: I don't *feel* as others do." He rubbed his heart and went to look out over the courtyard. "I think you are like that, too." He turned and looked at her. "You know, I have kept a close eye on you since your marriage to Horemheb. I found out you were previously married to Menna, though you were quick to move on. Did you feel even the slightest remorse about tricking Menna into marriage?"

Mut felt her heart swell within her. "It was my mistake to marry Menna."

"But did you feel any remorse? Or only embarrassment?"

Mut had not felt remorse in the fact she had caused him to embrace another woman, but only embarrassment—embarrassment at having to move back to her father's house—but she wasn't going to tell this madman about it.

"I did."

Pawah only grinned and shook his head. "No, Mut. You lie. You and I are alike. You would make a great Queen by my side."

"I can only assume you killed Beketaten. I would end the same way."

"I had no more use of her. Or so I thought at the time. It would have proved well to have the daughter of Pharaoh Amenhotep III when Tut and Horemheb were killed in battle." Pawah punched the air. "*That* is what I regret."

"I am not royalty. You would need to marry Ankhesenamun."

"Don't you think I have tried? When the old man dies, she will be my last resort. And then"—he let out an angry growl—"and then . . ."

"Then what? Are you out of options? Out of ideas?" Mut taunted, but at the growing rage in his eyes, she shrank back, regretting her mistake. The thought of calling to the guards lingered on her tongue, but his sheathed dagger scared her.

He leapt on the bed and straddled her, again covering her mouth and nose. "I would not say such things!" he said through his teeth, pressing his hand tight over her face. He grabbed the wet linen rag by the bed and replaced his hand with the rag as he stuffed it into her mouth. "You know, I think I might give you a taste of what it will be like as my wife."

She shook her head and tried to yell. He ripped her dress. Tears streamed down her face.

But then a knock came at the door of the main house.

Pawah patted her cheek. "We will get back to this."

He got up and looked out the courtyard window, and peered down to see a royal messenger standing at the door. He crept back and pointed a finger in her face. "Not one word," he whispered. He went and stood next to the window, out of sight, as another knock came. He watched the messenger walk around the home and spot the secondary house, to which he went and knocked. Pawah strained to listen when Tener opened the door. Bits of their conversation floated to him.

"Pharaoh Ay . . . daughter . . . come at once."

Tener bowed. ". . . very ill . . ."

Then Tener came to the main house and opened the door, the messenger following her.

Pawah crept over to Mut and removed the linen from her mouth. "You tell them not to enter and that you need your father here, as you are very ill." He grabbed her chin, pulled the dagger from his belt, and held it beside her cheek. "Or the last thing you and they will feel is my blade across your throats." Then he went and stood against the wall by the door in case they entered, his dagger pointed up and ready to strike.

The knock at Mut's door came, and he looked at Mut with a calm evil in his eyes.

Her chest heaved. She knew that if she sent them away yet again, he would do the worst to her . . . but she also knew that if she didn't, someone would lose their life, perhaps all of them. She didn't even know who had come. What if it was Ankhesenamun or her mother? A tear slid down her cheek as another knock came.

"Mistress of the House?" It was Tener.

Her voice croaked out. "Yes?"

The door began to move.

"Don't come in," Mut forced out as more tears fell. "I'm not well."

"You have not been well. Please let us take care of you." The door began to move more.

"No!" Mut cried. "I am very ill. Please send for my father to come."

It was done. She had done it. She'd lured her father to this fatal trap to save her own life. And she hated herself for it. Maybe she was just like Pawah: selfish and looking out only for herself.

Mut's eyes never left Pawah, and she prayed to the gods she had almost rejected that no one enter; but, with the same thought, she prayed they did.

The door paused and then closed.

Relief swept over Mut's body. At the same time her stomach grew hard—she knew the terror that would await her in the decans, maybe months, it would take for her father to arrive. And then . . . knowing she had betrayed the throne and her father to this man, Pawah, who had killed her sister . . . it was beyond her in that moment. She tried to move her fingers, but the pain and the ache took control of what feeling she had left in her hands.

She heard Tener murmur something indiscernible and then she said through the door, "I will do as you wish. I also shall bring you more bread." Her steps echoed down the stairs, and a short murmur of a conversation took place.

Pawah nodded to her and smiled.

Tener came back and Mut heard her place a plate of bread next to the door. "Mistress of the House, I have sent a royal messenger to Malkata. I also have asked the royal guards to stand guard at the front of the main home, instead of the courtyard, so that they may hear if you call for help and come get us." Tener paused, as though hoping for a reply. "Bread is outside the door. Also some wine for your stomach."

"Thank you, Tener."

Pawah's hand clenched into a fist. Mut let out a shaky breath, thanking her servant and maybe the gods—maybe they had given her some wisdom, some insight. *I will figure it out later, but for now, I will be safe from Pawah, as the guards would hear him if he tried anything more.*

Tener left the main home and returned to the second house. Pawah crept to the courtyard window and saw the messenger leave, and the guards walk to the main home. He let out a huff and then came near to Mut. "I guess that means our little fun is over, and we shall have near-silent conversations from now on." He stuffed the linen rag in her mouth and punched her a few more times to let out his frustration. "We could have been a great team, you and I." Then he retrieved the bread as Mut's eye swelled up. He sat in his chair and ate it as his eyes ran up and down her body.

Mut now only wished he would let out the ropes. Her arms ached as they had never ached before, almost to the point of complete numbness. Her rumbling stomach also wished for bread, but she knew not to hope for such kindness from this monster.

5

THE TIME OF CAPTIVITY

IT TOOK FOUR DECANS FOR THE MESSENGER TO GO TO MEN-NEFER and come back to Malkata. The morning after receiving Mut's message, Ay told Tey as they readied for the day, "Mut is ill. She requests me to her side, too sick to come to Malkata." He patted her freshly bathed skin. "I have arranged to travel to Men-nefer this morning."

Tey stood as her steward and servants finished oiling her body. "I will go with you."

Ay shook his head. "No, my love, you are safer in Malkata. Pawah is out there somewhere. My hope is that he has run off to Nubia or met an ill fate by Hittite or Libyan hands."

"Pharaoh, Mut is my child, too," Tey said as the servants pulled on her linen dress. "I am going with you. If Pawah is still alive, I do not want him to hurt you either."

Ay patted his dagger at his belt. "He can try."

"Pawah is a much younger man—"

"Pawah is a lazy prophet with a soft body. He has never seen war and only attacks from the shadows like a coward," Ay said, his knuckles going white around the dagger's handle. The briefest image of Nefertiti's body in the council room flashed in his mind. A piece of him died that day. He couldn't burden Tey's heart with the truth.

"Which is why I am going with you," Tey said, breaking his thoughts as she placed a hand on his bicep. "You are older now, Pharaoh. Yes, you have seen many wars, you have led your divisions, and victory has followed you, but this is a warfare unknown to you—he who attacks in the dark like a coward. You need someone there to watch your back. That will be me." Tey cocked an eyebrow as she locked eyes with him.

"That will be my royal guards." Ay patted her hand on his arm.

"No, that will be *me*." Tey placed her other hand over his.

Ay paused, pursing his lips, and shook his head.

Tey glared. "She is my daughter, too."

Ay knew after many years of marriage to Tey that the chance of taking no for an answer was slim, even as Pharaoh. He blew out a huff of air and narrowed his eyes.

"You may come, chief royal wife." He nodded, leaving Tey to ready herself.

They made their way to the Malkata harbor, where Ankhesenamun waited for Ay and Tey by the royal barge.

"What are you doing here?" Ay asked, snapping his head to Tey and then back to Ankhesenamun.

"Pharaoh." Ankhesenamun lowered her chin out of respect for him, but she stood with her feet planted on the dock and her hands curled into fists by her sides. "I heard the message that Mut is ill. You said yourself that Pawah is free. I am going to make sure he does not have his hands on her as well."

"No. No. No. You"—Ay pointed a finger to Ankhesenamun and then to the ground—"stay here." Turning to Tey, he said the same. "You stay here as well. Be the example for your granddaughter."

Tey spoke low so the guards could not hear. "You will let

me see my daughter or else I will make the rest of your life miserable." She eyed him like the lion eyes its prey.

Ay clenched his jaw and let out a heavy breath through his nose. "We don't have very many years left, so I can live with that if it means keeping you both safe."

"Ay," Tey said through her teeth, and lowered her chin, keeping her eyes locked on him.

Ay let out another heavy breath, and his eyes darted between Tey and Ankhesenamun. "Fine." Ay motioned to Hori and Ineni and four other guards to board the royal barge. "Then we take additional guards."

<hr/>

PAWAH SLAPPED MUT IN THE FACE ONCE AND THEN AGAIN UNTIL she opened her eyes.

"They're here," Pawah whispered to Mut, who blinked her eyes open at the stench of his breath. He opened her mouth and poured some stale wine in. "I need you awake enough to speak."

She coughed and he placed his hand over her mouth until she stopped. He placed some bread on the tip of her tongue and made her chew by forcing her jaw open and closed. She swallowed; it only caused her to want to vomit.

What seemed like a lifetime had gone by, with little food and wine. She'd lost count of the days, and some nights she wished for a quick end of this life. The heavy aftertaste of the stale bread remained on her tongue, which licked her dry, cracked, and bleeding lips.

He cut the ropes with his dagger and her arms fell to the bed, paralyzed. She rolled her head to the door, but he rolled it back to look at her. "Remember our deal?"

She blinked, unable to summon any more strength to nod her head.

"You weak child," he spat at her, and poured some more wine down her throat. She coughed and he put his hand over her mouth again. "Now, do you remember our deal?"

At a great expense of strength, she nodded.

Pawah caressed her face. "Convince your father to hand over the crown, and I will not kill you."

Then, as steps came from the stairs, he yanked her out of bed and held her up, as her legs were weak, and her arms hung by her side. As he positioned them to hide behind the bath chamber wall, she caught a glimpse of the bed. So much blood stained the sheets. She fell to the floor as he threw a blanket over the bed to hide the blood. He pulled her back up to standing. Pain entrenched her hands and fingers as they swung with his positioning of her. He pulled his dagger and placed it under her chin.

"You will do and say as I tell you." His hot whisper burrowed in her ear canal. She felt the room spin around her, but she blinked and swallowed to keep the bit of bread and wine from coming to the top of her throat.

A knock came at the door. "Pharaoh Ay has come to see his ill daughter," a royal guard said, and then entered. Pawah and Mut could see what happened in the room from a previously positioned copper mirror Pawah had adjusted. The guard looked around.

Pawah whispered to Mut: *"Tell him you are not clothed and ask for your father to wait in the living area of the bedchambers."* Mut swallowed a thick lump of saliva before she attempted to speak. Pawah shook her to hurry her up.

"I am not decent." Her voice came out barely a whisper.

"Again," Pawah instructed.

"I am not clothed!" Mut yelled with all her strength, but it came out as a normal voice. Her breath hitched.

The guard stopped.

Mut felt the room spin and her head ended up falling back

into Pawah's shoulder, and she stared at the ceiling until the ringing in her ears stopped. Pawah was whispering something, but she couldn't tell what. Her eyes rolled to the copper mirror and saw the guard advancing.

"Say yes."

"Yes," she whispered as a breath.

"Louder," Pawah nudged her on.

"Yes!" she blurted out, and felt herself lose control of her stomach.

The guard took a step back. "Yes, Mistress of the House. I will escort Pharaoh into your bedchambers."

Mut could not even wipe her mouth, for the stabbing pains in her arms and hands were too much to bear. Pawah wiped her mouth for her, though, to her surprise. But as soon as the vomit was free of her face, he pulled her back into his arms. She summoned every strength within her to keep her head from falling as the dagger's tip pressed upon the underbelly of her chin.

"Forgive me, Father," she mouthed as she watched the royal party enter. Mut's heart fell into her stomach. Her mother had come, and so had Ankhesenamun. She closed her eyes in dismay.

Ay, Tey, and Ankhesenamun entered with the guard Amenket to stand next to them.

"Mut, we are here," Tey called, and began to hurry to the bath chamber.

"Tell her no," Pawah whispered.

"No!" Mut said in a cracked voice.

Tey stopped. "Mut, please let me help you."

"Ask the guard to leave." Pawah's voice annoyed her ear.

"I don't want the guard to see me," Mut said. Even though her legs were weak, the tip of the dagger next to her chin forced her to position one of her legs to give her better balance.

Tey turned to look at Ay.

Ay chewed his lip. "Mut, are you dressed? The royal guard, I would like to stay."

"Get rid of him." Pawah's grip hardened against Mut's body.

"Please, Father." Mut licked her lips. She longed for something to drink. Pawah had been so cruel, beating her until she passed out, most likely so that he could have his way with her and say that he had not touched her. *I would never know the difference.* Her body ached regardless.

Pawah shook her again, which only exacerbated the spin of the room.

"I am not well. I . . ." Mut's voice trailed off as she once again let her head fall back on Pawah's shoulder. "I am embarrassed," she finally forced out.

Mut squeezed her eyes shut, knowing if Ammit were real she would devour her heart in the afterlife for the lies she told her family, baiting them to this man who had murdered her sister and now her husband.

Tey looked to Ay until Ay finally dismissed Amenket. He left the room, and at the close of the door Pawah pushed Mut out into the room, holding her tight against his body.

"If you call your guards, I'll kill her." Pawah's voice held low in the room as Ay shot up out of the chair.

"What do you want?" Ay's hand clenched into fists, hovering over the dagger at his belt.

"Take off your weapon. Throw it on the bed," Pawah ordered, and ran his thumb over the handle of his own dagger that touched Mut's chin.

Ay did as he was told.

"That's a good start," Pawah said. "I hope you take to the rest of my commands as easily as you took to that one."

"What do you want?" Ay asked again.

Pawah's eyes drifted to the crown Ay wore. "You know what I want, old man."

Tey followed Pawah's gaze. She stepped to Ay and

whispered, "Give it to him. Ay, please. I can't bear another daughter—"

Ay pushed Tey behind him and whispered over his shoulder, "Not another word, Tey." Then he focused his gaze on Pawah. "If I were to give you the crown, the guards would still arrest you. Wearing the crown means nothing if you have not been coronated by the Amun priesthood."

"Then I want you to order your guards to take me to Malkata and have First Prophet of Amun Wennefer crown me Pharaoh." Pawah's words dripped with annoyance.

"But *I* am Pharaoh."

Pawah sneered. "Yes, that does present a bit of a problem, doesn't it? Let's see how this works. You are old. You will die soon—"

Tey shook her head and her shoulders shuddered.

"Oh, I'm sorry, my *Queen*, should I use the correct vernacular? You will *journey west soon*. So here is what will happen: I am named Hereditary Prince and crowned Coregent, and then I watch you drink poison to end your own life, leaving me as Pharaoh." Pawah shrugged his shoulders casually, as though they would all sit down for a bite of bread and a drink of wine for the day. "And, the best part, husband to *you*." Pawah cocked a grin and winked at Ankhesenamun.

Ankhesenamun pressed her lips into a flat line as her hands curled into fists.

Ay said, "Are you going to be crowned holding a dagger against my daughter's chin?"

Pawah chuckled. "Yes, Pharaoh, I will."

Ay shook his head. "All of Egypt will see—"

"I don't care what the Egyptians see. I will be their Pharaoh, and they will answer to me. They will fear me. They don't fear you. Even your own palace still has *my* loyal subjects."

"Malkata is free from your control." Ay's eyes darted about the room as if trying to form some means of a plan.

"How did I escape then, Ay? You senseless child! Do you think I was able to fight the guards off of me? No, Ay, they let me go. Because they love me. I am their savior. *I* am the one to whom they have pledged their loyalty."

"You *were* their savior. But now you have no loyal subjects." Ay glanced at his dagger on the bed.

"The bottom line is this, Ay: Would you die to make sure your youngest daughter lives?" Pawah looked at Ankhesenamun and added, "Would you marry me to make sure your beloved aunt lives?"

Ay ran his eyes over Mut's beaten, bloody, and bruised body. Her arms hung without movement next to her sides; her hands bore the color of purple. Her knees buckled. He noticed the ropes on the bed as he looked more intently. "You held her for days, did you not?"

"Yes. More likely a few months . . . I've lost count . . . it takes so long for a messenger to come and then go back and then for you to journey back . . ." Pawah nodded and ho-hummed, sneering and running the dagger's blade along Mut's cheek, nicking her a few times. "We had a lot of fun together, though. Didn't we, Mut?"

Mut's jaw clenched. All she wanted was some wine and for the room to stop spinning and to stand . . . yes, to stand.

"Why did you beat her?" Ay asked, shaking his head.

"Last time I threatened, no one listened. I had to go straight to killing. This time I didn't want you to think I was not serious." Pawah waved his dagger as he spoke. "So I just wanted to show you how serious I am." He placed his dagger back under her chin.

"Did he defile you?" Ay asked her.

Mut's lip trembled, but the words never came: *I don't know, Father.* The ground seemed to spin as her stomach wanted to empty its contents but found itself empty, but fear of the dagger's tip beneath her chin made her try with every shred of her strength to keep her stomach settled.

"Our dear little Mut can't speak right now," Pawah said, and laughed. "She's had too much wine, I suppose." He pointed the dagger at Ay. "But to answer your question, I did not. I told her I would, though, if she did not do as I said. Let's just say she is much smarter than her sister." Pawah chuckled and twirled the dagger in his hand. "Oh, Ay—" Pawah pointed the dagger at him again, and then at Tey behind him. "Who does she get her smarts from? You or your wife?"

Tey inched toward the door.

"Wife of Ay," Pawah sung. "If you call the guard, she dies."

Tey stopped in her tracks.

"Now, Ay," Pawah started again. "Let's go over this one more time. You tell your guards to escort me to Malkata. Mut will stay with me in case you decide to change your mind. You then call for Wennefer. You name me the Hereditary Prince. I am crowned Coregent and then you take poison and die. You've lived a long life. We'll just end it a little earlier."

Ay swallowed and then shook his head.

"What? You want two daughters' deaths on your head?" Pawah asked, and pushed the dagger a little more into Mut's chin so that a tiny drop of blood fell down the blade.

Mut whimpered. She pushed the stabbing pain in her legs out of her mind so she could stand a little taller to keep the dagger from going further into the underside of her chin.

"Stop!" Tey put her hand forth and pulled on Ay's arm. "Please give him the crown. Just let him have it. I will drink the poison with you. I can't see my youngest daughter be murdered like this."

Ay faced Tey. "If I give Pawah what he wants, then

Nefertiti was murdered in vain. He killed her because she kept him from the crown."

Tey widened her eyes and her jaw dropped. Her hand clutched her heart. "You told me she was ill and passed in her sleep."

"No . . ." Ay's voice dropped. "That man, Pawah, killed her. He will not hesitate to kill Mut either."

Pawah shrugged. "I will not." He drew the dagger over Mut's shoulder, drawing more blood.

Mut grimaced as she peered down at her useless puppet arm, dripping with her blood.

"And I grow tired of waiting." Pawah yawned. "Give me the crown and we both live."

"Pharaoh does not abdicate." Ay stepped toward Pawah.

"Yet you are a *father*! What father would not drink poison to save his own daughter? I'm letting you *redeem* yourself for Nefertiti." Pawah shook Mut's body. "Look at it this way. Name me Hereditary Prince. I'll marry Ankhesenamun over there—" Pawah motioned to her with the dagger before snapping it back under Mut's chin. "I'll even marry this poor widow, too." Pawah rubbed his cheek against Mut's. "Then we can all be family."

Ay's shoulders rose but then fell as he appeared to debate his options.

"All of your army, *Pharaoh*, is at the southern and northern borders. All you have here are your royal guards. Now, do what I demand." Pawah sliced Mut again on her shoulder.

Mut cried and did not look her father in the eye. She only shook her head. *Pawah should never be on the throne. I would die for that, I know this now, and Father must know too.* Her heart wished, though she believed Horemheb never loved her, that he were there in that moment to keep his word and keep her safe. But he had been murdered as well. She only saw one option: if she regained feeling in her arms, she would take

Pawah's dagger and stab herself, ending it, leaving Pawah vulnerable to be taken and executed for his crimes.

She spoke to Ay through her eyes: *I am sorry, Father.*

She closed her eyes and waited until she could feel her fingers.

I am coming, Horemheb. I am coming, Nefertiti. I will see you shortly if an afterlife does indeed exist.

𓆸 6 𓆸
THE TIME OF RETREAT

THREE SEASONS EARLIER, GENERAL HOREMHEB WATCHED IN hiding as Tut's body traveled through the army's campgrounds and began the journey back to Malkata. His leg and knee pained him with each step back to the cot. His cane wobbled as he found the pain in his shoulder and leg to almost match the pain of guilt within his chest. Horemheb sat and rolled to his back, leaving his cane beside his cot. Like his knee, his shoulder and neck throbbed with each turn of his head and each movement of his arm.

I deserve this pain. I deserve every pain life has to offer me. I let them be killed.

Commander Paramesse entered Horemheb's tent once Tut's body had left. "You will need to heal, friend," Paramesse said as he poured some wine. "Before you go back and claim your throne, you need to heal."

Horemheb slightly shook his head at the offer of wine from Paramesse. "I know," he said in a low voice. The camp was eerily quiet other than the occasional clanking of weapons outside; the men were all silent out of respect for their young deceased Pharaoh.

"Paramesse, my brother-in-arms . . ." Horemheb watched

as Paramesse drank. A thick lump formed in the back of Horemheb's throat as he thought. *Tut . . . I loved you as a son, but never told you until your last moment. Forgive me . . . forgive me for not being there to save you.*

Paramesse hummed in acknowledgment as he drank.

"Please, tell me how he was attacked." His words came out quick, like the thrust of a dagger.

Paramesse coughed and wiped his mouth with his forearm. "Are you sure you want to know this now?"

"Yes. I need to know." Horemheb averted his gaze to the ceiling of his battlefield tent. "I need to know," he whispered.

Paramesse nodded and put his cup back on the table. He sat next to Horemheb's cot, digging his heels into the dirt, and rested his arms on his knees, his spine bending as he sank into his position. He peered over his shoulder to Horemheb and sighed.

"You bear almost the same look of pain now as you did when Pharaoh Neferneferuaten was murdered. I know you and Pharaoh Tutankhamun were close. It is not my place to say anything, but this account may not be what you need to hear right now." Paramesse's voice lowered. "You are my friend. You are in pain, and I don't wish to see you—"

"Please." Horemheb's gruff voice was laden with devastation. His eyes watered. He'd lost everyone. His love, Nefertiti, and their son . . . His wife—he had caused her early journey west . . . and now the man he called son, his Tut. He needed to hear how he was injured, so he could feel the depth of pain he was supposed to feel—he deserved to feel. Horemheb blinked to keep tears from falling in front of his comrade, friend, and subordinate. "Please tell me."

Paramesse's brow furrowed as he studied Horemheb, unmoving on his cot. Then he turned his head to look straight ahead and drew a deep breath, letting it out in almost a whistle. Slapping a hand to his neck, he pursed his lips.

"He was with the longbow archers," Paramesse began,

and Horemheb clenched his jaw, bracing himself for the account of Tut's attack. "I saw from far off." Paramesse shook his head. "*I* am to blame. I did not think our brothers would attack their own Pharaoh, especially one as loved as Pharaoh Tutankhamun."

"No," Horemheb said. "This was Pawah's doing. I should have been next to him."

"Friend, if you were next to him, they would have stabbed you in the back," Paramesse said and rubbed his neck. "The remaining longbow men killed the traitors who attacked Pharaoh. We sent the traitors who attacked you back to Malkata to be executed for their crimes against the throne."

Horemheb remained silent, but gave a slight nod, despite the pain. *Traitors should die. Traitors should be punished.* Yet his mind drifted to his own acts of treason, acts of conspiracy, against Pharaohs Akhenaten and Smenkare. His body sank into his straw cot. *The gods punish me. They take away all I ever cared for. They see my agony and deem it better than death.*

At Horemheb's silence, Paramesse dropped his head and hand. "I . . . I am sorry, Horemheb. It shouldn't have happened. None of this. The battles are not going in our favor. Then, this . . . I only pray the gods give us a renewed vigor when you heal and come back from the dead."

They listened for a moment to the despondence in the camp. There was no laughter, only hushed whispers.

Paramesse cleared his throat and continued telling the story. "I could only look from far off. We tried to backtrack to him, but we could only watch as Pharaoh fell to the ground. He parried another blow with his dagger. The archers shot and killed some of his attackers, but some remained. Pharaoh managed to stab one, but then two others held him down. I knew it was the end, but those loyal to him managed to save him from the attack. I worried about you, so I took a few loyal men and went to find you. Then I saw them coming for you in the far distance. I saw the sun glint on your armor. I yelled your name, hoping you could fend for yourself until we could get there."

A scowl came over Horemheb's face. "Pawah will die for this," he mumbled under his breath; his hands turned to fists.

"You must heal first."

"I can never heal from this."

Horemheb's mind raced back to Tut's last moments. He had called him *son*, and Tut had called him *father*. He had failed Nefertiti, and now Tut. He'd failed Amenia and his father. What future did he have? At least Mut was safe now that he was known as dead. There would be no reason for Pawah to go after her.

He sat up.

She was the daughter of Ay, though.

"What is it?" Paramesse asked, straining to hear and looking around.

Horemheb took a deep breath. "Pawah has taken everything from me, and I now worry for my new wife. She is a daughter of Ay."

"She should be fine. Her father would send guards." Paramesse stood up. "Besides, you are injured. You cannot even walk without a cane. If you do not quit moving, your wounds will break open again. Your body will break even more." Paramesse shuffled his feet and put his hands on his hip as he watched the dirt circle around his toes. "Horemheb, you need to heal physically. Also, we are in the middle of war. A *losing* war, if I might add. Men are dying away from home, in a foreign land, Mitanni land. They are afraid their bodies will not make it back to Egypt as Pharaoh's did. Without their bodies, they risk not journeying to the Field of Reeds." Paramesse grimaced. "It is a fear we all share. You need to get your mind right. You need to get your spirit right with the gods. You need to heal. This army needs you. You are all that we have left. They think you are dead. When you are reborn, it will not solely be to take revenge for Pharaoh

Neferneferuaten and Tutankhamun, but to unite this army, to take back what was lost, to gain victory. There are many who are counting on you. Egypt is counting on you to heal—"

"We have received no word to come back to Egyptian lands?" Horemheb asked, lying back down. He felt the wound tear on his neck from moving and let out a frustrated sigh. He knew Paramesse spoke true, but he didn't want to hear it. His hate for himself drowned out the needs of the many.

"No." Paramesse shook his head and let his hands fall to his sides. "Horemheb, don't move. Don't hurt yourself more. We can't change the past." He knelt next to his friend and lifted the bandage on his shoulder. A grimace followed. "But we have the future," he said, pouring a bit more of the honey-based wound ointment on Horemheb's shoulder. "Heal." He smoothed the bandage back down. "Then fight back. Only a few of us know you are still alive. When the time comes, we will need you to come back from the dead. We will need you to reinvigorate our men. *Your* men."

Horemheb raised his hand in the air and Paramesse took it and squeezed.

"Promise me," Paramesse said as he locked eyes with Horemheb.

"I will heal, and then I will fight back," Horemheb said and returned Paramesse's squeeze of the hand.

"Good." Paramesse released and stood. "Hopefully I will return from battle in the morning. Do you want the servant to cool you?"

"No. I want to be alone now." Horemheb stared again at the ceiling. "Fight well, my friend."

When the tent flap closed, signaling Paramesse was gone, Horemheb pulled Nefertiti's letter from his shendyt. He hated Ay for tearing Nefertiti's letter in half, as one half of it now fell to the floor, but the other half he put up to his nose. The lotus blossom scent waned.

"I didn't keep anyone safe, my Nefertiti," he whispered. "And now I risk losing you forever." He took a deep and long inhale of the scent, trying to imprint it upon his memory. "I will avenge you. I will avenge our son. I will avenge Tut."

Horemheb put the letter back into his shendyt.

"Heal," he told his body. "Heal, so I may avenge them."

He closed his eyes and envisioned Tut fighting for his life against those men.

All we can do is pray.

Numbness started in Horemheb's belly and slowly spread to the rest of his body. Closing his eyes, he relived Nefertiti's last moments and then Tut's; the complete rage and breaking of his spirit in both moments competed with each other within him. Where would he find the strength to continue, to stand again? His body was broken from his own men's khopesh attacks.

In the briefest of moments, the urge to give up his spirit came over him, but he opened his eyes, glaring with renewed vigor, as if the gods had granted him a new life-force to exact his revenge and correct the wrongs done to them. A captive breath released through his lips.

"Heal me, so I may serve you," he prayed.

A season later, word came that the Mitanni had fled back to their capital city of Washukanni.

Paramesse flung open Horemheb's tent flap. "They leave their ally in the midst of war. They leave us to fight their battles!"

"We will not," Horemheb said, sitting up and rubbing his neck, almost healed. "Order the men to retreat to the northern border."

Paramesse gritted his teeth and snorted through his nostrils. "With pleasure."

Horemheb looked at the scar on his leg just above his knee and remembered the sting of the khopesh. His skin had healed on his leg, shoulder, and neck, but every day he had fought through the pain of regaining his mobility.

He stood without the cane now, even though the pain still caused his eye to wince. "Soon," he whispered, and began to gather up his items, making sure the two most important were on his person: the two halves of Nefertiti's letter, still tucked in his shendyt, and her gold-and-blue lapis ring, still placed upon his pinky finger.

IT TOOK SEVERAL DECANS TO REACH AND SECURE THE NORTHERN border, but the Hittites still pressed upon the fortresses. Paramesse came into Horemheb's tent just as Horemheb was practicing the swing of his khopesh.

"The Hittites might have us by the morning sun."

Horemheb ran his thumb across the blade. He had sharpened it the day prior. "No, they will not." He took a firm hold of his khopesh and lowered it to the ground. "I am ready."

Paramesse drew his own khopesh. "Let us see."

Then he swung at Horemheb's head.

Horemheb parried and halted his khopesh before it smacked Paramesse in the nose.

Paramesse smiled as they lowered their weapons. He nodded, placed his hand on Horemheb's shoulder, and squeezed. His eyes ran over Horemheb's face as though looking for signs of pain.

"I have no more pain, my friend," Horemheb said. "I am healed, and once I kill Pawah my spirit shall be, too."

Paramesse drew a long inhale and nodded. "Then let me declare that your journey with Osiris is now complete, Hereditary Prince." He removed his hand, stepped back, and bowed. He went to leave the tent and then looked over his shoulder. "Come out when I say."

Horemheb nodded and then swung his khopesh again; it made a shrill hum in the new dawn's air.

Paramesse smirked and then left. Horemheb followed him but stopped when the moonlight and the torchlights of camp almost touched his nose.

The Overseers of the Garrison and their troop commanders rallied the men together. The Overseer of the Fortress stood at the wall in the distance, his men behind him, on guard for a Hittite attack.

"Men of Egypt!" Paramesse's voice boomed in the torch-lit air. "Warriors for the throne! We have lost our Pharaoh Tutankhamun! We have lost our General Horemheb! We have fallen into retreat! The enemy is knocking at our door!" He paused, looking a few men in the eyes. "Yet! The gods have sent us a redeemer!"

He paced to one side of the dirt pathway as he spoke. The men's eyes lifted and the camp could feel the build of excitement, a renewal in energy.

"They have sent back a warrior so brave, so strong, so fierce, that the underworld spat him back to lead us to victory!"

Paramesse waved his khopesh in the air.

The men's eyes lit ablaze in the torchlight.

"Victory!" Paramesse yelled again, and the men nodded and looked to each other and chanted along with Paramesse.

"Victory!"

Paramesse turned to face Horemheb, and then turned back to the men. "The gods sent back Hereditary Prince and General Horemheb of Men-nefer!"

The men erupted in victorious shouts as Horemheb drew a deep breath and stepped into the light. He swung and slashed his khopesh in front of his body and thrust the blade's tip into the air at the peak of the fiery roar of the crowd.

"The Hereditary Prince lives!" Paramesse's voice boomed above the cry of the men.

The yells got even louder as the men banged on their wooden shields and stamped the ground. Their voices boomed and the ground shook as the Hittites looked from the shadows, nervous at the commotion.

"We will have victory!" Horemheb cried, and pumped his fist into the air. "As sure as Osiris brings me back from the dead, we will have our victory!"

The first of the sun's light tipped over the horizon and gave an auspicious glint off the tip of Horemheb's khopesh.

"VICTORY!"

THE BREAK OF MORNING MET WITH A BRUTAL BATTLE, BUT THE men, inspired by the gods' renewed faith in them, pushed the Hittites back. Horemheb led his men to push them even farther, out of the Mitanni lands, not even a few decans later, until Suppiluliuma, King of the Hittites, ordered a retreat and sent a peace agreement with the Egyptian military to take to Pharaoh.

"YOU WERE MEANT TO BE A WARRIOR. YOU WERE MEANT TO lead," Paramesse told Horemheb as they neared the northern fortress again on their return to Egypt.

Horemheb contemplated the statement. His father had wanted him to marry and have a family—after all the pushing for his military career, training him day in and day out, shouting insults, telling him he was such a failure that he could not even ride a chariot.

I am what my father made me, he mused.

His thoughts drifted to his younger years and caused his

heart to ache for Amenia. He never should have married her. He never should have agreed to his father's marriage proposal.

He never should have loved Nefertiti.

He never should have loved Tut.

Yet . . . here he was, having failed all three of them, and now his wife Mut sat home alone thinking him dead.

What was he meant for?

Not this. Not in his mind. He could not even save those closest to him.

This is my punishment, my god Amun, he silently prayed. *I can see now. This is my punishment. I shall lead thousands upon thousands of men to victory, yes, but I will fail those closest to me.*

"Now you shall return as Hereditary Prince and take the throne once Pharaoh Ay passes." Commander Paramesse rode next to him, surveying the land of Egypt as it came into sight. "You will be remembered, my friend."

Tut's last words came to him then: *Remember me, my father.*

Then, to answer Tut's request more than respond to Paramesse's comment, he whispered, "Yes, I will."

COMMANDER PARAMESSE AND GENERAL HOREMHEB MADE THEIR way back through Egypt, gathering followers and supporters for the resurrected Hereditary Prince as they traveled through Canaan and Goshen. They came upon Men-nefer, and Horemheb took a deep breath as they readied themselves to disembark.

He twisted Nefertiti's gold-and-blue lapis ring on his pinky finger as time slowed in that moment. He wished he was going to get her, Nefertiti, his desired wife. He wished to see her again, to hold her, to touch her, to kiss her. To love her. Every night, still, she came to him in his dreams, wrapped in white and gold, her skin glowing with her smile, holding his son, but she was always just out of arm's reach. As she drifted away he could only watch, weighted down by the bleeding scars of his body. In his dreams, he was broken. Awake, he guessed he was broken, too.

He stood in the barge's cabin, somewhat hidden from the people's view. Staring in the direction of his estate, he envisioned the life he never would have had with her even if she had lived. Instead, her half-sister awaited him there, thinking him journeyed to the land of the dead and back. Any remaining love Mut had for him would be all but gone by now. It had been a year since Tut's body was sent back, and almost three years since he had married her.

His thumb ran over the gold band of Nefertiti's ring.

I miss you, Nefertiti.

He pushed the dream from his mind yet again, on this new day, as he had always done. Egypt needed him; his men needed him; and it was enough to continue getting out of bed every morning.

Paramesse stopped and looked back at him. "What is it, Horemheb? Horemheb?"

Paramesse's question knocked him from his trance. His fingers broke the connection to Nefertiti's ring, and he dropped his hands to his sides, finding Paramesse's eyes.

"What is it?" Paramesse repeated.

Horemheb shook his head, trying to form something coherent to convey his thoughts, until he finally said, "How do you face your wife when she thought you had journeyed west?" He looked over Paramesse's head, once again in the direction of his estate. "How do I tell her I lied, that I never was killed on the battlefield?"

He added in thought: *Or rather, that I lied since the beginning. How do I tell her I loved Nefertiti? Do I even tell her?*

Paramesse chuckled and smirked. "You face her by telling her she will be Queen of Egypt." But his face fell at Horemheb's lack of enthusiasm.

Only a grimace came from Horemheb. Nefertiti, near the end, did not want to be royalty. And neither will Mut.

After a few moments of silence, Horemheb said with a slow shake of his head, "No. After all her family has been through, I do not think she will want that."

"Well, then . . ." Paramesse shrugged. "Be honest." He shook his head as if he had no other advice. "But not too honest. Women remember every word you tell them." Then he hit Horemheb's arm as he came to stand beside him to peer out of the boat, as if trying to encourage him. "I'm not saying *lie* . . . simply do not tell the whole truth."

The sun barely touched their toes; the shade of the cabin kept the sun's rays from falling on them.

Horemheb stayed silent for a moment. "I haven't been back since I married her."

Paramesse rocked on his heels. "Such is the life of a military man."

"I could have come back on many occasions, but I didn't want to leave Tut alone in the palace with that monster." Horemheb dropped his head, knowing that wasn't the real reason he had not returned. "A good man loves his wife, and I have neglected her."

Paramesse crossed his arms as he stared in the direction of Horemheb's estate. "You'll know what to do."

"No, I won't." Horemheb's voice dropped. "Two women have journeyed west because of me. One because I did not love her, and the other because I loved her so much that I lost my focus and did not protect her. My current wife, I married at my love's last request, not because I loved her."

He paused and shook his head at his own actions. Amenia and his father had told him not to do to Mut as he had done to Amenia, and yet, here he was, years later, having done it nonetheless.

"Am I a good man when I can't love those who need my

love and I can't protect the ones I do love?" His stomach churned. "How can I be a good man?"

Paramesse took a deep breath and squared his shoulders to Horemheb. Placing both of his hands on Horemheb's shoulders, he looked him in the eye. "You, my friend, are stuck in the past." He nodded. "The past is our worst enemy and sometimes our best ally. We learn from the past, certainly, but you need to let this go. You can't change who you loved or didn't love. Those women are gone now, but your wife, Mut . . . she is alive, she is here. Learn to love her. Learn to protect her." He smiled. "Time is redemption's best friend."

Horemheb lifted his head. "So you don't believe me to be a good man?" His father had not directly answered him, either, when he posed the question to him after Amenia's burial.

Paramesse patted his shoulders. "I think you are a *great* man. Maybe a lousy husband, but a great man. I've seen you risk your life for me, for Pharaoh, even for a troop commander. You have a sense that tells you when people are hurting. You try to comfort them. A great man sees the pain of others and tries to help, whether he is successful or not." Paramesse's hands fell to his sides. "I've seen your pain, Horemheb, at both losses of your two women and now the passing of Pharaoh Tutankhamun. A good man would be sad, but you have been entombed with them each time. You carry many burdens. You do the best you can. You never give up." He held a finger to Horemheb's chest. "That is the mark of a great man, a man I will be proud to call Pharaoh one day soon."

The tension in Horemheb's shoulders released. He nodded and put his hand on Paramesse's shoulder. "Thank you, my brother."

"Go in peace, Horemheb."

Paramesse's warm smile and slight nod caused Horemheb to draw in a cleansing breath. Horemheb gave a slight squeeze of Paramesse's shoulder, then turned to face the sunlit pathway to the harbor, packed with their countrymen and women to welcome their victorious army home.

"Now, let's resurrect our Hereditary Prince." Paramesse grinned and stepped first to proclaim the Hereditary Prince and General Horemheb had been risen from the dead by the god Osiris, and has come to succeed Pharaoh Ay.

Horemheb realized, in that moment, that he would have to marry Ankhesenamun, as well, to claim his right to the throne: the Hereditary Prince must marry the Hereditary Princess. He dropped his head as a new crashing weight fell into the pits of his stomach. His eyes shut tight.

Nefertiti, I cannot marry your daughter. I have already married your half-sister. I can fight many wars, but this . . .

He drew his khopesh and stepped into the sunlight as the people gasped and pointed. Women fell to their knees, screaming in joy and awe. Children ran away to spread the news. He slashed his khopesh in the air, and the blade reflected the sunlight in ethereal flashes of light. He sheathed his weapon and stepped forward as the people laid their hands on his bronze armor and touched his arms, crying. Paramesse came to stand beside him as soldiers pushed away the crowd.

Horemheb only looked in the direction of his estate in the distance. "I need a chariot."

"You don't want a litter?" Paramesse asked him under his breath with a smirk. "You are the Hereditary Prince, after all."

Horemheb shook his head at the thought of being carried. One day he would give in to it to keep embarrassment from the position of Pharaoh, but not today. "Just give me a chariot."

Shortly thereafter, a solider brought him one and he mounted. "I will be back with my wife," he told Paramesse. "We will then continue to Malkata to meet Pharaoh Ay."

Paramesse nodded. "We shall await your arrival."

Horemheb took off through the crowd toward his estate. His mind reeled at how he was to tell Mut of his so-called resurrection and how he would keep his promise to Nefertiti to take care of Mut—and now Ankhesenamun. As he rode, part of him feared Mut had found another man after she had received word of his passing, and then he wouldn't be able to keep his promise to Nefertiti. But part of him wished Mut had found another man. He had not touched her yet, and they had never consummated their marriage. He still couldn't bring himself to do so, and this was in part the reason he had never returned home.

But I am returning home now.

𓆸 7 𓆸

THE TIME OF VENGEANCE

HOREMHEB DISMOUNTED THE CHARIOT AT THE GATES OF HIS estate, surveying the royal guards at the entrance. His perplexing gaze fell upon each one. Their jaws dropped, and eyes widened as he walked past, handing the horses' reigns to a royal servant.

"Why is the royal guard at my home?" he asked, looking up and down the rows of royal guards.

They shuffled their feet and murmured amongst themselves, but he managed to hear their words.

"Is that the Hereditary Prince?"

"Is that General Horemheb?"

"Yes, it is I." Horemheb took a step backward to showcase himself to them. "Now tell me: Why is the royal guard at my estate?"

One guard found his voice and let out through a shaky breath, "Pharaoh Ay and his family have come to his daughter's side, as she is very ill."

"Mut? Ill?" Horemheb's voice dissipated in the air. He let out a heavy sigh and shook his head, stepping inside his courtyard.

Not Mut. Please, Amun, do not let her go to the Field of Reeds because of my absence, too. I cannot bear it.

Horemheb ran past the guards, who all looked at each other and pointed, whispering:

"Is that General Horemheb?"

Two guards blocked his path to his main home.

"Let me through. This is my home," Horemheb said, not even winded.

These guards look familiar, he thought as he ran his eyes over their faces.

"No. Pharaoh has ordered everyone out." One tilted his spear toward him.

"She is my wife," Horemheb said through clenched teeth.

Even though she will probably reject me now, if she lives. Amun, let her live.

The guard scoffed at him. "We were told Hereditary Prince and General Horemheb passed in battle. Mortal men are not resurrected from the dead. You cannot be him. You are an imposter."

"But I *am* him." Horemheb tapped his fingers on the guard's chest in challenge. "Osiris has granted my passage back to claim the throne as Hereditary Prince and lead Egypt to victory."

The taller man, who stood almost a head taller than Horemheb, peered down at him with narrowed eyes. "Prove it."

His mind searched every memory to remember their names. "You are the royal guard for Queen Ankhesenamun. I saw you in Aketaten," he said to one, then, to the other, "and I saw you in Malkata."

Hori's eyes did not waver. "A lot of people saw me there."

"This is nonsense." Horemheb shook his head, frustrated to be at a loss for their names. "How long has my wife been ill?"

They did not respond, and the guard's spear tilted still lower toward him. "You need to leave, imposter."

"You know I am General Horemheb." Horemheb looked at both of them, and then, at last, was almost certain he had the right names, and said them with confidence: "I even stood by you, royal guard *Ineni*, in the royal hall of Aketaten, and by you, royal guard *Hori*, at Malkata."

"How did you survive when Pharaoh Tutankhamun was killed?" Hori asked, furrowing his brow, keeping his spear lowered. "Were you not by his side?"

"I was not . . . per his command." Horemheb studied Hori's face, remembering he was the one who had to release Pawah the night Nefertiti was murdered based on lack of evidence to restrain him. "You were there that night when Pharaoh Neferneferuaten passed, were you not?" Horemheb asked Hori.

Hori nodded with a pressed grimace.

"The same man who . . ." He peered to Ineni, not remembering if he was also there that night. He thought he had remembered every detail—the same night replayed in his mind every time he closed his eyes—and yet, now, he faltered in remembering if Ineni had been there.

"He was there. He knows the truth," Hori said, and finally relaxed his spear, apparently believing him now.

"Pawah had us both ambushed. See my scars." Horemheb pointed to his neck and leg. "I needed time to heal before coming back from war. I was by Pharaoh's side when he journeyed to Re. He survived the attack, but he succumbed to a fatal evil spirit." Horemheb silenced his memory. He did not want to remember Tut's last moments, for that wound was still too fresh.

Hori snorted and shook his head. "I should have known Pawah was behind it." He grasped his spear with both hands and looked off into the distance. "We had him . . . but he escaped."

Ineni looked to the ground and clenched his jaw.

"He *escaped*?" Horemheb shifted his weight and broadened his shoulders.

"Yes, so now he is loose. Pharaoh had ordered his execution, but the next morning came and he was not in the pit." Hori locked his gaze with Horemheb's.

Horemheb swallowed, remembering his fears of Pawah coming for Mut since she was Pharaoh Ay's daughter. "Do you think he came here?"

Hori looked to Ineni and then back to Horemheb with widening eyes. "We searched Waset and all of Egypt. There was no sign of him. I assumed he had left for Nubia."

"Not a man like Pawah." Horemheb's voice fell low as a sudden cold took his core. "How long have they been in there?"

Ineni glanced at the position of the sun in the sky. "A long time."

"Follow me." Horemheb motioned for Hori and Ineni to come with him to the nearest wall that surrounded his estate's courtyard. His eyes soared to the top and he looked over the courtyard; that would be the position to see into the main bedchambers window. "Help me up."

Hori took Horemheb's foot and he jumped, grabbing the top of the wall with an extra push from the taller Hori. He pulled himself up and gained a footing on the top of the perimeter estate wall. Horemheb peered into the bedroom and he squinted, making out two figures in the corner. Were they hugging? Were they . . . dancing? He squinted again and put his hands over his eyes. Still unable to make out who was in the room, he made fists and peered through the holes in his palms. Finally, he was just able to make out what looked like Pawah holding Mut in the corner of the room.

His blood boiled; he dropped his hands and forgot to breathe. A bow and a quiver of arrows were slung over his back. He pulled an arrow and notched his bow, but as he pulled back, he second-guessed himself.

I am not an archer, he thought, *and if I hit Mut, I will never forgive myself. It is a long shot, too. My arrow needs to pass over the courtyard, and even if it made it all that way, Pawah would need to remain still to keep my arrow true to its target.*

He lowered the bow as still more royal guards, these along the wall, turned up to look at him.

"Is that the Hereditary Prince?"

"General Horemheb lives?"

They began to hold their hands up to him, but he jumped to the ground. They put their hands on him, and then on his shoulder, seeing his scars in awe of his rebirth.

"You are the rightful heir," they whispered. *"Named by Pharaoh Tutankhamun."*

Horemheb nodded to thank them for their acknowledgment of his claim to the throne, but he placed his hands out to quiet them. "My brothers-in-arms—yes, I have come back, resurrected by Osiris. But that must wait. Pawah, conspirator to the throne, holds my wife, Mut, hostage. I have seen with my own two eyes. Pawah, the man who escaped Pharaoh's edict of death." Horemheb nodded to Hori, making sure he had understood him correctly. "I can only assume Pharaoh Ay and his family are also in that room."

"We need to storm the bedchambers," a guard whispered, and garnered some head nods.

"No. Pawah is desperate now." Horemheb looked around to the royal guards. "There is no telling what a desperate man might do." Horemheb studied his estate and wished he had been home more to know its layout, but he could remember few details. There was a window to the bath chambers of the main bedroom. That would be his point of entry. "The bath chambers are on the backside of the main home. Hoist me up into the window. Hori and Ineni, come with me!"

Stepping lightly, Horemheb unhooked his khopesh from his belt as he crept into the main room with Hori and Ineni behind him. The faces of Ay, Tey, and Ankhesenamun went white at the sight of him, and Pawah laughed, thinking he had finally scared them speechless. He rose, his hand in the air as he spoke.

"Now that we are agreed, I can—"

Horemheb raised his khopesh and let it fly, chopping Pawah's hand off.

Pawah let out a blood-curdling scream and let go of Mut, who fell forward, her legs and body too weak to run away.

Ankhesenamun pulled the dagger from her belt as Pawah turned to face Horemheb.

Pawah's face paled to white. "You?" he gasped, clutching his now-crippled forearm against his body in a weak attempt to stop the bleeding. "You are supposed to be dead!"

"The gods granted me a new life to avenge the murders of Pharaoh Akhenaten, Pharaoh Smenkare, Pharaoh Neferneferuaten, Pharaoh Tutankhamun, and the attempts on the life of Pharaoh Ay and on *my* life, the Hereditary Prince." He held his khopesh up to Pawah's chin. "You have murdered them all, you have used my wife to torture Pharaoh Ay, and now you shall die."

Ankhesenamun growled; her knuckles went white around her blade's handle.

Tey had crept toward Mut and was pulling her away from Pawah.

Pawah peered behind Horemheb to Hori and Ineni and then over his shoulder, wincing, as he wrapped his wound with the end of his robe, attempting to make a tourniquet. Then he sneered and looked to Horemheb. "I could only murder them all thanks to my conspirator here, the mighty General Horemheb."

Ankhesenamun's jaw dropped. "No," she said in a breathless whisper. "You lie."

Horemheb narrowed his eyes and readied his khopesh to strike. "Enough of your lies, Pawah."

Pawah bellowed a deep-bellied laugh as his eyes danced. "I reveal to you the true mastermind behind it all!" He gestured with his bleeding forearm to Horemheb as he turned to face Pharaoh Ay.

"I said *enough!*"

Horemheb went to strike, but he stopped. He knew that if he struck now it would only increase the small seed of doubt this man had just planted.

It is better to let him use his silver tongue to dig his hole.

"You see, Horemheb was part of Pharaoh Akhenaten's murder, as well as Smenkare's—a fact I understand you, Ay, know to be true. Tell your wife how you convinced your dear, sweet Nefertiti to take the life of her own husband."

Tey looked to Ay over the crumpled body of her daughter. "I know Nefertiti did such a thing . . . but *you* asked her? Tell me it's not true!"

Ay's gaze slowly lifted from Tey to Pawah, his jaw firm in his hatred.

Pawah continued with glee, "And General Horemheb happened to be *absent* in Nefertiti's death, happened to *survive* this past war, but the young Pharaoh did not? It is not a coincidence. He and I worked together. He is just as guilty as I! He is only angry now and seeks my life because he didn't expect me to double-cross him!" Pawah stomped his foot as if stamping away the pain in his arm.

Ay looked to Horemheb and shook his head. He'd seen Horemheb's pain. He'd seen the way he looked at Nefertiti. He alone knew of their son together. He'd seen the way Horemheb had picked up Nefertiti's letter Ay had torn out of anger when Horemheb told him he was going to marry Mut. And now he saw the rage behind his eyes. Ay looked at his youngest daughter, lying on the floor, nearly unconscious, her head in Tey's lap. Horemheb had told him he would keep Mut safe. He'd failed both of his daughters—but at least Mut was alive. In the deepest of his heart, he knew Horemheb mourned Nefertiti, just as he himself had mourned his first wife, Temehu.

Pawah's laugh rang throughout the room. "Oh my dear Pharaoh Ay, who can you trust?"

"I trust General Horemheb. I *know* he did not conspire to kill my daughter, and thus, nor did he conspire to kill Pharaoh Tutankhamun." His voice held a firm tone as he locked eyes with Horemheb.

Pawah gritted his teeth. He pulled a dagger from inside his belt and lunged, with a maniacal yell, toward Horemheb, who was looking at Ay. But then Pawah let out a scream as Ankhesenamun sunk her dagger into his back. He turned to stab her, but Horemheb caught his arm and wrenched the dagger from his hand.

Pawah fell to his knees and laughed, shaking his head. Tears brimmed his eyes. "The little girl attacks again."

"I cursed you." Ankhesenamun spit at him. "I foretold that you would come close to the crown but you would die never having attained it."

His face paled as his breathing grew heavy.

"General, kill him for my family." Ankhesenamun gritted her teeth as Pawah fell to his knees. "Kill him for his treason to the throne."

Pawah snapped his head to Horemheb. "Yes, General, and be quick with it." Pawah sneered and eyed Ineni behind him. "But If I die, so will someone else. I have letters that tell of all the conspirators—"

"I will burn all of those cursed letters!" Ankhesenamun yelled, and Ineni lowered his eyes. "You will not use them to extort those to do your bidding."

Pawah's mouth curled into a grimace. "You know

nothing, child! Those letters are *real*, and they tell of everyone who helped dispatch the royalty—including your precious Tut and children."

Ankhesenamun's breath grew shallow as a tear welled in her eye yet refused to fall. "My children . . . ?" She clamped her mouth shut and gave a slight shake of her head. "You used your *false* letters to turn my husband away from me. Nothing you say, and nothing you may have, is true. Your letters are *lies*, and I will burn them all."

Pawah sneered. "Then you will never know who murdered your husband and children."

"*You* did."

Horemheb spun him away from Ankhesenamun. "Ammit will not have the chance to devour your heart." Horemheb punched him square in the chest. "I told you I'd rip it from your chest before the demoness feasted."

Pawah chuckled through hitching breaths of pain. "There are no gods, you fool!"

Ay wanted to inflict pain on this man as well, but Pharaoh managed to only stand watch with clenched fists. Then he remembered his dagger on the bed. He grabbed it but paused, noticing the dried blood on the headrest. He threw back the blanket and then stepped back with eyes wide. Ay breathed with an open mouth as hot tears welled in his eyes at the sight of his daughter's blood. "You savage," Ay whispered.

Horemheb growled upon his glance at the bloody bedsheets, tightening his grip on the khopesh.

Pawah's eyes darted around the room and landed on Ineni again. Ineni only smirked in return as he bowed his head to Pharaoh Ay and said:

"Pharaoh . . . if I may suggest a public execution?"

Still staring at the bloody bedsheets, Ay said through his teeth, "Drag him through the streets of Men-nefer and Waset, and then impale him outside the temple. I will order all the people to observe, and I want you, Horemheb, to ensure he dies and his body burned."

Horemheb bent over, pulling him up by his collar, and whispered to him, "I will relish the fact you will die a slow, painful death. I will take pleasure in watching you be torn limb from limb and burned and forgotten."

Pawah smiled at him. "And I will relish the fact you failed all four Pharaohs before."

Horemheb dropped him so his head made a *thud* on the wooden floor. A laugh in Pawah's chest convulsed his body.

Ay looked at Mut over Pawah's mad laughter, and vowed that since Horemheb had not been there to save her, he would not let the General have the crown. Horemheb would not succeed him. He would not put Mut through Nefertiti's pain.

"Hori! Ineni!" Horemheb barked.

The two guards picked the still-cackling Pawah up and dragged him out to the royal guards in the courtyard.

⚊⚊⚊

HORI ORDERED A SERVANT TO BRING OUT A HOT PLATE AND SEAR Pawah's arm while Ineni tended to his back wound. "So you will live longer," he told him, sneering. "You are lucky Queen Ankhesenamun's dagger was not that long. You shall survive long enough to endure your punishment."

Ineni peered down at him as the servants pressed Pawah's arm against the hot plate. The smell of burning flesh filled the air as Pawah's scream echoed within the courtyard walls.

Pawah's arm fell. As he breathed through his pain he began to snicker, then shook his head as his eyes trailed up to Ineni.

"You, Ineni!" he breathed. "You are my subject." He threw his head back, wrenching his arm to his chest. "You are my supporter! You owe me your life! I own you!"

As more royal guards approached, Ineni looked to Hori and nodded. "My loyalty is with the throne."

Pawah spat at him. "Liar!" Then he threw a pointed finger to the royal guards of the crowd and called out their names: "Amenket, Tchay, Renni, Yuni, all of you—you are my supporters, you are loyal to me!"

But the men only glanced at each other and shook their heads. They had all been conspirators at one point, but Pawah's threats were over now. Ineni had let him go; Hori had allowed Sitamun into Pharaoh Smenkare's chambers to kill him; both had been there to persuade Nefertiti to poison her husband, the Pharaoh, and the others conspired to kill Pharaoh Akhenaten. There were no clean hands among them.

"Those loyal to the throne," Hori said, stepping back, "string him to the back of the horses and parade him through the streets, proclaiming the former vizier and former Fifth Prophet of Amun, Pawah, has been found to be a conspirator and murderer against the throne and shall die by impalement for his crimes."

The whole of the royal guards came and laid their hands on him, tying him, binding him to the back of the horses, as Pawah yelled curses upon each of them, spitting and yelling.

Hori came back to the upper room and bowed before Pharaoh. "Pawah has been tied to the back of the horses. Is Pharaoh to lead the procession?"

Ay glanced at Tey, knowing he needed to lead the procession, as was his position as Pharaoh, but Tey's gaze fell to her daughter, whose head was still in her lap. Horemheb knelt by her side, helping Mut drink some wine. Ankhesenamun stood behind him, having retrieved her dagger from Pawah's back.

Ay closed his eyes before turning back to Hori. "The Hereditary Prince and General Horemheb will accompany Pharaoh to lead the procession. Take the royal family back to

Malkata at once. Have the best physicians look over Pharaoh's daughter Mut."

Hori bowed and left to carry out Pharaoh's orders.

Horemheb nodded as he peered up at Ay.

Hate flooded Ay's cheeks as he stared down Horemheb. He stole his Nefertiti. He failed to protect her. He married Mut as Hereditary Prince and promised to keep her safe. Now Mut lay beaten, starved, dehydrated, and only the gods knew what else had been done to her. If it was the last thing he did, he would not let Horemheb take the throne. He would not force Ankhesenamun to be Horemheb's wife as well.

Horemheb touched Tey's arm and then caressed Mut's shoulder. She whimpered under his touch, and he pulled his hand away.

"Have I gone to the Field of Reeds?" Mut whispered. Her eyes rolled under her eyelids and finally settled on Horemheb's face.

"No . . . you are still among the living," Horemheb said softly.

"But . . . you have passed. *You* have already gone." Mut reached out to touch his cheek, and when her fingertips felt flesh, she pulled her hand back to her chest. Her eyes made their way up to her mother in askance.

"You are alive and safe now, my daughter," Tey crooned, rubbing her back.

Mut sat abruptly and pushed herself against the wooden bed to steady her shaking body.

Her mother leaned forward to touch her bruised and sliced face. "Pawah will never touch you again, Mut. You are safe now."

Mut only clenched her jaw and moved away from her mother's hand as the tears broke and fell down her cheeks. Her eyes cut to Horemheb. "Where were you?" Then she snapped her gaze back to her mother and then to Ankhesenamun. "Where were you?!"

Her words ate through Horemheb's bronze armor and struck his heart. It was the very question Nefertiti had asked him when Khabek had almost killed her in his assassination attempt. The very question he knew Nefertiti, having been stabbed by Pawah, wanted to scream at him as he held her, but didn't. The question he knew Amenia wanted to throw in his face, but journeyed west from a broken heart before she could. The question he asked of himself when Tut passed.

Where were you?

The question repeated in his mind as he held his breath, answering in his own mind.

Not where I should have been, he wanted to reply.

"Where were you?" Mut cried as her shoulders collapsed, and she sobbed.

The royal guards came in and tried to help Mut into their leather-and-wood stretcher, but she screamed and struggled away from them.

Tey closed in on her and grabbed her flailing hand. She pressed her forehead to Mut's. "I will not leave your side," her old voice whispered as tears streamed down her cheek. "I will not leave you."

Mut cried as they carried her away, Tey beside them. Ankhesenamun stood back to let them work. Horemheb stayed on his knees as he watched. Ay still stood by the bed, his own eyes welling with tears. He looked at Horemheb and raised his dagger to him, repeating his daughter's question:

"Where were you, Hereditary Prince?"

Horemheb knew the sentiment behind his words. They'd had this conversation before.

Ay will never take responsibility for his hand in this. I know I failed, but I alone will always be to blame in Ay's mind. He is their father. He outranks me with both Nefertiti and Mut. Mut was under his care while I was at war—a war that he kept us in once Pharaoh Tutankhamun journeyed to Re. He is just as guilty as I am.

He repeated the words he had spoken when Ay had

comforted him over Nefertiti's murder: "I accept my failures. Have you, Pharaoh?"

Ay squared his shoulders to him as Horemheb stood. "You will watch your tongue, General Horemheb."

Horemheb narrowed his eyes. "Thus Pharaoh says."

ANKHESENAMUN WASN'T LISTENING AND KNEW THEY HAD forgotten she was still standing in the corner of the room. Her eyes ran up and down Horemheb's back as a crushing wave of sorrow pressed upon her soul. Green envy wrapped around her legs and her hands and squeezed her chest.

Why couldn't Tut have been resurrected from the dead instead? Why didn't Tut come home instead of this man? This man didn't even love Mut. Tut loved me, and I him. Why do the gods still punish me? For the sins of my father? My mother?

Her grimace overwhelmed her face as her eyes glistened in the sun's rays piercing into the room.

I hate you, Horemheb.

AY AND HOREMHEB LED THE PROCESSION THAT PULLED PAWAH, who finally collapsed and was dragged through the streets of Men-nefer, leaving a trail of blood from his reopened stump. At the sight of Horemheb, the people pointed.

"Hereditary Prince!"

"He lives?!"

"It's true! General Horemheb lives!"

"The Hereditary Prince lives!"

Then, even before the declaration of Pawah's crimes, they spat at the menace and kicked dust on him. The people had known his ways, and now he was reaping his reward. The army pranced in the streets alongside their Pharaoh and

Hereditary Prince, declaring their victory against the Hittites and the return of Horemheb from the dead. The procession took place throughout the whole of the city. Paramesse and his divisions waited for them to escort the royal barge. The evening came and they boarded the royal barge and sailed up the Nile toward Waset as the military men and royal guards took turns beating Pawah in front of Pharaoh's throne. Pawah only laughed in his agony. It would be at least a two-decan trip back to Waset, so the royal guard kept his wounds well cared for so that Pawah would not die before his execution.

THE NIGHT THEY HAD ALMOST REACHED MALKATA, PAWAH pointed a long finger at Ay and then dragged it to Horemheb. "You may kill me," he spat, losing a tooth after the last beating, "but you will always know I took what you treasured most!"

Both men stood. Ay's hands clenched to fists around his dagger and Horemheb's hand grabbed the handle of his khopesh. "It's what he wants, Pharaoh," Horemheb muttered through a clamped jaw. "He wants us to end him now, so he does not have to feel the pain of impalement."

Ay released his dagger, and Horemheb his khopesh. Ay stepped forward; his age had leaped upon him since Horemheb had been at war.

The guards grabbed Pawah and forced him to his knees. Pawah's head remained unbowed, and he smirked at Ay. Pawah's blood looked black in the shadows of the royal barge's torchlight. "I killed Nefertiti, and I took *everything* from Mut." The blood in his mouth bubbled out as he talked. "And I even made your granddaughter a widow. But you . . . you, old man, helped make her an orphan."

Ay held no restraint any longer; he put his entire weight

and life-force into his fist as he punched Pawah across the face.

Pawah's head flew almost to the floor if the guards did not catch him and bring him upright. "You hit like an old man." He chuckled breathlessly, spitting out another tooth. Ay went to punch him again, but Pawah spoke, his dark eyes peering up at him: "My last gift to you, *Pharaoh*. I curse your name and the name of Nefertiti to die in the memory of the people forevermore. You take my life, and I will take your memory."

Ay punched him again square in the jaw and then slung the blood from his knuckles. "You came so close, Pawah, but you don't scare anyone anymore with your threats and curses." Ay motioned to his guards to stand him up, and then Ay punched him over and over as though he were a straw dummy like the ones used in military training, until finally Pawah collapsed and could no longer laugh.

Sweat dripped from the tip of Ay's nose; his own labored breathing started putting stars in his vision. He turned and came back to his throne. He found Horemheb's eyes. "Age has taken my strength. Will you finish what I started with him?"

Horemheb could see the slow burn of hate in his eyes and knew it was directed toward both Pawah and himself. Horemheb squinted his eye in thought. "No, Pharaoh, I cannot. If you let me near him, I would kill him." His jaw clamped. "I would rather see him suffer from impalement."

Ay nodded and then motioned for the guards to continue their beating.

Horemheb watched the savagery and his mind drifted back to his dreams of Nefertiti, holding their son and welcoming him home. A future that Pawah had taken away.

No . . . he thought. *Not even Pawah could take that away. Such a future could never have been. Even her letter told me she would marry Tut, would give the child to Amenia if a daughter, or let Tut raise the child as his own if a son. If only I could feel her against me once more.*

He closed his eyes, remembering his dreams further—she was there, floating above him, her white and gold linens flowing around her, and still, he was weighted down, his body broken, unable to reach her. She was so close but just out of reach. She was gone.

He'd felt he'd lost everything, but he was wrong: still then he had lost Amenia . . . and further still he had lost Tut. Mut was alive.

His black eyes watched Pawah's beatings behind an expressionless face.

And Pawah took Tut away from me. I saw a future there. Tut, the man I called son. Tut, the boy I helped raise into a man. Pawah took him from me. Pawah took his future . . . his bright, auspicious future.

His teeth ached from the weight of his clenched jaw; he wished he were alone with Pawah to make him feel the same pain he had bestowed upon Horemheb.

And now Mut . . . he beat her and probably took her in bed for his own pleasure.

His mind went blank, only knowing the beating Pawah was enduring paled in comparison to what he would do to him if no one were watching.

THEY REACHED WASET JUST AS THE SUN ROSE. THE MILITARY MEN and the royal guards dragged a barely alive Pawah from the barge and escorted Ay and Horemheb to the front of the temple. They tied Pawah's feet and began the process of hoisting him up.

"You—" Pawah pointed at Pharaoh with his one good hand. "I took what you treasured most. And you will never forget it! You shall always remember me!!"

A blood-curdling scream left Pawah's lips as they sat him atop the spike.

Horemheb and Ay stood along with the people of Waset and watched Pawah scream all day, enduring his final breathless curses until the sun began its descent and Pawah breathed his last.

"Burn his body. Give his ashes to the crocodiles of the Nile," Horemheb ordered Paramesse.

Ay nodded in agreement. Together they watched as Paramesse and the military men took pleasure in setting Pawah's body ablaze.

Ay and Horemheb boarded the royal barge once again, to return them to Malkata, as the distinct burn of flesh filled the night air.

Ay turned to Horemheb and put a finger to his chest. "You make this right with Mut." He pressed hard and then pulled his hand away.

Horemheb said nothing, as no words were needed.

🕊 8 🕊
THE TIME OF APOLOGY

THAT EVENING, HOREMHEB CAME TO THE GENERAL'S APARTMENT at Malkata just as the physician was leaving.

"She is not doing so well." The physician took a deep breath, his voice low. "We are applying bandages, but her heart is fearful."

Horemheb's gaze fell, nodding, as the physician continued.

"I cannot imagine what she has lived through . . . torture, most likely. She must be favored by the gods to still have life."

The physician walked away.

And Nefertiti . . . was she not favored?

His heart broke again at the memory of that early morning he had watched her life leave her eyes. He swallowed the memory, focusing his mind on the present—his wife, who had just endured an entire season of Pawah's torment. He had promised she would be safe there. His head fell.

No more promises I cannot keep, he told himself before he entered.

Mut eyed him as he drew closer to the bed, her swollen eyes narrowing. "I thought you had left . . . it's what you're good at doing."

Horemheb remembered Amenia pounding on his chest, yelling that she hated him, and the same sting befell him now. "Pawah is gone. He will never hurt you again. I made sure of it." His voice fell flat.

Mut clenched her jaw and then winced as a servant wrapped a linen cloth over a gash in her arm. "You come claiming to be the hero, but the damage is already done." She threw her hand up to show him the bruises and gashes across her body, but seemed to immediately regret the action as she pulled back, wincing in pain. Her fingers twitched from their affliction.

"I'm sorry—"

"Get out." Her voice, gruff from the pain, resounded against the stone walls.

"Mut, please—"

"Leave me!" She shook her head, her jaw clenching in anguish. "Leave me!" she spat again through her teeth.

Tener hurried over to him and whispered, "General." She bowed her head but then looked him in the eye as Mut yelled "Leave me!" again through her teeth. Tener glanced to Mut as she spoke to Horemheb. "Perhaps it would be better if the servants stay the night with her and you find somewhere else to sleep."

Horemheb looked also to Mut, who now had her eyes closed tight as a servant poured castor oil and honey on her wound before wrapping it in a linen bandage.

I will not cause her further pain, he thought, and nodded to Tener.

He left and then leaned his back against the closed door of his apartment as he repeated Mut's words in his mind: *I thought you had left . . . it's what you're good at doing.*

Maybe she speaks the truth. I was too late for Nefertiti, not there for Tut, absent for Amenia, and now I have let harm befall her as well.

He stumbled to the courtyard and found an acacia tree to

lay down against. He didn't want the comfort of a bed. He didn't deserve one. He put his hands behind his head and looked up to the stars peeking through the tree's branches, trying not to feel, not to think, not to breathe . . . but to no avail.

What have I done? I have lost everything. Where do I go from here?

His thoughts, just as they did every night, brought Nefertiti back to him. He envisioned her in his dream: floating in linens of gold and white wrapped around her.

I miss you so, my love. I'm sorry I have failed Mut. I'm sorry I have not done as you requested. I did not keep her safe. I wish I would have kept you safe. I wish you were alive. Then Mut could be with someone she deserves. Mut would have been protected. And I . . . I would . . .

He wondered how, if his Nefertiti had lived, he would have stayed away. Would his heart ache as it did now? Would his mind constantly be reliving their last moment together? Would her letter hold the same importance to him? Would he have lost himself in war? How would he have sat through council meetings? How would he have not longed to touch her hand? Would he dream of her almost every night, as he did now? The dreams had been, in the beginning, of him coming home to her and his son. But then Pawah had murdered them in front of him. He had begged himself to not dream of her murder anymore. He couldn't bear it. As if the gods had answered him, those dreams transformed into the same eerily peaceful yet discouraging dream every night: Nefertiti, holding his son, floating in a void with white and gold robes flowing around her. The wound to her chest bled. She was so close, and yet he could not reach her. His body lay weighted and seemingly in pieces, falling away from her. Every effort to reach out to her ended in failure. Every night, the dreams ended the same. He often wondered if her ka was trying to speak to him, trying to comfort him, through Bes, the god of dreams. Even though he'd awake with pain in his heart, he longed to dream, to see her one more time. He'd beg Bes to see her, hold her once more. The god would always half-answer with the same dream.

He pulled out one half of her torn letter, her final lasting words to him, and placed it near his nose to try and breathe in the little scent of Nefertiti that remained.

It doesn't matter what I would have done if she had lived, for she did not. I let her be murdered. I let her last requests go unfulfilled. Tut is gone. Amenia fell ill because of me, and Mut . . . Mut never should have married me. I could not keep her safe. No . . . I did not keep her safe. Nefertiti, please comfort me. It is such a weight on my soul.

THE NEXT MORNING CAME TOO SOON. HOREMHEB AWOKE TO Ankhesenamun tapping his shoulder with her foot. How had he not heard her approach? A bead of sweat appeared on his brow as he looked around, trying to find the half of the letter he had fallen asleep with. The dream had come again; Ankhesenamun had awoken him just as his body fell into darkness, watching Nefertiti and his son dissipate.

"You should be careful with this," Ankhesenamun said, holding the torn half of her mother's letter.

Horemheb scrambled up, his face slack with panic. His breath hitched as he bowed his head to his Queen; his heart beat quickly within his chest as he wondered if she had read it.

"I will," he said and reached for it.

But she yanked it back and peered at him.

He noticed Hori and Ineni in the distance, but thankfully out of earshot.

"I remember this letter." Ankhesenamun's eyes ran over the content. "It said 'Commander' on the front. It laid sealed on my mother's bedside table. I had even asked if I could deliver it to you, but she said she would ask Grandfather to give it to you." She turned the letter over in her hand as her eyes snapped to his. "You loved each other, didn't you? Or I suppose I could assume as much by what my mother wrote."

Her voice wasn't as upset as he thought it would be. Horemheb paused before he responded. She had read it. She knew. No words came to his mind.

"Who else knows about this?" Ankhesenamun's tone softened.

"Only your grandfather and my commander."

Ankhesenamun nodded. "That's why he was so sure you had nothing to do with her murder."

Horemheb's head fell. "We were in Pawah's chambers that night. We were going to do away with him." He shook his head and looked in the direction of Aketaten, feeling the warm breeze in his face. Pressing his lips into a grimace, he took a deep breath through his nose. "But he had other plans."

"Did you truly love her?" Ankhesenamun asked, her eyes searching.

Horemheb looked his love's daughter in the eyes. "Yes." His response was a whisper. "I'll never forgive myself . . . for not being there when she needed me."

Tears gathered in Ankhesenamun's eyes as she nodded. She skimmed the letter again. "You . . . had a child in her womb." Her half smile drew out her tears. "My youngest sibling."

He wanted to reach out and press his hand on her shoulder to comfort her, but refrained as the guards, although out of earshot, could still see him.

"I'm sorry, my Queen," he whispered.

She clutched the letter to her chest. "It doesn't seem nine years have passed."

"No, I suppose it does not."

Nine years? Horemheb thought. *Had it been that long? It seems as if it were yesterday . . . but no, I watched Tut grow into a man. Nine years since Pawah took Nefertiti from me. One since he took Tut. Curse your heart, Pawah, for what you have done. I hope you die a thousand deaths, each inflicting worse pain than the last.*

His fists released and his shoulders fell. Pawah was dead, yet Nefertiti and Tut were still gone. At Ankhesenamun's silence, Horemheb looked to his bedchambers door. "Please don't tell Mut."

"She should know."

He shook his head and looked to the ground. "No, she shouldn't . . . not for a long time, at least." His thoughts drifted to Amenia as he found Ankhesenamun's eyes. "You read the letter. Marrying Mut and taking care of her was your mother's last request. I wouldn't be able to fulfill that request if Mut knew. She would never believe I love her."

"Do you?"

"I care for her as Nefertiti's sister." Horemheb dipped his chin. "I will not lie to you."

"That is not fair to her. You need to learn to love her . . . for *her*. Tut is gone, and you must live the life set before you."

"Tut?" Horemheb asked.

"I mean . . . my mother." Ankhesenamun leaned her head back and closed her eyes. "My *mother* is gone." She paused. "And so is Tut. He's not coming back, either." Her breath hitched, and her voice fell to a whisper. "You came home and Tut did not."

"I wish it were the other way around." Horemheb's brow furrowed.

"Me too." A tear ran down her cheek. "But"—she looked back to Horemheb—"this is my life now, and this will be my future. And Mut—she is your wife, and you now have a second chance. She is your future."

"Then don't tell her about your mother and me. Please."

Ankhesenamun bit her lip. After a few moments, she

nodded. Her gaze fell to the ripped piece of papyrus in her hand. "I was only able to read half the letter. But I understand." She folded it along its well-worn creases, closing her eyes, and drew a deep breath. "You are the Hereditary Prince now. I shall be married to you when my grandfather passes." The uptick in her voice at the end mimicked her eyes, but it did not pass as sincere.

Horemheb half-grimaced, remembering Nefertiti's same marriage plight. "You can be with whomever you want. It was what I would have asked Tut for when your mother married him."

"No, I cannot. I am the last living bloodline to the throne. I am here to stay. I am here to marry the Hereditary Prince."

"I meant you can *be* with whomever you want. I will look the other way. I won't say anything. I'll never hold you in contempt of our marriage."

Ankhesenamun pressed her lips into a sad smile. "If that is what you were going to do with my mother, why didn't you do it much sooner?"

"Because Nefertiti . . ." His voice trailed off. "Nefertiti was worried that if word got out the Commander had Pharaoh's wife, the struggle for the throne's power, the image in the people's eyes, everything, would be lost, and Pharaoh would have to order us both executed."

"The same holds true today, for me." Ankhesenamun lifted her chin. "My mother was content in her letter to marry Tut and live celibate for the rest of her life, so I assume I must do the same."

Horemheb shook his head. "If there was any way—"

"You promise me, General Horemheb, that you will love Mut. Don't love her because my mother asked you to. Find a way to love her the way Tut loved me at the end, the way you loved my mother." Horemheb looked away when Ankhesenamun's eyes filled with tears, but her tone pulled him back. "Promise me."

"I cannot make any more promises I don't know I can keep. Not anymore." Horemheb took a breath as he lifted his head. "But I promise I will make every effort."

Ankhesenamun nodded, as if accepting his proposal. "My mother is gone, General. She is not coming back. Make the most of what your life is today and tomorrow, for we only have so many days." Her finger ran along the letter's edge. "May I keep this?"

Horemheb paused, looking to it, feeling as though a part of him were about to be ripped away.

"I have nothing to remember her by, and I noticed this letter still smells of lotus blossoms." Her voice soothed the tear in his heart, but at the same time pained his soul.

Horemheb glanced at Nefertiti's gold-and-blue lapis ring on his finger. Which would he rather have? Then, with the full weight of his heart, he nodded his head, and watched her place half of Nefertiti's letter to him in her belt, already longing to ask for it back.

"Thank you," she whispered.

He nodded and watched her leave. He drew the other half of Nefertiti's letter from his belt, and his heart fell, for Ankhesenamun had taken the side of the letter with her salutation to him: *My Dearest Horemheb*, and her name: *Love, Your Nefertiti.*

HOREMHEB WENT BACK TO HIS BEDCHAMBERS, AND ONCE THE door closed behind him he stood in the shadow of the room, looking across the living area to the bed. Servants were tending to Mut's wounds with honey and plaster and tending to the bruises with castor oil and linen.

Horemheb walked toward the bed, hoping not to frighten her, but stopped short of the light. She would have many scars. He rubbed the side of his arm, feeling the two there,

one much older than the other: the first from Pawah's dagger
when he ran to Nefertiti's side as the life left her; the second
when he saved Tut from the Hittites. He drew a deep breath.
Now he bore two more scars: one on his neck and shoulder
and the other above his knee, when he and Pharaoh were
attacked by Pawah's men. The reason why he could not
return home to protect Mut. If he had been by Pharaoh's side,
if Tut had not wanted to fight with the archers, they both
could have come home, and much sooner, before all of this
could happen.

He let out a breath and dropped his arm. He did not want
to remember the scars now. Mut was his wife, and as
Ankhesenamun, Paramesse, Ay, and even his own father had
all told him, he needed to learn to love her.

As the sun rose, the room filled with more light and the
servants finished their dressings. Horemheb dismissed them.
"She will need to be kept cool," Tener whispered, and pointed
to the linen cloth and water basin beside the bed. "She has
been given a sedative of mandrake fruit and poppy to help
ease her pain. You cannot let her get too warm." He nodded
as she bowed her head and left.

Horemheb didn't move until he heard the door close
behind him.

Mut slept and Horemheb came near to her side and knelt
by her. She looked so much like his Nefertiti. He looked upon
her for a long time, remembering watching Nefertiti sleep
and then holding her as she slipped away.

You made me feel alive. Her last words to him.

"Marry Mut," he mouthed, and then rubbed his face.

*For you, Nefertiti, I will learn to love your sister because of your
last request.* He hung his head in his hands. *I do love Mut. I will
tell myself that until I believe it.* He let out a breath as he
examined her wrist that lay within his sight. There would
most likely be scars. The rope had left her skin bloody, raw,
and twisted. It would be something she always carried, and

he hated himself for not coming back to her, for not being there to protect her. *I do care for her, Nefertiti, and I'm sorry I have let Pawah hurt her, too.* There were so many bruises and cuts on her face and body—even on her toes.

"Where were you?" Mut's whisper cut through the silence of the room.

The question lingered in both the present and his memory. He closed his eyes to gather himself before turning to face her.

"You told me I'd be safe there."

He clenched his jaw as he wrapped his hand over hers, but she pulled her fingers out from underneath his palm.

"You let that monster beat me, and once I fell unconscious . . ." She struggled to speak and her voice fell into silence as her body shook from the horrors Horemheb could not even imagine had befallen her body.

"I'm sorry," he whispered.

She wrinkled her nose and blinked back her tears. "Is that all you can say?"

"There are no other words." His guilt hung over his head as he studied her bruised face and neck; his gaze fell to her wrists, her fragile and perfectly wrapped wrists.

She scoffed, her eyes sliding over to the window. "I thought I loved you, but my mother was right all those years ago. It was nothing but a blind infatuation, a childish fantasy. You care nothing for me." Her lip trembled as her voice ended with a hitched breath.

She was waiting for something, he saw. He lowered his head and gently pulled her hand into reach of his lips and placed a kiss there. She turned her face to him, her eyes hooded.

"You're a liar," she said with venom.

Horemheb drew a deep breath before he raised his head to her. He winced.

How to correct this? How to learn to love her?

He tried: "I never gave you any reason to believe I cared for you. I'm sorry I did not protect you, that I lied about being killed on the battlefield, that I did not come home, and that I left you for so long."

Those were almost the exact words he had written to Amenia in the last letter he had left for her. He grimaced, thinking himself horrible. He couldn't even come up with a genuine apology for his current wife. His head fell into his hand as he sighed in exasperation.

Amenia and Nefertiti are gone. Mut is my wife. Learn to love her. How do you fall in love with someone? How did I fall in love with Nefertiti? I admired her for her strength and her beauty and her love of Egypt. I mourned with her. I struggled with her. I fell in love with her touch and her smile. I spoke to her and found out who she was as a person, as a woman.

He pushed off from his knees and came to the other side of the bed and climbed in next to Mut. He propped himself up on his elbow and then reached over her to the damp linen cloth next to the water bowl on the bedside table. Taking it, he dabbed her face to keep her cool, moving as if he handled a piece of ancient papyrus.

"You can stop now, Horemheb," Mut said through her teeth, and looked away from him so he could only see her profile. "Why did you even marry me? What am I to you?"

"I married you—"

"You know, I didn't even think you loved me. I mourned you when they said you'd been killed, but I wondered: Would you have mourned me if the roles were reversed? Or would you just be sad that I was gone? Would you even care?" She licked her lip to catch some of her fallen tears.

How do I make this right?

His father's words came back to him: *A good man loves his wife.*

Horemheb swallowed as he thought about what to say.

"I care about you, Mut."

"Is that all?" she asked.

"I did lie to you. I will not try to hide it anymore. It is a mistake I regret." He watched her jaw clench as he continued. "I married you so you wouldn't be in Pawah's grasp here in the palace if you bore Tut's child for Ankhesenamun as his royal wife. I tried to keep you safe." He let out a sad sigh. "I never thought he would go after you in my home."

He saw the anger build behind her lips and her chest rise.

"I'm sorry, Mut. It is not fair to you."

Her mouth contorted as she took a sharp inhale, fighting off tears.

"If you want to separate, I will pay all that you need . . . but I am here now." He dabbed her forehead with the cloth. "If you desire, I will *never* leave your side. I will court you like I should have before we married." He tenderly turned her face to him. "I promise you, Mut, I will try my hardest every day for the rest of my life to receive your trust and love and respect and forgiveness."

Her eyes narrowed until she finally forced out: "It may never come."

"I will work every day nonetheless," he whispered, his eyes locked with hers.

Her jaw released some of the tension it held; her eyes ran over his face as if studying him for deceit. He did not even need to hide his eyebrow tell, for his heart spoke the truth. It was no lie. He would try until the day he journeyed west to earn her love and somehow redeem himself to her and the ones he had failed. In this way, he could earn some semblance of peace before he that time.

He continued to dab her face and neck and shoulders until the linen cloth became dry. Leaning over, he wet it again and wrung it with one strong squeeze of his hand.

Her eyes never left him. Finally, she asked, "Why didn't you come home? Why didn't you write me? Why did you let me believe you were dead?"

"Pawah's men attacked Pharaoh and me." He dabbed her cheek, his gaze somewhat veiled over as he remembered. "I was heavily injured. Pharaoh went to Re of infection from his wounds. I could not walk without a cane and had little use of my arm. I came to with just enough time to make it to Tut's side before he passed from this life." His voice shook as he let out a breath. "Before, when I thought we would both live, I thought it would be wise to finally seal the power for Pharaoh if he could be seen as reborn from Osiris, a true testament to the gods' divine blessing."

He left the cloth on her bosom as he outlined her jaw with his finger, taking note of a deep scratch the servants missed. He picked up the linen cloth and applied a slight pressure to the scratch to try to get the bleeding to stop. "It's been a nasty unspoken war between Pharaoh and the Amun priesthood, and quite a literal one between Pharaoh and Pawah. The last thing I wanted was to involve you in this tumultuous life, Mut. The last thing I wanted was for Pawah to hurt you, too."

He found her eyes as tears pooled in them. "But he did."

"Yes," Horemheb whispered. "And I'll never forgive myself, just as I will never forgive myself for the others. But I promise you, I will do whatever you need me to do to make sure you feel safe. I won't leave your side."

No smile came, but Horemheb thought the hate in her eyes died a little. He continued to dab the damp linen cloth on her upper body to keep her cool. He stayed silent, letting Mut decide if she wanted to speak or not.

THE MAJORITY OF THE DAY CAME AND WENT BEFORE MUT FINALLY spoke in a broken voice. "I just knew he would kill me at some point."

Horemheb hung his head. "I'm sorry, Mut. I don't know what to say."

"Don't say anything," Mut whispered. "Just listen."

Horemheb nodded and dabbed her brow.

Then Mut was silent and she closed her eyes as tears burst forth. She didn't know where to start. She didn't really even know Horemheb or whether she could trust him. He had lied to her! But it was to protect her—but he failed her! But he was here now, and he promised to stay here with her.

He will blame me for not defending myself. I should have had better control of his house. I should not have stayed at Malkata for so long. If I hadn't, maybe the servants would not have let Pawah in or left. I should have called the guards. I should have called the servants. I should have called for help—something. Instead, I let Pawah do what he did and I lured my family into his trap. Horemheb will just think me a child.

Her cheeks grew pink from embarrassment.

I am a child. I am a childish fool! I didn't even struggle that much when he first put my hands in the rope. I didn't know it would be like that for days, and then they told me it had been a season. How did it seem . . . ? It felt as if years had passed. I was so afraid. I shouldn't have been afraid. Horemheb has been in war, fighting a whole army, and I'm afraid of one man.

She chewed her bottom lip, but then the pain of biting her injured lip made her shoulders rise to her ears, which brought even more pain upon her body. She soon felt the cool cloth on her lip and her shoulders.

But he is here now. He is taking care of my wounds. He at least seems to care now.

"He tied me to the bed," Mut blurted out, but then stopped and waited for Horemheb to laugh or ask why she didn't try to break free.

He said nothing.

After a few moments, she continued: "And when I lost feeling in my hands and my arms, I knew I couldn't defend myself. When I lost strength in my legs, I knew he had complete control over me." Her voice cracked. "It was at that point I wanted to go west, but I knew he would keep me alive until he had no more use of me."

She paused, waiting for Horemheb to call her weak, but he never did. There was only sadness in his eyes, so she found the strength to continue.

"The ease with which he beat me, Horemheb . . ." Her mouth contorted in a grimace. "I've never seen someone so wicked in all my life. I thought they were just tales you told children to make them mind." She dabbed her tongue over the cut on her lip and winced. "I can feel my arms now, but they feel as weights, as if I can't move."

Her heart raced; her breath became quick and shallow to the point she couldn't speak any longer; images flooded her present, images of Pawah beating her with the wooden plate, with his hands, with anything he could find.

Horemheb placed a tender hand on her chest and dropped the other to her forehead. He locked eyes with her and slowed her breathing until she calmed. He moved his hand from her chest to her hand and brought it to his lips.

She wriggled her fingers and watched them intently as she thought. *At least they are not blue. I can move my arms. I can defend myself. If I'm not tied. If I'm not manipulated. If I'm not—*

"You are very brave to tell me this," Horemheb whispered and rubbed the back of her hand with his thumb. "I'm so sorry he did this to you. Pawah is dead now. He can never hurt you again."

Mut swallowed, haunted by her musings. *Am I brave? Perhaps. But I also led my family into a trap . . . I can't talk about this anymore.*

She said, "I'm tired."

"Then sleep, my wife," Horemheb whispered. "I will be here."

Her eyelids felt heavy, but she couldn't let them fall. Pawah lived in her dreams.

But as the day waned, she fell into a restless sleep with the help of more sedatives made with poppy and the mandrake fruit.

DECANS LATER, MUT HAD PHYSICALLY HEALED—EXCEPT FOR HER wrists, which bore the repulsive scars of the restraints that held her to the bed for the season she thought would never end. Scars still adorned her body, but the ones on her wrists were the most noticeable by far. Nausea swept over her as she stared at them.

She sat on the edge of her bed, rubbing her wrist, trying to rub off the scars, but to no avail. Tener and Raia were preparing her a bath. It would be the first time she bathed since the attack. The servants had wiped her every day, but she looked forward to the warm water.

Maybe, she thought, *the water will remove the scars.*

She took a quick inhale and a grimace fell upon her lips at the absurdity of her thought. Her mind tried to focus on the coming bath, but she was lost in the tortuous memories as they came in flashes back to her: the sting of the rope tied against her, the hiss of Pawah's breath in her ear, the blood running from her lip, the numbness setting into her fingers. No tears came, as they had already been cried, so she only sat on the edge of the bed, stiff-backed and stuck in her memories.

Horemheb had stayed true to his word and had not left her side. He leaned against the doorway to the bath chamber, watching her rub her wrists with a faraway look in her eye. As if he read her mind, he said in a low voice, "We always hope the wounds won't scar." He stood and came near to her, falling to a knee in front of her. "But the scars of our wounds shape our future."

He remembered speaking almost the same words to

Nefertiti, and as he remembered the feeling of Nefertiti's hand in his, he reached for Mut's.

"They are so visible," Mut whispered as her gaze seemed to pull out of the memories she visited and came to rest on her wrists. "Everyone will see, and everyone will ask." She looked at Horemheb. "I am not brave enough to tell everyone. I am not ready for this. It still hurts me so."

Horemheb rubbed her thumb with his and inched his way down to her wrist until his fingers wrapped around it. Her dainty wrist fell perfectly enclosed within his hand. "We can hide them like this." He smiled up at her, but instead of a laugh like Nefertiti's, Mut pulled her hand away.

"You jest now?" Mut rubbed her wrist and pulled her hands to her chest.

"I'm sorry, Mut. I . . ." His voice trailed off. His humor had always pulled Nefertiti from her sorrow, if only for a moment. But he had to remember that he was married to a woman who only looked like her. "I thought it may take your mind off the days you endured."

Mut chewed her lip and then closed her eyes.

Horemheb took her hands and pulled them to his lips. He kissed them before lowering them into her lap. "You are brave to tell me. That is enough." He waited to see if she would open her eyes, but she didn't. "Mut, I know you are hurting. We don't need to leave the bedchambers if you are not ready."

She opened her eyes, but her face remained expressionless.

Horemheb pulled something wrapped in a linen cloth out of his belt. "But if you are ready to take a walk in the courtyard, you can wear these to cover the scars so no one will know they are there." He opened the linen cloth to reveal two thick gold bracelets.

Mut bit her lip as a new kind of tear formed in her eyes. "Thank you."

Her whisper brought a half grin to Horemheb's face and a swell to his heart.

Tener appeared in the bath chamber doorway. "Mistress of the House, your bath is ready."

Horemheb patted Mut's thigh and placed the bracelets on the table by the bed.

He helped her to stand and then watched her enter the bath chamber. His words to Nefertiti flowed back to him as if he had spoken them yesterday: *We hope the wounds won't scar, but regardless, they still shape our future. We can hide scars, display them, learn from them, or repeat them. They are with us forever, but it is up to you what you do with them. I try to learn from my scars . . .*

He rubbed the scar on his arm that Pawah gave him when he found Nefertiti bleeding from Pawah's stab wound to the chest. His arm fell; he did not want to think about all the scars that tattooed his body and, even more so, his ka. He had many scars to learn from, and now he needed to right one: love Mut and take care of her.

Earning Mut's forgiveness would somehow, in his mind, equal the forgiveness of Nefertiti and Amenia. "I vow to the both of you that I will make Mut happy. She will be safe," he whispered. "She will be loved. I will find a way to love her."

❦ 9 ❦

THE TIME OF RELEASE

ANKHESENAMUN REREAD HER MOTHER'S LETTER, TRYING TO GUESS the other half of it. Regardless, she understood the main points.

She sat in her royal harem room's chair with her elbows resting on the table in front of her as she toyed with the letter. "Am I to doom myself to the same fate my mother accepted for her life?" she whispered as she ran her finger along the torn edge.

Tears welled at the knowledge her mother held Horemheb's baby in her womb, and that she was willing to live without both of them to keep power with Pharaoh and marry Tut.

"You still had your secrets, didn't you, Mother?"

The weight of her mother's burden fell heavy in her stomach, like a rock thrown in the Nile. She had loved Egypt that much. Ankhesenamun envisioned her mother crying as she wrote her letter, knowing she might die, knowing she carried a child who could never be told the truth, knowing she would never again be in the arms of the man she loved, or any man she might have ever fallen in love with in the future.

"I am so sorry," she whispered to her ka. "Mother, I wish

you were with me, if at least to help me through what I am feeling. You were there . . . you made this decision before. How? What strength did you have to accept your fate? I cannot endure. I cannot do this. Mother, I am not as strong as you were."

Her whisper died on a gentle warm breeze from the open window as it graced her brow, but she ignored it, becoming lost in her thoughts.

Marry the man who loved my mother, she thought at the irony of it, and shook her head, longing instead for Tut. *Why did he not survive?* she asked the gods, unable to speak the words aloud. *Has Tut not paid enough? Now you take his life as well?*

"He was good to you!" Her hot whisper flowed from her hard lips. "He worshipped you. He was a good King. You sent the ba-en-pet to show your blessing on him. Why did *he* not survive Pawah's attack?" Tears burned down her cheek as she swiped the shimmering blue faience statues of the gods from her table with a yell. "Why did you not save him?!"

Her tears became uncontrollable as her ribs constricted around her chest. As the room spun into a blurry vision from her indignation, she buried her head in her arms, remembering the day they laid him in his tomb. She cried at the lack of splendor it beheld, the lack of ornamentation, the lack of detailed instructions for him to follow to the afterlife.

"Not fit for a King," she whispered; her shoulders shook with her sobs. "Not fit for my Tut."

Then she did something she believed no Queen had ever done: she cursed the gods.

She cursed them with every fiber of her ka and flesh.

"I want no part of you if all you do is take and never give. You only punish. You never reward. You trick with your gift of ba-en-pet—you lie! All of you, even the Aten disc!" She slammed her fists into the table as she threw her head up. "Show me! Show me you are the mighty gods of Egypt!"

She cried, hating herself for speaking such wrath upon them, but still, she felt dignified in her words. She swallowed the lump in her throat, not bothering to wipe her face. Her voice fell monotone, her arms went slack, but her chin lifted.

"I want no part of you."

A KNOCK CAME AT ANKHESENAMUN'S DOOR A FEW HOURS LATER, and her grandfather entered. He looked old and frail. She had curled up on her bed with her mother's letter near her face. He walked to her and rubbed her shoulder.

"Ankhesenamun," he began. His aged voice told her his years were dwindling. She closed her eyes, knowing what that meant. But then Ay's tone took on a curiosity. "Is that . . . ?" He pointed to the papyrus in Ankhesenamun's hand.

"A letter from my mother." She did not look at him.

"To you?" He gingerly took it from her hand.

"No. To Horemheb." Her voice held no emotion, nothing. She didn't try to stop her grandfather from taking it.

"How did you find it?" He studied it, and his eyebrows raised. "How did you find this?" he repeated, as if the letter sparked a memory.

"Horemheb was sleeping with it on his face, and I picked it up. I asked him if I could have it, and he said I could." Ankhesenamun's distant gaze matched her distant voice.

"Ignorant fool," Ay muttered under his breath. "Did he not think someone would see him? Irresponsible. Where was he sleeping? Was he not with Mut?"

"Grandfather, please . . ." A long, low sigh followed. "He was outside under the acacia tree next to his apartment the first night he returned to Malkata."

"I am sorry, Ankhesenamun. His irresponsibility . . . that may give me an excuse to remove his Hereditary Prince title."

Ankhesenamun's eyes rolled to her grandfather's face. "Why would you do that? He is the father to your grandchild."

Ay's jaw clenched as he ran his eyes over Nefertiti's letter. His fingers twitched as if he wanted to crumple it, but at finding Ankhesenamun's eyes on him, he lowered the letter back to her hand. "He is also the negligent husband to my daughter."

"Did you know about this letter?" Ankhesenamun narrowed her eyes. "Did you know of his love for her? Her love for him? Outside of the child."

"Yes," Ay said after some hesitation. "When I heard of Mut and Horemheb's decision to marry, he showed me what Nefertiti had written. He promised me he would take care of my little girl, and he now has failed me twice."

"At least Mut lives," Ankhesenamun said, wishing her mother were there.

"Mut lives, but is scarred," Ay said through his teeth. "She will not see me. She will not see anyone. But Horemheb, she will see him. I do not understand her. Why him?"

"Did you know about my mother and Horemheb before you read the letter?" Ankhesenamun asked her grandfather, dismissing his anger, for Mut still lived, and her mother was gone. The past year had revealed many secrets about her grandfather. What was one more?

Ay jerked his hand away. "Yes, I did." He looked out the window. "I knew she held his son when they prepared her body for the afterlife."

After a few moments, Ankhesenamun whispered, "She . . . she was finally going to have a son." Her voice wavered as tears choked her up; she remembered what her mother told her about her father's betrayal when she could not bear a son for him. "She was going to have a son with Horemheb."

"I know." Ay's voice cut through her empathic feelings toward her mother.

"Then why would you take away his title?" Her brow furrowed as her words flowed out.

Ay sneered but did not answer her question as he turned and began to pace. "I often wonder what would have happened if she had married the crown prince Thutmose. Would she be alive today? If Thutmose would have seen the evilness of Pawah and killed him at the rebellion at Malkata so long ago . . . if Thutmose had not journeyed to Re, Pharaoh Amenhotep III would never have had Smenkare with Sitamun in his sorrow." Ay looked to the past. "Nothing would be as it is today."

"I would not be here, either." Ankhesenamun held her hand up to peer at the sunlight falling through her fingers. "Might as well. No one else has lived. I am the last one." She added in thought, *Except Nefe, and I hope to whatever true god there is, she is happy and well.*

"I would not trade you," Ay said, sitting next to her and placing his hand on her shoulder.

She finally looked up at him; she spoke slowly and with intention. "Grandfather, I have no desire to be royalty anymore. All I care about has been stripped from me. I am an orphan of the palace. You and grandmother will be gone soon, and I will have no one left. I do not wish to marry Nakht, nor Nakhtmin, nor Horemheb—especially now that I know he loved my mother and even fathered a child with her. I cannot be his wife. I will never come to love him. I will never bear his children. I might as well be entombed with Tut."

"Say no such thing, Ankhesenamun," Ay said as he pulled her into his arms. "Do not wish your life away. Tell me who you want to marry. Tell me who to name Hereditary Prince. Tell me what I can do to make you happy."

"I have no more happiness." Ankhesenamun's defeated tone brought no more tears from her eyes, as they had already been cried. She thought about the only man she might have had a life with, the Overseer of the Tutors . . . but he would never be accepted as Pharaoh. "Pawah took most everything from me. He took the people I treasured most in this world. This life has brought me nothing but pain. Do not name a Hereditary Prince for my sake." She squeezed her arms around Ay. "I will not find happiness here. Too much sorrow and pain fills my heart."

Ay rubbed her back and squeezed her even more. "Please, Ankhesenamun, tell me who to name Hereditary Prince."

"It does not matter. The Hereditary Prince must be someone whom the people will accept. We already know they will not accept a woman Pharaoh. Why would they accept anyone less than powerful as Vizier, General, Commander, or Master of Pharaoh's Horses? Anyone else will not be seen as divinely appointed."

Ay drew a deep breath and squeezed her tighter. "This is absurd. When Pharaoh Amenhotep III was King, the people would have no say in who was Pharaoh." Ay gritted his teeth. "Curse you, Akhenaten, for what you have done."

Ankhesenamun pulled away from him and lay back down, her back to him. "Yes, curse my father," she whispered under her breath. "For everything."

"Nakhtmin is the youngest . . . almost as old as Horemheb, though," Ay said. "You and he could live a long life together."

"Nakhtmin has a wife and several children already. He will not be with me. I will stay here in this room for the rest of my life." Her voice stayed flat. "In the royal harem, with all of Pharaoh's unloved and unvisited wives."

"Now, Ankhesenamun, do not put off your future before it has even begun." He rubbed her back and then squeezed her shoulder.

"I will do whatever you wish, grandfather." She had given in to her resignation. Egypt had won, yet again.

Was this how her mother found her strength?

A FEW DAYS LATER, WITH NO BUSINESS BEING THERE, Ankhesenamun stepped into the training yard. She needed one more time to say goodbye. Every time they passed each other in the corridor the past year, now that she again lived in the royal harem, she would act as if he did not catch her eye, but he did. She would peer over her shoulder as she rounded a corner and see him do the same. The guards were with her; their presence kept her from falling into his strong arms and weeping away her sorrow. She admired him from afar, just as she knew he did her. Since their last real conversation, he had stayed loyal to the throne and never broke his rank again. He did not touch her. He did not speak to her unless spoken to, and even then, his words were objective and restrained. But his eyes . . . his eyes told her he thought of her always. She had come to see him periodically in the training yard to keep up with her skills, and it was as it was in Aketaten: he a tutor, she a student; nothing more.

Sennedjem was teaching the nobles' fourteen-year-old sons, who might become more high-ranking officials in the military someday.

He could have made General if he had stayed in Pharaoh's army, she thought as she watched him take on four young men, coaching as he went.

One of the students who sat on the sideline waiting his turn hit his companion's elbow and nodded in her direction. She saw them smile and whisper to each other out of the corner of her eye. The training yard was no place for a Queen, yet earlier in the past year it had almost become a sanctuary. A place, especially here at Malkata, where there were no memories of Tut. Her bedchambers, now in the royal harem instead of the main palace, as she was no longer chief royal wife, held no memories, either; only emptiness. At least here in the training yard, she had new memories of Sennedjem, a *friend* who understood the pain of losing a loved one.

A friend.

She watched him and ignored the students as she became lost in her own mind.

She dreamt of Tut often and imagined their daughters, if they had lived, but every now and then Sennedjem made an appearance. Those dreams always ended the same: Sennedjem executed for taking Pharaoh's wife. She would wake in a cold sweat, as if morning dew gilded her body, and then she would cry herself back to sleep. Her heart contorted, knowing Tut was gone, along with her daughters, and then the guilt of her feeling the way she did for Sennedjem, after every accusation of infidelity with him that plagued the greater part of her marriage to Tut. She'd half laugh, half cry at the sick irony of it all. And now that Tut was gone, she could not find happiness—and could never find happiness married to Horemheb. A tear filled her eye as she remembered wanting Mut to marry Tut so she could adopt one of their children.

Now they would share a husband, but Mut will be the one to keep her own children, for Horemheb would never come to Ankhesenamun—nor did she want him to. She shook her head, hoping Mut never found out about her mother and Horemheb. *It would doom her to a life like mine.*

Sennedjem called out a "parry" command, and he drew her attention. She studied his athletic frame and well-defined body, oiled well so his sweat curled into droplets and rolled off his skin. She heard one of the students laugh, and she looked in their direction; they dropped their hands, shut their mouths, and sat erect, looking straight ahead. She stared at them for a long time, and they did not move until Sennedjem called for them to switch with the students in the training yard.

Her mind became lost again as she sat watching the lesson from the shade.

Sennedjem . . . Why? Why? Why?! Oh Mother, I know now a glimpse of what you felt with Horemheb. At least there could have been a chance with him. If she had married Tut, and Tut still traveled to Re, she could have married Horemheb. She could have been happy. But I would still be without Tut. Without anyone. Is the rest of my life going to be spent alone?

The tear that had filled her eye rolled down her cheek, and she wiped it away quickly before the students could see. It might have been acceptable to her, to live a celibate life alone as a priestess to Isis, if she had not tasted a man's love and the spark of life in her womb, but now a heavy weight sat on her heart as the day of her marriage to yet another Pharaoh grew closer: first her father, then Tut, now her grandfather, and soon, another. There was no future in her marriage to Horemheb, Nakhtmin, or Nakht—or whomever her grandfather decided to name. She knew it. They knew it. She was a token in the bid for the throne. And now she only wished for a life of insignificance with Sennedjem.

She watched him best the four young men, and her gaze dropped to the ground in front of her as she realized her trips to the training yard would need to soon come to an end to make it easier on her already-aching heart.

I should not be here.

She stood to leave, but then Sennedjem dismissed the young men and looked at her. His eyes said *Stay*, but he only bowed and waited for her command. The students left, and Hori and Ineni stayed at the entrance to the training yard.

Take me away from here! she yelled at herself—she yelled at Sennedjem.

This huge palace, its sprawling complex, its massive manmade lake, its soaring pillars, its golden, hand-carved delicacies—only served as a large prison. The training yard, her newfound sanctuary, now felt like a trap, with Sennedjem standing in the middle of the yard like a precious bait.

You and I can never be, they had already said.

She took a deep breath. Her mind told her to leave, but her feet took her to Sennedjem.

"In peace, my Queen," Sennedjem whispered, and bowed before her, his eyes lingering on hers.

"I have come to say . . ." *Goodbye.* But the farewell did not pass her lips.

Sennedjem waited for her to finish, as a good servant should.

"I have come to . . ." *Say goodbye.* But again the farewell did not pass her lips. She took another breath and rather said, ". . . have one last lesson."

Sennedjem lowered his head and pressed his lips into a straight line before he spoke. "As my Queen commands."

He picked up a pair of fighting sticks from the ground and handed one to her. She placed her hand over his in the trade-off as they locked eyes, speaking nothing and everything at the same time. He slid his hand away and grasped his fighting stick with both hands.

"My Queen, shall you attack or defend?"

She smiled at him as her eyes glistened.

He took a deep breath and nodded. His words came back to her: *And most of all, I wish you to find peace in whatever life the gods give to you.*

The future seemed bleak, but she knew she would persevere.

"I shall always attack."

A rekindled fire lit in her heart and in her mind, as she readied herself for the training lesson.

I will break free. Somehow, I will break free.

Then she raised her stick to strike.

NEAR THE END OF THE SECOND YEAR OF AY'S REIGN, A messenger bowed low before Pharaoh.

"Pharaoh of Egypt, King of the Upper and Lower, I have come from the Mitanni empire. Your brother, King Tustratta, has been assassinated by his son. The country is in civil war. His brother Shattiwaza is supported by the Hittites, and if he is victorious, the Mitanni empire will become a Hittite vassal state. The armies of Artatama II, brother to King Tustratta, request Egypt's aid to secure the borders against the Hittites."

Ay lifted his chin. "We have sacrificed much Egyptian blood to keep the Mitanni secure. We have proved our border to the Hittites and have secured a treaty with them. The Mitanni have never proven their borders without the aid of their allies. We will not reopen old wounds with the Hittites by sending aid to their enemy. Pharaoh of Egypt, King of the Upper and the Lower, declines the request of the armies of Artatama II."

The messenger bowed and left.

Horemheb stood in the shadows, watching the messenger leave, and then stepped forth. He came up to the platform steps and bowed to Ay and then to Tey. "May I speak freely to Pharaoh and his Queen?"

"When have you not, General?"

"Pharaoh Tutankhamun was taken in the Mitanni lands in a war you advised to engage. Why the change of mind?"

"Because before General Horemheb came back from the dead and with the full force of Egypt's military power to scare the Hittites into a treaty, it would have been a detriment if the Hittites took the Mitanni empire. Now, I believe, if we were to send aid, we would breach our treaty and end with another war on our hands. For once in a long time, since the news of your crushing victory against the powerful Hittites has traveled through the lands, our borders have stayed secure."

"I see." Horemheb bowed again. Upon rising, he took a

deep breath, and his brow furrowed. "I would also like to request forgiveness from Pharaoh and his Queen. I have failed two of your daughters."

"Yes, you have." Tey's harsh whisper cut through Horemheb, and his gaze fell to the floor. But then she stood and came to him. She placed her hands on his shoulders. "But they each made their decisions, too. I have no ill will toward you. You acted as you felt you had to for the greater of Egypt, and I cannot hold that against you."

Horemheb smiled as a glisten graced his and Tey's eyes. There was no need to fill the silence between them. Horemheb's chest swelled with gratitude—an unworthy gratitude, he knew, but a gratitude nonetheless—and a lining of peace captured his heart. Their mother had already granted him pardon.

Ay's eyes darted between the two of them before he stood. "Well, I do not grant my forgiveness. Pharaoh declares Master of Pharaoh's Horses, Nakhtmin, as his successor, as Hereditary Prince, and as his adopted son."

Both Tey and Horemheb snapped their heads to Ay.

A tight anger strangled the gratitude in Horemheb's chest. "You strip away Pharaoh Tutankhamun's appointment?"

"Pharaoh," Tey began as she squared her shoulders to him, "General Horemheb is the rightful Hereditary Prince."

"Silence," Ay said as a rage burned in his aged eyes.

I have lost too much to be denied this right, Horemheb thought as his eyes narrowed at his former comrade—his former friend.

Horemheb raised a fist in front of his chest. "Pharaoh Tutankhamun named me—"

"What is that?" Ay pointed to Horemheb's hand.

Horemheb's eyebrows drew together in confusion.

Ay walked closer and yanked Horemheb's hand to look at the gold-and-blue lapis ring that adorned his pinky finger.

"This is mine!" Ay threw Horemheb's hand away. "You thief!"

"I am no thief. Nefertiti gave it to me to remember her by." Horemheb's corded neck matched that of Ay's.

"I gave that to Temehu, and then to Nefertiti. It should be on my hand!" Ay pushed Horemheb in the shoulder.

Tey grabbed Ay's shoulder. "Pharaoh, enough of this."

Her harsh whisper sent his hand up to silence her. His hand moved again, to an outstretched palm in front of Horemheb's chest. "Give me the ring."

Horemheb shook his head, and his voice fell low. "It is not mine to give. Nefertiti gave me this ring to remember her by. I have worn it every day for ten years. I will not give you this ring."

"I am Pharaoh. I order you to give me the ring."

Tey's eyes glistened, and her jaw tensed as she watched Horemheb's muscles grow stiff. She turned her head to Ay's ear and whispered, "Temehu is gone and has been gone for more than half your life. Why do you rip away what is so treasured by someone else? Have you no heart?"

Ay's nostrils flared, but after a few moments, he dropped his hand into a fist by his side. He turned to go, but then stopped and stared at his wife and bore into her eyes with a taut jaw. He sat in his throne, as rigid as the pillars that held the roof.

"Mut will not live in Nefertiti's shadow anymore, nor will I force my granddaughter to marry you so you can neglect the both of them."

Horemheb stood resolute. "I am doing the best I can to treat Mut well, and I would do the same with Ankhesenamun."

"No, you loved her mother, and you will never truly love either of them. Mut had a choice, and she chose to marry you despite my pleas and my concerns, but Ankhesenamun does not have a choice." Ay waved his hand to dismiss Horemheb.

"You are no longer Hereditary Prince. Live your life well with my daughter and my first wife's and firstborn's ring upon your finger."

Horemheb narrowed his eyes and clenched his jaw. His next words came through his teeth: "As Pharaoh commands."

A FEW DAYS LATER, AFTER HIS ANGER HAD SIMMERED, AY CAME to Ankhesenamun's bedchamber in the royal harem to tell her of his declaration. Ankhesenamun stared out the window. He took a deep, satisfying breath, knowing he had he done well by her.

"I have named Nakhtmin as Hereditary Prince."

"Why?" Ankhesenamun asked, her stare intently focused on something out the window.

"So you would not have to marry Horemheb."

Ankhesenamun was silent.

"I think you will be happy with Nakhtmin. He is younger than Horemheb and handsome and has been good to his wife."

"Yes," Ankhesenamun said, crossing her arms, "he will be a good husband to his wife, but I will spend the rest of my life in this room."

Ay bowed his head and took a deep breath. "I never wanted that for your mother, and I do not want that for you."

"I know." She squeezed her hands into fists. "That is why, after I am married to the Hereditary Prince and forgotten in this place, I plan to leave Malkata."

Ay turned her to face him. "I see Nefertiti in your eyes. Looking back, I wish she could have done the same. I want you to be happy, Ankhesenamun. But where will you go? Is there anyone you trust to protect you that I can send with you?"

"I will go find Nefe in Canaan," Ankhesenamun said in

response to the first question, but to the second, she remained silent, her thoughts drifting to Sennedjem and Hori. Not Hori —she could never ask him to leave his family.

"As long as you are alive," Ay began, "you will be in danger of any who wish for the throne." He pulled her hands to his chest.

"Then what do I do, Grandfather? Live always in hiding?" Her eyes searched and pleaded with him.

"No," Ay whispered and shook his head. "I will do for you what we should have done for your mother." He paused, as if reflecting and wishing the past had been different. "I will tell the people you have journeyed west from illness before you are married to the Hereditary Prince, just as we did for Nefe. Then you leave Egypt under the cover of night." He cupped her face. "Go live a life you make for yourself."

"Can we do that? Will Egypt not fight over who takes the throne without someone of royal blood?" Ankhesenamun's voice filled with panic. "I was going to leave after I was forgotten by Nakhtmin or whomever the next Pharaoh is, not before."

"It is not your problem anymore." Ay kissed her forehead and released his shoulders, as if a burden had finally been lifted. "My only concern is that your body, when you journey west, will not be laid with royalty."

Ankhesenamun lifted her chin. "Neither will Nefe's."

"Neither of you will have anyone to perform the funerary rites," Ay warned.

"I know." That warning put a bit of fear in her ka, but part of her still wanted nothing to do with the gods. And if she only had this one life, she wanted it for herself.

"Without a preserved body, without the rites to regain your senses, you may not be able to journey to achieve immortality. There will be no afterlife for you."

"I know." The perilous journey to immortality never seemed appealing to her anyway. Sailing with spiked servants and five-headed reptilian beasts, chancing a second death at each of the gates that followed, and then, at the end, to be tested and interrogated by forty-two gods for crimes against the divine and human social order . . . and then finally having the heart weighed against the feather of Ma'at. She already knew that her heart would fall heavy. She had cursed them. She had wanted to do away with them. She knew her heart was already condemned to Ammit at the journey's end. There was no eternity for her—and even in the off-chance she did pass the tests, she would never be with Tut as much as she told herself she would. He would be one with Re and sail on his sun barge to raise the sun once again. She would be in the Field of Reeds. No, she would captain her own life away from bitterness, away from pain, and away from the corruption that held in recent memory.

"Then who will you take with you?" Ay asked, breaking her thoughts.

"I will ask Sennedjem, Overseer of the Tutors. If he does not accept the same risks as I, then I will go by myself."

"You will not survive by yourself," Ay said with a firm tone and wagged a finger in her face. "I will order whoever, this Sennedjem, to go—"

"No!" Ankhesenamun put her hand over his. "I want him to choose to go. It will not be the same if he does not. I cannot order him to accept that risk, that life, if he does not want it."

"As you wish, my granddaughter, but you will not go alone." Ay shook his head. "Not by yourself."

"Then I will find someone."

But a heaviness set in her stomach, for who would she find?

Who would chance their afterlife?

Sennedjem watched Ankhesenamun walk toward him with purpose, leaving Hori and Ineni at the entrance of the royal harem training yard. Sennedjem squared his shoulders to her and then bowed as she approached. He had only passed her a few times since her last lesson; he kept his distance so as not to cause any more feelings between the two of them. The days and nights had been hard, but he had started to feel the same numbness growing again. He cursed the day he had broken his status and spoken to her as though she were his equal. He cursed himself for touching her skin, kissing her hands.

Seeing her walk toward him made him hope, in some way, or some *how*, Pharaoh Ay had allowed her to be with him in secret. Why else would she be back? She had no real business in the training yard. Pawah was gone. There was no real threat to her. She needed no training from him anymore. She had even said that her previous lesson was to be her last.

As he rose from his bow, he found her eyes. A desire to touch her, to kiss her, to caress her, burned within him each time she had come to visit him, and it didn't differ this time. But acting on any of his impulses could land him in prison or dead, and, even worse, it would make Ankhesenamun endure more sadness. Her long linen dress flowed in the slight breeze, and her gold-beaded collar caught the sun's rays illuminating her perfect face as she walked.

She is so stunning, he thought.

Stop, he told himself. *Admire from afar.*

His face held a restrained smile. "In peace, my Queen."

"Walk with me," she said and walked past him to the shade. He followed her until they were out of sight and out of earshot of the guards. She abruptly turned to face him, and he almost bumped into her.

"Is something wrong, my Queen?" he asked in a low voice.

"Sennedjem, please call me Ankhesenamun when we are

alone." Her lip trembled, and her eyes lingered on his chest before she looked him in the face.

Sennedjem nodded, but he was still a little hesitant to call her anything but "royal wife" or "Queen." *She has to know that my calling her without her title will only make things between us more difficult. Unless . . .* He quieted his thoughts, not daring to give rise to false hope.

"I need to ask you a favor that involves much risk to your afterlife," Ankhesenamun began.

He stiffened a little at the thought of risking his afterlife, and wondered what she could possibly ask of him that would require such a sacrifice.

"Pharaoh has said he will tell the people I have gone to the Field of Reeds, taken by illness. Then I will be able to leave Egypt and go to Canaan and make for myself a new life." Her eyes found his as she bit her bottom lip. "But he wants me to have someone with me who will protect me. He will not allow this to happen if I go by myself."

She took a deep breath, as if to summon the courage to ask her favor. Sennedjem waited for her to speak, but when she did not, he guessed, in a whisper:

"You want me to go with you?"

She nodded and a tear fell from her eye. "I feel so selfish now for asking you, but when you said you had thought about you and me . . ." Her voice trailed off. "I . . ." She crossed her arms, unable to finish.

"Do not feel selfish, Ankhesenamun, for you are not." He grasped her hand and her arm fell uncrossed. "I took an oath to protect Pharaoh and his family, to die for them. I will go with—"

"No, Sennedjem." Her jaw held taut, forcing him to silence. "If you go, you may not be buried in Egypt, you may not have a body for your afterlife, you may not have the funerary rites performed for you . . ." Another tear fell down her face. "If you go, I want it to be because you want to go, not because of some oath—"

Sennedjem instinctively grasped the side of her face and then froze. He wanted to kiss her with every beat of his heart, but knew she was still a wife of Pharaoh. He wanted to look around to ensure no one was there to see them in case his will failed him, but he kept his gaze locked on hers.

She looked around, as if reading his mind, and then, when she met his gaze again, she smiled and touched his chest. He smiled, too, wrapping his other hand around her waist and pulling her close. He looked into her eyes and felt the breath of her on his lips.

"A chance to live a life with you?" He pressed his forehead to hers, giving her every chance to stop him. "I will take it no matter the risk."

A half grin lit her face, and for once, since Tut's passing, her eyes held no sorrow.

Never did he think he would be able to kiss her, but now, as though the gods had granted him a second chance at life itself, he graciously took their gift and placed his parted lips on hers. She wrapped her arms around his neck and he around her waist as they pulled closer, fulfilling in each other what was lost to them both.

🜚 10 🜚

THE TIME OF BONDING

GENERAL HOREMHEB STEPPED INTO HIS ESTATE AT MEN-NEFER with Mut beside him. She had wanted to face the fears of that home before she could face the people of Malkata or even her own father. At Mut's request, Horemheb dismissed all of the servants of his household save Tener and Raia.

As the high steward, Bakt, passed by to leave, she grinned at Mut. "I am truly sorry for what that man did to you," she whispered.

Mut's jaw tightened, and she stared her in the eye. "You knew."

Bakt gave a gasp that Mut suspected was more theatrical than earnest. "I did not! I never go into the master's bedchambers without a summons!" Bakt pressed her lips into a grimace, but her eyes danced as if to say, *You deserved it.*

"You let me walk straight into his trap," Mut murmured. "You are the head steward. You should know who is in the main house."

"My apologies, Mistress of the House." Bakt bowed her head, but kept her eyes locked with Mut's.

Horemheb placed his hand on Mut's shoulder, coming up

153

behind her and only catching the last part of the exchange. "Why the apologies, head steward?"

Mut lifted a finger to Bakt. "She knew Pawah was here. She let him torture me."

Horemheb's brow knitted, and a scowl came over his mouth.

Bakt shook her head and then lowered it. "You, Mistress of the House, dismissed the servants to the second house. How was I to know you were under duress?"

"You let me go upstairs! You *came* from upstairs!" Mut said.

Horemheb knew that even if Bakt had done such a thing, there was no proof. If Mut had been royalty, he perhaps could have taken her to Pharaoh to have her punished, but as it stood, he could only end her employment in his estate.

"I did—" Bakt began.

"My wife does not trust you, and therefore *I* do not trust you," Horemheb said, putting his second hand on Mut's other shoulder. "You are never to return, and if I see you near this estate again, I will have you beaten."

Mut narrowed her eyes at Bakt.

Bakt's innocent expression turned cruel. "You throw me to the streets?!" She shot her glance to Horemheb. "You?! You, who cared not to grace this estate but a few times in the last twenty years?! You, who cared not what your wife Amenia did or how she fared or whom *she* trusted?!" A long finger pointed in his face. "I curse you to journey west, alone, like Amenia. You know not the depths through which you dragged her. *I* was here. *I* watched her pass from this life. *I* comforted her in her sorrow at every turn. Do you know how hard she worked for *your* love? Do you know how much she gave up for you? You worthless excuse for a man!" Spittle came from the sides of her mouth as she spoke. "Then you bring *her*"—she jabbed a finger in Mut's direction—"and pretend Amenia never lived?" She shoved Horemheb in the shoulder. "You deserve eternal *death*!"

With that, she spun on her heels and left, slamming the door behind her after stealing one last glare at the two of them.

Horemheb fell mute, replaying Bakt's words in his mind.

Oh, Amenia. Forgive me. I'm sorry I never knew your true feelings for me until the end. I thought I did right by you. I thought . . .

He dropped his chin to his chest.

One of Mut's tears fell on his fingers as she looked down and away from the remaining servants, who were now leaving with Bakt, sneering at Mut and Horemheb as they walked out.

If Bakt could let such horrors befall Mut, we are not safe here. They will never understand. They will never forgive me for what I did to Amenia. They can never come back.

Horemheb went to the door and yelled after them: "None of you return to my estate!" His voice almost gave out near the end, for his heart broke remembering the absolute pain Amenia unleashed as she pounded on his chest.

I'm sorry, Amenia . . . I'm so sorry.

He turned to face Mut as he closed the door. They held each other's gaze momentarily as the silence ate through the space between them.

"She let Pawah hurt me because of you," Mut finally whispered. "Why couldn't you have loved your wife and been there for her?"

"I never should have married her," he whispered in return.

"Just as you should never have married me." Mut's eyes glistened, but she held her chin lifted parallel to the floor.

"Perhaps, but I am married to you now. I gave you my word that I would try every day for the rest of my life to earn your forgiveness—"

"What good is your word?" Mut asked and finally broke their eye contact as her gaze fell to the floor. "What good is your word?!" she whispered again, turning away from him.

He took a few heavy steps to block her path. "You have no reason to believe me, but I request a second chance to prove trust." He swallowed. "You are my wife, Mut. I swear to you, I will not treat you as I did Amenia. She weighs heavy on my heart and my mind . . . always . . . knowing that which I did to her."

Mut's lip trembled as she thought about his request; she finally took a deep breath and nodded her head.

A slight *rap-rap-rap* came at the door.

Horemheb rubbed her arms and pressed his forehead to hers. "Thank you," he whispered and then went to open the door.

A messenger waited for him. He bowed and then stood straight.

Horemheb cocked an eyebrow. "Messenger, I am no longer Hereditary Prince. You do not need to bow."

The messenger bowed a second time, keeping his eyes locked with Horemheb's. "General, I come bearing a letter from Commander Paramesse. He requests you read it in private and that you tell no one of its contents, and to burn the letter after reading."

He handed Horemheb the letter and then left.

An odd encounter. Is Paramesse's loyalty to me as Hereditary Prince?

He turned it over and saw the seal had not been broken. Opening it, he looked at Mut and smiled. She only returned a slight uptick in one corner of her mouth before her eyes wandered around the main house, freezing on the stairs.

Horemheb followed her gaze. "Let's go to the courtyard," Horemheb whispered and guided her there. She stood stiff and rigid and shook at his touch. "Let's not stay inside."

She closed her eyes as a tear fell.

"Please, Mut."

She finally nodded and took a breath, calming herself. They stepped into the dimming sunlight, and only then did Mut seem to be at peace, if for a moment.

He read the letter while she admired the beauty of the courtyard.

In peace, General and friend,

The whole of Egypt's infantry is not satisfied with the naming of Master of Pharaoh's Horses, Nakhtmin, as Hereditary Prince. Although he is a valiant and skilled warrior leader, he is not worthy of the throne. Pharaoh Tutankhamun named you. You are the rightful heir. We will support you in your march to Malkata once Pharaoh Ay journeys to Re and in your claim to the crown should you choose to take it.

Commander Paramesse

Horemheb took a cleansing breath, knowing his suffering might not be in vain. But then he looked at Mut. Pawah was dead now; she would be safe. Ay had it wrong.

To be Pharaoh would mean I never would have to leave her—at least not for years, as I would have to do if I were General. She would be happier in the palace. She would be at peace in the palace. Not here. Not with the memories of what happened.

He put the letter inside his shendyt. He would burn it upon the next flame he encountered, for it spoke of treason and conspiracy against the word of Pharaoh Ay.

As he watched her, Mut looked at the thick gold bracelets Horemheb had given her, now laced around her wrists. Then she peered over her shoulder at him. Her gaze drifted upward, toward the main bedchamber's large window, a frown on her lips.

Love her for her, not for Nefertiti, he told himself, but

nevertheless he still saw the resemblance she bore to that of his first true love. *Learn to love her.*

"Would you like for me to secure an inn to keep us for the night?" Horemheb asked her.

Mut shook her head. "No. I will stay here."

He came up to her and inched his fingers into her hand. "Are you sure, Mut? We can stay at an inn for as long as you like."

"No. This is our home. I must face my fears eventually."

She turned out of his embrace and walked inside. He followed at a distance and watched as she marched up the stairs to their main room and shut the door. He chewed his lip, wondering if he should follow her or let her be, as his feet inched toward the stairs.

I should go to her.

He took two stairs at a time and then softly knocked on the door to their bedchambers. No response, so he opened it to find Mut, standing still, staring at the bed. The room had been cleaned: fresh linen and blankets on the bed, neatly wrapped headrests, floors scrubbed to a smooth shine . . . the smell of blood was nearly gone. Nearly.

Her eyes blinked several times as her lips pressed into a thin line. "It's like it never happened," she whispered.

Horemheb came and placed a hand on her shoulder. She jumped away from him and screamed. Then she saw him. She clutched her chest.

"I thought . . . I thought . . ."

He pulled her into his embrace. "Pawah is dead. He can never hurt you again. And I will never hurt you. I promise."

He felt her nod and her tears wet his arm. Then she pushed away from him, and he gently guided her back into his chest, rubbing her back. "I am sorry, Mut. I'm sorry I was not here to protect you."

"You told me when I moved here with you as your wife that I would be *safe*. Not 'I love you.' Not 'You are beautiful.'

Not 'I am excited for the evening.' You told me I would be safe here." Her voice cracked. "You left me in your home as your wife and did not come back."

"I'm sorry." His heart ached for her, for their predicament. But, he reminded himself, he had asked to marry her. "I'm here now."

She pushed him away. "You only married me to keep me safe from what happened in Malkata." She hit him in the chest. "I know you don't actually love me. I was a fool to think so." She hit him again. "Why should now be any different?" She hit him a third time. "Did you think I would not hear the whispers in the halls of this home? For *years*? Did you not think the servants would compare me to Amenia? Did you think I knew not what happened to her? Did you think me a *fool*? Am I to follow in her footsteps? You *still* keep the truth from me! You told me you married me to keep me safe from Pawah and so that I would not have Tut's child. Yet I heard the rumors around this estate about the woman you loved. You promised to marry me only after she went to the Field of Reeds! What woman did that to me? Tell me! I deserve to know—"

"I promised your sister."

Horemheb's whisper silenced her as she processed his words. She choked back her yells and shook her head as the tears fell freely.

"My *sister*?" Her throat was thick with her tears. "Why would you promise my sister that? Did you love her?"

"Nefertiti knew she was in danger. She did not want the same for you."

"Nefertiti? Were you on an informal basis with Pharaoh?" Mut's eyes raged. "Did you love her as the rumors—"

"I *admired* her, Mut." Horemheb said the half-truth with ease. "We were close friends. When you have only a few to trust, they become close. Every day I never knew if she and her daughters were going to die, be murdered—"

"Well, it looks like you failed her, too. Do you fail everyone you supposedly care about?"

Her words cut him deeper than the khopesh to his shoulder and knee. A cold wetness grew behind his eyes, and he clenched his jaw.

"Yes, I failed her." He suddenly felt the need to jab back. "I'm sorry, Mut, for marrying you. I should have let you bear Pharaoh's child and been away to war while Pawah killed you and your baby—"

Mut slapped him.

"And yet he takes me in your own bed! He beat me nearly to death! You promised my sister to keep me safe?! You protect *nothing*! My father was right to appoint Nakhtmin as Hereditary Prince. How will *you* protect Egypt? I want you out of my sight! Get out!" She hit him in the chest.

This was his home, but she was right: he protected nothing important to him. Part of him wanted to yell back, but his hot ears simmered to nothing. She was hurting and lashing out, he realized, as was her right, and so he dipped his chin in humility. "I will leave you as you request. If you want to separate ways, I understand, as I told you before. I will pay whatever you want, though I know it will never compensate for what I have done. I am sorry."

He looked her in the eyes and then left, closing the door behind him. Her sobs came as soon as the door closed. He leaned against it, dropping his head back to the wood frame, and remembered Amenia's cries. He had left her by her lonesome. What if he had gone back to comfort her? What if he had not left the next morning? Would she be alive today? What if he had shown her anything to prove he did in fact care for her?

He took a deep breath as his father's words came back to him: *A good man loves his wife.*

Mut is my wife. I married her. I promised to keep her safe. I failed once, but I will not fail again.

Her sobs had turned to soft cries. He decided to open the door, which was met with her scream: *"I said get out!"* She lay on the floor. He walked to her as she cried some more. *"I said leave me!"* He knelt beside her and then rubbed her back. The cries shook her shoulders as she finally gave into his touch and pressed her head against his stomach. Peering to the bed, she whispered, "I can't sleep there." Her words came out barely audible. Horemheb wrapped her up in his arms and carried her to the second bedroom. He placed her on that bed and stood up.

She whispered, "I'm afraid, Horemheb."

"I will stand guard outside your door so you can sleep," Horemheb offered, remembering his same offer to Nefertiti all those years ago.

"No—" Mut's breath hitched. "Please stay here with me. I . . . I'm sorry for what I said."

"You spoke the truth." Horemheb tried to hide the pain in his voice, for he believed what he said. "There's no apology needed." He went to sit in the nearby chair.

"Horemheb, please . . . I'm afraid. You are my husband." Mut paused, frowning. "Stay here in my bed with me as you did in Malkata. I'm so afraid."

He looked at her and then came to slide in next to her so they both faced the door. He tenderly wrapped his arm around her waist, careful not to touch her scars in case they might have been painful still. "You don't have to be afraid." He pushed his forehead to the back of her neck. "I am so sorry, Mut." He drew an inhale . . . the same scent as Nefertiti: lotus blossoms.

I failed you both, he thought.

"I don't want you to leave. I was angry." Mut rubbed his arms wrapped around her.

"I'm glad you want to stay with me." Horemheb felt his eyelids already growing heavy in the dimness of the room. It had been a long ten years.

"What are you thinking?" Her soft whisper made his eyes open fully.

"Nothing."

"Are you mad I did not defend myself against Pawah? Are you thinking I am weak?"

"No, nor do I believe either of those things. You are brave to have survived him and have told me what he did to you."

More silence came, and Horemheb knew Mut was thinking, so he asked her the same. He felt Mut draw a deep breath before her question lingered in his ears:

"Did you love her?"

"Love who?" he asked, wondering which woman she referenced.

"My sister. Pawah said you only married me because you promised a woman you loved. That was the rumor in the house, too, with all the servants . . ." Her voice trailed off. Her body tensed in his arms. "That is why Amenia left this life, is it not?"

He paused, trying to think of how to phrase it so the full truth wouldn't hurt her. "I loved her as Pharaoh," he said finally.

"Then why would she—"

"I admired her, Mut. She trusted me . . . she asked me to take care of you and keep you safe by marrying you should she be killed. I told Amenia . . ."

What would he tell Mut? Would he lie to her yet again? She would leave if she knew the truth—wouldn't she? He would end whatever could be with her before it even began if he told her the truth. So he fumbled out some version of it.

"I told Amenia that someone I loved asked me to marry you, a friend of hers. She did not want that because of how I treated her." He winced at the lie but soldiered on. "I couldn't tell her that Pharaoh asked me . . . it would only complicate things and potentially draw you and her into danger . . . so I told her it was a woman I loved. I loved your sister as

Pharaoh. It was a misunderstanding—one that she paid dearly for, at my own fault."

She remained silent; her body stayed tense.

"You remind me of—" *Her*, he wanted to say but instead, "Of my failure to protect Pharaoh."

At least that was an accurate half-truth.

No words came from her still, though he felt her tears on his arm.

He leaned and whispered in her ear. "I promise I will spend the rest of my life striving to accomplish the impossible goal of making up for my failure to you. I can never go back. I can't change what happened. I can only work my whole life to receive your forgiveness."

Finally: "I know." She rubbed his arm and then turned into his chest.

He soon felt her breath fall into a rhythm on his neck as he rubbed her back. A brief flash of a future with her filled his mind. They had not yet consummated their marriage, nor had they kissed. He couldn't bring himself to do either one and was sure it was the furthest notion from Mut's mind as they lay next to each other. Her body began to tremble, and her brow knitted. He took a deep breath, knowing Pawah still plagued her in her dreams. He swept his hand over her brow to loosen it as he had done every time Pawah revisited her dreams. It seemed to relax her, so he kissed her forehead before closing his own eyes.

❧ 11 ❧
THE TIME OF REBIRTH

EGYPT WEPT AT PHARAOH AY'S DECLARATION THAT ROYAL WIFE and Queen Ankhesenamun had fallen ill and gone to the Field of Reeds. After the preparation time, Ay laid to rest an empty sarcophagus inside a tomb in the Valley of the Kings. He had made plans to leave Sennedjem's tomb intact, as his wife lay there, but to remove Sennedjem's name, erased as if never existed.

That night, Ankhesenamun and Sennedjem took off under the cover of darkness. She looked back and saw her grandfather standing and watching them. She squared her shoulders and waved one last time. He raised his hand to her.

"Tell my mother I love her," Ankhesenamun whispered, "for I shall not see her again."

She took a few steps backward and drew a deep breath.

There was no turning back now.

"I want to live my life."

She glanced to the man with whom she could see a future, and with a hard-set determination in her eyes, she turned her back on Malkata, on Egypt, on her past.

With Sennedjem beside her, she snuck off to the private

modest barge Ay had prepared with three Fleetsman sworn to secrecy. They were to take them to the land of Goshen in the Lower. They would then cross on foot to Canaan and begin their search for Nefe and General Paaten and the one named Atinuk.

THEY CAME UPON MEN-NEFER A FEW DECANS LATER AND, PER Ankhesenamun's request, they docked and walked the long path to Horemheb's estate. They came upon the gate.

"Are you sure?" Sennedjem asked. "We haven't been seen by any who recognized you. We are taking a chance coming here."

He peered over to Ankhesenamun, dressed as an officer's wife: long linen dress, no gold-beaded collar, and, since it was the cold season, a long, thick linen cloak. Her wig had gold beading, but not the elaborate detailing of the one she had worn as a royal wife.

"I need to let Mut know I have not journeyed west. I remember wanting to end my life should she have gone before me. I don't want her to feel the same." Ankhesenamun locked eyes with Sennedjem.

Sennedjem nodded his head toward the main house. "Then let us go sit with them."

A smile lit her lips, and her shoulders felt free. The future was unknown, but at least she knew whatever it was would be of her own choosing.

They approached the door just as the sun held high in the midday sky. Tener opened the door, and her face, after a moment's confusion, went white with recognition.

"Is it . . . is it . . . ?" She stumbled backward, leaving the door open.

Ankhesenamun and Sennedjem hurried in and closed the door behind them.

"Is the Mistress of the House here?" Ankhesenamun asked, keeping her voice low.

Tener's lips trembled upon an open mouth. "They . . ." She pointed up. "They are on the roof." Her breath at last caught, and she breathed.

"Thank you. Tell no one we have come." Ankhesenamun locked eyes with Tener until Tener nodded and bowed.

Sennedjem followed Ankhesenamun to the rooftop living area, where Horemheb and Mut were eating a small meal of bread and fish. Horemheb looked up first, and then Mut. She shot out of her chair and raced to Ankhesenamun.

"I thought you were gone!" she cried, and buried her head in Ankhesenamun's shoulder.

"I am not, but you mustn't tell anyone." Ankhesenamun pulled her back to find her eyes. "I came to tell you . . . never give up. You never know what the future holds."

Hope brimmed in her eyes and curled her lips. "Thank you," Mut finally whispered, and she wrapped her arms around Ankhesenamun's neck. She pulled back suddenly and asked, "But why? Why the false journey west?"

Horemheb came to greet them as well, and Ankhesenamun glanced at him. "Many reasons."

"Please stay and eat. Please," Mut begged. "You must be hungry."

Sennedjem stepped forward and said, "I have paid for a full day at the harbor."

Ankhesenamun smiled and nodded at Mut's request.

They sat and ate with Mut and Horemheb. Mut finally could no longer eat without asking:

"Why did my father do this for you?"

"He said I reminded him of my mother . . ." Ankhesenamun forced her eyes to stay on Mut instead of drift to Horemheb, who suddenly tensed. "He wanted me to avoid the same life of loneliness that my father subjected her to after Setepenre was born."

Mut nodded in understanding.

Ankhesenamun lowered her gaze to the half-eaten loaf of bread between the four of them. "Anyway . . . do you remember when you gave me my mother's blanket for our second daughter at the feast Tut held in her honor?"

"Yes . . . ?" Mut tilted her head as if trying to follow the change of subject.

"I want you to keep it." Ankhesenamun's hand went to her travel sling and pulled forth the faded blue-and-white-stitched linen and wool blanket.

"But, Ankhesenamun . . ." Mut shook her head. "I gave it to you. Nefertiti would want her grandchild to have the blanket."

"You gave it to me during a time that I would like to forget. I am leaving everything behind. I want no more of it." Ankhesenamun's eyes held firm as she handed the folded blanket back to Mut.

Mut's fingers wrapped around the blanket, but her arms stayed straight as if giving Ankhesenamun one more chance to take it.

But Ankhesenamun held firm. "Besides, it was made in Egypt . . . it should *stay* in Egypt."

Ankhesenamun let go and took a deep breath. She gave Horemheb a slight nod as Mut admired the blanket once again. Horemheb's eyes glistened, and Ankhesenamun couldn't tell if it was because of the sudden chilly breeze that came into his face or because his son would have been wrapped in that blanket had her mother lived to give birth. His head dropped, and he ran his finger and thumb over his eyes before locking eyes with Ankhesenamun once more.

"Where are you going to go?" Horemheb asked as Sennedjem noticed the exchange between Horemheb and Ankhesenamun.

"Canaan, to find Nefe." Ankhesenamun's voice cracked at the sight of Horemheb's continued love for her mother, even eleven years later, but her eyes darted to Mut. She looked somewhat happy. Perhaps he was keeping his promise to make every effort to love Mut.

"You should take some horses. I heard two horses can buy you a lot of land in Canaan."

"We have a donkey, but he is small," Sennedjem said. "Our barge might fit one horse, but not two."

"Then take one of my horses. You can still get a good plot of land for even one."

Sennedjem nodded to Horemheb. "We appreciate your generosity."

Horemheb's eyes drifted back to Ankhesenamun. "Anything for our Hereditary Princess."

"I am no longer that," she replied. "The Hereditary Princess is entombed in the Valley of the Kings."

"Of course." Horemheb smiled softly. "Then consider it a parting gift. I'll go get a horse ready for your travel." He excused himself and left for the stables.

Ankhesenamun's gaze followed him out.

"Mut, is he good to you?" she whispered.

"Ever since he has come back from war, he has been." Mut found her eyes. "He acts as the man I imagined him to be when I was nine years old and first laid eyes on him. He is good to me."

"Are you happy?" Ankhesenamun's brow knitted, and her eyes searched Mut.

Mut pushed her lips into a tight line as she considered this. "Some days, yes. But Pawah's attack . . ." Her eyes glistened. "Sometimes I think there's nothing I can do to be truly happy. I blamed Horemheb for a long time, but he did what he thought was best for me in keeping me safe. He married me when he did not love me—"

"What?" Ankhesenamun feigned disbelief and pressed further to see what all Horemheb had told her. It soothed her soul a little that he had not lied in entirety to Mut.

"He married me to keep me safe from Pawah, and so that I would not be entangled in the mess you and Tut were in. He later admitted that my sister had asked him to care for me." Mut looked at the wooden roof over their living area.

"You decided to stay with him?" Ankhesenamun leaned forward to find Mut's eyes once again. "Why?"

"He promised me that every day, for the rest of his life, he would try to earn my forgiveness and love and respect."

Sennedjem had stayed quiet, but now spoke in a whisper. "I knew General Horemheb to be a great leader, but he also sounds like a great man."

Ankhesenamun wanted to thank Horemheb for keeping his promise, but didn't want Mut to hear, so she excused herself to the bath chamber and instead went to the stables and found Horemheb loading bags of gold, copper, and bronze in travel slings on the horse's back.

"You don't have to do that," Ankhesenamun said, coming up behind him.

He stopped, dropped his head, and then continued loading the horse. "Yes, I do."

"No, you don't. My father made sure we had plenty of gold."

He sighed and shook his head, putting the bag he had held over the horse's back. "I'm sorry Tut did not come back to you. I'm sorry you are being forced to run away. Sennedjem seems to be willing and capable of taking care of you—hopefully, better than I took care of your mother."

Tears filled her eyes. "Although I want Tut here by my side, I am hopeful for this future."

Horemheb's head snapped to face her, as if a memory sparked. "Tut . . . he asked me to tell you something—" He paused, trying to remember Tut's words. "He wanted you to find someone who loves you as he did and can grow to love you even more." Horemheb smiled at the memory. "I am sorry I did not tell you sooner. But . . . he wanted you to be happy, my Queen Ankhesenamun. He wanted you to find happiness."

Her breath hitched as she smiled and wiped the tears from her cheeks. "My Tut . . ." She closed her eyes. "Thank you for telling me. I needed to hear that." She peered up at the roof to where Sennedjem and Mut were. "After all the accusations, after all the lies of infidelity, do you think it is wrong of me to find happiness with Sennedjem?"

"No. I think he would have wanted it for you. As long as Sennedjem takes care of you and loves you, I think Tut is smiling down upon the two of you from Re's barge every day the sun comes in the sky. He is happy for you."

Ankhesenamun took a cleansing breath and fell into Horemheb's chest. "My mother would think the same for you and Mut," she whispered. "I have something for you." She pulled something from inside her cloak and then handed him her mother's letter. "I was wrong to ask you for this."

He looked at it for a moment and then pulled the other half from his shendyt. "This side has *your* name in it. You should keep it."

He smiled, and so did she.

A moment of silence passed over them, before Horemheb said, "Thank you for the blanket as well."

"My mother would have wanted your *son* to be wrapped in it."

Horemheb looked to the floor, and his chest and shoulders rose with all the air he could fill his lungs, then he looked back at Ankhesenamun as they shared the memory of Nefertiti.

"Be good to Mut, Horemheb, as you have been these past two years. Wrap your child in my mother's blanket. That way you'll be reminded that she is happy for you." She smiled again. "I know it is hard."

He smiled at her comfort and then turned at the horse's hoofing and patted the horse, keeping him steady. "It *is* hard.

There are times I wish Mut to be with a man like Sennedjem. Someone much closer to her age. Someone she wouldn't outlive by a long time."

"She is taken with you still," Ankhesenamun said.

Horemheb shook his head. "She has become disillusioned —and for good reason." He took a sharp inhale as he glanced toward the rooftop. "I don't think I deserve happiness." He turned to face the horse again, smoothing his hand down its mane.

She stood for a moment, trying to gather her thoughts. What would she say to this man clearly ridden with self-condemnation? Finally, it came to her.

"I read the letter . . . or rather, half of it." She half smiled, remembering its bittersweet contents. "I think my mother would have wanted you to be as happy now as she was with you."

Horemheb blinked back the slight glisten in his eyes before locking them with Ankhesenamun. "But I let her be murdered."

"No, you tried to save her," Ankhesenamun said, shaking her head. "My mother loved you. She would not want you to spend the rest of your life in guilt."

"Mut deserves someone else, someone who can fully love her." He temporarily broke their connection, glancing back at the horse.

"*You* can love her." Ankhesenamun's words held firm, confident in the future; they came out as clear as the crisp air around them. At his silence, she continued. "Maybe you are in your own way of loving Mut."

Horemheb's brow furrowed at her words.

"Don't push her away, like Tut did me, because you think she should be with someone else. It only causes pain." Ankhesenamun thought about telling him what Mut had said just moments before, but decided to leave it at that. Mut would tell him in time, and it seemed he needed more time as well.

"You are wise," he finally said.

"As are you," she whispered.

He gave a sad smirk and grabbed the reins and walked the animal to the doors of the stable. "Be safe, my Queen, on your journey and in your life. Find your happiness."

Ankhesenamun nodded as they walked back to the main house. "You as well."

MUT WATCHED ANKHESENAMUN AND SENNEDJEM LEAVE AS THE sun sank in the west. Horemheb stood behind her and placed his hands on her shoulders—gently, as if not to scare her. She placed her hand on his, and then her eyes fell to the large gold bracelet on her wrist, and she dropped her hand.

I hate the reminder . . . but I hate the scars, too.

Horemheb turned her to face him and drew her to his chest in an embrace. Wrapping her arms around him, she felt herself squeezed. Part of her wanted to ask him to let her go with Ankhesenamun and Sennedjem and maybe find someone who would love her and marry her for love, to get away from the memories here and to start over, to start anew; but another part of her melted into the warmth of Horemheb's embrace and remembered his patience with her nightmares, his gentle touch, his sincerity and his genuine kindness toward her. The gods, she felt, had left her, if they even existed, but at least, in this moment, she thought they might be real, and so she prayed for forgiveness of her doubts in them.

Horemheb held her as long as she held her arms around him. He ran his eyes over her face. "I'm sorry, Mut."

"What for?"

He winced and looked to the two shadowy figures that

were now on the distant road, traveling toward the harbor, and then looked back to her. "She gets to start over."

It was as if he had read her mind; it caused her heart to jump and her breath to hitch.

"When Amenia passed and I spoke with my father—before he passed as well"—a pained grimace sprang forth on his face—"I saw an entirely different future I could have had. All of my childhood and time as a young man, I thought my father wanted me to climb the ranks in the military, but then he told me he wanted me to have a life outside the military, and *that* was why he had pressured me to marry Amenia." He searched her eyes. "I thought about all the things I had done wrong, or what life would have been like if I had made different choices." He took a deep breath as he rubbed Mut's arms. "A good man loves his wife."

Mut pressed her lips into a small smile, unsure where he was going with his speech, but was comforted in the fact he was opening up to her.

"It may be out of order of the usual progression"—he grinned, but his eyes still held a certain sorrow in them—"but, Mut, I want to start over with you. I care for you, and I *want* to fall in love with you. Will you give me a second chance? Will you let me prove my worth to you as your husband?"

Mut's eyes glistened as she nodded. Maybe the gods did exist.

He took a step back and dipped his chin, holding out his hand for her to take it. "Will you join me for dinner, Mistress of the House Mutnedjmet?"

Mut laughed for the first time in a very long while. "Of course, General Horemheb."

SHE HAD A HEARTY LAUGH LIKE HER SISTER, BUT NOT QUITE AS deep. Horemheb smiled at the memory, but pushed Nefertiti away. To redeem himself to all three persons he had failed, he needed Mut's forgiveness—and he needed to find a way to love her for her. There could be no more comparison to Nefertiti.

They sat at the table as Raia served them a plate of lamb and honey bread. Horemheb halted Tener before she placed the wine cups and water bowls, and moved his chair to sit by Mut. Tener smiled at a grinning Mut and then placed the items on the table. Horemheb and Mut each dipped their fingers in the water before sharing their bread and pinching off pieces of lamb.

"So, Mistress of the House, tell me something about you." Horemheb held a warm smile on his lips. He chuckled ashamedly. "I don't really even know that much about my own wife."

Mut shook her head. "And I don't even know that much about my own husband, except that after he came back from the dead, he has taken care of me. Which I would guess tells me that he has a kind soul." Mut didn't let him respond as she took his hand in hers and continued. "I also guess you should know that I fell in love with you when I was nine years old, the first time we met." Her cheeks gave rise to a pink blush. "I bet you don't even remember."

Horemheb chuckled. "No, I do." He leaned back in his chair and stared off in the distance, finding the memory. It was before the garden with Nefertiti.

Don't think about Nefertiti, he chided himself.

"I remember the gaping jaw and star-dazzled eyes of a young girl."

Mut buried her face in her hands and giggled. "I wish you didn't remember."

He chuckled before he asked, "Why did I draw your eye?"

"*You were the Commander!*" Mut laughed. "There is only

one Commander of Pharaoh's Armies, and"—she peeked an eye through her fingers—"you looked really good in leather and bronze."

"So you were struck by dashing good looks and the military uniform?" Horemheb laughed as he spoke.

She batted her eyelashes, and a smug smile fell on her lips. "Not only those things . . ." She pulled away, as if debating to speak her mind, but then she said, "I had made up this image of perfection in my mind of you, as well. Things you would say, things you would do, always standing for right and fighting for Egypt and protecting the weak . . ." Her voice trailed off again. When she spoke further, her voice had lowered: "Even after I heard about what you and my sister had done, I never blamed you. I blamed *her*. I was mad at you for keeping secrets, but in my heart, I still loved you—or rather, I loved the image I had made of you." She shook her head. "I don't know why."

Horemheb's face froze. Did Mut know about his love for Nefertiti? Did she know about his son? "What had we done?" His voice wavered. "What secrets?"

Mut waved off Tener and Raia so that they were alone in the dining room. "Pharaoh Akhenaten."

A slight relief passed over him, but he hid it so that she wouldn't guess there was something else.

"What Pawah said about you conspiring against the throne . . ." Mut took a deep breath before continuing her question: "Was any of it true besides Akhenaten?"

Horemheb lowered his head. "Some of it." He looked up to the wall in front of him and took a deep breath, clasping his hands in front of his mouth, before turning to face her.

She sat staring at him, her lip trembling, as if he she were afraid to hear the truth.

"Egypt was not in a good state. Pawah forced our hand, and we murdered Pharaoh Akhenaten with poison. Pawah did the same to Smenkare with our full knowledge.

Meritaten's murder was an accident. Your sister never forgave herself."

Mut lowered her gaze. "I tried to warn Meritaten, but she didn't listen to me."

Horemheb placed his hand over hers. "You were better than all three of us."

"Three?"

"Your father, your sister, and me."

"My *father*?" her eyes grew wide. "He was a part of it too?"

Horemheb swallowed. "I thought you knew."

Mut blinked back tears, and Horemheb knew he had shattered the last good image she held of anyone. Not knowing what else to do, he continued.

"I didn't have a hand in any other conspiracy. Pawah alone acted against your sister and Pharaoh Tutankhamun." He shook his head. "If he had only gone to sleep that night—that night he killed Nefertiti—I could have killed him. We spent months trying to find weak links in his network to get rid of him, but he found them out every time, so that those loyal to him stayed loyal out of fear. That night, we had finally made it—we were going to strike—but he, the cursed snake, instead went to the council room and lured Nefertiti to her murder. The one night I was not there to protect her . . ."

He stopped speaking as his chest constricted and his breath hitched. He couldn't let Mut know he loved her, so he continued with the story, pushing past his guilt.

"And then, with Pharaoh Tutankhamun . . . Pawah tried several times to persuade Tut to name him Hereditary Prince. When Tut finally saw through all the lies, he dismissed him and sentenced him to exile. So Pawah escaped somehow and sent his men to kill both Tut and me. Tut did not survive, and I was severely injured. I would have been killed if Paramesse had not saved my life."

"Then I owe Commander Paramesse my gratitude," Mut said, her eyes filling with tears.

"Mut, I'm sorry you knew this. It was something I never wanted you to know." He rubbed her hand.

Mut nodded and blinked back her tears. "My sister told my mother and me about Pharaoh Akhenaten and the plot against Smenkare. My mother never looked at Nefertiti the same after that, and even more so after Meritaten was murdered as well. I felt sorry for Nefertiti, but in my own selfish ways, I was . . ." She shook her head, not wanting to finish.

"You were what?"

"You are going to think me cold and heartless," Mut warned as she sat back in her chair and placed her hands in her lap.

"Mut, we've all done and thought things we are not proud of," Horemheb said, reaching out and placing his hand over hers. "I will not judge you."

Mut smiled hesitantly, and, with her voice just a whisper, she responded, "I was *glad*."

Horemheb pressed his lips together, tightening his hand over hers.

Why were you glad Nefertiti suffered?

He quelled his sudden action and kept his question within himself. Instead nodded, trying to listen and understand.

"See? I shouldn't have told you." Mut pulled her hand away, sensing the tension in his hand.

"Why?" Horemheb sat back, wishing he had not let himself get bothered by what she said.

"You think me evil." Mut peered at him. "I can see your shock."

"No, I don't think you evil." Horemheb released the tension in his shoulders.

Maybe she has a reason. I need to listen.

Mut threw her hands in the air as she looked around, as if

trying to justify herself to him. Then she blurted out, "I felt that way because I was glad Nefertiti finally felt like me."

His head tilted. "How do you mean?"

Mut crossed her arms. "I finally have someone to tell all of this to, and I am afraid of what you might think of me."

Horemheb turned her chair to face his and pulled it close so their knees almost touched. "You said yourself that you heard the whispers in this house about how I treated Amenia. I can only imagine what you think of me." He tapped the sides of the chair. "I no longer have the gleam of a child's admiration in your eyes."

She lowered her head and rubbed the bracelets on her wrists. "No, but you are making up for it."

Horemheb half grinned as he found her eyes. "I am glad to hear that."

A moment of understanding passed between them, and then, afraid of what might come next, Horemheb broke the silence. "So how do you mean—you were glad Nefertiti finally felt like you?"

Mut smirked. "Curse your listening," she jested, but then her smile fell. She took a moment to find her words, but finally spoke. "I know it sounds silly, but I always felt like my mother and father loved Nefertiti more than me." She rubbed the bracelets as she spoke. "I was only ever *Mut*. My sisters and I were only ever called by our names, but Nefertiti . . . she was father's '*lotus blossom.*' My mother looked upon Nefertiti like she was her own—and her favorite—and, well, I don't know . . . in my older years, I tried to reason with myself why. Maybe she was trying to prove to my father that, even though she wasn't Nefertiti's true mother, she loved her as her own, and so she had to show more love to her than to the rest of us. But when Nefertiti told us what she had done, my mother never looked at her the same. She looked at her like the rest of us, but with more disappointment in her eyes. But my father . . . my father only loved Nefertiti more."

Horemheb nodded. "I'm sorry, Mut."

"I . . . I know they love m-me—" Mut pressed her lips together as she tried to steady a stutter. "I just have always felt in Nefertiti's shadow—even now, that she has journeyed to Re. I mean, look . . . look at us. You only married me because she asked you to." She shook her head vigorously. "My sister . . . she was Queen, chief royal wife . . . she was *Pharaoh*! She had beauty and grace and eloquence in words and wit and intelligence, and she made no mistakes. She could do no wrong—even when she committed murder! And I, the last and oldest to get married, the only child of my parents to divorce, the longest to learn the trade of the scribe, the one who didn't know what to do with her life . . . I felt like they didn't love me as much." She paused, but then quickly added, "But I know they did. It's just—"

"It's just how you feel. There's no shame in that," Horemheb offered.

"Even Pawah called me 'dear Mut.' " Her face went white at the memory. "How is it *he* could call me something other than just *Mut* and my own family could not?"

Horemheb touched her cheek to comfort her. "Let's not think of that right now. We are starting over. Pawah is gone. He will never touch you or hurt you again."

She nodded and closed her eyes, drew in a deep breath, and let it out through her mouth.

"I remember when I first talked to you all those years ago," Horemheb whispered, realizing he had the perfect term of endearment for her. "I noticed how sweet you were, and I am glad to see how that has not changed. You—"

Mut opened her eyes. "You still think I'm *sweet*? Even after all I've told you?"

"Yes. You have a pure heart," he said and pulled her to standing. "My sweet one."

Her eyes lit, and her lips spread wide. He studied her

twenty-three-year-old face: bright eyes, full lips, straight nose, hooded lids, high cheeks—but not as high as . . .

Stop. Nefertiti is gone. Mut is here, and she is stunning.

His own face had aged, as some small wrinkles had set into his forehead, and his own lips weren't quite as full anymore. His body was racked with scars. Even in the last few years, the khopesh-strike to his leg had made his knee stiff. It was harder for him to kneel on that leg, and it ached in the mornings.

Why would she want to still be with me?

"Why do you look at me like that?" Mut asked.

Horemheb outlined her face with his finger. "For the first time, I am taking in how truly beautiful you are."

"Stop it!" Mut hit his chest with a light slap of her hand. "Even *I* know when you are jesting."

He snatched her hand. "No, I speak the truth." He put her hand to his eyebrow. "You can tell when I lie because my eyebrow twitches."

Not as much anymore, but I need not tell her that.

He leaned forward to whisper. "Don't tell my tell, though." She smiled at the wordplay. "It's not very noticeable, but when you know to look for it, you'll be able to read me like a scroll."

Her hand slid down to his cheek. "I didn't need to see if you were lying. Your actions toward me these past two years have already told me the truth." She pressed her hand to his chest. "I always hated you for leaving me, but I've never said 'thank you' for coming back."

"Please don't thank me. It only adds to my guilt."

Horemheb covered her hand with his—

And remembered when he did the same with her sister.

Stop. This is Mut. Mut is here with me now.

He rubbed her thumb with his.

"You didn't have to, though," Mut said, giving a short shake of her head. "You could have left me when my father brought me back to Malkata. You could have treated me as you treated Amenia. Forgotten about me. But you bandaged my wounds, tended to my recovery, listened to me *without* judgment, stayed by my side, made every attempt to make up for past mistakes . . ." She wrapped an arm around his waist. "Thank you for caring for me when you didn't even want to marry me."

He wrapped his arms around her waist and said, "You don't ever need to thank me for caring for you as a man should his wife. I was selfish, and I am sorry. As I've told you, I will spend every day trying to make it right."

She smiled up at him, and he knew he should probably kiss her. *I cannot use her for my own desires, and I cannot pretend she is Nefertiti,* he thought, and decided against kissing her. He couldn't bring himself to do it—not yet.

"Horemheb," she began.

The tension in his jaw grew: he could guess she would probably say something about it: *How can you say that and not kiss me? I'm your wife. You are a liar. I hate you—*

"Thank you for not being intimate with me until you feel you love me. I think that is what I've admired most about you during our time together. You never took advantage of me. You never asked me to bed, even when I was vulnerable. And I know you do not stray because you sleep beside me every night. You've honored me, and you've told me the truth. I don't want you to feel like you have to kiss me. I only want you to when you find you truly love me."

The tension in his jaw disappeared, and he searched her eyes. *The gods surely are soothing this open wound,* he thought. Even though his lips did not smile, his heart did.

"I only want to be fair to you, Mut, since I have treated you so unfairly."

"In the beginning, yes, you were very unfair. But now we are starting over, and . . . I'm glad you are the man I get to call my husband." She placed both of her hands on his cheeks; her eyes quickly glanced to the bracelets on her wrists and then back to his eyes. "I will wait for you."

In that moment, his heart opened to her. He placed a hand over one of hers and kissed the inside of her palm. "My sweet Mut."

12

THE TIME OF PASSING

Two seasons later, word came to Men-nefer that chief royal wife Tey had fallen gravely ill, and the royal physicians did not think she would live in this life much longer.

Mut threw her dresses into a travel sling as her servants Tener and Raia packed up the rest of her items. She walked from the secondary room past the main room, and found that she didn't shudder upon seeing it. She hadn't even been inside its walls since they first came back to Men-nefer, nor had she ever planned to, but it was enough to know that its hold on her might someday pass.

She ran down the stairs and found Horemheb waiting for her. He grabbed her hand and led her outside. Placing her and their travel slings into his chariot, he turned to the servants, who were coming with them.

"We will go on ahead. We may make it earlier by a day or two. Meet us in Malkata, at my apartment there."

They nodded and began to pack away the litter that would have been carried by the donkeys, as it was no longer needed since Horemheb and Mut were traveling by chariot.

Horemheb jumped up behind Mut and took the reins, and together they rushed off toward the Nile.

TWO DECANS LATER, THEY ARRIVED IN WASET AND WERE FERRIED across the Nile to Malkata.

"We are lucky it is flood season—otherwise, it could have taken us a lot longer," Mut said. She thought she should probably send a prayer of gratitude to Hapi, the god of the annual floods, in case he existed.

She and Horemheb came to the palace apartments, and they walked along to that of the chief royal wife. Mut entered the bedchambers, where she found her mother and father. Her mother lay in bed, and her father in a chair by her side. She hated that she immediately thought of Pawah beside her own bed, but she eagerly pushed away the memory. She cautiously approached them, as they both slept.

Her hand went to her mother's as she knelt beside her between her father's chair and the bed. "Mother," she whispered and saw her mother's eyes dart underneath her eyelids. "Mother," she whispered again, this time a little louder.

Her mother's eyes peeked open, and upon the recognition of her face, she smiled. "Mut . . ." Her hoarse and rough voice sent a shudder through Mut.

"I'm here, Mother."

"You are the last to come," her mother said and then began to cough.

Mut's gaze dropped to their interlaced hands, and her shoulders slumped.

"But the one I wanted most to see," Tey whispered.

Mut's gaze snapped back to her, and her chest lifted. Wanting to know why, she raised her eyebrows in question.

"Of all my children, you were the one I worried about the most. The one I didn't want to leave." Tey coughed some more; her energy waned with each one.

"Why were you worried about *me*?"

Mut thought, *I am the only one divorced. I am the only one married to someone so much older than me. I am the only one who was tortured*—she made her mind stop thinking this as tears welled in her eyes. *Even my own mother can see what a sorry excuse I am, for she is only worried about me.*

"I told you that you would never be happy waiting for Horemheb." Tey's eyes gave warmth to Mut's soul. "I told you to marry Menna. And now, you are married to Horemheb." She pressed her lips into a smile. "I need to make sure you are happy. After what happened, I was so worried for you. I was worried he would not take care of you, that he would leave you again. I need to make sure I was wrong."

Mut covered Tey's hand with both of hers. "He has been good to me, and even though I know he does not yet love me, he treats me as if he does. I am happy, Mother. Though, in a sense, I am still waiting for him. That is my choice, as it was my choice to marry the first time and then cause Menna to leave. You do not need to worry for me."

Tey smiled and rubbed her daughter's hand with her thumb. "I'm glad you are happy, my daughter." She took a shallow breath and suppressed a cough. "I knew you were going to be my last child. Age came after you were born, and . . . I wanted to apologize to you." She suppressed another cough.

"Why, Mother? You have no need to apologize to me."

Tey shook her head, then yanked back her hand to cover her mouth as the cough reigned supreme. "No . . . I need to, as I have apologized to *all* my daughters." Another cough came. Mut offered some of the wine that sat on the bedside table. Tey drank feebly and then shooed Mut's hand away. "I was unfair to you. I treated you less kindly than I did Nefertiti. I tried to prove myself to your father, prove that I would love the child from the woman he loved more . . ." Her eyes glistened.

"He loves *you*, Mother," Mut said. "Just as much, if not more."

Tey only smiled at her daughter's naïveté. "I wish it were true . . . but more so, I want you to know that I love *you*. I know we have had our differences, but you will always be my daughter and my heart will always be with you. You will always have my love, Mut. My heart nearly stopped the day I saw you . . . that horrible day—" Tey choked on her own tears as she rubbed Mut's gold bracelets. "You are so strong. A survivor. Stronger than I ever was or could have been. Do not let that time define you and your future."

Mut nodded. Tears streamed down her face as she unsuccessfully tried to push those memories of Pawah to the furthest recesses of her mind. Tey's eyelids became heavy again as she struggled to breathe.

There were so many things she wanted to tell her mother: about her husband, who still had not touched her; about her lost faith that had had a few resurrections here and there; about her fear of becoming a mother if her husband ever did decide to lie with her. She had questions she never thought to ask except now, when her mother did not have the breath to answer: where she came from . . . her childhood . . . her life before her father. The questions reeled in her mind. But as soon as she opened her mouth to ask just one, her father's hand came to her shoulder.

"Your mother needs to rest now." Ay stood to walk Mut to the door.

Mut nodded, wiped her tears, and kissed Tey on the forehead. "I love you, Mother."

"And I you," Tey whispered.

Mut lingered, looking down upon her mother, Tey's eyes now closed, and knew that if her strength could so easily vanish, her time would soon come. The questions—why didn't she ask the questions before? Why did she push her away after the time with Pawah? Tears replaced the ones she had wiped away as her father gently pulled her from Tey's side.

As they neared the door to the bedchambers, Ay placed his hands on Mut's shoulders. "I love your mother, despite what she told you."

Mut nodded again.

"I want you to be honest with me." Ay rubbed her shoulders.

Mut locked eyes with her father. *About what?*

"Is Horemheb a good husband? Are you happy?"

She nodded again. "Ever since he came back, he has treated me as a good husband should." Her mind raced back to the image of herself, younger, meeting Horemheb for the first time . . . and then that of him, now . . . and she realized he truly lived up to that earlier image, despite the flaws of his past.

"I am happy, Father."

Ay lowered his chin and focused his intense gaze upon her as he whispered, "And does *he* love *you*?"

Mut dipped her head. "He said he needed time to fall in love with me. He has been truthful to me, Father. I know he does not lie to me. He honors me and my body. I am waiting for him."

"Mut . . ." Ay shook his head. "What I've always tried to tell you is this: do not rely on someone else to make you happy. Do not wait to find your happiness. If you are happy with him, then I am ten thousand times joyful. But I wish this for you: to find your *own* happiness, *outside* of someone else." He kissed her on the forehead. "Your mother and I are old and tired, and we will be going to Re soon. I do not want to leave without knowing you are truly happy."

"I am, Father." Mut pulled into his chest, burying her head there. "I don't want you and Mother to leave. I have so many questions, so much I need from you."

He rubbed her wig affectionately. "Time takes all, and in

the grand view of life, all that matters is your faith, your heart, and your conduct. Those things have all failed me at one point in my life, as I am sure they have and will you, but know this: you will come back from failure for the greater. If you have lost your faith, regain it with more fervent dedication. If your heart has numbed, love more than ever before. If you have done things of which you are not proud, learn from them and make wiser decisions in the future. I have no worries about you, Mut. You are a strong and brave woman who has endured more than most. I love you, my daughter."

Mut beamed as she squeezed her arms around her father, and new tears emerged. She had never heard such words from him, such genuine words of advice, and certainly never addressed to her; nor had she ever felt as close as she did to her father in that moment.

A FEW DAYS LATER, PHARAOH AY ANNOUNCED HIS CHIEF ROYAL wife, Tey, had traveled to the Field of Reeds. Ay entombed her with all of the splendor a chief royal wife deserved. His thoughts drifted back to Temehu, buried as an official's wife with a tomb that underwhelmed his love for her. He had vowed to give Tey a burial of much more, and now he had kept his promise.

He sat on the throne alone now.

Horemheb approached and bowed before him. "My sorrows are with you, Pharaoh Ay."

"Are they?" Ay narrowed his eyes at the man who had stolen Nefertiti from him and treated Mut so horribly in the first years of their marriage. The man who had failed his daughters in every way—even now, Mut had to lie to him about her happiness with Horemheb. He knew his daughter and could see through her own words.

"Yes, my King." Horemheb stood at the step below the platform. His mouth pinched into a straight line as he locked eyes with Ay.

Ay leaned his chin on his hand, which rested on the throne's arm. "Why have you come?"

"May I speak freely?"

"Of course. Don't you always?" Ay asked, hoping to get a last few jabs in before he left Mut in his care, without her father to protect her.

Horemheb's eyes squinted. "I have come to ask Pharaoh for the return of the title Pharaoh Tutankhamun had bestowed upon me: Hereditary Prince."

"Why would I give this to you? You have already proven your worth to Egypt as General, but with a higher title, you would fail our great country, just like you have failed every other Pharaoh who has sat on this throne." Ay lifted his chin and sat back.

Horemheb's nostrils flared, and a distant gaze crossed his expression. He licked his bottom lip and then took a deep breath. "Had I sat on the throne, I would not have failed her . . ."

Horemheb did not need to finish; Ay knew the insinuation behind the words: he, Ay, had let Mut leave Malkata; he had let Mut fall into the hands of Pawah while Horemheb was away.

Ay chewed on his lip. "You told me—nay, you *promised* me —that you would care for my daughter after you failed to protect my Nefertiti." His words spat venom into the air.

"I was fighting a war in a foreign land, surviving an attack that left me maimed and unable to wield a weapon for a full season." Horemheb clenched his jaw, and Ay knew he wanted to say more but restrained himself.

Ay smirked at Horemheb, knowing he had the upper rank and Horemheb could not say what he wished as he had that day Ay had heard of Horemheb and Mut's pending marriage.

"You give yourself excuses."

Horemheb's eyes bore through him. *As do you,* they said.

"No. Master of Pharaoh's Horses Nakhtmin will remain Hereditary Prince." Ay shooed him away with his hand.

But Horemheb planted his feet as his hands curled into fists. "Why? Queen Ankhesenamun is gone—she will no longer have to marry me. Is that not why you stripped the title away from me? In addition, I outrank Nakhtmin. Pharaoh Tutankhamun promised the title to me. I deserve this throne. I alone know the sacrifice it took to get us to this point. Nakhtmin? He is a brave and skilled warrior, yes, but he lacks everything that I have in the way of true leadership."

"I don't want you on the throne." Ay's voice lowered. "You trick my daughter into thinking you might one day love her? You lead her down a path I know you cannot follow. You had no regard for my firstborn, and now you have no regard for my *last* born."

Horemheb dipped his chin. "I had every regard for Nefertiti, and I have been honest with Mut."

"So honest as to tell her of your *son?*"

Horemheb's shoulders shrank. "I promise you, I will tell her in time."

"You liar. You always lie. You fail to keep your promises. I loathe going to Re while knowing you keep my daughter."

"Mut will be treated the best I can give her—"

"Which is not as much as you would have given my Nefertiti. Mut will always be second in your eyes. I wanted happiness for her, and you will never be able to give that to her."

"I *will* give her happiness. She will travel to the Field of Reeds as a woman who has been loved and cared for. She will go in peace." At Ay's silence, Horemheb asked him, "Don't you want a Queen's burial for your daughter? Would you deny her the right? You would strip her of this luxury for the afterlife?"

Ay narrowed his eyes. "You use my daughter to bribe me to get what you want?"

"No. I do it to talk reason to you, *Pharaoh*. King Tutankhamun, the rightful heir to the throne, named *me* Hereditary Prince, and when you go to Re, I will uphold the right he bestowed upon me. To do otherwise would be to chance everything we have worked for, to forever lose the power of Pharaoh. You are not blood. Tutankhamun was the Crown Prince by birth, and he had named *me* Hereditary Prince. And when I take my claim to the throne, I will make sure your daughter is taken care of in every way that *you* have failed her."

Ay pounded a fist into the throne's arm. "You will watch your tongue, *General*." His heartbeat soared, and he clutched his chest. His age and his grief in losing Tey had made him weak. "Arrest him!"

But the royal guards hesitated, looking at each other and then at General Horemheb, who stared Ay down. There was a slight shuffle of feet, but the guards stayed put.

At the lack of the guards' response, Horemheb placed a foot onto the platform level of the throne and bent at the waist, leaning his elbow on his knee. "You will save much bloodshed if you return to me my right."

Ay sneered, dropping his gaze to Nefertiti's ring upon Horemheb's finger. "You will never sit on this throne. There are many loyal to Nakhtmin and to me. All of Pharaoh's chariots, at the very least."

Horemheb pursed his lips and looked to the floor before returning his gaze to Ay. "Are you certain?" He stood back up. He slightly bowed to Pharaoh, keeping his eyes locked with his. Then he turned and left the throne room.

"I am certain." Ay's whisper wavered as he reassured himself.

He took my Nefertiti. He has the ring I gave to Temehu and then to Nefertiti. He took my youngest as his wife. He lies to her. He gives her false hope. He let Pawah do unspeakable things to them both. I will never relent, even if it means his and his supporters' bloodshed. Those loyal to me will not let him see the throne.

PHARAOH AY'S HEART STOPPED THAT NIGHT, NOT EVEN A FULL year after Tey had been entombed.

Horemheb sent a trusted messenger to Commander Paramesse in Men-nefer as royal messengers sent word to Nakhtmin in Nubia. Horemheb guessed it would take about two decans for both to reach Malkata.

Who would be crowned Pharaoh? Him or Nakhtmin?

TWO AND ONE HALF DECANS PASSED AND THE TWO HALVES OF Egypt's army met in Waset.

Horemheb put on his armor in the middle of the night and then woke his wife, caressing her face. "My sweet one . . . I am so sorry."

"What is it? What's wrong?" Mut asked, coming out of her slumber, and then, feeling his armor, she sat up straight in bed. "What is wrong?! Why are you dressed for war?"

Horemheb rubbed her arm, trying to soothe her. "I must take what your father stole from me; otherwise, everything we have done will be in vain. I wish it did not have to be this way, but it does."

"No. I will go with you." Mut threw her legs off the side of the bed and went to grab her bracelets.

"Mut, it may not be safe. I cannot let you be hurt."

Mut looked him in the eye. "I will stand by your side, as you have stood by mine."

Horemheb narrowed his eyes at her and clenched his jaw. She was silent, staring back at him in the same way. Finally, he nodded, and Mut went to get ready as he called for the First Prophet of Amun Wennefer to get ready for the coronation and to come to Malkata.

They went to the throne room, and before Horemheb entered, he turned Mut to face him. He looked her in the eye. "Do you or do you not wish to be Queen?" He had always assumed it was what any woman would want, but then he remembered Nefertiti and Ankhesenamun. He touched her cheek. "I will give up this fight if you do not wish to be Queen. The command of Pharaoh has already waned. I will leave the struggle for the Pharaoh's power behind, leave the position of Pharaoh with Nakhtmin, if you wish to remain as we are."

Mut studied his face for a long time, but her gaze finally fell to the floor. "Egypt would be better off with you as its Pharaoh." Then she returned his gaze. "I cannot say no."

Horemheb shook his head as he cupped her cheek. "Egypt will take much and give little in return. I have learned this in my life. Egypt is our home, our country . . . *but you* are my wife. As Queen, you would have guards by your side at every moment, you would have more gold and riches than any of Egypt and be sent with such riches to the afterlife . . . but if a threat arises to the throne, you will be in danger, just as your sister was, and your niece. If we fail to have a son and daughter, you will be the Hereditary Princess. You will be married to whomever seizes the throne. You may be killed for the same reason." He stopped to caress the side of her face. "I will most likely go to Re before you, and you will have twenty or so years still by yourself. After my passing, the guards in Malkata would be limitless—you would be safe—but you could never remarry as great royal wife should we have a son. But in Men-nefer, after my passing as General, you would be as you are, with the option to hire guards and remarry."

Mut's eyes glistened. "It is a hard choice . . ." She lost her voice for a moment as her gaze drifted, but then, as though she suddenly knew for certain, her voice came back with strength and her eyes locked with his. "If you stay by my side all of your days, I will be Queen for you."

He pulled her close and kissed her forehead. "But do you *want* to be Queen"—his whisper filled the small space between them—"knowing both the good and the bad?"

She chewed her bottom lip.

"I have already told you I will stay by your side either way," Horemheb said.

She swallowed. "Yes, I want to be Queen," she whispered.

He narrowed his eyes at her, trying to make sure she knew what she said. "I will give this up if you do not want it. If you feel safer in Men-nefer as General's wife than in Malkata as Pharaoh's—"

"I want to be Queen."

He kissed her hand. "We cannot go back once I enter this throne room. Pharaoh does not abdicate." His eyes searched hers still.

"I know," Mut whispered, and then kissed him on the lips. For the briefest of moments, the warmth in his heart toward her blossomed, and he envisioned wrapping her in his arms and kissing her back . . . but he didn't. He had to be fair to Mut, had to be sure he loved her before he kissed her in such a way.

"Then follow me, my sweet one," he said, and let his fingers linger in hers as he pulled away from her. He walked into the throne room and finally let his hand fall away from hers.

They were the first to arrive, and her mother's throne held her gaze.

Horemheb came up behind her. "Are you sure?"

Horemheb ran his eyes down her back, tracing her round shoulder and down the length of her arm by her side to the gold bracelets that hid her scars. *Mut is strong and brave and beautiful.* A growing breathlessness and a quickened heartbeat made him realize the depth of care he felt toward her.

"Yes," she whispered and turned to face him. "For Egypt, for my home, for my country, yes. This is my decision. This is my choice."

Horemheb grabbed her hands and came closer to her. "Then stay behind me." His voice fell low as his eyes lingered on hers. "If fighting breaks, you run and hide. These are honorable men, and I don't believe they would kill you if I were to be killed, but nevertheless, I want you to hide if it comes to violence. You are still the daughter of Pharaoh Ay, a Hereditary Princess in your own right, had he not named Nakhtmin. If I were to be killed, you may be forced to marry him or suffer the same fate."

Mut nodded and pulled her hand from his grasp, only to place it on his cheek. His stomach hollowed at her touch, and his mouth grew dry. He kissed the inside of her palm before she spoke. "If you were to be killed, know this, Horemheb . . ." Her eyes glistened as her lips searched for the words she wanted to speak. "Know that—"

But then, Nakhtmin stepped into the throne room, as did Commander Paramesse, each surrounded by their subordinate commanders.

Horemheb looked to her lips and then her eyes and drew away to meet the new arrivals at the lowest level of the throne room. Mut stayed behind him.

First Prophet of Amun Wennefer entered and came to stand on the throne's dais, and the second and third prophets each stood on the level beneath him, one holding the great Pshent crown for whomever was to be crowned Pharaoh and the other the blue and gold Modius crown, for his chief royal wife.

Nobles and officials of the highest rank began filling the throne room's halls to witness who would become their next Pharaoh.

Horemheb and Nakhtmin stepped forth.

"Who shall be crowned Pharaoh of all Egypt?" First Prophet Wennefer declared. "Master of Pharaoh's Horses Nakhtmin, named Hereditary Prince by Pharaoh Ay?" He gestured toward Nakhtmin, and then to Horemheb. "Or General Horemheb, named Hereditary Prince by Pharaoh Tutankhamun?"

"Who shall decide?" a noble called out, and immediately a roar sprang up from the crowd, each man yelling over the other about whose word was law, who had the right, who Amun would divinely appoint.

Nakhtmin turned to Horemheb. "You should not be here."

Horemheb locked eyes with him. "Nor should you."

"I am the Hereditary Prince!" Nakhtmin yelled in a booming voice.

The room silenced.

"I have come back from the dead." Horemheb's deep voice did not need to boom as it echoed off the stone walls in the surrounding silence. "I have been divinely appointed by Amun-Re. I am the divine Hereditary Prince, named by Pharaoh Tutankhamun, grandson of Pharaoh Amenhotep III! I am the rightful heir to the throne!"

Nakhtmin drew his dagger. "No, *I* am the rightful heir to the throne. I am the Hereditary Prince, named by Pharaoh Ay, Master of Pharaoh's Horses to Pharaoh Akhenaten and Vizier of the Lower to Pharaoh Tutankhamun. I am Pharaoh Ay's adopted son! Amun-Re has divinely appointed me!"

"Shall we have bloodshed to determine this?" Horemheb asked, eyeing Nakhtmin's dagger. His hand went to the handle of his khopesh hanging from his belt.

"You will die for a chance at the throne?" Nakhtmin flipped the dagger in his hand.

Horemheb unsheathed his khopesh. "I do not wish to kill you, but I will defend the honor and word of the true divinely appointed, Pharaoh Tutankhamun."

Commander Paramesse and his subordinates, as well as some of the chariot captains, took the side of Horemheb. Commander Paramesse spoke: "We do not wish bloodshed among our brothers-in-arms. General Horemheb is the rightful heir."

Horemheb lowered his khopesh.

Nakhtmin thrust his dagger in Horemheb's direction. "Fools! He cannot defend Egypt! He could not even defend *Pharaoh*! He came back from the dead, and Pharaoh Tutankhamun did not?"

Paramesse's hand rested on his weapon's handle. "The gods resurrected him as the one true King. Lay your dagger down and kneel before him."

"I would rather shed blood than let him steal what is mine and divinely appointed by Amun!" Nakhtmin said and lunged for Horemheb.

Horemheb swung his khopesh, but Nakhtmin, the younger and less-injured man, dodged him and sliced Horemheb in the arm. Horemheb dropped his khopesh but pulled his dagger from his chest-belt and swung low, slicing Nakhtmin in the leg.

"My skin grew thick from war while you still suckled your mother's breast," Horemheb taunted to a limping Nakhtmin, knowing full well there were only a few years between them. He swung his arm to show he still had full mobility. "Lay down your weapon and accept me as the divine king!"

Nakhtmin only yelled and swung again. Horemheb dodged it by taking a single step backward. Nakhtmin tried to stab Horemheb's leg, but missed as Horemheb sidestepped his attack, again with a single step.

"I do not want to spill Egyptian blood. Lay down your weapon," Horemheb ordered. "The army stands with me."

"Not all!" Nakhtmin yelled. "And when they see me best you, they will know I am the true King!"

"Yet you limp," Horemheb said, encircling him, keeping his distance, sizing up his opponent. His slice to Nakhtmin's leg may have proved critical, but in war, one must never underestimate one's enemy, for a man's pride and ego could be his downfall.

"I deserve the crown. I am Pharaoh Ay's adopted son." Nakhtmin stood, seemingly ignoring his sliced leg. "I have sacrificed for this throne. I have ordered men to their graves. I have spent years away from my family. I have lost—"

"You have not sacrificed as I have!" Horemheb yelled even louder, his deep voice resounding in every ear of those in the great throne room hall.

At that, the men behind Horemheb drew their weapons, as did the men behind Nakhtmin. The nobles and officials began to scramble, trying to hide behind pillars and behind doors. Wennefer and the Second and Third Prophets took refuge behind the large thrones of Pharaoh and his Queen. Mut stood boldly beside Commander Paramesse.

"You lie!" Nakhtmin yelled amid the chaos, and then lunged toward Horemheb, striking with his dagger.

Horemheb felt his body do what it had always done as Nakhtmin's lean charioteer's body lunged at him, dagger raised. The memory of Horemheb's infantry training and experience took over his limbs, moving without emotion, blocking Nakhtmin's attack and returning it with the same force. But once Horemheb felt his dagger sink into Nakhtmin's chest, felt the *thunk* as its hilt hit the man's body, only then did he close his eyes, unable to breathe as his belly twisted into knots. A certain silence rang in his ears, although he could still hear the gasps and the clamor around him.

Nakhtmin's dagger fell to the floor with a *clang* of bronze against stone, and in its dying echoes, the audience was rendered mute.

"My brother," Horemheb croaked out a whisper in Nakhtmin's ear. "I asked you to lay down your weapon."

Horemheb withdrew his head, so he faced him. Nakhtmin's face paled as he struggled to breathe. "Why did you not lay down your weapon?" Horemheb winced and placed his hand on Nakhtmin's shoulder. "Why cause me to spill Egyptian blood for the crown?"

"Because I thought the gods . . ." Nakhtmin swallowed and took several shallow breaths. ". . . I thought they wanted me to be King." He grimaced as a few grunts of pain surfaced in his throat. "I thought I was divinely appointed." Nakhtmin's hands covered Horemheb's grip on the dagger in his chest. "Tell my wife and children, I love them," he sputtered. "Tell them . . . I am sorry."

"I will tell them." Horemheb grasped his hand behind Nakhtmin's neck and pressed his forehead to his. "I am sorry, too, my brother."

"Pharaoh does not apologize," Nakhtmin whispered, staring dazedly into Horemheb's eyes. "Please make sure power is restored to Pharaoh's throne."

"I will," Horemheb whispered fervently. "I will ensure you go to the Field of Reeds with all you need and more." He nodded and pulled his dagger from Nakhtmin's chest.

His brother-in-arms fell to the floor, first to his knees and then to Horemheb's feet.

Horemheb's dagger dripped with blood. He peered over his shoulder at Mut, a glisten in his eye.

The men began to chant, "Pharaoh Horemheb! Pharaoh Horemheb!"

But Horemheb only surveyed them all and then pointed to Nakhtmin's body. The room fell silent as Horemheb spoke. "You cheer me because I killed my Egyptian brother? This man gave much for Egypt. He should be honored." Then he turned and went to the steps, to the prophets, who emerged from behind the throne. "The gods have spoken. I am the rightful heir to the throne."

First Prophet Wennefer and the prophets who stood

beside him recited the ritual coronation and placed the great Pshent crown on Horemheb's head; then they did the same to Mut with the Modius crown to signify her place as chief royal wife.

Horemheb faced the crowd and recited the oath. Then he declared, "Pharaoh's first command: send our Egyptian brother, Master of Pharaoh's Horses Nakhtmin, with honor, for long past are the days Egyptian shall rise against Egyptian. Long ago, we were united as both the Upper and the Lower to form our great country and expand our lands into our empire under our great god, Amun-Re. Today shall symbolize that reuniting. The conspirator against the throne, Pawah, the former Fifth Prophet of Amun and Vizier of the Upper and Lower to Pharaoh Tutankhamun, is dead, and we shall curse his heart to Ammit. Let his ways perish with him!"

The army roared in agreement as the nobles and officials nodded their heads and clapped with vigor.

"Pharaoh Horemheb! Pharaoh Horemheb! Pharaoh Horemheb!"

WHILE PHARAOH AY'S BODY WAS PREPARED FOR BURIAL, Horemheb prepared himself for the Appearance of the King ceremony, first in Waset and lastly in Men-nefer.

In the meantime, Horemheb split the faction that supported Nakhtmin into three separate factions, placing them among his own supporters—one at the northern border, one at Men-nefer, and one at the southern border—so any coup that might arise would be more easily found out. After this was done, he rose Paramesse to the rank of Vizier of the Upper and Lower, and two trusted and loyal troop commanders, Khensuhotep and Mahu, to the ranks of General and Commander.

Thus Pharaoh said.

✵ 13 ✵

THE TIME OF ASCENSION

AFTER THE FINAL APPEARANCE OF THE KING CEREMONY, MUT stood at the entrance of their old home in Men-nefer for a long time before she finally shut the door. She returned to Horemheb and their litter, and the servants helped her inside.

"I am not sad to leave this place." Her voice fell low as she stole one last glance at Horemheb's Men-nefer estate.

The servants lifted the litter and began to carry Pharaoh and his Queen toward the harbor.

Horemheb whispered back, "Neither am I. The only good memory there was starting over with you." He dropped his hand to graze hers, but then pulled it back to his lap.

Mut smiled as she looked forward.

He thought about leaning over and kissing her, but that action was not for Pharaoh to do in public, and he still wasn't sure if what he felt was love. Whatever it was had the same sensation and commitment as love, yes . . . but still, he needed to know for sure that it was indeed love. He had made every effort not to think of Nefertiti or to compare what he felt with her to that of what he felt with Mut. But Nefertiti still graced his dreams, still in her white and golden robes, still clutching their son in her arms, still floating away as his body lay weighed down, seemingly in pieces, bleeding from old wounds that rendered him immobile, keeping him from even reaching out to her. His dreams prevented him from believing his mind when it told him he did indeed love Mut. He knew that if he kissed her, it would mean she would be expecting more. He had not been with a woman in years—he had not had the appetite for it since Nefertiti's murder—but now, the urge rose within him, and he wanted Mut. He tried his hardest to repress his desires, for he knew he not only had to be fair to Mut, but he also had to honor Amenia and Nefertiti.

They boarded Pharaoh's large royal boat, and he and Mut retired to the cabin, where Horemheb ordered the release of the opaque curtains to give them privacy. Light filtered in through the black, translucent linen hangings, where they could watch the Nile from their lounger. It was a long trip back to Malkata, and so, they made themselves comfortable. Horemheb pulled Mut under his arm, and her cheek rolled to his chest. They sat in silence for a moment as they adjusted their eyes from the blinding outside sun to the far more dim interior.

"Mut," he said, low so that those outside the cabin could not hear him.

"Yes, Horemheb?" she whispered and peered up at him.

He outlined the contours of her face with his eyes. "You are beautiful in face and in body and in heart, and I am glad you are my Queen. I am glad you are by my side."

"I am glad you are by mine as well," she murmured and wrapped her arms around him.

Horemheb debated asking the question that had lingered in his mind since his coronation. He figured she had thought he'd forgotten, but he had not. What had she been about to say to him before Nakhtmin and Paramesse entered the throne room? The question reeled in his mind. Had she been about to say she loved him? What would he have said in such a case?

Did he love her in return?

He rubbed his hand over hers on his chest as he looked to the Nile behind the boat as they disembarked and began the three-decan journey home.

Mut sighed.

He peered down at her. "What is it?"

"Nothing." She pressed her cheek further into his chest and gave his body a little squeeze as she got more comfortable.

"Mut"—he drew her chin upward so that she faced him—"what do you think?"

She bit her bottom lip as her eyes searched his; finally, she opened her mouth to speak, but it was the same response as before. "Nothing."

"I believe that to be a lie . . . but you do not have to tell me." He smiled at her, noticing she glanced down at her wrists. He brought her hand to his lips. "We don't ever have to come back to Men-nefer."

Her eyes brightened at this. "I would very much like to never come back. That place kept me a prisoner. I hated it."

Horemheb wrapped his hand around the back of her neck and kissed her forehead. "I should have sold it a long time ago. I'm sorry I made you endure years there."

"Pharaoh does not apologize," she whispered.

"I am never Pharaoh with you, my sweet one." He kissed her cheek and then looked to her lips. He had to be sure, although everything he knew about love told him he wanted to kiss her.

"Horemheb," she started, but he spoke first.

"I blame myself."

A moment of silence passed between them.

"I don't blame you. Not anymore." Mut caressed his cheek. "But I am thankful to leave that place."

THEY CAME TO THE VERY NORTH OF WASET, AND ONLY THE TOPS of Malkata's tall walls could be seen in the far distance.

Mut had cried the nights previous, telling Horemheb about her father and her mother and how she missed them. She told him of her scars and how she hated when he looked upon her without her kohl makeup, without her jewelry to hide them. She told him of her lack of faith. He comforted her by telling of his own struggles with his faith, but that his faith had seen him through the darkest of nights, and he encouraged her to seek her own faith out again.

They had passed by Aketaten, now abandoned, its tall walls slowly being retaken by the desert. He had thought of Nefertiti, in Akhe-aten. His heart longed for her. His ka ached for her. They had passed by in silence. Nefertiti was gone, but Mut was here, and somehow, in his efforts to gain Mut's forgiveness, he saw her in a different light—not as Nefertiti's sister, but as Mut. As sweet Mut.

And as the sun set high in the sky, Mut awoke lying on his chest.

He peered down at her and smiled. "I'm glad you can sleep. You did not sleep much on this journey."

"I suppose I did not," she whispered.

They ate, then reclined again in their private lounger as the boat came near to the Malkata harbor.

"I wanted to tell you something," she began, and they locked eyes. "Do you remember before your coronation, when you asked me if I wanted to be Queen?"

"Yes. I have wanted to ask you what you were going to say as we stood in front of the throne." His heart beat fast within his chest. He'd done it; he'd asked the question. But now he knew what she had been going to ask. What was his response? What would he say?

"I was going to tell you . . . I love you," she said, her voice as calm as the sun in the sky.

The words *As I love you* came crashing behind his lips.

But those words never completed their journey, for at that moment the boat docked and the servants asked to bring Pharaoh and his Queen to the pier.

His mind raced.

Did he love her?

How should he respond?

Oh, why had he *asked*?

Her eyes bore into his as she whispered, "I only wanted you to know." She pulled away from him. "Thank you for being the man I envisioned so long ago."

Her lips held a small smile, but there was only want in her eyes. He felt she needed him to tell her she was loved, but he had to make sure to be fair to her.

She slid away from him and out into the shining sun.

Ankhesenamun was wise in her advice, he thought. *Perhaps I am simply getting in my own way, and it is not my love of Nefertiti that keeps me from her.* As he watched Mut step from the royal boat, he realized he indeed loved his wife.

MUT, HAVING ALREADY SHOWERED, WANTED ANOTHER BATH, FOR it had been a long journey. She stood in the bath chamber of the chief royal wife's apartment. Her servants now had at least quadrupled in number, but still, she kept Tener and Raia near her and named them both Head Steward. She looked at herself in the polished copper mirror. Her reflection bore no makeup, no kohl, and no oil, revealing the scars that usually hid under their façade. Four scars, to be exact; four ugly scars on her face, and many more elsewhere. She removed her bracelets to reveal the most hideous of all the scars she bore on her body. She'd only let Tener and Raia draw her bath, and once it was done, she dismissed them. Only they and Horemheb had she let see these ugly reminders of her torture.

"I am Queen now. Chief royal wife." Her whisper ate at

her ka as she pushed Horemheb's lack of response to her declaration of love from her mind. "Soon, if they don't already, everyone will wonder, 'Why does our Queen wear thick bracelets made of gold? Why does our Queen wear so much makeup? Why does our Queen stay by Pharaoh's side all the time? Does she not attend to matters to which the Queen should attend? She should be a powerful Queen, not one solely dependent upon Pharaoh.' " Her wrists burned, just as they did four long years ago. Her hands clenched into fists. "Now everyone will know."

Horemheb stepped into the bath chamber. "Now everyone will know what? That Pharaoh has the most beautiful wife in all of Egypt?"

Mut did not turn around. Even though he had seen the scars, she wanted to limit the number of times he saw them, and the torches still were ablaze, as were the evening sun's rays that fell into the room. She watched him in the reflection of the copper mirror as she thought, *I love you, Horemheb. I wish you could love me. It's been three years since you came back. Three years of unconditional devotion to me . . . and yet, you still cannot tell me you love me. Am I so horrible to look upon that you cannot tell me, that you must lie to me about being beautiful? These scars . . . these scars I wish I could erase. I wish I could go back and never tell you about my crisis of faith, about what happened, about anything. You comforted me then, but I need you now. I opened up to you and you still cannot say you love me, even though you act as if you do. My mother was right . . . I will grow old waiting for you. I will not be happy waiting for you. Yet I will wait.*

His smile fell at her silence, and he came up behind her and kissed her on the neck. "What is wrong, my sweet one?"

His endearment tortured her soul. She turned her face from the mirror so he could not see her reflection.

Do you love your "sweet Mut"? she wanted to ask.

"You kept your word," she whispered as a tear fell down her cheek. "You have striven every day to treat me as a husband should treat his wife, to receive back my trust, my love, and my forgiveness." She swallowed; the quick debate to continue with her question was over before it began. "Now that you have those from me, what is it that you are to do each day?"

He placed his hands on her shoulders and tried to turn her to face him, but she resisted.

"No, Horemheb. I don't want you to look at me."

"Why not?" He pressed his forehead into the top of her wig.

"I want to hide my scars. I don't want to remember. I don't want them. I wish I could cut them from my face and body. I wish I could remove my hands just above the wrists so I wouldn't have to look at them anymore." Horemheb rubbed her upper arms as he opened his mouth to speak, but she cut him off. "I don't want you to say anything. There is nothing to say. We can't change the past. I just hate when you look upon me without any covering. I hate my reflection."

"I don't." Horemheb finally succeeded in turning her to him, and he coaxed her chin up so he could see all of her face. She peered up at him, a frown on her lips. "I see a beautiful, strong woman who survived something no one should ever have to endure."

Her heart broke, remembering the pain, but wishing he loved her, too, and was not only comforting her in her time of sadness.

"These scars that you hide . . ." He gently pressed his finger over each one and then grasped her wrists. "These scars tell me you survived." He then cupped her tearful face with his hands. "You will make for a powerful Queen—one Egypt is fortunate to have."

The corners of her mouth turned up as she pulled him into an embrace. She wished he would kiss her—not even for the intimacy but just to know she was loved by someone who still lived, someone she loved in return. Yet part of her wished he never saw her because of the scars. They were ugly, and her face felt on display.

Horemheb kissed her wig and then tilted her head so she faced him. She tried to pull her face away from his view, but he kept ahold of her chin so she could not. "I *see* you. Please do not hide from me." He traced the contours of her face with the backs of his fingers.

Her breath became shallow as her heart beat faster.

Her eyes told him what she needed.

He came closer, but she refused to get her hopes up. He would probably kiss her forehead or her cheek, just as he had done so many times.

He kissed her cheek.

Her heart fell back to a normal rhythm as she closed her eyes. *I told him I would wait for him, but how can he say all of these things to me and treat me the way he does and not love me? What is wrong with me—*

Then he did something he hadn't done before. He kissed her other cheek and then her forehead and then her chin and then he pressed his face to hers, his lips hovering over her lips.

"My sweet one," he whispered, "thank you for letting me fall in love with you."

A smile bloomed, as did her heart, as he pressed himself against her, and then his lips followed suit, softly at first, as if he didn't want to break her, and then, just as the sweetness of the moment peaked and the tingling spread from her lips to her toes, he cupped her cheek and his kiss progressed until the world around her faded away.

Suddenly she hated the need to breathe; she clung to him for fear of falling from this dream she had found herself in. Her body trembled, as did her lips, and her ka felt renewed and alive.

This was what she wanted. This made her forget all the years before.

This was what she had waited for.

HE KISSED HER UNTIL HE WANTED TO CARRY HER TO HER BED. Her lips were as sweet as honey . . . and her scent of lotus blossoms filled his mind with thoughts of Nefertiti. He pulled slightly away from her, although abruptly. *Nefertiti is gone.* He grounded himself and pushed away the memory of Nefertiti. *I love Mut. Mut is my wife.*

"What is it?" Mut murmured, her eyes lost in a daze.

"I needed to breathe," he whispered—not at all a lie.

"Me too." She giggled and, her arms draped around his neck, pressed his head back to hers.

"I have a most demanding wife," he teased with a smile and a soft bite of her lip.

"Don't you?" A sly grin graced her face, and she rolled to her toes, placing her lips fully on his once again.

He loved her, but Nefertiti still hung in the back of his mind. Was he being truly fair, or had his desire for Mut's body blinded him? Maybe he needed to rethink his certainty in his love for Mut—maybe he was not as certain as he thought—for why would he recall a memory of his past love while with Mut? The pang of guilt regarding Nefertiti's murder and his loss of her still stung his heart, and it was enough to cause him to stop kissing Mut.

"Your bath grows cold," he whispered in between her kisses.

She pulled away and let out a soft laugh. "I am Pharaoh's wife. The bath can always be reheated." She studied his eyes, as if rethinking his comment. "Do you not want to be with me tonight?"

"I do," Horemheb said as he rubbed her back.

It wasn't a lie . . . but was it fair?

He kissed her, but she did not kiss him back this time. He

knew when he came into her bath chamber that he would kiss her and that it would most likely end in the consummation of their marriage. But his fleeting thought of Nefertiti had thrown him, and now he wondered if there had perhaps been a slight lapse in his judgment.

The fact that I loved Nefertiti does not mean I cannot love Mut too.

His thoughts focused on Nefertiti and Amenia as he watched the hurt pass over Mut's face. Nefertiti and Amenia had both been in unfulfilling marriages for reasons they could not control. Now he had found a way to love Mut, and he did love her—he was certain of it now. He would not let her fall victim to the same entrapment in marriage. So as he looked Mut in the eyes, he planted both of his feet on the floor and cradled her face in his hands.

"My sweet Mut," he whispered. "I promise you today what I should have promised you the day we married. I want you to know this before we go any further: I will never leave you, you will be the only woman who has my love, no other woman will warm my bed at night, and my love and loyalty to you will not be dependent on whether or not we have children, whether or not we have a son. There will be no conditions, for I love you, all of you."

He saw the tension in Mut's shoulders slide away as her smile returned. Her eyes soft, her fingers caressed the back of his neck as she pushed her chest into his.

He kissed her, a long, slow kiss of passion, which her mouth graciously received. His hands moved from her face to run down the length of her back and then press her whole body against his.

"My sweet one," he whispered, getting lost once again in her lips.

✻ 14 ✻

THE TIME OF PUNISHMENT

AY'S DAUGHTERS MADE SURE HE WENT TO RE WITH A BLUE LOTUS blossom in his right hand and a white one in his left: one for his Nefertiti and his Temehu, the other for Tey, who had bridged the gap in his heart. The people entombed him alongside Tey in the grand tomb meant for Pharaoh Tutankhamun.

Mut had stood in front of the tomb as it was sealed; no tears graced her eyes.

Horemheb glanced at her.

As if sensing his stare, she whispered, "They were old for a long time. I had already said my goodbyes. I will see them in the afterlife."

Horemheb brushed her hand, careful not to show too much affection in the public eye. "*We* shall," he whispered back, glad Mut had been making more offerings to the gods in her worship and was speaking of the afterlife again.

But a fear trapped his mind. Would his heart survive the test against the feather of Ma'at? Would his heart, at the end of the journey, be devoured by Ammit? He had committed a sin against the divine and human orders: he had conspired to kill Pharaoh Akhenaten, he had stood aside as Pharaoh

Smenkare was murdered, and he had been too late in keeping Nefertiti and Tut from the same fate. What would be his justification? There was no redemption—only a justification. If all forty-two gods agreed and his heart passed the test, then he would find immortality and become one with Re. Only then would he see Nefertiti again.

He shook his head, chiding himself for remembering her in that regard.

He looked at Mut.

"I love you," he whispered, so low she almost didn't hear, but her response came back.

"As I you."

A FEW MONTHS LATER, IT BECAME KNOWN THAT PHARAOH'S WIFE was with child. Horemheb and his Queen sat on their thrones, ruling Egypt each day.

He noticed many things upon the throne—mostly that his command was often questioned, the use of the phrase "Thus Pharaoh says" or "As Pharaoh commands" had waned. Messengers and servants had begun to leave without waiting for Pharaoh's dismissal. He had seen it culminate and dissipate under Ay's reign, but it seemed that now it was going in an endless downward spiral. He was unsure how to proceed, but knew that if this continued, the position of Pharaoh—and all that had been done to restore power to the throne—would be in vain. The priesthood of Amun might once again become the most powerful. But as long as the monies came through Pharaoh and then redistributed back to the priesthood, he knew he still held some power over them. That was one good thing that came from all of it, and he thanked Nefertiti for initiating the policy during her reign. His poor Nefertiti endured so much—*gave* so much—and in the end, it cost her her life. He gritted his teeth as he remembered the waste that had been Pharaoh Akhenaten. He had forced all of their hands. They'd had to take extreme measures for the betterment of Egypt, and those measures spat in the very name of what they all had agreed to do in the plan to restore power to the position of Pharaoh.

Maybe extreme measures would need to be taken once again . . . but what?

He glanced at Mut, with their child in her belly. His jaw loosened as he reached over and squeezed Mut's hand. He hoped for a son so there may be some political stability, but he vowed to Amun that he would never stray from Mut if she did not bear a son. In his own mind, he had reasoned that if the gods needed him to right the wrong of Akhenaten and still be punished for his hand in the conspiracy against their divinely appointed, it was very likely they would not grant him an heir.

FOR MONTHS ON END, HIS MIND HAD REELED AT HOW TO CORRECT the situation at hand, until one night when his wife yelled out in pain. Horemheb called for Tener and Raia. They ushered the royal midwife into the bedchambers.

Nofret had aged since she had delivered Ankhesenamun's children, yet this time she stood aside as Weret, her prodigy, now took her place, coaching Mut through the labor pains. They gathered her up and took her to the birthing pavilion outside where the night breezes cooled Mut's flashes of heat that usurped her body.

Horemheb stayed by her side.

"Will Pharaoh follow tradition and leave us, or be as Pharaoh Akhenaten and Tutankhamun and stay through the delivery?" the midwife asked him with a firm jaw.

Horemheb's face remained calm, but his heart dropped at the comparison to Akhenaten. *The people should not remember him,* he thought, but snapped his attention to his wife. "If the Queen will have Pharaoh."

Mut winced and breathed through a new stab of pain, but then nodded.

The morning sun arose as the child's head emerged.

The new midwife-in-training placed the Bes amulet over Mut's brow; Nofret oversaw Weret, nodding at her good performance.

"A few more breaths, my Queen," Weret soothed, coaxing out the remainder of the baby's body until finally the whole of it lay in Weret's arms.

"A son!" Mut's breathless cry escaped her lips as a laugh fell on her tongue. She turned to Horemheb as the sweat plastered her wig to her face.

His mind, in a fleeting moment, jumped back to the day he had found out Nefertiti held his son within her womb, but he pushed it from his memory. He would not let the sorrow of his past hinder this joyous day with his love, with his sweet Mut. He ran his hands over her head and kissed her on the mouth, in the moment, not caring who saw such displays of affection.

Tener and Raia laid Mut back on the cushions they had set for her. The midwife had the limp baby laid across her arm, rubbing and patting his back.

After a few moments, Mut's smile faded. "Why isn't he crying?"

The words stung the ears of those who had heard the same words from Queen Ankhesenamun. Only this time, silphium was not to blame.

"Sometimes we need to work to get the baby to breathe." The midwife rubbed a little harder as the wet nurse stood off to the side.

Horemheb dropped his head. His son did not breathe, did not cry, did not take to the wet nurse. He heard Mut's cries as though he had been lost in a dust storm.

Surely I am being punished again for not saving Nefertiti and my son, and for my infidelity with Amenia and causing her early journey west. I am being punished for striking my hand against Amun's divinely appointed. We are all being punished for our murder of Pharaoh Akhenaten and Pharaoh Smenkare. The gods make sure we know and feel pain. They still need me to correct the wrong. I must correct the wrong, but how? Send me a vision. Tell me what you need me to do! Don't make Mut suffer as well. She is the only innocent one left.

In his peripheral vision, he saw Mut clinging to the bundle they handed her. Tears welled in his eyes as he closed his eyelids to keep the tears from falling.

He moved to her side and wrapped her in his arms. He couldn't bear to look at his son's face. He only rocked with Mut's trembling body, trying to absorb as much pain as he could from her. Their son's early journey west was caused by his sins, he knew.

Amun-Re, highest god of all gods, please, I beg you on my life, however insignificant it may seem, do not let the punishment for my sins be carried to Mut, do not burden her with the consequences of my transgressions.

After they were assured of Mut's physical health, the servant women left the royal couple in their grief.

Mut's cries became whimpers in Horemheb's arms. "I'm so sorry, my love," she whispered. "I could not bear your firstborn, a son."

"No, Mut, don't." His voice wavered in his guilt and sorrow as he rubbed her back. "No, this is not a tragedy of your doing. Please know this. I do not blame you, nor will I ever blame you." He kissed her forehead and her lips.

I blame myself, he thought.

Then he found it within his heart to look upon his son, still held tightly in Mut's arms, and the tears finally fell.

☙ 15 ❧
THE TIME OF ACCEPTANCE

WITH HIS SON'S PASSING, THE GODS SENT HOREMHEB A revelation:

> In order for the future of the position of Pharaoh to be successful, the past must be erased.

Sleepless nights followed the revelation as he wondered if he had become mad, like Pharaoh Akhenaten, believing visions that were just delusions of his own mind.

But the longer he obsessed and with each passing day, each passing decan, month, and season, he noted the position of Pharaoh was lesser in the eyes of the people. Some of his more loyal officials reported rumors of priests and officials taking advantage of the poor and pocketing the offerings for themselves. People seemed to be giving fewer offerings to the priesthoods—perhaps they were afraid of corruption; perhaps Pawah's affiliation with the priesthood of Amun had tainted the people's beliefs and trust in the priesthood.

Paramesse, with his newly appointed General Khensuhotep and Commander Mahu, told Horemheb of the laxity and abuse with which their ranks treated military-owned property. Additionally, after intermingling Nakhtmin's supporters through his trusted ranks, more abuse had been reported. He had suspected some corruption had taken place while he commanded Pharaoh's armies, but when Pharaoh Akhenaten was in charge, nothing could be done. With the subsequent Pharaohs, he had been too involved with Nefertiti to notice or care. His heart tugged at the betrayal against him and the man he'd called son, Tut—against Pharaoh. He'd ignored it most of the time as General and knew he was partly to blame for the continuing corruption in the military ranks. Perhaps, if he had been diligent, Tut might still be alive today. Guilt crept into his shoulders as he shook these thoughts from his mind—he could not change the past.

His Overseer of the Treasury, Satau, told him the royal treasury was not growing as it should. He suspected the numbers were being falsely submitted by the states and provinces as they had been since Pharaoh Akhenaten. Satau's old fingers shook as he scribbled with his reed brush, recalculating again and again yet coming to the same conclusion. The taxes and the offerings per person were just not adding up.

Horemheb walked the halls at night, his lips pursed, his brow furrowed, as he wondered how to implement the correction of these errors. He prayed to his patron god, Horus, for whom he had been named, and to Amun-Re, for guidance, for strength, for clarity in his next actions. He needed more time to set his mind before he could ever think of erasing the past.

Mut had become with child again, and fear that his past sins would take away their child a second time began to hurry his heartbeat as dread filled his ka. So, as their child grew in Mut's womb, the more he thought about what needed to be done, the more Pharaoh and the state slowly fell in the eyes of the people.

The more he prayed, the more he confirmed to himself the

past had to be erased. He, as Pharaoh, had to cover the period of time during which the people had lost faith in Pharaoh. It was not enough that Tut had publicly rejected his father—it needed to be struck from memory entirely. Akhenaten's scar upon the people of Egypt had to be forgotten, hidden for all eternity.

But, at the realization of this truth, he felt the sting of the khopesh against his leg and neck and shoulder once again. He felt it rip through to his heart. To erase the past meant to erase the names of those who had lived. Those Pharaohs who had lived. As Pharaoh, the speaking of their names, their images in stone, was to be spoken and revered forevermore, so that Pharaoh may truly live a life eternal. Horemheb would be robbing them of that highest earthly honor, and the thought shook his spirit to its core.

His Nefertiti . . .

His Tut . . .

Never to be remembered?

He dreamt one night soon after the realization came to him. He'd already been walking the halls until the old injury in his knee, at last, could not carry him any longer. He'd collapsed into the queen's bed. Mut rubbed his chest, asking him why he was in such distress, until he had fallen asleep, unable to answer her.

Then, almost as quickly as he had closed his eyes, there she was:

Nefertiti, floating in all of her white-and-golden glory, clutching their son, her chest wound still a stark contrast to her robes.

He tried to call to her, but his voice would not come. He tried to reach her, but his arm would not move. I'm sorry, he wanted to say. I won't do it! he wanted to cry.

Her eyes only peered at him through the dark void in which she abided as she reached out her hand to him. So close . . . but she never touched him.

He was falling away from her.

"Nefertiti!" he called out, but the words mangled in his throat.

"Hide the scar, Horemheb." Her voice floated to him in a whisper that resounded like a thousand drums. He lay there, weighted down, bleeding from his scars, and falling to pieces as her words reverberated in his body. "Hide the scar."

He awoke with a start, Nefertiti's command pounding in his ears. He sat straight up. Beads of sweat piled on his brow and his breath came out in shaky spurts. Bes had sent that dream. There was a message the god of dreams let Nefertiti tell him.

He studied Mut, asleep, before pulling himself from bed.

He wandered the halls aimlessly until he came upon Malkata's temple, which housed a solid gold statuette of Amun. He came to stand in front of Amun, opened his mouth with an offering, and, just as suddenly as he'd woken, he dropped to his knees and wept.

For how could he do that to Nefertiti, to Tut, to all of Nefertiti's daughters, to Ankhesenamun? To erase their pain, their plight, their love, their purpose? What monster would he be to do such a thing?

"I know now, my god Amun-Re, I know now why you left me as the sole survivor of all the conspirators to the throne. You have to make sure our deeds are covered, erased, so that no doubt lingers in the minds of the people regarding your divinely appointed and your priesthood. But must this fall to me? I *loved* her. I loved Tut. I loved them all. I would be their executioner. Spare my sweet Mut. Spare her, please. I alone deserve to suffer. Do not take any more children from her."

He prayed and begged Amun to pass this from him. But the memory of Mut's cries as she held their lifeless son and the fear of it happening again overwhelmed his prayers and his desires to have this burden passed to someone else. When tears became scarce, he placed his forehead to the stone ground.

"For you, my god Amun, for Egypt, I shall do this."

He let the remainder of his tears fall and soak into the stone. He sat back on his heels and raised his head to look at the statuette.

"For you. For Egypt," he whispered.

SOMEHOW, HE MADE IT BACK TO MUT'S APARTMENT JUST AS THE dawn filled the room.

Mut awoke from her slumber upon hearing him enter.

"Horemheb?" she asked, rubbing her eyes. "What is it? Horemheb, what's wrong?" She placed her hand on his shoulder as he sat down with his back to her, his tongue rendered mute.

"The position of Pharaoh . . ." he began, trying to piece together his justification to her, knowing her family would be the victims in all of it. She quieted as he finally began to reveal to her the cause of his distress. "The position of Pharaoh will never be as it should if I do not erase the people's fears of Pharaoh Akhenaten. The scar of his reign cannot be remembered." He wiped his eyes. "*He* must not be remembered. No one associated with him . . . can be remembered."

"What do you mean?" Mut wrapped her arms around him as she pressed her cheek to the back of his neck.

"The people . . . their respect for Pharaoh is not as it should be. The elevation of his throne is not as high. The position does not command reverence as it once did."

"Yes, it does," she whispered, her voice wavering.

"No, Mut. I was alive under Pharaoh Amenhotep III's reign. I trained in his army. There is a difference." His voice fell.

She remained silent. She was born halfway through Pharaoh Akhenaten's reign and thus had nothing to compare. "Do you really need to erase the names of my sister and nieces for this? What of *my* name?"

He closed his eyes, the truth attacking his heart.

Yes.

He stood up, letting the blanket fall off the side of the bed.

"I need to pace the halls and think some more on this."

"I'll come with you." Mut moved her legs out from underneath her newly pregnant belly.

"No, my love," he said. He pressed her back to bed and rubbed his hand on her belly and then her cheek. "You need sleep." He looked to the dark circles under her eyes and knew they mirrored his own. "I have kept you awake too many nights in my pacing, in my absence. Please sleep for me and our child."

She at first insisted but then obliged, too tired to argue.

He left to ready himself for the coming day.

THE SUN ROSE IN THE SKY, AND HOREMHEB SAT IN THE COUNCIL room with Vizier Paramesse, his scribe, and First Prophet of Amun Wennefer. He sat in silence for a while, planning out every detail of the questions he would ask and the plan he was about to order.

Paramesse sat searching his face, silent, as if he felt Horemheb's burdens as his own.

Wennefer only tapped his finger and took a heavy sigh. "Are we going to get on with it?"

Paramesse cocked his head toward Wennefer. "You, First Prophet, are to address the King as *Pharaoh* and with the proper respect."

Wennefer glared at Paramesse and curled his lip back in a sneer. His eyes still on Paramesse, he spoke to Horemheb. "Pharaoh, what is it that you wish to speak to us?"

"The proper action, First Prophet, would be not to ask a question until Pharaoh has spoken," Paramesse chided.

Horemheb finally looked at Wennefer. "Why are the people not flowing to the temples of Amun as they did before Pharaoh Akhenaten?"

The question seemed to take Wennefer by surprise. He mumbled an incoherent response.

Horemheb said, "Those trusted to me have told me that the people are hesitant with their offerings."

Wennefer narrowed his eyes, and his jaw tightened. "The people have found a number in our priesthood who did the same as former Fifth Prophet of Amun Pawah, taking too much for themselves and then using it against the people. They fear us and are wary of our devotion to Amun."

Wennefer's statement stung Horemheb's soul, as it only confirmed what he hoped to be a glimmer of his own insanity; he recognized now that the reports were true . . . total erasure had to be done for the greater of Egypt.

"So there is corruption in your ranks?"

"No. No." Wennefer shook his head. "We can take of our own—"

"There are none greater than Pharaoh! Pharaoh is Amun's divinely appointed, and as such, Pharaoh makes the prophet appointments." Horemheb's firm gaze set upon Wennefer. "If there is corruption, Pharaoh must correct it."

He recalled from his early memory of Amenhotep III how Pharaoh was to speak and how Pharaoh was to act. The King never displayed emotion other than rightful anger. The King was always referenced to as "Pharaoh." If this new future were to flourish, all traces of Akhenaten and his laxity on the throne must be put to death.

"There must be no memory of the king who left this position in disregard and took the people's faith from Amun's priesthood."

"Are you speaking of Eternal Execration, erasure of names, the final curse?" Wennefer held a small smirk on his face.

"You, First Prophet of Amun, shall address Pharaoh as *Pharaoh*." Horemheb lifted his chin to show the height of his crown. His bloodshot eyes made Wennefer dip his chin and avert his gaze.

"Pharaoh," Wennefer began again, and again locked eyes with Horemheb. "The priesthood has debated erasure on multiple occasions. We agree that it makes the most sense. It may be prudent to tell the people *we* initiated this idea."

Horemheb stared him down. Amun had given his revelation to his priesthood as well—after all, why *wouldn't* the god do so? At least he was not alone in his visions like Akhenaten had been. Horemheb thought back on his struggles with the vision: all the sleepless nights, the loss of his son, the pain and agony he'd prepared himself to endure until he finally accepted Amun's revelation . . . but it seemed to him that Wennefer held no second thought, guilt, or remorse about enacting this horrible punishment. Perhaps Amun wanted the apathy of the priesthood to ensure Pharaoh carried out the god's wishes fully.

He said now: "Why, First Prophet? So you can be seen as a savior in the people's eyes? No, *Pharaoh* shall make this so."

"Pharaoh does not have the power to do so. We would both benefit greatly from erasing the past. You get more prestige and honor, and we regain the people's trust—and offerings, which we can then use to feed our families at night."

Yes, their families grew fat from the people's offerings. Horemheb looked the plump prophet over as he thought, *I shall make sure the priesthood no longer takes advantage of the people and their faith . . . yet he might be right. Pharaoh's power has waned, but I feel there is just enough so that I may do it alone.*

Horemheb motioned to the scribe. "Pharaoh shall now make a declaration."

Wennefer sneered as the scribe held his reed brush at the ready.

"From the date Pharaoh places his seal upon this edict, there shall be a firm government in which legal and religious abuses that have arisen since Pharaoh Akhenaten will not be tolerated."

"Pharaoh—" Wennefer started but was silenced by Horemheb's glare.

"A new reign has come to bring glory back to Egypt, as it was under Pharaoh Amenhotep III." Horemheb's mind reeled as he spoke the words he had decided to say earlier in the morning.

"Officials of the states and provinces, prophets, and military captains and commanders found cheating the poor, pocketing offerings, taking bribes, blackmailing, or misappropriating slaves, ships, or other properties, will be subject to swift judgment and execution."

"Pharaoh—*execution?*"

"Pharaoh is speaking." Paramesse leaned forward and held his pointed finger to Wennefer's face. Once Wennefer's mouth stayed close, Paramesse brought his hand down to the table.

Horemheb looked at Wennefer, as the next statement would affect him as well. He wasn't sure how he would enforce this edict, but knew much of the military was on his side. It would prove the true test of Pharaoh's power, and if it failed, Egypt would suffer for it.

He said, "Pharaoh, as Amun's divinely appointed King, shall alone appoint all prophets, officials, and military commanders."

"This is absurd!" Wennefer shook his head. "We do not need Pharaoh intervening in *our* priesthood. We have everything under control."

"You will do well to keep your mouth shut, First Prophet. Pharaoh has spoken, and he can and will remove you from your appointment as he is Amun's divinely appointed, the truest First Prophet." Paramesse glowered at Wennefer. Even dressed as a vizier, his military-commander body and expression rendered Wennefer silent, though Wennefer still shook his head and bit his lip, as if debating chancing his appointment at speaking against Pharaoh once more.

Horemheb continued, "Balance will be restored unto Egypt. Monuments, temples, and stelae that were erected under Pharaoh Akhenaten, Pharaoh Smenkare—"

His heart gave pause—*Nefertiti!*—but his lips continued Amun-Re's request of him:

". . . Pharaoh Neferneferuaten, Pharaoh Tutankhamun . . ."

Now he had said their names, but a part of his heart still twitched, knowing he still had to sign and seal the edict for it to be law; he could still take their names out. Still, he continued speaking:

". . . and Pharaoh Ay shall be destroyed. All references to the Aten and the Aten policies shall be removed and erased from all landscapes. The blasphemous abandoned city of Aketaten and all that remains there shall be wiped clean from its foundations. There shall be no reference to any policy, any monument, any property, or any person"—his heart wrenched again, but his lips continued for the love of his country—"living or journeyed west during the time after Pharaoh Amenhotep III and until this day."

Horemheb stopped speaking; his heart beat out of his chest. He had declared it, the scribe had written it, and the edict lay before him, ready for his cartouche and seal.

Wennefer sat back and folded his hands over his large belly. "Pharaoh does not have the power to carry out this edict. It must be a joint effort. And as such, we demand that there be no execution."

"You dare demand from Pharaoh?" Horemheb asked him, and Hori and Ineni stepped forward and planted their spears on the stone floor in unison, creating a resounding echo throughout the throne room.

Wennefer pressed his lips to a thin line and brought his hands to his chin. Leaning his elbows on the table, he said, "No, Pharaoh, I do not demand anything."

He might be right, the better part of him reasoned; the edict would be easier carried out if it were a joint effort, and perhaps with less bloodshed, since Amun's priesthood was also seen as divine. He also wasn't sure just how much of the military was loyal to him—how much he could push until their loyalties were rescinded. He remembered Smenkare's purge and did not want to be regarded as he was. A joint effort may be easier on the people, as there would appear to be more divine leadership and authorization behind the edict . . . more endorsement . . . more acceptance . . . more license to carry out the edict.

It would also be a massive undertaking. It would be good to have a few highly ranked prophets such as Wennefer, even though he lacked respect, to oversee the areas Pharaoh could not personally attend to. But to say it would be a joint effort would be a self-fulfilling prophecy of Pharaoh's power never returning to its fullness in the eyes of the people.

He glanced at Paramesse, and upon connecting their gazes, he knew the same thoughts ran through Paramesse's mind as well. They both looked back to Wennefer.

"Leave us, First Prophet," Horemheb commanded.

"Pharaoh will discuss with his vizier a path forward. A joint effort we may consider."

"Of course Pharaoh will. It is the only logical choice." Wennefer smiled. "We will be waiting to hear about the erasure. We are eager to have it done and forgotten."

Wennefer's words tore at Horemheb's soul. "You only wish it to be gone so that your pockets can be full again."

Wennefer's brow knitted together as he placed a limp hand over his heart. "Pharaoh, such words cut me deep."

"The truth can hurt sometimes," Horemheb said, seeing through his façade.

Wennefer only stood, bowed with a sneer, and left. At Horemheb's dismissal, the scribe left, too, so only Paramesse and Hori and Ineni remained with him.

Horemheb's shoulders relaxed, as he felt he didn't need to act so much as Pharaoh in front of these men who had already proven so much to him.

"What shall I do?" he asked to no one in particular.

Paramesse cleared his throat and gestured to the guards.

"Hori, Ineni, sit at my council table," Horemheb ordered. "These men stood guard at Pharaoh Neferneferuaten's door, protected Queen Ankhesenamun while in Aketaten, and helped me avenge my wife and capture Pawah. They are loyal to the throne."

Paramesse acknowledged each of them as they sat and nodded.

Hori dipped his chin. "We are honored, Pharaoh."

"We need this to be a joint effort," Paramesse said, getting to the point. "It will be as if the gods—"

"I know," Horemheb cut him off. "I have not signed this edict yet." His finger gingerly touched Pharaoh Neferneferuaten's cartouche and then slid down to Pharaoh Tutankhamun's.

She told me to hide the scar . . . but she and Tut weren't the scar, he thought, remembering Bes' dream.

"Pharaoh." Paramesse clasped his hands on the table. "It must be done." Paramesse knew of his love for them both, but even Paramesse could see the need for erasure. Horemheb closed his eyes.

My Nefertiti . . . my Tut . . . forgive me, he pleaded in silence.

"When this edict becomes law," Horemheb mumbled, "they will destroy Aketaten and Akhe-aten."

"Yes," Paramesse said with a slow nod.

"I will not let their bodies be desecrated. I will condemn them to eternal death among the living for the greater of Egypt, but I will not condemn them to eternal death in the afterlife. How much time will you need to oversee the transportation of their bodies to the Valley of the Kings?"

"It is soon to be flood season, which will help cut down on our travel time." Paramesse scanned Hori and then Ineni. "And if we have all of our trusted military and royal guards in this effort, I believe a season should be enough time."

"A season." Horemheb closed his eyes. Mut would deliver their child just a few months after that. Hopefully, the erasure would be done before the child came, and the gods would grant life this time. "Make it so."

"Thus Pharaoh says," the three responded in unison.

Horemheb's finger still drifted between Nefertiti's and Tut's names on the papyrus, and the thought of his afterlife lingered in the back of his mind as he asked his next question. "How do we make it seem this was a joint effort with the priesthood of Amun?"

The three sat silently for a moment until Hori piped up. "We could send word with First Prophet Wennefer that Pharaoh asks outright about their problems. Wennefer then proposes erasure, but with the condition that Pharaoh alone has the right to enact the edict and put all of the safeguards against corruption like in this edict." He pointed to the papyrus laid in front of Horemheb.

Paramesse nodded. "It could work. We would need to add

to the edict and lay out the roles and responsibilities of each to carry out what part—who would oversee what, how it would be enforced, how to prevent an Akhenaten from rising again." Paramesse's nostrils flared as he mentioned the former Pharaoh's name.

Horemheb gave this some thought. "We must buy time so that we can relocate the tombs."

"Well," Ineni spoke up, "we could just use the excuse of modifying the edict. Tell the priesthood it will take a season to get it just right."

Paramesse nodded in agreement.

"Thank you, royal guards, Hori and Ineni." Horemheb took a deep breath, and then dismissed them to stand outside the door. He and Paramesse needed to write a script to be delivered to Wennefer that would be recited at a meeting so that it may seem a joint effort.

After the guards left, he stood, followed by Paramesse.

"One more favor, my brother, my friend." Horemheb came to him and put his hands on his shoulders. "Promise me something."

"Anything, Pharaoh." Paramesse lowered his chin, waiting.

"Bury my Nefertiti in a secret place," Horemheb whispered, "and when I journey westward to Re, you have the funeral procession, and so on and so forth, but then you go in afterward and take me out and place me alongside my Nefertiti and my son."

Paramesse's eyes grew wide. Horemheb suddenly remembered he had never told Paramesse about his son in Nefertiti's womb. But just as his eyes widened, they relaxed. "Yes, my Pharaoh."

"And what of Mut?" he asked, more to himself, though he figured Paramesse would ask the same question soon enough. "Mut will outlive us for a long time. As great royal wife, I expect her to find happiness with someone else, even though she can never marry. But she will not have to marry the next Pharaoh when we have an heir. She will be able to be with whomever she wants, and whomever that is, leave instruction to place her alongside him."

"Thus Pharaoh says."

HOREMHEB MET THE FIRST FIVE PROPHETS OF AMUN IN Malkata's council room at public decree. In an unprecedented turn of events, he requested the statue of Amun to be present, for what he was about to discuss, he wanted Amun there to guide him. The people began to whisper in the streets, wondering what this Pharaoh would do. His guards, Hori and Ineni, stood on either side of Pharaoh and Mut as the five prophets entered. Paramesse had left the night before to begin overseeing the secret order of Pharaoh.

The five prophets took their seats after Pharaoh sat down.

"Prophets of Amun." Horemheb's deep voice stilled the confusion in the room. "Pharaoh has noticed a lack of respect for his throne. Has the priesthood experienced the same?"

The prophets looked to each other, debating whether they should tell Pharaoh their concerns, until finally, First Prophet Wennefer spoke, reciting the script he had received from Pharaoh the prior day.

"Pharaoh, King of the Upper and the Lower . . ." He took a deep breath. "Yes, we have experienced the same. The people treat us with caution. They are wary of us in our devotion to Amun. We believe they fear we are as corrupt as the former Fifth Prophet Pawah. Our offerings are lacking, and the priesthood's treasury wanes."

Horemheb nodded. "The people fear the past. They fear what can be done by Pharaoh. They fear the greed and corruption of the gods' prophets."

With barely a half smile, Wennefer said, "Perhaps Pharaoh

should erase the past, so that we do not have to endure the people's fear. For what is Egypt without Pharaoh? What is Egypt without Amun-Re and his priesthood?"

Horemheb's finger curled down into his hand, making a fist at his chin. The moment was upon him. There was still an opportunity to let it pass to the next Pharaoh . . . if the next Pharaoh was even to be honored. The moment needed him to speak, and even though he had authorized the script for Wennefer to recite, its words still levied a great tax on his heart. Lowering his hand, he pushed his lips together, knowing the words he must speak, but halted at the memories of Nefertiti and Tutankhamun flooding the forefront of his memory:

Nefertiti weeping in his arms, the silk of her skin, the taste of her lips, the ring of her laugh, her last words: *You made me feel alive.* And Tut, the frightened little boy in the chariot all the way through to seeing him a man, as Pharaoh, blessing him on the battlefield, and then his last words flowing into his ears: *Remember me, my father.*

It was almost enough to make him lose his morning's breakfast.

I made her feel alive and now I take away her last life. He asked me to remember and now I must forget. A grimace crept over his lips as a glisten came to his eye. *Why must it be me?*

He closed his eyes and bowed his head to Amun's statue seated behind the five prophets.

Amun-Re, do you still punish me for my hand in Pharaoh Akhenaten's murder? How much more can I bear for Egypt? How much more must I pay?

He remembered the night with Nefertiti as he pushed her body close to his to leave her lasting imprint, for she would have had to marry someone else. The same dread, the same longing, filled his ka once again. All those months and seasons of his constant agony engulfed his present. Heavy weights set into his jaw as cold chased the warmth from his chest until he finally repeated his own scripted words in nothing but a whisper:

"Pharaoh agrees."

He licked his lips and breathed to ease the tears that halted at the rims of his eyes. Upon his exhale, he peered up at Amun-Re. His heart broke again as the answer to Wennefer's questions came out from his lips:

"For Egypt would be nothing. We will enact Eternal Execration so that Egypt may find restored faith in Pharaoh, the gods, and priesthoods without remembering the stains of the past."

He knew then had Amun-Re asked him, begged him, to erase the misdeeds so that Egypt would thrive as it always had.

Egypt, you take much. You take much from me.

He heard Mut whisper, sitting beside him, so low only he could hear it: "Please. We don't have to do this."

Horemheb swallowed as he tried to push her plea from his broken heart.

Will you ease my pain, my god? Will you give me the strength to carry out your order? The silent plea lived in his eyes.

"We are agreed," Wennefer said, nodding and smiling, and the four other prophets nodded with him. "At morning light, we are to begin the erasure—"

Horemheb held up his hand to halt Wennefer.

"Pharaoh, we are to begin the erasure at morning light," Wennefer said again, and stood to leave.

"You are not dismissed." Horemheb's voice boomed throughout the room.

Wennefer may have gotten his way with the joint effort, but this edict shall be mine and mine alone.

"Pharaoh has not dismissed you. Pharaoh has not commanded anything. You, First Prophet of Amun, will respect the throne and Pharaoh's words."

His purposeful tone and the single unified strike of the

guards' spears against the stone floor caused Wennefer to swallow.

"No more shall Pharaoh be dishonored. No more shall Pharaoh be diminished. If we are to erase this past, you, First Prophet of Amun, shall honor Pharaoh as Amun's divinely appointed, his truest first prophet." He stopped and lifted his chin even higher and bore his gaze deep within Wennefer's eyes.

He will obey me. He does not have the power to do this alone either.

After a moment, Wennefer bowed and took his seat. "Thus Pharaoh says."

Horemheb did not let the small victory show on his face as he leaned into his golden throne and rubbed the gold in the chair's arms—just as Tut used to.

My son, my Tut, forgive me. I shall always remember, and so will they, these who are eager to erase your name. I promise this to you.

"Pharaoh shall prepare an edict of the actions to take to destroy the records of those who lived before us. This will take time. Meet here on the first day of the next season, and then I shall sign the final edict.

"Why wait?" Wennefer shook his head and narrowed his eyes. "You already have an edict."

"You will address Pharaoh as *Pharaoh*."

Wennefer took a breath. "What purpose is there in waiting, Pharaoh?"

"The King owes you no reason but shall share the purpose. The edict needs to prevent tyranny and anarchy when it comes to the destruction of monuments and records. Everything shall be accounted for, and each task will be outlined so that nothing is overlooked, and it shall be done with dignity, as is fitting for royalty. As the economy is flourishing, as peace lives at our borders with the Hittites, the Libyans, and the Nubians, we have time to do this with respect. It shall be methodically carried out and overseen by ourselves."

He saw Wennefer's lip turn to a half scowl as he bobbed his head, clearly only regretfully agreeing with him. After a quick moment, he muttered:

"Thus Pharaoh says."

16

THE TIME OF THE FIRST
REMEMBERING

A SEASON CAME AND WENT, AND THE SECRET MOVE OF THE
royals' bodies to the Valley of the Kings was almost complete.
Horemheb had ordered Nefertiti's body to a secret burial,
overseen by Vizier Paramesse. Pharaoh wanted to make sure
no one would harm her.

He had been told the entrance to Tut's tomb had been
covered by a mudslide, and Horemheb took it as a small gift
of appreciation from the gods. He ordered the erasure of the
entrance from the records and ordered his tomb to be
untouched.

*This at least gives my heart some consolation for what I am
about to do.*

The first season's stalling did not come without cost. The
prophets asked daily when he would create his edict, when
he would carry it out, when they could regain the people's
faith. The more they asked, the more Horemheb knew they
only asked because of greed. The people's offerings were still
not as abundant, as they remembered Pawah, and so the
prophets' pockets remained further emptied. They thought
Horemheb would back out of his agreement and so pressed
him.

The day of the next season came, and Horemheb had not received word yet from Paramesse that the transfer was complete. He needed to stall further—and yet again, the gods granted him consolation, for now, he could tell of the past and rid some of his burdens. He had told them he would execute the edict with all respects due to royalty, and that, before the erasure, all must be told to those overseeing its implementation, so that they would truly feel the lives they were erasing.

The five prophets sat in the council room on the first day of the next season as Pharaoh had ordered. The edict of Horemheb's own creation lay before him, waiting for his sign and seal.

They think I am here because of their actions? Amun-Re, give me the wisdom to handle their kind, to show them who is your divinely appointed.

Horemheb observed the five prophets' pale faces: lips, trembling with victory; eyes, tinged with triumph. The reed brush drizzled ink into a slosh on the table as he held it, re-reading the papyrus scroll for the fifth time. His stomach turned over on itself, and his heart beat slowly, heavy with the burden he agreed to.

The sharp intake of breath behind him made him grip the brush harder. Mut stood there. Her tears were as his own, but he was in the wolves' den and hardened his resolve. In his hand, he held the legacy of those who came before him. Pushing the chair back, he stood with a graceful grandeur and placed the reed brush in its well.

The five prophets of Amun leaned forward in their seats, gnashed their teeth, ready to pounce, but Horemheb raised his hand to silence them. His guards stood at either side, spears in hand and khopeshes within reach.

"You said you would sign," one of the pale prophets said in the silent moments after. "For the greater of E—"

"There are none greater than Pharaoh." His stare cut

through the tension in the room, centering on the one who had spoken; the man drew his jaw in and forced his lips closed. "Before we sentence the past to death, you"—he raised his finger to all five prophets in the room—"*you* will remember."

Wennefer narrowed his eyes at Horemheb. "But we all know the past. It is for the future generations not to know about the weakness of Akhenaten or the transgressions of those who opposed him. It is for Egypt."

"You will hold your tongue, First Prophet." Pharaoh's glare met Wennefer's. The two most powerful men of Egypt stood, seeing who would break their stare first. Finally, Horemheb struck the other down with his words: "I, Pharaoh, the sole divine ruler of all of Egypt, appointed you, Wennefer, as First Prophet of Amun, and I can remove you."

Wennefer's upper lip twitched, but he slowly bowed to Pharaoh and then took his seat. "As Pharaoh commands."

The other four prophets' faces paled. *This* Pharaoh, unlike so many others before him, would keep his reclaimed power over their leader.

"By signing this edict . . ." Horemheb's finger jammed again and again into the papyrus on the table. "By signing this, we are condemning the memory of those now gone to Eternal Execration, condemning their memories to the bottom of the Nile, never to be remembered again."

"Yes, Pharaoh," the prophets muttered. A few heads began to shake, but at the glare of Pharaoh, all movement ceased.

I just threatened their leader, Horemheb thought. *They so easily forget.*

Wennefer said, "We discussed this edict. It is what is needed." The other prophets nodded and murmured in agreement.

"And yet you feel no remorse?" Horemheb's eyes were centered on Wennefer, but his words were to all. "I, Pharaoh, have seen your drooling, your dancing feet, your hunger for this everlasting punishment to be pronounced. You, oh great, wise prophets of Amun—*you* desire this . . . but you are no better than those we are about to erase. You do not deserve to be remembered. Your wickedness lives on, but your deeds will be covered."

Horemheb's voice was no more than a whisper, yet strong enough to move mountains, causing Wennefer to shake at the knees and sit back down. They all muttered indecipherable words to explain away their demeanor.

Once again Pharaoh silenced them. "Only because this history undermines the power of Pharaoh—not just in the eyes of our own but also those of our foreign allies and enemies—will I, Pharaoh, sign it."

Mut let out a despairing breath behind him. He forced himself to ignore her.

"But first," he continued, "we will remember those to be denied a place in history. We will know the truth, and we will acknowledge they lived and breathed. They are worthy of much more than this pitiful end. You will remember, and their lives will stay with you until the day you travel to Re. They will weigh heavily on your hearts, and they will haunt your minds even as you journey to the afterlife."

A silence settled in the room, inching its way further inside the bones of those attending there.

"As . . . Pharaoh . . . says." Wennefer clenched his jaw and crossed his arms over his chest. Leaning back, he nodded. "Where shall we begin with this . . . chronicling?"

Looking to the statue of Amun standing behind the prophets, Horemheb drew in a deep breath. Amun had granted him his small victory of power over the priesthood. "We shall begin with Pharaoh Akhenaten and the birth of his beloved . . . Queen Nefertiti," Pharaoh said as he rested back into his chair.

Mut's hand came to his shoulder as if to thank him for starting with her half-sister.

Horemheb felt the guilt in his heart betray him—for he had other motives for starting with Nefertiti. He drew a quick breath.

I am not ready to let Mut know of my love for her. Maybe tomorrow I will have the strength to tell of what happened between us . . . and then Mut will know.

He began to speak, and he told the tale until the day had almost ended.

"Queen Neferneferuaten—our long-past Queen Nefertiti, the most upright of us all—chose not to be a part of their deeds of the dark," Horemheb announced to the five prophets of Amun. They had all leaned forward, eagerly listening to his recounting. *Yet, eventually, she did indeed take part,* he thought, *but for today's telling, she did not.*

"*Your* deeds of the dark." Mut pointed to the First Prophet Wennefer. Her eyes held a rage against the priesthood. Horemheb knew her rage against Pawah—not only for her sister but for herself.

"Not mine," Wennefer said, his arms still crossed over his body, as if to protect himself from his brother-prophets' mistakes.

"*All* of your deeds are done in the dark," Mut hissed, referring to the sins the priesthood had committed against her family. Her eyes turned to Horemheb, begging her husband to continue the recounting, to shed light on the priesthood's greatest transgression, before he cast it out to be forgotten by history and buried by the passage of time.

Wennefer jabbed his finger in the air. "There is no proof!" He knew of which deed she spoke. Hatred lingered in the air between her majesty and the priesthood.

"No proof is needed," Mut forced out between her teeth. "I was there!"

"We are a different hierarchy of prophets, my Queen.

Placing the blame for past events on us is unwise, especially as we move forward to erase—"

"Silence!" Horemheb threw his hand in the air.

The sun sank lower. Servants dashed in to light the oil lamps and alabaster lampstands.

Horemheb leaned back in his throne. His lips were parched, as he had been speaking for the greater of the day. For now, their memories were safe . . . but he had much left to tell before he signed the edict to erase them from their records.

They sat in silence until the sun left them for the night.

Wennefer stood. "We thank Pharaoh for his recounting. However, Pharaoh will now sign the edict."

"There are none greater than Pharaoh. You will not order him to take any action!" Horemheb said, knowing Paramesse needed a few more days to complete the transfer of tombs. "You are so quick to forget, First Prophet. Perhaps Pharaoh should dismiss you and find a replacement, perhaps someone who values the sanctity of the legacy of the kings, and who knows there are none more powerful than Pharaoh."

"My apologies, Lord of the Two Lands." Wennefer bowed and took his seat.

Horemheb rubbed his bottom lip with his finger in thought. *I must stall until I hear from Paramesse that the bodies of the royals are safe . . . that my Nefertiti is safe.*

He spoke aloud. "There shall be no signing of the edict tonight as there is still much left to tell. We will retire for the night and meet again at the first morning light, for the complete legacy of the kings still has yet to be told. Pharaoh will continue the recounting tomorrow."

He stood up, bringing his arms outspread as the prophets also rose. Horemheb took a deep breath and lifted his eyes to the statue of the god behind the prophets. "May Amun be with us all."

The prophets left, and then Horemheb and Mut retired for

the evening. They picked at their meals in silence in the dining hall; they walked to the Queen's bedchambers in silence; they bathed together in silence; they got ready for bed in silence.

Mut finally turned to Horemheb and hit him in the chest. "Why are you smearing my sister's name? Why are you telling of Akhenaten's murder? Don't tell of their transgressions. If you are to erase them, at least give them dignity!"

"We must tell the truth, for their memory to be truly honored before—"

"No!" Mut yelled as the redness in her face grew bright, and her chest pumped like the flutter of a bird's wings. She hit his chest again.

"Mut, I cannot do this right now. Do you know of the burden that rests on my shoulders?"

"But everything? Must you tell *everything*? Must you erase even their names? Must this fall to you?"

"Yes . . . everything." Horemheb clenched his jaw.
Everything.

Mut would soon know the whole truth. He could only deal with one tragedy at a time. If Mut were to leave him because she knew he indeed loved Nefertiti, then he would cope with that another day; but these next days were to focus on telling of the lives they lived so they could remember one last time. To the goddess of truth and balance, Ma'at, he had prayed for wisdom, and in his heart, he knew this was what was needed. The searing pain of the next days would test both his strength as Pharaoh and the love of his chief royal wife.

He glanced at his gold ring on his finger with the blue lapis stone. All this time, he had never taken it off. *Nefertiti, I miss you so. Forgive me.* He looked at the ivory and gold chest and knew at the very bottom lay the last half of Nefertiti's letter to him.

Mut had been speaking, but he had not been listening. He came out of his thoughts as Mut pushed him away, tears streaming down her face. "Why, Horemheb? *Why?*"

He grasped her hands. "You know why, my sweet one." He cupped her cheek with his hand. "You know why."

She buried her head in his chest and wept. "But . . . my family . . . their names stripped bare and erased . . ." She cried between breaths.

Horemheb rubbed her back and squeezed her as close as her pregnant belly would allow them. "At the end of this life, we will stand before Ma'at and Ammit, our hearts weighed. It is no different than what I do by retelling the past. All of our deeds, both wrong and right, will be uncovered for one last time. Those who champion the edict will know exactly what they are erasing. The lives of those we erase will be on all of our consciences. We shall always remember what we have done. *That* is why I must tell everything."

Mut cried again, "But why Eternal Execration, Horemheb? They have done no wrong!"

"I know," Horemheb said, closing his eyes to hold back his own tears. He knew exactly of whom she spoke, but he had to be strong for his wife, for himself. "But if we do not erase them all, the people will remember Akhenaten. All of our loved ones were related to him—if one is remembered, then Akhenaten will be remembered. For who is Tutankhamun without Akhenaten? Who is Nefertiti without Akhenaten?"

"My sister," Mut said through her tears. "Nefertiti is *my sister.*"

And my first love, he added in thought.

Horemheb picked Mut up, swinging his arm under her legs and sweeping her off her feet. He walked with her in his arms as she buried her head in his shoulder, still sobbing.

"You will see the pain it causes me too soon enough," Horemheb whispered to her as he laid her in their bed, his heart breaking, with each step, even more than it already had.

"You will see why I do not want to do this, either. And I hope, in time, you will see why it needs to be done."

He kissed her forehead.

"Now it is late. Let us sleep."

She shook her head. "I will not be able to sleep."

He came and laid down next to her. "Neither will I."

But after a while, Mut's puffy eyes slowly began to close; despite her words she drifted to a restless sleep. Horemheb watched her as he ran his fingers lightly down her arm.

"I love you, my sweet Mut," he whispered.

She only hummed in response.

"I don't want to lose you . . ."

He dreaded the next day, for he would have to tell Mut all that had happened between him and Nefertiti. He wrestled with the temptation not to tell but reasoned he would be a cursed man if he did not, potentially having his heart devoured by Ammit on the scales of Ma'at. The secrets he held bore down on him, and part of him wished they could be known so he would not have to carry their burden any longer. But at that thought, guilt crept over his body. He said a prayer to the goddess Bastet that Mut would understand. His heart could not lose both Nefertiti and Mut, for he did love them both: the first by an utter connection of souls, and the second through a learned love, but a deep love nonetheless.

☙ 17 ❧
THE TIME OF THE SECOND
REMEMBERING

THE SUNRISE CAUGHT THE GLINT OF HOREMHEB'S STARE INTO THE empty room. His royal guards stood at attention behind his throne. The statue of their great god, Amun-Re, towered above the five vacant seats in front of him. He lowered his elbow to rest on his knee, cradled his head in his hand, and peered through his fingers.

There is so much left to tell, he thought.

His mind filled with images from the previous tumultuous night. The screams and tears of his precious wife, his sweet Mut and the beating she gave his chest, begging him not to condemn her family to erasure, raced through his recent memory.

The morning's grain-rich breakfast rolled in his belly as he sat on his throne. As he had commanded the day before, the five prophets of Amun gathered in their seats at the morning's first light. They looked well-rested, eagerly awaiting any mistake he might make.

I was there, he told himself. *I remember. They will remember as well. I am Pharaoh. There are none greater.*

Mut entered from the shadowed doorway behind him and took her place behind his throne. Her eyes and cheeks sat puffed and inflamed. Silence lingered in the hall as Horemheb straightened his back and brought his hand to his side, revealing his eyes. The early-morning sun kissed the feet of the great god Amun-Re, the rest of his stone-gold body still cast in shadow.

So much blood spilled for you. So much sacrifice to keep you as the premier god of Egypt.

He took a deep breath and closed his eyes to gather his thoughts. He clenched his jaw, wishing Pharaoh Akhenaten had never assumed the throne. Had his brother, the Crown Prince Thutmose, lived, history would not have to be erased. They could have declared the Aten as the premier god, restored the power stolen by the Amun priesthood to the position of Pharaoh, and returned Egypt back to Amun, all within a few years, and have been done with it.

But no . . . Pharaoh Akhenaten had to spend seventeen years tearing apart Egypt, disassembling its economy and faith, lost in his obsessions to the sun, the Aten disc. He brought his murder upon himself, and now condemned his entire family to eternal erasure.

He forces me to purge our records. Curse him! By my hand, the people will forget them.

He squeezed his eyes, and his brow furrowed. He took a deep breath amid a tight chest and continued to think.

But it is necessary. The people cannot remember what he did, what Pawah did, what I did. For the sake of the future of Egypt and Amun's divinely appointed Pharaohs, I do this—I do it so there is no weakness in the people's judgment.

He opened his eyes, noticing the ache in his jaw from gritting his teeth while he thought. The prophets began to fidget in their seats, uncomfortable with Pharaoh's silence, until the sun uncovered the knees of Amun. Finally, Wennefer stood and spoke.

"Great King of Egypt, we have all gathered to hear what is to be erased. Will Pharaoh continue from yesterday's

LAUREN LEE MEREWETHER

recounting of Pharaoh Akhenaten and his Queen Neferneferuaten-Nefertiti?"

Nefertiti, he thought, taking another deep breath, *the one who sacrificed everything for Egypt and Amun.* He swallowed the growing lump in his throat, his heart breaking for her and what she had gone through—bringing Pharaoh poisoned wine on the threat of rebellion.

Duty and love for country made Horemheb speak against the will of self:

"Pharaoh shall now speak."

He took one final calming breath.

"Sit down, First Prophet, and all shall hear Pharaoh's words as we begin with the People's Restoration of Egypt and their threat of rebellion if Pharaoh Akhenaten were not removed from the throne."

He told of Pawah, he told of Nefertiti, he told of Ay, and he told of himself. Mut was silent throughout it all until, when Horemheb told of his son within Nefertiti's womb, he heard a gasp of pain. He lowered his head—it was all told now; there was nothing else left to hide. He could only pray Mut could understand and not abandon him like he had Amenia. He pushed past the memory, the agony of remembering, and began the story of the Crown Prince, the boy King.

He stopped the tale when he and Tut had left for the northern border shortly after his coronation, for he could not go on. He could only suffer one former heartbreak at a time. Staring at Amun, he wished death had come to him instead and that the gods had allowed Nefertiti and Tut to continue in this life. He wished Mut, a husband who could have loved her as he had loved Nefertiti. After such a day of retelling, emptiness filled the shell that was his body. Pain made way to numbness. He wanted nothing more than to lie down, to do nothing but blink and breathe.

Silence reigned in the council room. The sun had already begun to dip behind the great horizon. Servants attempted invisibility as they lit the torches in the room.

A weight dropped in Mut's stomach; she had not realized Horemheb had fathered a child with her half-sister. He had told her he loved Nefertiti as a Pharaoh . . . but never to this extent. She had assumed it was nothing more than admiration, as he had said; she'd never had reason to suspect otherwise. Mut looked at her own growing belly and peered over at him. Was she only a replacement for Nefertiti, a cheap copy of her half-sister?

Will I always live in her shadow? she wondered. *I cannot even have an original love. It must always follow Nefertiti.*

Wennefer stood. "My Pharaoh and his Queen: we, the Amun priesthood, do not agree with what the former Prophet of Amun, Pawah, did, nor with what the people demanded, nor with what Pharaohs Akhenaten and Smenkare believed. So, as we all are in agreement"—Wennefer looked around to make sure his fellow prophets' heads were nodding with him —"we all know very well what happened to the two Pharaohs after Pharaoh Neferneferuaten. Perhaps now, before the sun sets on this second day, Pharaoh can sign the edict."

Horemheb looked around at those in the room. "The First Prophet shall sit until Pharaoh dismisses him—only then, shall he stand." Horemheb eyed Wennefer until he dipped his head and sat down. Then, Horemheb continued. "Pharaoh shall not sign the edict. All of the Pharaohs deserve their account to be retold for the last time. We will honor them before we rid them of our historical records."

"My King—" Wennefer began.

Horemheb held his hand out to silence him. "None are greater than Pharaoh."

Wennefer bit his tongue and took a deep breath; the other prophets did the same.

Horemheb continued, "We shall continue the recounting at first light." A few grumblings made their way to Horemheb's ears. "Honor the slain," he commanded. The grumblings ceased. "Remember their legacy before we rid them from our children's memory." The two guards behind him stepped forward as he raised his voice. "First light." He pointed a finger in the air.

Mut stood behind him. Her feet ached from standing all day, but such was her place as her husband spoke of the family who would never be remembered. Silence came from the priesthood, so she spoke. "Your Pharaoh has commanded first light. Or do you speak treason against Amun's true First Prophet, his divinely appointed King?"

"No." Wennefer nodded in reverence to the position of Pharaoh, but he spoke through clenched teeth. "There are none greater than Pharaoh."

"Then we shall resume at first light," she said, her back straight and her hands to her sides.

They agreed and left for the temple.

Horemheb turned to Mut after their exit. His eyes held her pain. She had tried in the days before, pleaded with him for another way, begged him on her knees, but there was nothing else he could do. He closed his eyes and dropped his head. She put a hand on his shoulder. He looked up to find tears streaming down her face. She wasn't sure if they were tears of uncertainty—not knowing if he loved her as a replacement for her half-sister—or tears upon seeing his own pain. Part of her heart bore his sorrow in losing the woman he loved; the other part, however, wanted nothing more than to hit him across the face for keeping this from her. Every muscle drew tight in tension as she pushed her anger away, for the guards stood there. And in her own mind, to resolve her pleading from the night before, she accepted that there was no other way to restore the divine power to Pharaoh. She couldn't ask her questions in front of anyone, lest it be seen as an undermining of his throne, so instead, she only spoke in a low voice.

"I know why you must do this, Horemheb. I see the way they question you. The future people of Egypt can't know about this period of time, or else Pharaoh will always be questioned," she said as she wiped her eyes and her nose, realizing now, after all these years, why her sister did the things she did—she loved Egypt more than all else. "But it doesn't take away the pain."

"Be strong, Mut," he said as he cupped her cheek with his hand. "You are courageous. It is why I fell in love with you."

Nuzzling her nose into his palm, she breathed a sigh of relief at his reaffirmation that his love for her was not a replacement; and yet, as her gaze focused on the gold-and-blue lapis ring upon his pinky finger that she now knew was Nefertiti's, she wondered further. "I am trying."

He brought her into his chest and kissed her forehead.

"May Amun be with us," Horemheb whispered to her.

Mut looked up to her husband with a wary eye. "May Amun give us strength."

The words came as if from an old memory of her illegal studies with her mother when Pharaoh Akhenaten and Smenkare sat on the throne. Horemheb's faith had rekindled her own over the past years . . . but after so much pain, after learning the truth, it seemed her faith was failing her again. She found the eyes of Amun staring back at her as she looked past her husband, and then his face came back into focus. This man, so full of faith—so powerful and so righteous, she'd thought—had lied to her . . . had he not?

Her mouth contorted into a grimace as he dismissed the guards to stand in the hall as if anticipating her backlash. At the close of the door, he kissed her. Her mouth stayed closed, and her back stood straight.

"Mut," he whispered and pressed his forehead to hers. "I know you have so many questions. I—"

"Why did you keep the truth from me—for all these years?" Mut's breath hitched as the words flowed in a whisper.

Horemheb's eyes bore into hers, his brow furrowed, as if trying to formulate the right words to say to her. She shook her head as her eyes filled with tears. She pulled his hand toward her so that she could look at Nefertiti's ring upon his finger. She bit her bottom lip as the tears finally broke the barrier of her eyes.

"Do you even love me?"

"Yes, Mut." He squeezed her hand. "I love you."

"Then why?" She took a step back.

"Please," he begged, and took a step with her, clutching her as if he could not let her go.

"Why?" She leaned away from him.

"I told you I married you because Nefertiti asked me to. I told you I did not love you when I married you—"

"I thought you truthful." She shook her head. "But you manipulated me! You tricked me into loving you. I will never compare to Nefertiti in your eyes. How can I compare to Pharaoh, the woman revered by all as the most beautiful woman in all of Egypt?! How can I compare to the woman who would have given you your . . ." Her breath hitched as she remembered her own unborn child. " . . . your firstborn *son*? How can I compare with the woman who told you, as her dying words, 'You made me feel alive'? How can I *compare*?!" She pushed him away. "I cannot and will never compare! Do not lie to me more! Tell me the words that I speak are not true." She stifled her tears for a moment and lifted her chin to her husband, to brace herself for the truth—or his lie.

He let out a breath and lowered his head. "I love you, my sweet one." His eyes filled with tears as he found her gaze again. "And so I will tell you the truth. In the beginning, I compared you in every way to Nefertiti."

Her lips trembled as she felt her chest collapse, yet she stood tall.

"I miss Nefertiti every night and every day. I still hear her laugh in my memory." He stopped and swallowed as his own tears fell. "But I fell in love with you, Mut, because of you. There was no comparison in that regard, not then or any day since. I love both of you in my own way."

"You lie!"

Her arms held a slight tremble as she tried to hold her thoughts at bay, but to no avail:

I have never not been compared to Nefertiti. That is nothing new under the sun. He lies to me yet again!

She turned and left him in his council room as the thoughts barraged her mind.

He is lying! He is a liar. He lied to me then. Why would he not lie to me now?! To keep his oath to Nefertiti fulfilled!

The ache in her feet screamed at her as she hurried to her apartment. Air could not come quickly enough to her lungs as she closed the doors behind her. Her shallow breaths caused the room to spin as she threw herself on the bed, mindful of her unborn baby. She curled on her side and wept.

I thought I had found love. I thought he loved me. I thought I was happy. I thought he was a good man. But he is dishonorable. He did the same to Amenia. Why would I think I would be any different?! You fool! You ignorant child! Infatuated with a monster —a monster who will erase the woman he claimed to love. Amun forbid, he should have to erase me!

She rammed her arm across her face, wiping her tears.

Amun, if you are there, take me. I do not wish to live with these lies anymore. I have no one left who cares for me. I would have been better off to have had Pawah's dagger slice my throat. This child in my womb is a lie. He will be born into a false marriage. Spare him! Spare him like you did my firstborn!

"Do you hear me?!" she yelled at the pinnacle of her rushing thoughts.

"Yes."

Horemheb's deep voice caught her off guard, and she screamed in her temporary fright. She sat up and calmed her breathing. Her eyes narrowed at the man who'd lied to her all these years.

"Leave me, *Pharaoh*."

Horemheb only stood, his jaw visibly clenched. After a few moments, he came and sat next to her. "What I said was the truth, Mut." He rubbed her hand, but she yanked it away.

Liar.

"I told you, when you found the truth for the basis of our marriage, that if you wanted to leave me, I would pay for whatever you needed. I kept this from you because I thought you wouldn't believe me. I prayed to Ma'at. I prayed to Bastet. I prayed to Amun." He stopped and nodded. "All that I wouldn't lose you."

Liar.

"I give you the same option now. If you want to leave me, I will ensure you are taken care of for all of your days." He found her eyes. His eyes held her sorrow once again. "But you will leave me a broken man, for you truly have my love."

He is just manipulating me, she reminded herself, *like he has always done.* But the sorrow in his eyes never wavered, and that eyebrow never moved. *Maybe he is telling me the truth. Maybe he is lying. Maybe he told me about his tell, so I would believe him, so I wouldn't leave, so he needn't break his promise to my sister.*

She finally responded, "Leave me . . . tonight."

Horemheb dropped his head. "As you wish, my sweet Mut," he whispered and stood to go.

She watched him go halfway to the door until her heart could take no more.

"What made you love her so?" she called to him. He

stopped and turned to her as she crawled out of bed and came to stand before him. Her questions came in one long slur through her clenched teeth. "How long were you in love with her? Was there more than what you said to the prophets? You say you do not compare. But what makes you love *me*? Would you have ever married me if Nefertiti had lived? Would you have ever even spoken my name again if Nefertiti had lived? I thought *I* bore your firstborn son. You took that away from me. *She* took that away from me! Do you love me as you did Nefertiti? Can you even love me as *your* Nefertiti? Will you—"

Horemheb only took a deep breath and put his hands on the sides of her arms to silence her. "I know you have many questions. But if you do not believe me when I tell you 'I love you,' then I can never truly answer your questions. Right now, I need time to think about the days ahead. I hope you can come to believe me, for I cannot see my life without you." He dropped his hands and left the room to Pharaoh's bedchambers.

Mut whispered as the doors closed:

"You cannot answer me because you do not love me."

18

THE TIME OF THE THIRD
REMEMBERING

THE NIGHT HELD A TUMULTUOUS FIGHT AGAINST SLEEP, HER MIND racing, until finally, she thought it in vain to try to sleep. Tener and Raia came to her per her command to ready her for the day. The door to the council room was open, and she saw in the alabaster torchlight Horemheb already on his throne.

He must not have slept either. Does he not sleep for me . . . or for Nefertiti? Does it even matter? Yes, it does matter. No, it does not.

The one question she must ask if she were to believe him still lingered in her mind as she watched him stare into the empty room. It finally found the courage to escape her lips:

"Did you love her more than me?"

Mut fixed her gaze upon her husband, seated on his throne and staring at the five empty seats before him. She pinched the skin between her thumb and forefinger as she rested a hand on her pregnant belly.

The sun had not yet risen; its preceding glory fell through the columns of the council room at Malkata. They waited for the five prophets of Amun to enter before the morning light, as ordered the day before.

Horemheb dropped his chin for a second at the strain in her voice. The answer he gave the night before rang true through his heart: *I love you each in my own way.* He had already answered her the night before, but she'd refused to listen. So, he gave her the answer she wanted—*needed*—to hear.

"No, my sweet Mut. I love you more than her."

He glanced up and saw her chewing her lip. His mouth grew a pensive smile as he stood and drew her into his chest. Smoothing the strands of her golden-laced wig with one hand and rubbing her back with the other, his memory of his Nefertiti caused a deep ache in his throat as he pressed his lips to Mut's.

At the kiss's end, he placed his hands on her belly. Even though he was twenty years her senior, he did love Mut. He loved her because Nefertiti had asked him to take care of her when she left this life, but also because he had found admiration in Mut's eyes and a warmth in her heart.

"You carry my child. You are the only woman who warms my bed at night. I will take care of you and provide all that you could ever ask or need," he told her as he ran his fingers down the side of her cheek.

She smiled a half smile, but her eyes averted to her half-sister's gold-and-blue lapis ring on his finger. "Though, you still wish for Nefertiti, do you not?" Mut asked, her voice soft.

He remembered the prior night—he'd left her questions about him and Nefertiti unanswered. He had only asked for silence, saying he needed to think about the hard days ahead because she already held a perceived truth in her heart and wouldn't believe anything he said.

A mistake to stay silent, perhaps . . . but maybe not? She had at least come to the third day's retelling. Some part of what he had said must have resonated with her; otherwise, she would not be here, asking these questions.

Horemheb rubbed her arms. "Nefertiti is gone." His voice cut through the air between them and contradicted the softness of his touch. "She will never be remembered after I sign this edict. After we are gone to be with Re, no one will ever speak her name again—" A lump formed in his throat, and his words were forced mute at the realization of her true eternal death among the living.

"Don't press me further, Mut, please, my wife."

Mut seemed to shrink as her spine and shoulders slumped.

Horemheb opened his mouth to speak as he tried to rub her arm, but she pulled away and the door to the room opened, jarring their moment together. Horemheb dropped his hands and took his seat on his throne as his gaze lingered upon his wife. *I am sorry,* he wished he could say, but not now, not as the five prophets of Amun gathered to their seats for the day.

He pulled his stare from his wife to the prophets as he stalled, hoping another idea could come to him before he signed that cursed edict. The weight of the past and the weight of the future burdened his shoulders. He clamped his jaw shut, knowing the more he spoke the story of those to be erased, the closer their condemnation would ensue.

He looked at the face of Amun for the second time that morning.

He asks for much.

He took a deep breath and closed his eyes to gather his thoughts. To seal Pharaoh's power over the priesthood, he had to blot out their names:

Pharaoh Akhenaten, who in his own madness worshipped the Aten far longer and with much more zeal than planned . . .

His brother, Pharaoh Smenkare, who fell into his trap of false faith and murdered his own people for their faith in Amun . . .

The one he loved, the mother of his unborn son, Pharaoh Neferneferuaten—his Nefertiti—murdered by Pawah, the former vizier and Fifth Prophet of Amun, in his struggle for the throne . . .

And, finally, Pharaoh Tutankhamun . . . Tut. *My son.*

He remembered each of their faces, lingering the longest on his Nefertiti and his Tut. A tightness overcame his chest.

Forgive me.

He opened his eyes and looked again at the face of Amun. The people could not be allowed to remember what Akhenaten and Smenkare did, and in so doing, could not be allowed to remember those who encompassed the two cursed Pharaohs. There mustn't be weakness from Pharaoh in the people's eyes. He pleaded with the god, *Is there another way? Please give me wisdom to see before I sign this edict!*

Amun only stood tall in his stone image.

A touch on his shoulder alerted Horemheb to Mut, eyes wide and glistening. She pushed out a whisper, saying, "Be strong, Pharaoh."

His brow furrowed in appreciation of her gesture, knowing those words meant more than their sum. He thanked Amun for granting him an understanding wife—a wife to whom he had been unfair. He took a cleansing breath, grasped her hand, and brought her fingers to his lips, never losing eye contact with her.

"My sweet Mut," he whispered, and kissed her hand, this time, not caring what the prophets saw. "What would I ever do without you?"

Her smile did not reach her eyes. However, Horemheb knew the prophets sat waiting for him, on this third day, and so he would need to wait to comfort Mut. He patted her hand, and she pulled it back to her side. He turned to address those prophets who sat with unamused faces.

"Today"—Horemheb felt a sharp pain in his chest as he spoke, his eyes surveying each of the five men—"we shall recount the life of the boy King, Tutankhamun, firstborn son of Pharaoh Akhenaten." He stopped and closed his eyes one final time; simply speaking the young boy's name drew a painful tug on his soul. His voice wavered, knowing the time drew ever nearer that he would be their executioner.

"Be still and hear his tale . . ."

He opened his eyes to the day ahead.

". . . before we remember no more."

He told of Pawah's doings: the never-ending doubt Pawah placed upon the young Pharaoh, the wedge Pawah drove between Pharaoh and his one true love, Ankhesenamun, Pawah's murder of Tut's daughters, and Pawah's conspiracy and acts against the throne. He told of his own deeds—not to gather pity but for the cleansing of his soul. He told of his marriage, and his abandonment of his new wife, Mut. He told of Pawah's attempted murder of Pharaoh and himself. He told of the plan to allow Ay to become Pharaoh. And he told of Tut's last words:

Remember me, my father.

Horemheb fell mute after his retelling, and silence overcame the room.

His eyes welled with tears as he remembered all that had been lost and would be remembered no more: his love, his Nefertiti; his unborn son he had never known; the man he called his son, Tutankhamun; Ankhesenamun and Ay.

They would all be lost to time.

Their names never uttered again.

A true eternal death.

His gaze fell to the feet of Amun's statue.

Forgive me.

"Pharaoh," Wennefer spoke, "will you continue into the night, or shall we reconvene tomorrow?" He tapped his finger on his knee. Wennefer shook his head, as if disapproving of how many more days this Pharaoh would draw out a story soon to be forgotten.

Horemheb knew they all grew increasingly frustrated

with these days of retelling. But he ignored this as he lifted his chin once again.

"Pharaoh Ay did what he thought was best—" His voice cracked. "But we shall speak of it tomorrow." He licked his lips and let out a heavy breath, holding his tears at bay. Clamping his jaw shut, he peered at his wife.

The sun dipped low over the horizon, its shadow cast throughout most of the room. The five prophets of Amun sat with slouched backs, tiring of his tales as their feet waited in eagerness to go destroy the past.

Horemheb looked to the papyrus edict in front of him and the sloshed ink in the well. His eyes darted between the reed brush and the place for his cartouche and seal on the edict.

One more day, he thought. *One more day . . . and then I will be able to say goodbye.*

His teeth gritted together as his jaw clenched tighter.

I only lie to myself. I have already said goodbye, and yet I cannot bring myself to say goodbye again. I will spend the rest of my life saying goodbye.

He forced out: "We shall meet at first light."

Horemheb's words hung heavy in the air, and his chest drew stiff. He knew he could not go on to a fifth day, as there was no more story to tell after tomorrow. His stalling was becoming evident, and he knew he would have to sign the edict at tomorrow's sunset and hope Paramesse had finished the transfer before then. Numbness overtook his fingers and toes as a chill in the air enveloped his body and pulled the corners of his contorted mouth downward. The words of his love, his Nefertiti, came back to him in the moment.

Will I ever just have love?

He had responded: *You have my love.*

But he realized now that she meant *peace*, not love. She wanted peace in this life. Now he understood her unfulfilled desire, for after tomorrow, he would never have peace again, knowing he had erased their memory.

For Egypt, he thought, and then: *Egypt takes much. How much more will Egypt take from me?*

He looked at Mut and his unborn child, and took a long breath as the prophets exited the room. Mut walked to face him and put her hands on his shoulders as he stood. He leaned his forehead to hers.

"I am sorry, Mut, my Queen. This . . . this weighs so heavy on me. I have fought many battles. I have won many wars. But this . . . *this* . . ." He closed his eyes as his ribs constricted around his lungs.

"I know," she whispered at his silence. She stroked his cheek. Tears pooled in her eyes as well.

In that moment, seeing her still standing by him, he realized how deep his love for Mut truly was. She comforted him even though she doubted his love for her. Despite the half-truths he had told her, even as she took the truths as lies, she still stood there with him in his pain.

He did not deserve her.

"But may Amun be with us and give us strength," she said.

He shook his head as the next words flowed on his breath:

"No. May Amun grant *peace*."

MUT DISMISSED THE GUARDS ONCE AGAIN; THEY SHOULD NOT BE there to witness her husband's pain. Her heart broke for him. Both a woman and two sons—one of his own blood, the other a beloved adoption—he had to erase. She didn't bother to wipe his tears; they needed to fall. He pressed his forehead to her shoulder and wrapped her in his arms. No sound came from him as his silent tears fell on her golden collar.

Questions came to the tip of her tongue. How had she not known any of this? The man she held in her arms was a strong military general, Pharaoh, tall, with a physique to match his warrior reputation, and yet . . . he held so much pain and love inside. Her mind drifted back to what he told her the day before. Was it true? Dare she believe him? Did he truly love her . . . for her?

His arms squeezed around her even more, and she felt his tear-drenched kiss on her neck. *Does he care for me? And if so, does he only care for me because Nefertiti asked him to?*

"Thank you for standing beside me," he whispered, his hot breath in her ear. He pressed his cheek to hers and then placed a soft kiss on her temple.

Mut stood rigid. He had lied to her, though. She knew that much. When she asked him if he loved her sister right after she had escaped Pawah, as they traveled back to Men-nefer, he had said he only admired her . . . that he only loved her as Pharaoh. Yes, she remembered. It wasn't that he had just withheld the truth—he had *lied* to her.

"I have lost a son, too," she responded. "I know the pain. I am not strong enough to erase his name, however. You are a strong king. I hope your strength takes you far in your rule over Egypt." Her eyes, now dry, contrasted his. "Goodnight, Pharaoh. May Amun grant you peace."

She left to her apartment and only once the guard opened the door did she realize Horemheb had followed her. Lowering her head, she took a breath. He would not stay in her bed tonight, she told herself. Horemheb closed the door behind him as Mut turned around to face him in the privacy of the bedchambers.

"I don't want you here," her venomous whisper hit his back.

She saw his back muscles tense and then relax. He peered over his shoulder and then turned to face her.

"I want you to leave."

He took a step toward her.

"You will not manipulate me anymore. Not with your

body, not with your words, not with your false affections!" Mut took a step back and sliced her arm through the air.

Horemheb stopped in his advance, his lips trembling. "If that is what you *truly* believe, then I have failed you as your husband." He grimaced. "I am sorry, Mut. I promised you I would spend the rest of my life making sure you felt safe, never leaving your side, and loving you unconditionally." Horemheb's gaze fell to the floor.

"You lie to me like you always have." Mut's jaw tightened. "I will stand by your side as your Queen. I will comfort you these next days as you erase my family, because I know it is what is needed for Egypt. I see your pain." Her ribs constricted as their baby kicked her in the stomach. "I see your pain," she repeated, trying to keep herself composed. "But after this, I want nothing more to do with you."

A new glisten built behind his eyes. "At least I come to you stripped bare. I have nothing more to hide." He opened his arms to her. "You know all now. I have told you every truth, and I hope one day"—his breath caught—"you realize it as such." He pressed his lips so that they made a straight line and curled his fingers so that they made fists. He took a step back and lowered his hands to his sides. "I will keep my promise to you. I will fight for us . . . even if your forgiveness never comes."

She tried to hide the tremble in her own lips as she remembered warning him when he first made his promise, warning him that her forgiveness may never come. This time she was no longer sure he was lying. Wasn't she? Would he say these things if he were lying now? Or was this just another ploy to appease her sister's last wish? There was no way to tell. She would never know.

He left her in her bedchambers, and then she realized she was rubbing his gift to her, the bracelets that covered the horrid scars of her wrists, courtesies of Pawah. Her body shook as she remembered the months of horror she spent with him. She frantically looked around the empty room.

"Horemheb! Wait!" she called, out of sheer fear, if nothing else.

The door opened. Part of her leaped for joy that he had not truly left and hoped she would change her mind; part of her wondered if he had known she would call for him. He stepped to her and wrapped his arms around her.

"Why are you shaking so?" he whispered.

"I . . ." Mut stopped and calmed her breathing. "It's nothing for you to know." She pulled from his arms, realized her subconscious rubbing of the bracelet, and stopped.

His gaze fell to her wrists, and then he unsheathed a dagger from his belt. He walked the entire bed and bath chambers, checking behind every reed curtain, every door, and then came back to her.

She watched him, and part of her thanked whichever god would listen to her after her near dismissal of them. The same debate went on in her mind, however, as he approached her:

Is he only doing these things to trick me so he could keep his promise to his Nefertiti?

"Your room is empty." He bowed his head to her.

She licked her lip. Maybe this one night, he could stay, just in case someone wanted to hurt her. She had not even thought of it the night before, but tonight . . . tonight, the cuffs had enslaved her to her fears once again.

"Mut," he whispered. "Please do not send me away again. I could not bear it a second time."

That was when she realized: He was Pharaoh. He could have any woman he wanted. He could have stayed against her wishes the night prior. He could have said no just now. He could have done many things. He could have forced her to do many things. But he didn't.

I'm still mad at him, but maybe he does care for me? Maybe. Time will tell. I hope, at least.

She finally nodded.

A small smile came to his lips.

"No," she said, shaking her head at his smile. "This does not mean anything. I want you here because I do not want to be alone."

She realized the irony in her statement. She was using him, but he had used her for all these years, and that fact in her mind soothed her conscience.

"For you, anything." Horemheb's smile vanished. "Would you like me to stand watch at your door?"

Mut shook her head, unable to speak.

Why would he demote himself to that of a guard for me? Chance someone seeing Pharaoh standing guard at his chief royal wife's door? Is he trying to win back my loyalty? For me, or for my sister? Goddess Ma'at! If you are there, if you live, let me see the truth, and if he lies, goddess Seret, bring swift justice to him!

The pain in her feet broke her prayers, and she walked past Horemheb and went to lie down, her back to him. The soft wool mattress tucked densely in the fine linen sheet felt so good and so cool against her skin. She didn't even want to use the headrest; her cheek just wanted to be on the cool linen sheet.

The *click* of his dagger in its sheath echoed through the empty room, and then came the familiar sound of him placing his weaponry on the table beside the bed. She felt the space beside her sink a little as he lay down, and she heard him take a deep breath. He placed a hand on her back between her shoulder blades.

"I will always love you, Mut."

He did not try to kiss her, and she was thankful. He'd respect her body until he knew she believed him, if their past path to intimacy held any insight. She stayed her tongue, and the warmth from his hand left her.

Do I believe him? That doesn't matter. What matters is if he tells the truth. Does he tell me the truth? I cannot tell.

THE TIME OF THE FOURTH REMEMBERING

A SWARMING WAVE OF NAUSEA OVERCAME HOREMHEB'S STOMACH the next morning, for it was the last day of retelling. He wanted to comfort Mut, but these days drained him. He wasn't sure how she would believe him, but at least now she had seen his love and wouldn't forsake it immediately as she would have four years ago—or so he hoped. Sleep eluded him again as he lay awake before the sun even began its ascent. Mut lay next to him, also awake.

"We shall not remember them after this day," he whispered.

"My father, my mother, my friend," Mut whispered, and then, finally: "my sister."

"My son." Horemheb remembered his final adoption of Pharaoh Tutankhamun in his last moments. *My love.* He mouthed those last, remembering Nefertiti's warmth against his but not wanting Mut to hear. He rolled to his wife and stroked her side. "I dread today, and I shall dread tomorrow."

"As do I," she whispered, but kept her back to him.

"I hold their lives in my hands once again, and I fail them . . . again." A grimace accompanied his cracking voice.

Mut sat up and patted his hand. "It seems you fail everyone in your life." Her hand withdrew as quick as the asp's bite.

Horemheb drew a quick inhale from the sting, but after a few moments realized it was the very reason why he hated to look at himself in the mirror all of these years. "It seems I have." His voice fell low.

She looked away from him and placed her legs out of the bed and then continued to sit on the edge, as if contemplating what to do next.

He'd lost Mut as of now, but it didn't mean she wouldn't come back to him one day . . . he hoped. He went to her side and, despite the stiff ache in his long-past-injured knee, knelt in front of her. She tried to stand and push him away, but he grabbed her arms and kept her still. The oil lamp had almost died out but gave enough light to reflect in her eyes and give a soft glow to the highlights of her face. She pulled away, and his hands slid to her knees. Her gaze fell to Nefertiti's gold-and-blue lapis ring on his pinky finger and then returned to him.

He pleaded with his eyes for no more questions—at least not today. He could only deal with so much heartache. "I love you, Mut. I am sorry I have lied to you, and I have failed you and your family." He moved his hands to rub her arms. "I have no greater pain than this."

Mut pushed him away. "I wish I could believe you."

"Mut, you carry my child! I *love* you." He cupped her face and then her shoulders. "I am here. I have kept every promise I made to you since we began again. I don't know what else to say."

"You kept *every* promise?!" Mut's breathing labored.

"Yes." Horemheb kept his voice firm but soft. He didn't want the stress from the prior days to further damage his relationship with his wife.

"You took me in bed when you did not love me." Her words cut through her teeth. "When you loved my sister!"

"No! Only when I realized I *did* love you and not a moment before. I waited several—"

"Oh, *you* waited?!"

"—to be sure I loved you." Horemheb took a deep breath.

Mut tried to stand, but the weight of her belly and the proximity of Horemheb made it difficult, so she stayed seated.

In Mut's silence, Horemheb continued. "It would not be fair to you if I had not. Is that not why you said you admired me? Because I waited?"

Her silence gave him some relief, and then a question he wished she would not have asked fell into the space between them:

"And you did not think of Nefertiti at all?"

"No." It was a lie. He *had* thought of Nefertiti. But at each instance, he had pushed her from his mind. He was with the living; he loved Mut. Mut was his wife. *A good man loves his wife.*

She huffed. "You are a liar."

"I kept my promises to you, and I intend to keep them until my last breath, whether you believe me or not." Horemheb stood and offered a hand to help her stand.

But she refused him; she stood by herself and pulled her shoulders back. "You cannot simply forget someone you loved."

She pushed his chest to move him out of her way to the bath chamber. A few steps in, she stopped and said, "Who knew the General-turned-Pharaoh could be so coy of tongue? To what ends will you go, Horemheb, in order to trick the little naïve child into loving you just so that you may appease a dead woman's last wish? That is why you try to trick me, yes? Only now, I am older and wiser." She turned and pointed a finger at him. "I don't want anything more to do with you."

His breath caught in his throat as he watched the glimmer of her lamp lit shadow enter and disappear into the bath chamber.

"No," he whispered—to himself only, as Mut could no longer hear him. "Maybe in the beginning, but not now. Most assuredly, not now."

He sent for Raia and Tener so she could bathe. He left to the king's apartment to bathe as well.

A messenger found him and bowed as he walked the Malkata corridor. "I bring a report from Vizier Paramesse."

Horemheb stopped to hear the messenger's words. "What does he say?"

"He says 'It is done.' "

Silence befell the torchlit hall as Horemheb's heart stopped.

"Pharaoh, is there something you wish to say in return?"

"No." The word crept out of his dry mouth.

The messenger bowed and left before Horemheb could dismiss him.

He blew a burst of air from his lips. "This is why history must be changed: even the messengers do not respect Pharaoh," he muttered under his breath.

Once inside his bedchambers, the servant heated the water for his shower as he undressed.

There is no more need to stall.

He placed his royal shendyt on the large chest and leaned against it, drawing his head to his hands.

"Pharaoh's shower is ready." The servant's voice came meekly to draw him from his thoughts.

He stepped under the trough, and the servant began dumping the buckets of water over Horemheb's head.

"You can't simply forget someone you love," he repeated as the lukewarm water ran down his back.

But Egypt will forget. They will never remember her . . . them.

He closed his eyes and steadied his breathing. "I miss you, Nefertiti. Do I wish you here? Yes, but you are not." He barely mouthed the words so that the servant would not hear him. "But if your ka still roams this palace, be with your sister. Comfort her, as she will not let me. Make her see the truth."

He balled his hands into fists against the stone wall.

"The *truth*," he whispered and thought of the retelling. He had told all; he had spoken every truth he had known. The weight of what he would have to do that evening pressed against him. "Forgive me, my love."

He shaved, oiled his face and body, and applied his own kohl and scent, after dismissing the servants. He dressed in silence, his mind numb as he tied his royal shendyt.

TIME SEEMED TO STOP AS HE SAT IN HIS THRONE WAITING FOR THE first day's light.

Mut entered before the five prophets of Amun and took her place by his side. Lotus blossoms covered her freshly bathed body in their perfume, and he closed his eyes and dipped his head as his mind struggled to separate Nefertiti from her sister.

"Thank you for coming this last day," he whispered, peering at Mut. Horemheb gestured for his guards to stand outside the council room.

"I told Pharaoh I would stand by his side as his Queen. *I* keep my promises."

"As do I." Horemheb's brow furrowed as he watched her lips contort in a scowl. "One day, I hope our goddess Ma'at shows you the truth."

"She already has," Mut spat, and looked him up and down. "By your own words."

"My words were of a love that happened years ago, and

just this morning, my words were of a love I feel today, for my wife, who stands before me calling me a liar." Horemheb stood to face her.

"I can't believe you anymore. I have always been in Nefertiti's shadow. I even told you that my own parents favored Nefertiti over the rest of us. She was the standard. She was the one to live up to—and she was *Pharaoh*. We would *never* compare. It is no different with you. I heard the way you spoke about her. I heard the longing for her in your voice. You fathered a son with her. You promised her you would marry me and take care of me. The only reason you say you love me is so you can feel assured that her last wish was met." Mut shook her head at him. "You disgust me. After everything you told me all of these years . . . you *disgust* me."

Horemheb chewed on his bottom lip and then scratched his chin.

How to make her see the truth and believe it?

He opened his mouth to speak, but Wennefer stepped into the council room's light, quickly followed by the remainder of the five prophets of Amun.

Horemheb's guards entered behind the prophets and took their place behind the throne. Horemheb looked at the prophets, focusing his glare on the one who attempted to sit while Pharaoh stood. When he made sure they knew who was Amun's divinely appointed, he sat, and the five prophets followed.

"Pharaoh," Wennefer spoke, and bowed his head. "Surely this is the last day of retelling? There is but one Pharaoh left whose account is to be retold."

Horemheb rubbed the gold in the throne's arm as Tut had done only six short years ago. There was no more need to retell of Pharaoh Akhenaten's heresy, nearly causing the empire's collapse. His wife, his brother, his son . . . all would meet the same fate as he. Akhenaten cursed them all to a truly eternal death among the living, for to live eternally was to have their names spoken on every Egyptian tongue for all eternity. *You have forced my hand to take that from them, Akhenaten. He makes me erase their names. Curse you, Akhenaten. Curse you.*

"Pharaoh," Wennefer spoke again at Horemheb's silence, "the last three days have been long, and we prophets have grown old. We must finish the recounting and begin the erasure, so that we may restore faith in Amun's priesthood and reverence and power for Pharaoh."

"Yes." Horemheb nodded, knowing his days of stalling had come to an end. "Today, we shall remember Pharaoh Tutankhamun's chief royal wife, Ankhesenamun, the last child of Pharaoh Akhenaten and his Queen Neferneferuaten-Nefertiti. We shall also remember Pharaoh Ay. But after today, we shall remember them no more."

Mut's breath hitched, but Horemheb ignored her. He spoke.

He told of his injury and his subsequent perceived rebirth from the god Osiris. He told of Ay marrying Ankhesenamun to gain the crown when Pharaoh Tutankhamun had been slain. He told of his failure to his wife, now his Queen. He told of Pawah and the deserved agony he endured in his death. He told of Ankhesenamun's entombing but kept the young queen's wish and did not tell of her and Sennedjem's self-exile to Canaan. He told of Ay's replacement Hereditary Prince, Master of Pharaoh's Horses Nakhtmin. He told of his fight for the crown. His eyes glazed over. He had never killed a fellow comrade in all his years, save Nakhtmin. He still remembered Nakhtmin as he had lain there, still remembered pulling the dagger from his chest.

Horemheb dropped his head and took a deep breath.

"And then I seized my rightful claim to the crown."

His eyes lifted to the statue of Amun behind the priests.

It was done.

The past had been told.

Time had run out.

The edict lay before him.

It was time to commence the Eternal Execration, the erasure of names, the final curse.

Paralysis took his hands. Mute was his tongue.

History would remember Horemheb as Pharaoh Amenhotep III's Hereditary Prince, as both of his sons, Thutmose and Amenhotep IV, journeyed to Re young. History would never remember Akhenaten; nor his bride, Nefertiti; nor his brother, Smenkare; or his children, his only son, Tutankhamun; nor his father-in-law, Ay. Mut's father would be lost to history, as history would now tell that she never knew her father. Mut's full name, Mutnedjmet, would change to Mutbenret to remove any record of her relation to Ay and Nefertiti. Egypt's records would be purged of the heresy, the pain, the betrayal, the conspiracy, the death, the slaughter, the murders, and the economic downfall that plagued the last three decades.

Before the prophets could urge him further, he reached out and, with a stroke of his reed brush, signed the edict and sealed it with his cartouche.

He wished to vomit but had not eaten breakfast or dinner the night before. Swallowing the lump in his throat, he stood after placing the reed brush back into the well.

"Prophets of Amun, Pharaoh has signed this edict. We alone know the true history of what we have now removed from our records. Let your hearts be heavy during this time, and pray they do not feed Ammit at the end of this life."

Horemheb gestured their dismissal and watched with hatred as they left with smiles on their lips, an edict in hand for the scribes to copy to clay tablets and distribute to the provinces. He looked at Mut as he gestured to the guards to stand outside the council room yet again.

"Is there anything else you wish for me, Pharaoh?" Her words were light, but her face spoke of pain and resentment.

He wished for her to believe him.

"I wish you happiness, my Queen." He squared his shoulders to her. "I wish you happiness," he repeated, "and I cannot give that to you."

"No, you cannot," Mut said, but then froze as she remembered her father's words: *Do not rely on someone else to make you happy . . . but I wish this for you: to find your own happiness.* She lifted her chin but stilled her tongue.

His weight shifted from one foot to the other but kept her gaze. "Then what becomes of us?" Horemheb finally asked.

Mut pressed her lips together and gave a slow shake of her head.

Horemheb lowered his chin. "Then, if you are to truly have nothing more to do with me, at least stand by me as we carry out the edict. Even though you do not believe me, I still need you by my side. Bear my child, and then I will leave you to your own life in the royal harem or wherever you wish to go." His voice caught at the very end.

The pang of his words hit her hard in the chest.

He is just lying again to try and trick me, she told herself, but the defeated voice that accompanied his furrowed brow told her otherwise. Just as she was about to believe him, her gaze fell to Nefertiti's ring on his finger, which again hardened her heart against him.

"I will stand by you because I am the Queen of Egypt, *not* for you. I will bear your child because this child is also mine, but I do it *not* for you. Then I want nothing more to do with you. I cannot divorce Pharaoh, I refuse to be exiled, I never want to live in Men-nefer again, and so I must remain here . . . but *not* for you."

His face crumpled as though she had stabbed him in the heart.

"Thank you, Mut."

She shook her head. "You will refer to me as chief royal wife or Queen, and I will speak to you as Pharaoh."

Horemheb nodded as his eyes glistened. "Thank you, my Queen." His words came out thick.

They held each other's gaze for a long time. She studied him as they stared at each other, lost in their own thoughts. It appeared as if the weight of the world sat on his fallen shoulders, and the dark circles under his eyes kept the light from his face. His mouth appeared too tired to smile. She half thought he would try speaking to her again, telling her of his love for her, but he didn't. She was glad he didn't. She could only take so much heartache. Every time he told her he loved her, a little dagger pierced her heart, for she knew, was absolutely certain, that it was a lie.

He loved Nefertiti, the half-sister with whom she could never compare, even in the eyes of her own father and mother. How would Horemheb be any different? A façade had kept her happiness, and now, without it, she found life with Horemheb far less desirable. How had she fallen in love with a man twenty years her senior who had failed her sister, the Pharaoh, and let her be killed? Who took part in the conspiracy against Akhenaten and Smenkare and let her niece, Meritaten, be killed as well? He who had left her in Men-nefer without so much as even a goodbye kiss to be tortured by Pawah?

A tear formed in her eye as she remembered the ropes and the bed.

He who had let another Pharaoh journey west under his watch, the one he called son. He? He who had lived and yet refused to send word he was alive. Now, he! He . . . the man who now erased her family from the records . . . no images of them ever to be seen again. He!

How had she fallen in love with him? Because of his handsome face? Because of his fit body? Because of his uniform? She refused to remember all of the kindness and affection he had shown her.

He is a failure. He is nothing, and he is nothing to me. He used me to grant Nefertiti's last wish. That is all I ever was to him.

Her eyes narrowed. "Goodbye, Pharaoh."

She turned and left the council room that would forever hold the memories of the past.

Horemheb watched her leave, and then whispered:

"Goodbye, my love."

☙ 20 ❧

THE TIME OF ERASURE

A FEW DAYS LATER, HOREMHEB WAITED FOR HIS CHIEF ROYAL WIFE
by the royal boat that would take them to Ipet-isut, where he
would oversee the erasure of Pharaoh Tutankhamun's victory
wall and statues. He watched her as they carried her down
the dock on her litter. She stepped off and bowed her head, as
was her duty to him as Pharaoh, as he acknowledged her:

"Chief royal wife."

Without making eye contact she returned the
acknowledgment:

"Pharaoh."

Then she stepped onto the boat.

How do I make her see the truth?

He paused before following her and taking his seat on his
throne in the middle of the boat. His guards boarded as he
reflected.

*I should have left the past alone. The weight I have lifted from
my heart in telling her the whole truth now only burdens me more.*
He wanted to glance at her, but he kept his head straight
ahead.

His stomach went cold as he saw Ipet-isut's great obelisks
standing high against the rising sun. His heart ached for his

wife, but even more so, in the moment, for Tut. He deserved an honor among the Pharaohs who had left their mark in Ipet-isut. The air around Horemheb became stale as he closed his eyes, until finally he breathed.

They docked and they made their way to the great temple of Amun. Horemheb sat in a litter with his wife, surrounded by their guards, as they watched Tut's and Ankhesenamun's statues be chiseled away so that they were unrecognizable. He stared into Tut's face one last time, just before a stone mason finished hacking off his nose and chin. Horemheb had to look away; the deafening sounds of chiseling and grinding in the vicinity caused his head to spin in memory of the young boy he had learned to love as his own. His mind moved slowly from one image of Tut to the next, the sounds grating on his ears until an Overseer snapped him from his trance.

"Is this to your satisfaction?" The Overseer gestured to the now-unrecognizable statues. It took Horemheb a moment to process what the Overseer was asking him, so the Overseer continued in his silence. "Or would you like for us to continue?"

"You, Overseer, will address Pharaoh as *Pharaoh*," Horemheb told him through a tight chest and jaw. It would do no good to go through this entire ordeal and still let people get away with their irreverence. He looked to the Overseer—a young man, so perhaps he didn't know how to address the King of Egypt; he would not have been alive during the time when people did so correctly.

The Overseer bowed his head. "Or would Pharaoh like for us to continue?"

"They are unrecognizable." Horemheb pursed his lips and gave a curt nod. "It shall suffice for the erasure." His voice held as steady as the Nile and spoke with unwavering power. His shoulders were pulled back and his chin lifted, but his insides collapsed within him.

A stare bored into the side of his face and he turned to find Mut looking at him. They locked eyes for a moment. A slight frown on her lips and a soft, wet glimmer in her eye gave him some comfort. It seemed as if she felt sorry for him—or at least still hurt with him. His brow furrowed for a moment, and his lungs leapt for the chance to take a deep breath. Her head slightly bobbed as she pressed her lips into a soft, consoling smile. He responded the same.

Perhaps there is hope she will come back to me after all.

He pulled his back a little straighter and looked forward. "Let Pharaoh move on," he ordered, and the servants picked up the litter and began to walk to the next object of demolition.

They came upon Tut's victory wall he had built when he had defeated the Nubians as a young man. Horemheb looked at the depiction before him, of Tut in his chariot, standing guard over the mortuary temple Ay had erected for him after his passing. His edict had given the instruction to dismantle the victory wall's thousands of talatat stones and his mortuary temple and use them as filler in the gateway of the Ipet-isut temple and the surrounding pylons in the complex. Stone by stone they dismantled it, and with each sound of bronze chisel against stone, a deep stabbing gripped Horemheb's stomach. Numbness took him as he watched the seemingly endless number of masons work. His face fell slack at the sound of grinding to his left, and he knew they were erasing Tut's cartouche in the walls and pillar carvings and stelae, to be replaced with his own.

Mut stayed silent next to him as the sun reached high overhead and then began to set in the west behind them.

The stone masons worked and worked and worked, waiting for Pharaoh to give the word to stop for the day, until finally the Overseer approached with a shaky step.

He bowed low at the waist. "Pharaoh?" His words wavered with his knees.

Horemheb only stared straight ahead, watching the stones be dismantled one by one.

"Pharaoh?" the Overseer said again.

"What is it, Overseer?" Horemheb asked, still looking at Tut's mortuary temple. His tone was as numb as his body.

The Overseer cleared his throat. "Would you—Pharaoh . . . would Pharaoh wish his laborers to work into the night?"

Horemheb blinked and realized the light he saw was that of work torches—the sun had already left them. He drew a deep breath before he spoke. "No. They need sleep for tomorrow. Have them reconvene in the morning."

"Pharaoh is most kind," the Overseer said as he bowed a second time.

Horemheb flitted his hand to dismiss him.

The servants picked up their litter and carried them back to their royal boat to take them to Malkata for the evening.

HE FELT MUT'S STARE AS THEY ENTERED THE PALACE DOORS. They walked in silence to the queen's apartment, from which he assumed he would continue on to his, but his desire at that moment was to do nothing but be wrapped in her arms.

Please, he begged in thought. *Don't push me away again tonight.*

As if she read his mind, she brushed his fingers with hers and gave a slight gesture with her head. His soul leaped for the only piece of joy he would have that day as he followed her into her bedchambers.

He shut the door behind him and then turned to face Mut.

She stood rigid and then opened her mouth to speak. "The only reason you are here is because I *saw* you today. I felt your pain. It mirrored mine as I saw my new name, Mutbenret, replace that of Ankhesenamun. I know now of your love for Tut, and I understand the despair you must be feeling."

Horemheb's gaze stayed on her face as he realized her desire to keep nothing between them dwindled at her informal dialogue. "Yes, but it was easier knowing my chief royal wife was by my side."

Her lips trembled, and he guessed she wanted to say something about her sister but was trying to refrain, so he said it for her.

"Are you wanting to ask me if it would have been more easy with Nefertiti by my side?"

A grimace passed over Mut's face as she nodded, holding her breath as if in anticipation of his answer.

"I don't know, my Queen. Nefertiti is not here. *You* are here. It was easier with *you* by my side. I . . ." He closed his eyes and looked to the floor as his breath caught. "I didn't even think of Nefertiti today until now." He looked at her again.

Her lips trembled again, so he spoke for her.

"If you want to call me a liar, so be it. I was a liar. I've apologized, but I know I can't mend the hurt you feel. If you will have me, I will try every day for the—"

"Stop," she finally said. "Just stop." The corners of her mouth fell down as her body shook in its rigidity. "I don't know if you are telling the truth. I can't trust you. I am tired of being second place. I am tired of being afraid. And I am tired of debating whether or not to believe you."

"Then what shall we do?" he repeated the question from the day prior, hoping and praying that Mut would have some change in heart.

"I don't know, Horemheb."

She'd called him by his name, not *Pharaoh* as she had wished in the council room the day before. It had been an exceedingly hard day, and his heart leaped at this glimmer of hope.

She only shook her head as her shoulders fell. "I am tired." Her spine slumped as she shifted on her swollen feet.

He gave silent thanks to the gods as she didn't repeat her last answer. Not wanting to give her the opportunity to reject him in a secondary statement, he stepped forward, picked her up, and took her into the bath chambers. She looked at him as her fingers fell on the scar on his neck and shoulder, raised in a ghastly ridge. He let her down and then began to heat the water.

She stayed mute even while he poured the water into her stone bathwell.

"Why do you do this?" she finally asked, staying dressed. "You could have called Raia or Tener."

He put a few drops of her pressed lotus blossom oil in the water. He popped the cork back into the jar's top and placed it on the stone rim of the bathwell. Looking into her eyes as she stood across the bathwell, he smiled, knowing his true answer: *Because I love you.* But, knowing she'd think him a fraud, he simply responded: "The Queen has shown kindness to me in staying by my side, and I wanted to show kindness in return." He dipped his head to her.

She nodded, seeming to accept that answer, and then he left her to bathe.

AFTER HE HAD SHOWERED, HE CAME BACK TO FIND HER LYING ON her side and crying in bed.

"What is it?" he whispered, and put a hand on her shoulder.

"Nothing." Her cries stopped. "I'm tired. Let us sleep. We have a long journey tomorrow."

He smiled, realizing she had not asked him to return to his bedchambers. As he lay down beside her, he thanked Bastet for Mut's small token of grace.

He closed his eyes, for what Mut had said was true. They had to travel to Aketaten in the morning to oversee the beginning stages of the destruction of the once-royal city. His mind briefly turned to Nefertiti, but he pushed her away.

I'll mourn her again . . . later.

He looked upon Mut and longed to kiss her, even on the cheek.

Please be with your sister, Nefertiti. She will not let me comfort her.

"Yes, my chief royal wife. Please sleep."

A few moments later, after he had let the soft wool mattress conform to his aching body, she whispered, "You can call me Mut."

His lips and his heart smiled in the darkness, and he closed his eyes, hoping to not dream. He couldn't bear to face Nefertiti in the night before he witnessed her second death.

<hr>

YET NEFERTITI CAME AGAIN IN HER WHITE AND GOLDEN ROBES *floating around her in the dark void of his dream. She held his unborn son in her arms.*

He tried to yell out, "Forgive me!"

But she only peered at him as her ghastly chest wound grew in size, staining her dress. Tears fell from her eyes.

"You told me to hide the scar!" he tried to call to her, but the weight upon his lungs kept him from calling across the void. His scars still bled, weighing him down and rendering his body useless in trying to reach her.

She stayed mute.

And then something happened that had not happened before.

Tut appeared beside her, his eyes pleading with him, begging to know why Horemheb had destroyed his memory.

"Tut!" He felt the sting of the khopesh in his leg and shoulder once again. "I had to . . . my son! Forgive me!" Fighting with more vigor to try to reach them, he only bled more, his voice never reaching past his lips.

Then each of Nefertiti's four late daughters, Meritaten, Meketaten, Neferneferure, and Setepenre, appeared behind her, each holding a long, pointed finger at him—even the babe, Setepenre.

He felt them close in around him as he lay unmoving.

"Hide the scar!" he finally croaked out, and closed his eyes tight, unable to bear the crushing silence around him.

HE AWOKE AS THE SUN FELL ACROSS HIS EYES.

"Hide the scar," he whispered and took a deep, shaky breath.

"What?" Mut murmured as she drifted awake.

Horemheb calmed his senses as he patted his arm and let his fingers glide over the two scars—one from Pawah in his failure to save Nefertiti, the other from the Hittite as Tut saved him.

"Nothing," he whispered.

Mut left to go to the bath chamber after asking Horemheb to send for the servants.

Horemheb sat back down afterward. He closed his eyes and tried to envision peace, as if it were the dawn before a battle, to numb his emotions, so that he could do what he needed to do for victory. Or, in this case, for Egypt. For the future of Pharaoh.

His mind raced over the past, unable to complete his task.

"Will I ever have peace again?" he whispered to the gods. "Or is this my punishment rather than death?"

Mut emerged, no smile on her face. "I am ready."

He nodded, and they left to board the boat to Aketaten to oversee the progress of dismantling the city dedicated to the Aten.

❦ 21 ❧

THE TIME OF AKETATEN

THEY TRAVELED MOST OF THE DECAN-LONG TRIP IN SILENCE. When they disembarked to Aketaten, Mut finally turned to Horemheb, who sat beside her in the litter. His face had fallen slack; the dark circles under his eyes told anyone who dared look upon him the depth of his grief. His body swayed slightly on his feet. His royal shendyt, she noticed, was pulled tighter around his thinner frame.

I wonder if he would lose his appetite over my passing and erasure as he does with Nefertiti . . .

She dropped her head before looking ahead, down the dock, to the royal palace, which was already covered with stone dust as it rose above the city like the light ash of a small sandstorm. It was time. She would witness her sister be erased. Her heart loved Nefertiti, but her mind resented her. The comparison held even in Nefertiti's absence.

They neared the palace and Horemheb halted his company. Paramesse stood at the palace doors and bowed to the royal couple. The servants, by order of Pharaoh, lowered the litter and Horemheb and Mut began to walk toward Paramesse. Concern held in his eyes as he studied Horemheb's thinner frame.

He sees it, too. She glanced at her husband.

Horemheb only stood, and then, with a weak voice, asked, "Vizier Paramesse, what is the status?"

"We should have the Aketaten palace and city razed by the end of the flood season."

Horemheb's jaw clenched. "Good. Pharaoh needs to see the progress."

"Thus Pharaoh says."

They passed through the great hall, stepping over the large chunks of rock and debris. The roof additions Nefertiti had put up were gone; masons and laborers worked on the roof to dissemble the palace from the top down. Horemheb had his guards stay behind.

They came upon a sunken relief carving in the corridor where he and Nefertiti had met many times. It had been quiet and almost forgotten, and nothing had changed: an eerie silence still, now, accompanied the hall. Only two laborers actively chiseled away, the only two figures still left in the stone, Nefertiti and her daughter Meritaten.

Mut looked to him as one laborer began chiseling away Nefertiti's crown. He held tears in his eyes and his chin trembled. He stepped forward, leaving Paramesse behind them, but Mut kept by his side.

"I love her, Mut," he finally whispered, watching the laborers remove Nefertiti's image from the stone.

Mut held her tongue as she looked at her sister's face. *Why, Nefertiti? Why would you make your lover marry me? Did you not know he would never love me as you? He compares me and he lies to me. He used me! He only cares for me because you asked him to. Why would you do that to me? Why—*

"Her only transgression to deserve this erasure was marriage to Akhenaten. She will be forgotten. They will be forgotten." He kept his voice low, clearly to keep anyone from hearing their conversation. He looked at Mut and outlined her face with his eyes. He opened his mouth to speak but then closed it and turned his attention back to Nefertiti.

"You think I look like my sister?" It was the truth. What did Pawah tell her? *A cheap copy.* Those words burned in her soul as she imagined her husband with her sister.

How can Horemheb love me when he had Nefertiti? He can't. He only lies to me. That is the only explanation for why he tells me he loves me. Yet here is he is, telling me he loves her. Why? To rub it in my face?

"You are almost the age she was when I fell in love with her."

"You didn't answer my question," she asked.

He chewed his lip but said nothing.

"I know what she looked like, and I can see my reflection. I know you loved her. I know you loved her with a love you have never known before. I know I will never compare to your first love. I know I am just a replacement to you. Just a cheap copy."

"Mut, that is not—"

"I don't want to be Nefertiti in your eyes, Horemheb. Love me for me, or don't love me at all."

The memory of Nefertiti warning her to not be the second wife came back to her in that moment. She took a step backward, nodding, already having made up his answer in her mind.

She turned and left him.

Horemheb watched her leave. "But I do love you . . . for you."

But she was already gone.

He pressed his fist into the palm of his hand and looked back to Nefertiti's image. "I'm so sorry, my love." His heart was torn, wanting to go after Mut but feeling this need to stay with Nefertiti for one last time.

A tear slid from his eye as Nefertiti's face was slowly chiseled away.

Oh, my Nefertiti! His ka pleaded in silence. *I pray to the god Amun and the goddess Ma'at that one day, even though I have condemned you to a forgotten future, you may still reach eternal life on this earth. May your name be found again and be on the lips of all those who know your image, and may you forever be the most loved Queen in spite of me, in spite of all of this. I wish for you . . . peace.*

Paramesse had been standing off behind Horemheb, but approached now, walking almost to his side.

"All of them . . . I let perish, Paramesse. Nefertiti . . . Tut . . . and now I order their eternal death." His jaw clenched as the heavy weight he had carried in his stomach saturated his body.

Paramesse remained silent.

"The man I called son . . . his name, in Ipet-isut, I replaced with my own. I had his victory wall torn down and reassembled for my own achievements. The woman I first loved . . . I had her face ripped from the walls of Aketaten and her image torn down in Waset, her children now nothing but ghosts. I will have wiped them all from the memory of Egypt." Horemheb, the mighty warrior, could not keep the tears from falling even as he stood as Pharaoh, shoulders tall and back straight. "I cannot bear this burden, Paramesse. It is far too great."

Paramesse dipped his chin and let out a heavy sigh. "My friend—" he began as the last of Nefertiti's face vanished with the crumbling rock.

"I can still taste the perfume of her lips. I miss her. I wish I had been there. Why weren't we there? We were one night too late. One night. One *night!* I will never forgive myself." He closed his eyes to pull the tears back into his eyes.

"She would not want that for you."

He shook his head in thought. *But the gods want it for me. It is my punishment to bear this guilt alone.*

After a few moments, Horemheb whispered again, "Do

you know what her last words were to me? 'You made me feel alive.' " He reached down and grabbed the rubble that was her image. "And yet I kill her memory." He let the stone dust and bits fall through his fingers. "This is how much I love her." He chucked it at the wall. "This is how I show her!"

His hot whisper drew the attention of the laborers. Paramesse dismissed them, and when they were alone in the hallway, Horemheb placed his hand on the wall where Nefertiti's image was and bowed his head.

"I cannot bear this, my friend," he said, surveying the destruction by his feet. "Instead of letting her be killed, this time *I* hold the dagger. You know the truth." He shook his head. "Why did Amun want me as his divinely appointed?"

"Because you were the only one strong enough to do what was needed to be done. It is not easy, but it is what is best for Egypt." Paramesse put a hand on Horemheb's shoulder, his own tears welling in his eyes.

"Egypt takes much."

"Yes, it does."

Horemheb and Paramesse walked the long corridors again as they were demolished. They happened by the abandoned Pharaoh's bedchambers. Horemheb placed a hand on the door just as a laborer removed it. The view of the room was nothing like what he remembered, for now it was torn apart and destroyed. He could feel her warmth again against him, but for fear of shedding tears in front of his subjects, he pushed the memory from his mind.

Forgive me, my love.

HOREMHEB WALKED THE REST OF THE PALACE WITH PARAMESSE before they descended into the city. His guards walked behind him until they came across a bust of Nefertiti in an artist's workshop. He peered over his shoulder at Hori, who came and bowed to him.

Horemheb spoke low: "Royal guard Hori, as a favor to Pharaoh, in your service, please hide that image of Pharaoh Neferneferuaten so that it may be saved from destruction. Tell no one."

Hori bowed, placing his arm over his chest and keeping eye contact with Horemheb as if to say *With honor,* but his mouth said, "Thus Pharaoh says."

Horemheb wanted someone at some point in the future to wonder, Whose beautiful face was this? This woman who wore the crown?

He turned to look at the destruction, well underway and soon to be no more. The stones would soon be rendered silent, no longer to bear their image, no longer to tell their tales. There would be no story, no account, no memory remembered here.

22

THE TIME OF NEW BEGINNINGS

AFTER THEY HAD RETURNED TO MALKATA, MUT FOUND THE letter Nefertiti had written to Horemheb. It lay in the bottom of the chest that Raia and Tener had opened to get another dress for Mut.

"Where is the other half?" She flipped it over, finding nothing. She read what remained of it, and her blood boiled as she read the evidence of the love between Nefertiti and Horemheb. She finished reading and repeated the greeting: " 'My dearest Horemheb'?" Her breath burned her lips at the full realization that he had kept this letter hidden from her.

He kept it all these years. Would he have done the same if I were the one to have passed? Why would he keep this letter if he loved me? No, because he lies!

Tener and Raia looked to each other. "What is it?"

"A letter from—" Mut looked to them, knowing she couldn't tell them of Nefertiti. "A letter from his late first love."

"Why are you so angry, my Queen?"

Mut wished they could feel what she felt, so they would understand. "He only just told me of her. This letter . . ." She wrinkled her nose in disgust as her chest struggled to breathe.

"I know he compares me. I know that now. He only married me because he promised her to take care of me. He loves her more than me."

"Did he tell you this, my Queen?" Raia asked.

Mut's nostrils flared. "I just know."

"My Queen—" Tener stepped forward, but Horemheb entered.

Mut spat at him. "You . . ." She trailed off, the rage blinding her mind from knowing what to say.

"Tener and Raia, leave us," Horemheb ordered, a sorrow again in his voice.

As the door closed, Horemheb stepped toward Mut, but she held up her hand to stop him. Her breath and body shook as her mind raced, until she finally settled on what to say.

"If you had to choose . . . a life with Nefertiti, or a life with me . . . which would it be?"

"My Queen . . . Mut . . ." Horemheb shook his head. "That is an unfair question."

"No, it isn't. Who would you choose?"

"I'd choose both."

Her mind reeled. She knew her question was unfair, but in her heart of hearts she wanted him to choose *her* . . . for this one time in her life to be chosen over Nefertiti. Yet her sorrow turned to rage: her shoulders rose and her fingers curled, wrinkling the years-old papyrus. Seeing the grimace on his mouth and his slight step toward it, her vision blurred as her words burst forth in a coursing wind from her mouth.

"Would you cry for me should I perish, too?"

"Yes—"

"Will you even love our child?!"

"Yes, I do—"

"Will you love our child as you loved the son you had with Nefertiti?!"

"Yes, why—"

"Do you grieve him more than *our* firstborn?!"

"I grieve for—"

"Do you love me?!"

"Yes—"

"More than Nefertiti?"

His shoulders fell. "I told you. I love you both in my own way. Please don't compare—"

"Is that why you didn't save me from Pawah?!" The real source of her pain emerged its ugly head. "You were alive, Horemheb!" Her lips trembled; her body trembled. "You *lived*! I was no widow! And yet you did not come back to me for three seasons after I received the news of your battlefield passing! You let Pawah beat me and have his way with me! You do not love me! If I had been Nefertiti, you would have come—"

"I loved Nefertiti, and I let her DIE!"

His words resounded in the air between them.

"She was murdered because of *my* failure to protect her!" His brow hung heavy over his eyes. "I loved Tut and I let *him* be attacked! Amenia loved me and I not her and because of *me*, she met an early journey to the afterlife!"

He shook his head, and his gaze fell to the ground as he tried to control his breathing.

Mut stayed silent, but her mind accused him of every infraction against her and stacked it against his love for Nefertiti. *No . . . if the roles were reversed, you would have come back injured to your precious Nefertiti. You would have saved her. You do not love me. You have never loved me.*

"They left this life at my own hand." He was speaking as she thought. "And now those I love will never be remembered. Nefertiti, her daughters, your nieces, your father, Tut, Smenkare, Meritaten, Kiya, none of them will ever be remembered, all because of *me*!" He slammed a fist into his palm. "Because of *me*, Mut! *ME!*" He paced in front of her. "Their blood is on me. Their eternal unrest is on my head. No one else's. *I* must carry that burden!"

Tears welled in her eyes at her selfishness, but her anger toward him drowned it. *He does not answer my question. He knows the truth and tries to make me feel sad for him. He tries to trick me yet again.*

"You have already been hurt by Pawah, the man who took them all away from me. I had my vengeance with him, but the ache in my chest and the tear in my eye does not leave me." He stopped and squared his shoulders to her. "I am sorry I let him touch you. He beat you worse than a man in court for beating his wife. I am sure he took you in bed. He did unspeakable things to you. And I am sorry. *I am sorry* I was not there. I am sorry, many times over, that I did not come home to protect you and make sure you were safe."

You would have come home and made sure I was safe had I been Nefertiti, she thought.

"But"—his lips held a small smile—"you are *alive*. You are *here*. I am happy that the gods gave us a second chance. I am glad you are my wife." He paused, as if he wanted her to speak, but she stayed silent.

Gave you a second chance to fulfill Nefertiti's last request, she wanted to say.

"I do love you, Mut. I know you think I am lying to you."

"I know you lie to me," she muttered, her heart beating against her chest wall.

Like every time before. Everything I believed was a lie.

He shook his head. "You blame me for comparing you with Nefertiti, but I have set in my heart and my mind not to compare since the day you let me stay beside you as you healed from Pawah's attack. *You* are the one comparing, not I."

Her brow furrowed even deeper. *He accuses me?! He lies! He compares!*

"*Everyone* compares!" she yelled with all her breath, and then, without even thinking, she ripped the remainder of Nefertiti's letter in half; as though the adrenaline in her body kept her hands working, she ripped it over and over again until she threw the tiny pieces to the floor.

He only stood rigid and mute. His chin quivered as his eyes darted at each piece on the floor.

She breathed with a hot, trembling breath. "Now." A scowl passed over her lips. "Now you know what my heart feels like!"

Hot tears burned her cheeks at the shame and anger at ripping Nefertiti's letter. *But he deserved it! Treat him like he treats you!* she told herself.

"Ripped from your chest!" Her breath hitched. "Knowing you have nothing left!" After a moment, she screamed, throwing her fists to her sides, for her body had no other response. "You *liar*!"

Her eyes dropped to the floor to follow Horemheb's gaze.

He values that stupid letter from her more than he will ever value me!

The weight of regret mixed with the burn of jealousy in her heart as she surveyed the wreckage she had caused. Her unborn child kicked her hard in the ribs as if to add to the tension.

Nefertiti is gone now. He has already erased her memory. I only add to his pain.

She looked at him one last time, but his gaze stayed on the pieces of the letter on the floor.

I don't care. He never loved me. He only lies to appease Nefertiti's last wish.

Her breath caught in her chest again, and then she went to call Raia and Tener to draw her a bath.

***

HER HANDS TREMBLED AS SHE STEPPED INTO THE WATER.

"Are you well, my Queen?" Raia asked, and then peered

over her shoulder to Pharaoh, who still stood staring at the pieces of the letter on the floor.

"I am living, Raia, but my heart does not beat." Her whisper came out meek and low.

"Why so, my Queen?" Tener asked as she soothed Mut's forehead with warm water to wash the makeup from her face.

"My husband lies." Mut closed her eyes.

"My Queen, do not be angry with me, as I will speak freely without permission." Tener's smooth touch on her brow kept Mut from rebuking her as Tener continued speaking. "But I have seen how Pharaoh treats you after all these years. He does love you. I believe that now."

"No, Tener. I tire of you and Raia telling me what I want to hear." Mut sighed as her muscles twitched in the water, remembering the long nights asking them if she had been a fool to marry him, and knowing they lied to comfort her—just as they did now.

"I am not, my Queen." Tener looked back to Pharaoh through the crack in the door. "If he did not love you, he would leave you as he did in Men-nefer. Before, he only sent a letter or a messenger every now and then. Here in the palace, he might come by once or twice to ensure you were taken care of, but instead, he stays. He would not stay if he did not love you. He wouldn't—"

"You know nothing, Tener." Mut squeezed her eyes and balled her hands into fists.

Raia shared a look with Tener and then said in a soft voice, "It seems he is grieving, my Queen."

"Yes. For his first love."

"Or for his loss of you." Tener's words hung in the small space between them as Mut repeated them in her mind.

His loss of . . . me?

Mut's eyes slowly opened, and her hands quit shaking. She sat up in the bath and looked at Horemheb through the crack in the door. She had never thought of it that way before.

She saw his grief and had assumed it was wholly for Nefertiti.

"And even if he grieves for his first love, too," Tener continued, "grief never truly ends. It can only change. It is a journey, just like life. It doesn't mean he loves you less, or her more, or you not at all, or her not at all. If anything, he grieves both you and her."

Raia added, "A person grieves for those they love." She placed the last lotus blossom in the water. "He loves you, my Queen. Maybe by telling you about his first love, he hoped to show you his whole self and that your love for him would overcome any doubts. Did he have to tell you about her? Or did he *choose* to tell you about her?"

Mut answered every question in her mind as Raia asked it.

"Maybe he told you now so that you would know his love for you is true. If he had told you about his first love when he first came back and when he did not love you, then do you think he would have tried as hard as he does these days to comfort you, to be with you, and to honor you and your wishes?"

Raia placed her hand on Mut's and continued in Mut's silence.

"Tener and I have been with you all of your life, my Queen. We have watched you grow from a child to a woman to a mother. We have seen how he acted toward you when he did not love you and yet was still fulfilling his first love's last request to take care of you. Yet you believe now, after all he has done for you since he came back from war, that he still does not love you?"

Mut shook her head as she watched him kneel next to the pieces of the letter on the floor, her heart breaking for him.

Raia said, "My Queen, Pharaoh treats you with patience, gentleness, faithfulness, respect, kindness, honor, and humility. Even a good man does not act that way toward a woman he does not love."

Tears welled in Mut's eyes. She had ripped the letter to pieces. The letter he had carried and kept for more than a decade. Nefertiti's memory was erased. It and her sister's ring were the only reminders he had left of her. Yet he had not yelled at Mut or hit her or slapped her when she had done it. A man who did not love her would have, or worse. Her vision blurred through her tears.

"We tell ourselves what we believe to be true to the point where it becomes absolute." Raia stayed kneeling by the bathwell, and released Mut's hand in the water. "Then it doesn't matter what that person tells us, because we will never have believed them anyway."

Mut didn't realize she had been holding her breath as her lungs took a sweeping intake of air. Her tears began to stream down her cheeks as her mind filled with every act of love he had given her. Tener and Raia spoke the truth: someone who didn't care for her deeply would never have done those things, even if it were a promise to a first love, and never with the sincerity he had done them with, nor with the tenderness he had shown her.

She watched Horemheb stand and then leave the bedchambers with a sharp close of the door.

"What have I done?" she whispered, and buried her head in her hands, her tears only adding to her bath.

THE PAIN HE HELD INSIDE BLISTERED HIS SOUL AS HE WALKED with a straight back, clenched jaw, and clamped teeth, fists by his sides. He'd dismissed his guards and walked into the sunshine of the palace's training yard. He looked up and took a deep, pained breath. Servants were still around, so he swallowed his scream of anguish.

His fingers itched to hold a weapon once again. He pulled the dagger from his belt but then threw it on the ground upon seeing a khopesh hanging on the training wall of weapons. He marched to it with a heavy step, numbing his mind. He grabbed it and immediately began attacking one of the training poles. His form had become slack without practice, but he still managed to hack the pole in half with two mighty swings. He swung around with a backhand slice, again taking the pole to the ground.

The servants had stopped what they were doing and watched him until finally, he tired, having destroyed several training poles, and fell to his knees. Becoming aware of their stares, he bellowed, "Leave!" They scattered quickly until the training yard was emptied.

He cried out in agony as he stared at his reflection in the bronze blade. "I hate you," he told the man looking back at him. "Why did you tell of Nefertiti? Why would you push Mut away? Why would you take the letter off of your person? Why did you let Ankhesenamun find the letter and give half to her? Why did you let Ay read it and tear it in half in the first place? Why didn't you save Nefertiti when you had the chance? Why didn't you just kill Pawah the day he confronted you about Akhenaten? Why didn't you just love Amenia?" His corded neck twitched. "Why? So many things —why?"

His fingers let the khopesh roll out from his grip as he sunk his chin deep into his chest. The dull *thud* of the bronze on the dirt mimicked his heart dropping into his stomach. He looked to Nefertiti's ring upon his pinky finger. Clasping his other hand over it, he pulled his hands close to his chest. He felt the smooth blue lapis in his gold band pressed into his palm.

"Amun-Re, Horus, Hathor, Ma'at, whoever will listen," he prayed, a deep ache in his voice and a deep yearning in his body for any to hear him. "I cannot endure this punishment you've set before me. I am carrying out what was needed for Egypt, for you. Is there no reprieve? Is there no redemption? Now Mut is gone from me, and she takes one of my last memories of my Nefertiti. All I ask is that Mut find happiness and that our child live. In that way, I will know my punishment, at least, is not hers. Please," he begged as tears welled in his eyes. "Please," he whispered as the tears fell.

He turned his face into the breeze and looked up at Re as the sun began to set.

"For the sun shall rise again tomorrow, and Osiris has conquered death. If Pharaoh did not make it to the afterlife, the sun would not rise. Therefore, I have faith Nefertiti's heart was not devoured by Ammit, and they both completed the journey and are on the sun barge with Re. Every day they will look upon me and wait for me. I know this punishment is only for this life, but please do not subject Mut to it. She has done nothing wrong."

His father's words came to him as he sat back on his heels, staring at the setting sun:

A good man loves his wife. If you marry that young woman, love her, and then all of this will matter not. You have your past, but it is up to you what you do with your future.

Horemheb pressed his lips together as he wiped his face and calmed his breath. "What shall I do with my future?" His spine bent, and his shoulders curled forward, for the future looked too bleak to face. "You have appointed me to lead your people." As he spoke to the gods, he settled his chest and breath. "I shall do my duty to Egypt."

He stood and put the khopesh back on the wall.

"I shall make sure my edict is carried out in full. I shall personally oversee that it is done. Power will be restored to Pharaoh, and corruption will flee." He went to where he'd dropped his dagger, picked it up, and brushed it off. "The people will be empowered again. Our economy will flourish, and our borders will be secured. And our faith in you will not waver." He set his jaw and gritted his teeth as he sheathed the dagger back into his belt. "That is what I promise you, my gods. If it is acceptable, show me your favor."

HE WALKED AND STOOD OUTSIDE HER BEDCHAMBERS FOR A LONG while.

Hori and Ineni stood guard, saying nothing, until they stole a glance at each other, and Ineni cleared his throat to speak.

"Pharaoh, if I may ask, will you be entering?" Ineni bowed his head.

The corner of Horemheb's mouth twitched. "Has the Queen been out since I left last?"

"No, Pharaoh."

He debated leaving her tonight, for she would hear nothing he could ever say. Why subject her to more pain? Why try and then have the conversation result in Mut comparing herself again to Nefertiti? Why further drive a wedge between them?

Hori's gaze drifted over to Horemheb. "Pharaoh Tutankhamun stood outside this door many times contemplating what to say to chief royal wife Ankhesenamun."

"You mustn't speak of them, royal guard Hori." Horemheb's voice filled with sorrow.

Hori nodded but continued despite the gentle warning. "He always went in not knowing if it was going to be for worse or for better."

Horemheb smiled at the memory of the man he called son. *Even in his absence, he still manages to teach me.*

He smirked, remembering his own advice to Tut from so long ago when he wasn't sure if Ankhesenamun loved him or not: *There is meaning behind your woman's kiss.* There was something behind Mut's kiss. She did love him, and she only acted out because she thought he was a trickster.

I must make this right.

Finally, he stepped inside and saw, through the crack in the door of the bath chamber, Tener and Raia helping Mut to oil her pregnant body as she wiped away what he assumed were tears.

He watched silently in the growing shadows of the room, stealing a long glance to the ripped-up letter that still lay on the floor. No anger came—only longing. He steered his gaze toward his wife.

She is hurting. I have hurt her.

Mut came out and sat on the edge of the bed, looking at the bath chamber as if in a trance. Then, as Tener and Raia went to walk to the door, they jumped at the sight of him, having not seen or heard him enter. They bowed but then silently departed. At the soft close of the door, he walked around to the front of Mut. She opened her mouth to speak, but he dropped to one knee and grabbed her hand.

"Before you speak, I want you to know this, and please let me finish so that you can hear everything."

She nodded.

"I did what I thought to be right by you, Mut. I did not tell you of Nefertiti initially because I thought it would only add to your pain, that it would further drive you away from me. I felt the tremors of your body as you dreamed. I heard you cry out in your slumber. I saw and still see the way you meticulously cover each and every scar. I did not want to hurt you, especially after you told me your feelings about your sister. I wanted to keep you safe."

He grabbed her other hand as he stared into her fresh face.

"I tell you now of Nefertiti because I condemn her memory to erasure, and I have had her murder and her love and our son on my conscience for over a decade. I tell you now because I thought our love would endure." He paused as he watched her eyes begin to glisten. "I have so much guilt, Mut. So much guilt for it all, including you. I did not protect you from Pawah, and now I cannot protect you anymore from the truth, but I am glad you know. You know everything. Did I love Nefertiti? Yes. Do I still love her? Yes. Will I always remember her? Yes. I cannot change the past, but know that I love *you* in this present. I do not want to live my life without you, but I must, for Egypt, if you do not want me."

He squeezed her hands; he knew this would be his last plea, and then he would leave her alone if she rejected him again. His love would always be there if she ever came to seek him out.

"I swear to you, Mut, *I love you*, and I love our child. I do not deserve you, and yet the gods have granted me a life with you. *Please* do not take away your love for me, as you are the only one who brings a smile to my lips and warmth to my heart. You are my wife, and I will always, *always* love you."

Tears built behind her eyes as he continued.

"And to answer your question before—would I choose this life or one with Nefertiti?" He paused. "I cannot choose. I will always be sorrowful Nefertiti is gone and that I could never have this life with her, but I will always have peace and happiness knowing what my life has brought me . . . you and your love, even if only for a few years should you refuse me now." Tears welled behind his eyes, too, as he spoke. "Erasing them was one of the hardest tasks I have ever had to do, but living without you, Mut, will be the absolute hardest."

He searched her face as her tears began to fall.

"Please know . . ." His lip trembled. "I love *you*, Mut." He cupped her cheek. "My sweet and beautiful Mut."

She nudged her cheek further into his hand. Her gaze fell to his ring, and she took a deep breath. "I understand now," Mut whispered as she found his eyes. "You loved Nefertiti, and I am happy you found such love in your life."

"Mut, I . . ." Horemheb cupped her lower back with his

other hand, pulling himself closer to her. He wanted desperately for her not to compare anymore.

"I know." She rubbed his shoulder as another tear released and fell down her cheek. "I know," she whispered. She leaned her forehead against his. Her breath hitched as she gently shook her head. "I am so sorry, Horemheb." She closed her eyes. "I ripped her letter in my anger and my jealousy. I could not see the full truth in your words."

He cupped her face and then kissed her on her cheek and then her other cheek and then her forehead and then her chin. His lips hovered over hers.

"I will miss the letter, but I would have missed you more."

"Liar," she softly laughed through her sniffles.

"No, my sweet Mut . . . no."

Then, through both of their tears, he pressed his lips to hers.

"I love you, Horemheb," she whispered, kissing him back.

He pulled away and looked into her eyes, caressing the side of her face. "As I love *you*." He emphasized each word, then he again returned his lips to hers.

MUT FELL ASLEEP IN HIS ARMS THAT NIGHT, AND AS HE RAN HIS fingers down her face and chest and shoulder, softly so as not to wake her, his mind drifted back to the edict at hand and his prayer in the training yard.

He whispered to the gods, "Thank you for opening my wife's heart to me once again. If I have your favor, please let our child live."

He kissed her forehead, still careful not to wake her, and then let his body relax into the cool linen sheet on their bed.

✿ 23 ✿

THE TIME OF FORGIVENESS

THAT NIGHT, HOREMHEB DREAMED.

HE FELT HIS BREATH LEAVE HIS BODY AS HE REALIZED HIS ARMS and legs and face were ripped to pieces and bleeding from his scars. This mess of his life he had made. Heaviness set in upon his face, his mind, and his heart, yet he was somehow floating in a void of darkness.

Then a light shone in the distance. Nefertiti, wrapped in her white and golden robes and holding his son, appeared out of thin air. Her hand reached to him, as it had done in all of his dreams since her murder.

He tried to reach for her. They were so close, but he couldn't move his arms, or even his body.

"I'm sorry," he yelled through the void. "I tried so hard. I tried. I tried!"

Tears streamed down his face as he watched her robes whip around her body. Her ghastly dagger wound to the chest stained the purity of her clothes.

Her eyes danced in the light. "You made me feel alive," she whispered in the lightest of voices that resounded in his ears as if a tap against the purest of gold metal.

"I only failed you," he called to her, still being weighed down as she lifted ever higher.

"Horemheb," she called in an ethereal tone, and reached out to touch him.

Her finger finally grazed his arm and his arm was made weightless. He jutted his arm around her waist and pulled her close. Her hand grazed his face and shoulder as her knee grazed his. With each touch, the bleeding stopped and his body became whole.

"I found everything in you," she whispered to him, and gave him a soft kiss on his lips.

"As I you," he whispered to her, but she shook her head.

"You still have your life yet to live, my love." She pressed her hand to his chest. "Your heart is not wholly mine anymore. It has not been for a long time."

He grimaced as he pressed his forehead to hers and wrapped his arms around her, wishing what she said were not true.

"This is what I wanted for you," she whispered, and smiled. "Mut is happy. Let yourself be happy, my love." Her head tilted at his silence, her eyes glancing down to his son. "We are gone now, Horemheb. We are in the past." Her voice seemed to float in the space between them.

"A past that I have erased."

She smiled so that her skin glowed. "As long as you remember us, that is all that matters."

She began to float away, and his fingers slipped past her waist until he held no one. Stray pieces of hair floated in front of her face.

"I will wait for you in the afterlife, my love."

Tut appeared beside her and nodded, smiling as well.

"Tut, I'm so sorry."

Tut came to him and kissed his forehead. "As long as you remember me, my father, I am at peace."

Horemheb brought him into an embrace, the scars of his body

being erased the longer he held him. He rubbed his cheek upon the top of Tut's head.

"I love you, my son."

Tut released him and Horemheb did the same. He traced the outline of their faces with his eyes, cupping their cheeks.

"I love you both."

"We know," Tut said, and smiled as his skin glowed. "We love you, too."

"Now live your life, Horemheb. We have all of eternity to wait for you," Nefertiti said, and her lips grew into a smile, which brought forth laughter. Her deep, hearty laugh rang true and pure through the innermost of his soul . . .

. . . until his eyes blinked open.

HIS CHEST ROSE WITH THE AIR THAT FILLED HIS LUNGS. THE PRE-dawn filtered into the bedchambers. He wiped the sole tear hanging from his eye, and then a smile grew on his face as he thanked the god of dreams, Bes, for letting him see Nefertiti and Tut one last time.

In that moment, he could finally breathe, after all these years. The weights of guilt on his body seemed to dissipate. He took another deep breath, and he couldn't be certain, but in the small light that crept above his head, he thought he could make out Nefertiti and Tut on Re's sun barge. He smiled, knowing they had made it. They had made it to the afterlife. His heart felt light. Perhaps there *was* redemption.

Perhaps there was peace.

He rolled over to look at his wife, his sweet Mut. He caressed her face and kissed her forehead, wrapping her up in his arms so that their faces nearly touched.

"I am happy."

She hummed and smiled in her sleep.

"I *love* you." He laughed as tears of joy burst forth, and he pulled her closer than he ever had before.

———

MUT AWOKE A FEW HOURS LATER. SHE LAY BESIDE HOREMHEB, her head on his shoulder, her hand on his chest, her pregnant belly touching his hip. She breathed in the clean morning air. There was a peace on his face and in her heart. The sun fell so perfectly in the moment. The sound of the Nile river filled the distant air. The birds sang their sweet tune.

"Don't you wish this to be every morning?" she whispered to him.

He smiled and kissed her hand. "I do, and it can be."

"Yes," she chuckled. "I suppose it can."

She lifted her head, and he leaned to kiss her.

———

AFTER A WHILE, THEY DECIDED TO GET OUT OF BED AND ATTEND to matters of the day, but the pangs of labor began in Mut's back.

"Is it our child? Or is it a strain from the travel?" Horemheb asked. He rubbed Mut's back as Mut leaned on the bedpost, breathing through her pain.

"Child, Horemheb!" Mut finally pushed from her lips.

A large grin grew on his face, but still, he rubbed her back until the pain passed. He ran to the door and threw it open to see Hori and Ineni standing there.

"Call the midwife!" he yelled and then slammed the door to go attend to Mut.

Hours came and went as Mut labored, until it was finally time. Mut had asked for Horemheb to stay, so he stood beside her as she squatted on the birthing stool in the royal pavilion. The midwife once again helped coax the child out. The midwife-in-training stood behind Mut, holding the Bes-amulet to her brow and chanting good blessings upon the mother and the one to come.

Mut let out a breath once the child had arrived, yet the baby was silent. A fear took root again in her mind as she flashed to her son, born lifeless while her stewards helped her to lean back on the cushions behind her.

Raia whispered in her ear, "You have a beautiful daughter, my Queen."

The midwife rubbed and patted the baby's back as she held her little body across her forearm, her head in her hand.

Mut whimpered and closed her eyes at the lengthening silence, tears welling within them. Finally, after her breath caught in her throat, she whispered, "Why isn't she cry—"

Then, with the joy of a thousand glorious days, Mut heard her baby girl let forth a lively cry. Her heart skipped as she took a deep, cleansing breath, and a smile filled her face.

Horemheb kissed her on the mouth and took ahold of her eyes, speaking of his immense love for her.

Her hands trembled from sheer joy as the wet nurse laid their daughter in her arms.

Her eyes, her nose, her lips: they were perfect.

"What shall we name her?" Mut asked Horemheb.

"We can name her after her mother's true name . . . Tanedjmet."

Mut's smile grew, for some of the past would still live on.

"I like that name."

"Then her name shall be Tanedjmet," Horemheb whispered, and slid his finger down her small cheek.

Mut turned then to Raia. "Bring me the blanket," she whispered, and a moment later, Raia came with an old blanket and wrapped their daughter in it.

Horemheb's eyes filled with pride as he looked at Mut holding their daughter wrapped in Nefertiti's faded blue and white blanket.

His dream had meant something. He felt the past slide from his shoulders as he wrapped Mut and his new daughter in his arms. Letting out a breath, he smiled. Mut found his eyes as she placed her head on his shoulder.

"I would never trade this for anything," he whispered to her.

Her eyes grew bright, and a never-ending smile graced her lips. "Neither would I."

THAT EVENING, AS MUT SLEPT AND TANEDJMET LAY SLEEPING IN his arms—at his command—he walked to the window of the queen's bedchambers. He looked back at Mut, his heart filled with gratitude, and then he looked out at the stars in the sky as the Nile breeze fell upon his face.

"Thank you for finding favor with me," he whispered, lifting his eyes to the skies. "Thank you for giving me back my wife and child."

He finally felt forgiven; he finally felt redeemed.

He finally had peace.

EPILOGUE
THE TIME OF THE LAST
REMEMBERING

THE SUN'S WARMTH FELL UPON HOREMHEB'S AGED SKIN AND THE Nile's breeze moistened what the sun took away. Time slowed as he looked out of the Malkata palace, north toward Aketaten; the city, now abandoned and destroyed, lay in ruins. He looked even farther north, to Men-nefer, where his wife Amenia was laid to rest. Then he turned to face east to the shimmering Nile waters, and then to the west were there lay the Valley of the Kings, where he had hidden his precious Nefertiti and where lay the tombs of Ay and Tutankhamun and now even Akhenaten and Smenkare.

He and Mut had lived a long time together, but though his foresight had told him he would journey west first, being twenty years her senior, she had gone before him. The gods had granted his request: to keep Mut from his punishment and to let their child live. But he knew now that he was still to be punished for his transgressions.

A few more years, he felt he had, but not many more. He had always expected to die childless in marriage with Amenia, but as this first year of loneliness became another without Mut, without Nefertiti, without Amenia, without Tut, his heart dwindled within him. His daughter, Tanedjmet

—his only child—brought him joy most days, but he still felt alone.

"Pharaoh?" a familiar voice called behind him. "You sent for me?"

"Yes." Horemheb turned to face his vizier and old friend, Paramesse. "Walk with me along the shore."

Paramesse nodded and fell into step next to Horemheb around Malkata's great lake.

After some moments of silence between them, Horemheb finally nodded to ready himself to speak.

"I will name you Hereditary Prince, Paramesse, my vizier and my friend," Horemheb said as the two old men walked along. "I have done much work to make sure Pharaoh stays the most powerful man in Egypt and to rid the corruption that plagued the priesthoods and the military and officials' ranks. You must continue that work. Do what you must, even if it means establishing yourself as a god. Do it and make sure your son, Seti, and your grandson, Paramesse II, know this. Make the people love and fear you."

His body felt like a shell, hollowed out, ready for the next stage. This life had been mostly filled with pain and longing, but he had found love, and twice. The gods had blessed him in that regard. He had always asked himself, out of all the conspirators against Akhenaten, against Smenkare, why was he the one to survive? Why was his name the one to be remembered? The only answer he could muster was that he had lived in his punishment through years of guilt, of pain, of false hopes, and would journey to the afterlife in the same manner.

"I am honored, Pharaoh, and I will do all that you have asked. But my friend, you can still have a son. You have some years left. Marry another young woman; have a son with your many wives. You are Pharaoh."

"Paramesse . . ." He gently shook his head, smiling. "You already have a son and a grandson. You will ensure the lineage of Pharaoh continues. As much as I hate for my daughter to be a second wife, she is the Hereditary Princess." He clenched his jaw, knowing he would be dooming her to the same life as that of Nefertiti. "Tanedjmet will marry your son, Seti. If he refuses her in love, please provide her a means to escape if she so chooses and not join the royal harem of lonely and unloved women."

"But . . . my King of the Upper and the Lower." Paramesse tilted his head to look upon Horemheb. "Why not yourself? Why not have a son?"

Horemheb drew in a deep breath and turned from Paramesse. "You remember the day Pawah slaughtered Pharaoh Neferneferuaten, my Nefertiti?"

Paramesse looked to the ground. "I do."

Horemheb let his words ride on his exhale. "Only you, Paramesse, could see my true pain." He crossed his arms over his chest. "There was my woman, and there was my son."

"Pharaoh—"

"Do you remember the day my Queen Mut went to the Field of Reeds?" Horemheb flinched, remembering her passing only, one year previous, in her last attempt to carry and deliver a child.

Paramesse stayed his gaze on the ground. "I do."

"There was my woman, and there was my son."

"But, Pharaoh—"

"Do you remember when Pharaoh Tutankhamun left this life?"

"Yes, I—"

"There . . . was my son."

Paramesse drew a deep, pained breath.

"Paramesse . . ." Horemheb shook his head again. "It still hurts as though they journeyed west in my arms this morning."

He looked to his friend again, and seeing that Paramesse still did not understand him, he began again.

"No . . . after I could not have children with Amenia, whom I could have loved but did not, and after I lost my first love, Nefertiti, and my unborn son, and after I lost the man I called son, my dear Tut, and after . . ." His voice trailed off as he thought back to his most recent loss. "My poor, sweet Mut . . . after her many times of trying to have a son for me . . ."

He shook his head, feeling his heart drop into his stomach —she had wanted a son. With her difficulties with the prior pregnancies, he had asked her not to, but she wanted to bear the next heir . . . for him. Her loss pricked his heart so that it nearly stopped.

"No. No, I have loved and lost too many times. I wish for no more heartache. I wish for no more loss. I wish this curse upon me to end. I do not want anyone else to suffer because of my sins."

Paramesse opened his mouth to speak, but closed it, his gaze dropping again to the ground.

Horemheb rubbed the gold ring with the blue lapis that still fit perfectly on his pinky finger. The pad of his pointer finger slid easily over the smooth lapis. He closed his eyes and thought of Nefertiti and then of Mut. He had always assumed Mut would outlive him. He had promised Nefertiti —or rather, her ka—that he would be with her in rest. "Promise me, my friend, when the time comes for me to journey to Re, that you will place a sarcophagus in my tomb, but that you will place me beside my Nefertiti."

"I have already promised many years ago." Paramesse's voice was unwavering.

"Please promise me again," Horemheb whispered, needing to hear those words.

"I promise."

He took a deep breath as the wind came into his face. "Amun punishes me, my friend."

"He does not punish his divinely appointed," Paramesse said, and placed a reassuring hand on Horemheb's shoulder.

Horemheb smiled a weak smile and opened his eyes. "Of course, Paramesse," he replied, knowing his lie, but after a lifetime of practice he had conquered his tell, and he took Paramesse's nod as a sign of acceptance. "May Amun be with us," Horemheb said, and he squeezed Nefertiti's ring once more before letting his hands fall to his sides. "And give us strength."

Paramesse, seemingly noticing Pharaoh's guilt-ridden shoulders, said, "May Amun give you peace, my friend."

Horemheb only dipped his chin, and with a slow shake of his head he whispered, "No." He turned his face in the direction the breeze was blowing. "I only ask that Amun may remember."

His voice carried on the winds, across the dunes of the desert, with the hope that one day the gods might perhaps bring those he erased forth from the dead once again.

THE STORY DEEPENS

THE LOST PHARAOH CHRONICLES
PREQUEL AND COMPLEMENT
COLLECTIONS

Want to follow Ankhesenamun and Sennedjem into the land of Canaan? Do not miss *Nefertiti's Legacy*.

Pain lives in the palace; rest and peace will never befall her there.

Determined to escape the horrors of her past, Ankhesenamun leaves Egypt to find her sister in the vast lands of Canaan and begin a new life with a man she might love one day. However, the neglect of her father has caused Canaan to fall into a tyrannical state, full of oppressive kings and raiding brigands.

After cursing the gods and forsaking her divine duty as Hereditary Princess, has Ankhesenamun further doomed their search and rendered any true escape from her past impossible?

In conclusion to *The Lost Pharaoh Chronicles* saga, *Nefertiti's Legacy* is a dramatic tale of a woman's struggle to find peace, inner strength, and the love her mother wanted for her.

Nefertiti's Legacy will contain spoilers for the complete *The Lost Pharaoh Chronicles* series and the complement, *King's Daughter*.

Go further into the past with
The Lost Pharaoh Chronicles Prequel Collection

Find out how Tey came to Ay's house in **The Valley Iris**, why
Ay loved Temehu so much in **Wife of Ay**, General Paaten's
secret and struggle in the land of Hatti in **Paaten's War**, how
Pawah rose from an impoverished state to priest in **The Fifth
Prophet**, and the brotherhood between Thutmose and
Amenhotep IV in **Egypt's Second Born**.

The Prequel Collection

Bundle and save exclusively at www.
laurenleemerewether.com.

Dive deeper into the story with *The Lost Pharaoh Chronicles Complement Collection.*

Find out exactly how Pawah transformed the naïve Nebetah into the conniving Beketaten in *Exiled,* where General Paaten and Nefe end up in *King's Daughter,* and if Ankhesenamun and Sennedjem ever find them again in *Nefertiti's Legacy.*

The Complement Collection

Exiled will contain spoilers for *Salvation in the Sun,* and the prequels, *The Fifth Prophet* and *Egypt's Second Born.*

King's Daughter will contain spoilers fo book one and book two of the series, *Salvation in the Sun* and *Secrets in the Sand,* respectively; and the prequels, *The Mitanni Princess* and *Paaten's War.*

Bundle and save exclusively at www. laurenleemerewether.com.

A LOOK INTO THE PAST

As readers may have gleaned from this novel and series, the account of Pharaohs Akhenaten, Smenkare, Neferneferuaten, Tutankhamun, and Ay were removed from history by Pharaoh Horemheb. Only recently, archeologists have uncovered bits and pieces of what happened during the Amarna period, the period of time this series covers. The author has taken liberties in *Silence in the Stone,* the last book of The Lost Pharaoh Chronicles series, where there were uncertainties and unknowns in the historical record.

Silence in the Stone covers the last period of time that was erased. Many theories posit that Ay sent Horemheb to war and then took his crown while he was away. Ay married the Hereditary Princess Ankhesenamun and by the second or third year of his reign, she was not mentioned again and had seemingly disappeared from the record. *Silence in the Stone* took liberties in having her leave Egypt. Her mummy, if she was not the mother of Tut's children, has not been found; if she was the mother of Tut's children, then she was not a daughter of Akhenaten or Tut was not Akhenaten's son, and her mummy has been identified. Either way, Ankhesenamun running off to Canaan was probably not what happened, as royal wives usually fulfilled the role of celibate priestesses of Isis if Pharaoh did not lie with them. The author did not want that for her precious Ankhesenamun character, and so wrote for her a happy ending after all she had endured. The tomb of Sennedjem, an Overseer of the Tutors, was excavated by Boyo Ockinga[1] in Awlad Azzaz (Akhmim). He notes it appeared Sennedjem's name was deliberately erased from the tomb's decoration. The tomb was heavily damaged, and it is uncertain anyone was ever entombed in it.

Find out what happens with Ankhesenamun and Sennedjem as they journey into Canaan and if they ever reunite with Nefe and General Paaten in *The Lost Pharaoh Chronicles Complement*: **Nefertiti's Legacy**. To avoid spoilers, please read the second complement, **King's Daughter**, first.

The author's research on when Tey died was conflicting. Some sources say she outlived Ay, since they believed her to be much younger, but others say she died shortly before Ay, who was most likely in his seventies when he died. The timeline in *The Lost Pharaoh Chronicles* puts his death at seventy-four. The average age for a male during this time was in the forties and fifties, although some sources say the god Thoth assigned sixty years as a full lifespan for a man, and to live past forty and even to one hundred was considered an accomplishment. So even if Tey was much younger than Ay, she would have lived a full life in ancient times if he had lived to his seventies. Even though not much is known about Tey, the author wrote a backstory for this series character in the first book of the prequel collection, **The Valley Iris**.

It is generally accepted Ay was on the throne for four years. Ay had named a relatively unknown person, Nakhtmin, as his successor, who was not mentioned again once Horemheb took the throne. As soon as Horemheb became King, he divided the military to prevent a coup.

Horemheb was married to a prophetess of Amun, Amenia, who presumedly died during the reign of

Tutankhamun. They had no children. It is assumed he married Mutnedjmet during Tutankhamun's reign (Mutbenret was formerly Mutnedjmet due to a translation error; *The Lost Pharaoh Chronicles* use Mutnedjmet as her name prior to the erasure and Mutbenret as her name after the erasure). Mut died in her forties, seemingly from childbirth, in Year 13 of Horemheb's reign. Horemheb's adjusted reign appears to be fourteen years, although some accounts say twenty-seven to twenty-eight, but those additional years are sometimes attributed to the covering of some of the time he erased. Mut's mummy was found beside Amenia in Horemheb's tomb in Saqqara that he had built before ascending to the throne. It appeared her body had born multiple children but did die in childbirth.

Horemheb instituted a strict edict that cut down on corruption and erased the past early in his reign. Details are found in a stele in Karnak. The author created the term "Eternal Execration" for the modern-day *damnatio memoriae* because she could not find in her research the term for the act of erasing one's memory before Latin became a language. The closest record of what the Egyptians described this act as was "execration texts" carried out in physical form. Execration texts were used in rituals where the names of enemies of Pharaoh and Egypt were put on tablets and then broken and buried to curse those names listed. They also served as warnings to tomb robbers and the like for what punishment or curse would befall them if they entered unwelcome.

Horemheb personally traveled and oversaw the erasure, the "Eternal Execration," to ensure his edict was being carried out in the big cities as well as the smaller towns and provinces.

Horemheb and Mut reportedly had an unnamed daughter. Some sources say her name was Tanedjmet due to a jar found in a royal tomb in the Valley of the Queens, which began construction in the 19th Dynasty. The tomb might have been intended for Mut, but the 19th Dynasty started with the Pharaoh after Horemheb. Some lesser-known theories speculate Tanedjmet might have been the mother of Ramses II, but since she was related to Ay, her memory was also erased and the mother of Ramses II is attributed to Tuya. Tanedjmet's mummy has never been found.

The mummies of Horemheb and Nefertiti have not been positively identified or located at the time of this writing. However, some assume the Younger Lady (a mummy) is Nefertiti because, even though there is a brother–sister DNA relationship between her and the mummy identified as Akhenaten, some speculate three generations of first-cousin inbreeding would show a brother–sister DNA relationship, and so they believe Nefertiti has already been discovered. Many others assume Nefertiti's mummy has not been found. Others assume she and her daughter Ankhesenamun were found a while ago—both mummies in very poor condition.

Once Horemheb died, Paramesse, the named Hereditary Prince, took the throne. Paramesse took the royal name Ramses. He ruled for two years before he died. He, his son Seti I, and his grandson, having taken the royal name Ramses II, started the 19th Dynasty and thus ended the 18th Dynasty. Seti I was most likely a troop commander when his father took the throne, who then subsequently named him Vizier and Crown Prince.

A little peek into the author's mindset based on her research:

- There are only a handful of named fictional characters in the story. The majority of the main characters are based on and named after their real-life counterparts. She wanted to stay as close to the historical account as possible, yet still craft an engaging story.

- Pawah was a lay prophet and scribe of Amun in the 18th Dynasty noted during the reign of Neferneferuaten, and although his quest to take the throne could have been a possibility, there is no evidence to support Pawah as the villain in *The Lost Pharaoh Chronicles*. The author wrote a prequel collection, and one of the prequels is the character Pawah's backstory, **The Fifth Prophet**.
- Pharaoh Ay's Vizier, General, Commander, and Master of Pharaoh's Horses are unknown.
- The author used "Pharaoh" as a title in the story due to the mainstream portrayal of Pharaoh to mean "King" or "ruler." Pharaoh is actually a Greek word for the Egyptian word(s) *pero* or *per-a-a* in reference to the royal palace in Ancient Egypt, or, literally, "great house." The term was used in the time period this series covers; however, it was never used as an official title of the Ancient Egyptian kings.
- Ancient Egyptians called their country Kemet, meaning "Black Land," but because the modern term *Egypt* is more prevalent and known in the world today, the author used "Egypt" when referencing the ancient empire.
- Regnal years were not used during the ancient times, but rather used by historians to help chronicle the different reigns. The author decided to insert these references throughout the novel to help the reader keep track of how much time has passed and to have a better idea of the historical timeline.
- Amun can be spelled many ways—Amen, Amon, Amun—but it refers to the same god. Likewise, the Aten has also been spelled Aton, Atom, or Atun. The author chose consistent spellings for her series for pronunciation purposes.

- Ancient Egyptians did not use the words "death" or "died," but for ease of reading the author used both in some instances. Rather, they would use euphemistic phrases to satiate the burden that the word "death" brought, such as "went to the Field of Reeds," "became an Osiris," and "journeyed west."

The author hopes you have enjoyed this story crafted from the little-known facts surrounding this period, and is hard at work writing more books.

Be sure not to miss the *The Lost Pharaoh Chronicles Prequel and Complement Collections*. Find out how Pawah rose from an impoverished state to priest, how Tey came to Ay's house, why Ay loved Temehu so much, General Paaten's struggle in the land of Hatti, and the brotherhood between Thutmose and Amenhotep IV in the Prequel Collection. Dive deeper into the story with the Complement Collection and find out exactly how Pawah transformed the naïve Nebetah into the conniving Beketaten, where General Paaten and Nefe ended up with mysterious Atinuk, and how Ankhesenamun and Sennedjem fared on their journey to Canaan to find Nefe.

Did you love this saga and are looking for more? Check out Lauren's *Egypt's Golden Age Chronicles* and *Ancient Legends* collection. Bundle and save exclusively on www.llmbooks.com.

---

1. Ockinga, Boyo. A Tomb from the Reign of Tutankhamun at Akhmim. Aris & Phillips, 1997. ISBN 0-85668-801-0

GLOSSARY

CONCEPTS / ITEMS

1. Amphora – large clay jar primarily used for transport and storage of wine
2. Ba-en-pet – iron from the sky; metal of heaven
3. Captain of the Troop – mid-ranking officer of the military; one rank below Troop Commander
4. Chief royal wife – premier wife of Pharaoh; Queen
5. Commander – second-in-command of Pharaoh's Armies; third-highest ranking beneath Master of Pharaoh's Horses and the general
6. Coregent – ruler second to Pharaoh
7. Deben – measure of weight equal to about 91 grams
8. Decan – ten-day period; three decans in a month
9. Dynasties – lines of familial rulers in the Old Kingdom, then Middle Kingdom, then New Kingdom (where this story takes place, specifically the 18th Dynasty)
10. Faience – popular blue-glazed ceramic
11. General – highest-ranking position of Pharaoh's Armies

12. "Gone to Re" – a form of the traditional phrase used to speak about someone's death; another variant is "journeyed west"
13. Great royal wife – chief royal wife of the Pharaoh before
14. "Greatest of Fifty" Commander – second-lowest military rank; a commander of fifty men
15. Ka – spirit
16. Kap – nursery and school for royal children in the royal harem
17. Khopesh – sickle-shaped sword
18. Master of Pharaoh's Horses – highest-ranking position of Pharaoh's chariotry; second-in-command to the general
19. Mistress of the House – the title for the wife of a non-royal estate owner
20. Modius – crown for the Queen
21. Overseer of the Garrison – second rank below Commander; under the Overseer of the Fortress
22. Pharaoh – the modern-day term for the ruler or King of Ancient Egypt
23. Pshent – the great double-crown of Pharaoh
24. Royal harem – a palace for the royal women, usually headed by the chief or great royal wife
25. Royal wife – wife of Pharaoh
26. Season – three seasons made up the 365-day calendar; each season had 120 days
27. Shendyt – pleated apron; the royal shendyt is lined with gold and worn by Pharaoh
28. Silphium – now-extinct plant used for contraception and/or to induce menstruation after conception
29. Steward – main person in charge of the estate(s); position held by a man or a literate woman

30. Talatat – standardized thin stone block used for building monuments and reliefs
31. Troop Commander – third rank below Commander; under Overseer of the Garrison
32. Vizier – chief royal advisor to Pharaoh

GODS

1. Ammit – goddess and demoness; Devourer of Hearts
2. Amun – premier god of Egypt in the Middle Kingdom
3. Amun-Re – name given to show the duality of Amun and Re (the hidden god and the sun) to appease both priesthoods during the early part of the New Kingdom
4. Anubis – god of embalming and of the dead
5. Aten – the sun-disc god of Egypt (referred to as "the Aten"); a minor aspect of the sun god, Re
6. Bastet – goddess and protector of the home, women, women's secrets, and children
7. Bes – god of childbirth
8. Hathor – goddess of joy, women's health, and childbirth, among other aspects of life
9. Ma'at – goddess of truth, balance, and harmony
10. Osiris – god and judge of the dead; god of resurrection and life
11. Re – premier god of Egypt in the Old Kingdom; the sun god
12. Seret – goddess of vengeance and protection

PLACES

1. Aketaten – city of modern-day area of El'Amarna
2. Akhe-aten – necropolis for the city of Aketaten

3. Ipet-isut – modern-day Karnak of Luxor; "The Most Selected of Places"
4. Malkata – palace of Pharaoh Amenhotep III
5. Men-nefer – city of Memphis; south of modern-day Cairo
6. Saqqara – necropolis for the city of Men-nefer
7. Waset – city of modern-day Luxor
8. Washukanni – capital city of the Mitanni empire
9. Valley of the Kings – royal necropolis across the Nile from Waset

PEOPLE

1. Ahset – steward of Ankhesenamun
2. Amenhotep III – deceased Pharaoh and father of Amenhotep IV and Thutmose III; died in Book I, *Salvation in the Sun*
3. Amenhotep IV / Akhenaten – deceased Pharaoh; second son of Amenhotep III and Tiye; journeyed west in Book II, *Secrets in the Sand*
4. Amenia – first wife of Horemheb; journeyed west in Book III, Scarab in the Storm
5. Amenket – royal guard
6. Ankhesenpaaten / Ankhesenamun – daughter of Amenhotep IV / Akhenaten and Nefertiti; royal wife of Akhenaten; chief royal wife of Tutankhaten / Tutankhamun; royal wife of Ay
7. Ay – Pharaoh; father of Nefertiti and Mut; brother to Tiye; vizier to Pharaoh Tutankhamun
8. Bakt – head steward of Horemheb's Men-nefer estate
9. Beketaten / Nebetah – deceased daughter of Pharaoh Amenhotep III; born with the name Nebetah; wife of Pawah; journeyed west in Book II, *Secrets in the Sand*

10. Djar – chief royal guard under Pharaohs Tutankhamun and Ay; successor to Jabari
11. Horemheb – military general (highest-ranking) under Pharaohs Tutankhamun and Ay; future Pharaoh
12. Hori – royal guard
13. Ineni – royal guard
14. Jabari – deceased chief royal guard under Pharaohs Akhenaten, Smenkare, and Neferneferuaten; journeyed west in Book II, *Secrets in the Sand*
15. Khensuhotep – military general under Pharaoh Horemheb
16. Kiya – deceased Mitanni Princess sent to seal foreign relations through marriage to Pharaoh; journeyed west in Book I, *Salvation in the Sun*
17. Mahu – military commander under Pharaoh Horemheb
18. Meketaten – deceased daughter of Pharaoh Amenhotep IV / Akhenaten and Nefertiti; journeyed west in Book I, *Salvation in the Sun*
19. Meritaten – deceased daughter of Pharaoh Amenhotep IV / Akhenaten and Nefertiti; chief royal wife of Pharaoh Smenkare; journeyed west in Book II, *Secrets in the Sand*
20. Merka – Malkata servant of Pawah
21. Mut / Mutnedjmet – half-sister of Nefertiti; daughter of Tey and Ay; wife of Horemheb
22. Nakht / Nakhtpaaten – Vizier of the Lower under Pharaohs Akhenaten, Smenkare, Neferneferuaten, and Ay
23. Nakhtmin – Master of Pharaoh's Horses under Pharaohs Tutankhamun and Ay
24. Nefe / Neferneferuaten Tasherit – daughter of Pharaoh Amenhotep IV / Akhenaten and Nefertiti; exited series in Book II, *Secrets in the*

Sand; returns in the complement book, *King's Daughter*

25. Neferneferure – deceased daughter of Pharaoh Amenhotep IV / Akhenaten and Nefertiti; journeyed west in Book I, *Salvation in the Sun*

26. Nefertiti / Neferneferuaten – deceased daughter of Ay; chief royal wife and Coregent of Pharaoh Akhenaten and Pharaoh Smenkare; Pharaoh in her own right, as Pharaoh Neferneferuaten; journeyed west in Book II, *Secrets in the Sand*

27. Paaten / Paatenemheb – military general under Pharaohs Akhenaten, Smenkare, and Neferneferuaten; exited series in Book II, *Secrets in the Sand*; returns in the complement book, *King's Daughter*

28. Paramesse – military commander under Pharaohs Tutankhamun and Ay

29. Pawah – former Fifth Prophet of Amun; husband of Beketaten; Vizier of the Upper to Pharaoh Tutankhamun

30. Raia – servant of Mut

31. Sennedjem – tutor of Tut; Overseer of the Tutors in the royal harem

32. Setepenre – deceased daughter of Pharaoh Amenhotep IV / Akhenaten and Nefertiti; journeyed west in Book I, *Salvation in the Sun*

33. Sitayet – deceased Captain of the Troop; journeyed west in Book III, *Scarab in the Storm*

34. Smenkare / Smenkhkare – deceased son of Pharaoh Amenhotep III and Sitamun; half-brother and nephew of Pharaoh Akhenaten; journeyed west in Book II, *Secrets in the Sand*

35. Suppululiuma I – King of the Hittites

36. Temehu – deceased mother of Nefertiti; journeyed west in Book I, *Salvation in the Sun*

37. Tener – servant of Mut
38. Tey – wet nurse and step-mother of Nefertiti; mother of Mut; wife of Ay
39. Thutmose – deceased firstborn son of Pharaoh Amenhotep III and Tiye; journeyed west in Book I, *Salvation in the Sun*
40. Tiye – deceased chief royal wife of Pharaoh Amenhotep III; sister of Ay; journeyed west in Book I, *Salvation in the Sun*
41. Tut / Tutankhaten / Tutankhamun – deceased Pharaoh; only son of Pharaoh Amenhotep IV / Akhenaten and Henuttaneb; journeyed west in Book III, *Scarab in the Storm*
42. Wennefer – First Prophet of Amun during the reign of Pharaohs Tutankhamun, Ay, and Horemheb

ACKNOWLEDGEMENTS

First and foremost, I want to thank God for blessing me with the people who support me and the opportunities He gave me to do what I love: telling stories.

Many thanks to my dear husband, Mark, who supported my early mornings and late nights of writing this book.

Thank you to my parents, siblings, beta readers, and launch team members, without whom I would not have been able to make the story the best it could be and successfully get the story to market.

Thank you to Spencer Hamilton of Nerdy Wordsmith, who put this story through the refiner's fire, making this piece of historical fiction really shine.

Thank you to RE Vance, bestselling author of the GoneGod World series, who offered guidance in the series' framework and structure.

Thank you to the Self-Publishing School Fundamentals of Fiction course, which taught me invaluable lessons on the writing process and how to effectively self-publish, as well as gave me the encouragement I needed.

Finally, but certainly not least, thank you to my readers. Without your support, I would not be able to write. I truly hope this story engages you, inspires you, and gives you a peek into the past. I've also created a Reader's Guide to help you delve into the history and into Book I a little bit more—just go to www.LostPharaohChronicles.com to receive it.

My hope is that when you finish reading this story, your love of history will have deepened a little more—and, of course, that you can't wait to find out what happens in the prequel and complement collection!

ABOUT THE AUTHOR

Lauren Lee Merewether, a historical family saga fiction author, loves bringing the world stories forgotten by time, stories filled with characters who love and lose, fight wrong with right, and feel hope in times of despair.

A lover of ancient history where mysteries still abound, Lauren loves to dive into history and research overlooked, under-appreciated, and relatively unknown tidbits of the past and craft for her readers engaging stories.

During the day, Lauren studies the nuances of technology and audits at her job and cares for her family. She saves her nights and early mornings for writing stories.

Get her first multi-award nominated novel, *Blood of Toma*, for **FREE**, say hello, and stay current with Lauren's latest releases at www.LaurenLeeMerewether.com

facebook.com/llmbooks
twitter.com/llmbooks
instagram.com/llmbooks
amazon.com/author/laurenleemerewether
bookbub.com/authors/lauren-lee-merewether
goodreads.com/laurenleemerewether
tiktok.com/@llmbooks

ALSO BY LAUREN LEE MEREWETHER

Egypt's Golden Age Chronicles — *Warrior King, Book I*

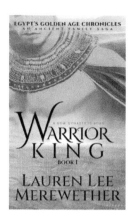

Expelling the foreign kings of Egypt is proving costly.

1575 BC. Surrounded by her enemies, the future of the rebellion is in the hands of Queen Ahhotep as her husband's body is laid at her feet.

To unite the divided kingdom, Ahhotep must be the commanding leader to those still loyal to her family, a guiding voice her children require, and meet the impossible expectations of her mother, the Great Wife Tetisheri. Feeling alone and finding no consolation in the palace, Ahhotep seeks counsel with a man she loves but cannot have, inviting conflict into her family and her heart.

With obsolete weaponry, inferior resources, and the royal family's divided front, their supporters dissent and leave. To keep their borders secure, Ahhotep must find a way to consolidate power, raise a capable army, and mold her son into a Warrior King before death comes for her and her people.

Warrior King is a beautiful ode to the powerful women behind the crown and how their love, determination, and sacrifice propelled the once-called Kemet into a golden era of ancient Egyptian history.

Ancient Legends — *The Curse of Beauty, Book I*

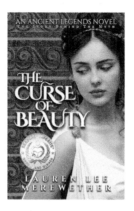

Before the Muses spoke of Medusa, a woman inspired the myth.

In a time of political turmoil and shifting power in Ancient Greece, Thais, daughter of the Tiryns chieftain, navigates a treacherous landscape filled with danger, betrayal, unexpected love, and shallow alliances.

When King Oceanus arrives with his army, intent on seizing control of Tiryns, Thais finds herself torn between her father's desire for peace and the council's thirst for war.

But even as the city faces a threat from without, the greatest danger may lie within, as long-held secrets and hidden agendas threaten to tear Tiryns apart.

Desperate to end the conflict, Thais strikes a deal with the enemy, setting in motion a chain of events that will change the course of history and test the limits of her strength, both in love and courage.

Winner of the gold medal for the 2022 Readers' Favorite Awards in the Fiction-Mythology category, *The Curse of Beauty* is a masterful work of historical fiction that will leave you spellbound.

WHAT DID YOU THINK?
AN AUTHOR'S REQUEST

Did You Enjoy *Silence in the Stone*?

Thank you for reading the fourth and last book in **The Lost Pharaoh Chronicles**. I hope you enjoyed jumping into another culture and reading about the author's interpretation of the events that took place in the New Kingdom of Ancient Egypt.

If you enjoyed *Silence in the Stone*, I would like to ask a big favor: Please share with your friends and family on social media sites like **Facebook** and leave a review on **book retailer sites**, **BookBub**, and **Goodreads** if you have accounts there.

I am an independent author; as such, reviews and word of mouth are the best ways readers like you can help books like *Silence in the Stone* reach other readers.

Your feedback and support are of the utmost importance to me. If you want to reach out to me and give feedback on this book, have ideas to improve my future writings, get updates about future books, or just say howdy, please visit me on the web.

www.LaurenLeeMerewether.com
Or email me at
mail@LaurenLeeMerewether.com
Happy Reading!

Printed in Great Britain
by Amazon

41259874R00199

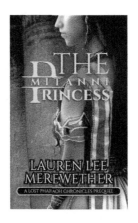

THE LOST PHARAOH CHRONICLES TIMELINE

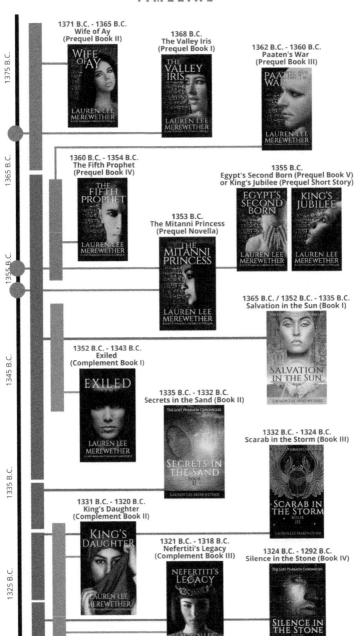

THE LOST PHARAOH CHRONICLES
COMPLEMENT COLLECTION

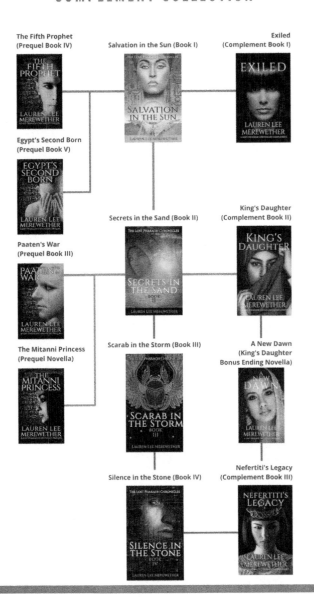

The Fifth Prophet
(Prequel Book IV)

Egypt's Second Born
(Prequel Book V)

Paaten's War
(Prequel Book III)

The Mitanni Princess
(Prequel Novella)

Salvation in the Sun (Book I)

Secrets in the Sand (Book II)

Scarab in the Storm (Book III)

Silence in the Stone (Book IV)

Exiled
(Complement Book I)

King's Daughter
(Complement Book II)

A New Dawn
(King's Daughter
Bonus Ending Novella)

Nefertiti's Legacy
(Complement Book III)